Breaking the Silence

Daphne Calder

Published by Daphne Calder, 2024.

BREAKING THE SILENCE

First edition. October 8, 2024.

Copyright © 2024 Daphne Calder.

ISBN: 979-8227659002

Written by Daphne Calder.

Chapter 1: Echoes of the Past

In the heart of Los Angeles, where the sun drapes its golden shawl over the city, I sit in my studio apartment, a mismatched collection of thrifted furniture and unmade memories. Dust motes dance in the afternoon light, swirling like forgotten melodies in the air. I'm Lila Monroe, a name that once echoed through the vibrant music scene, now reduced to a whisper in a ghostly echo chamber. The skyline outside my window reflects not just the ambition I used to wear like a second skin but the shadows of what once was—my late husband, Jake, my love, my collaborator, now just a haunting refrain.

I glance at the array of dusty recordings scattered across my coffee table, each a relic of a dream I once held close. The tracks we recorded together were infused with the kind of passion that made every note feel like a heartbeat. They were alive, vibrant, filled with laughter and love. Now, they sit silent, locked away in a world I'm no longer part of, as if they too mourn his absence. I close my eyes, pressing my fingers against my temples, trying to block out the memories. The laughter we shared, the arguments over lyrics, the late nights spent tweaking beats—each moment feels like a bittersweet song played in an empty room.

The clock on the wall ticks incessantly, reminding me that time, cruel as it is, marches on. I should be creating, should be pouring my heart into melodies that soar like the seagulls over Santa Monica Pier. Instead, I'm stuck in a loop, replaying the moments of our last days together, the final notes of our last song lingering like a painful reminder. I pull out my phone, scrolling through photos of us, his infectious smile frozen in time. A knot tightens in my throat. I'm not sure I can face the world beyond these four walls.

Just then, my phone buzzes, shattering the stillness. It's an invitation from Tara, an old friend I haven't seen in years. She's in town for a music festival, and her message bursts with enthusiasm:

"Lila! You have to come! It'll be like old times. Music, friends, life! Please say yes!" I read the message three times, hoping the words might ignite some spark within me. I can almost hear her voice, a melodic mix of excitement and urgency, coaxing me to join her.

For a moment, I consider the idea—standing in a crowd again, surrounded by the pulse of live music, the kind that used to course through my veins. But what if the notes are just a painful reminder of what I've lost? What if I can't handle the weight of nostalgia? Yet, beneath the layers of sorrow, a flicker of curiosity dances, whispering promises of rediscovery. Perhaps it's time to stop hiding from the world, to let the echoes of my past collide with the present.

I take a deep breath, letting the air fill my lungs, feeling the weight of indecision lift slightly. I text Tara back, my fingers trembling as I type, "Okay, I'll come." The moment I hit send, a rush of exhilaration tingles through me, mingling with the residual fear. What am I getting myself into? The prospect of seeing familiar faces, of stepping into the electric atmosphere of a festival, both terrifies and excites me.

The day of the festival arrives, and the city buzzes with an infectious energy. I throw on a sundress, something light and carefree, a far cry from the somber attire I've worn for far too long. The mirror reflects a stranger, a ghost of Lila Monroe, the girl who danced under the stars, who lived for the beat of the music. I hope to find a piece of her in the crowd today, to reclaim a spark I thought had extinguished forever.

As I step out into the warmth of the day, the air is thick with anticipation. I navigate through throngs of festival-goers, their laughter and chatter mixing with the distant strumming of guitars and beats pulsing from the stage. The vibrant colors of the crowd blur together, a living tapestry of stories and dreams, each person a note in a symphony I'm hesitant to join. My heart races, caught between the thrill of the moment and the fear of being overwhelmed.

I finally spot Tara near a food truck, her wild curls bouncing as she waves excitedly. She rushes over, enveloping me in a hug that feels both familiar and foreign. "You made it! I was beginning to think you'd ghost me like a sad ballad," she jokes, pulling back to study my face. "You look amazing! Ready to let loose?"

"Ready as I'll ever be," I reply, trying to match her enthusiasm but feeling a flutter of nerves twisting in my stomach.

"Trust me, Lila, this will be good for you. Music is the best medicine," she says, grabbing my hand and pulling me toward the stage. The sound grows louder, the crowd's energy palpable, and for the first time in what feels like ages, I feel a flicker of something close to hope.

The first act hits the stage, a local band whose soulful sound washes over the audience like a warm breeze. I close my eyes, letting the music seep into my bones, feeling the rhythm pulse beneath my skin. It's a reminder of everything I've been missing, a sensation that tugs at my heartstrings and dares me to open up again. The energy surges around me, and I can't help but sway, the music weaving a thread of connection through the air.

Tara glances at me, her eyes sparkling with mischief. "See? Isn't this exactly what you needed?"

I nod, my heart beating in sync with the melody. As the band plays on, I catch a glimpse of the carefree girl I once was, the one who danced without a care in the world, unencumbered by grief. The night unfolds in a series of vibrant moments—laughter shared over overpriced food, friends catching up, strangers bonding over music, and for a brief moment, the weight of my past lightens, just enough to let the joy seep through.

But as the final notes of the first set fade, the realization hits me: the shadows of my past still linger, whispering reminders that life can change in an instant. As the next band takes the stage, I can't shake the feeling that this day, this festival, might be the beginning of something unexpected. Something both thrilling and terrifying.

The festival grounds pulse with life, a kaleidoscope of color and sound that wraps around me like a warm embrace. Music reverberates through the air, a steady heartbeat of rhythms and melodies that beckon me closer. I stand with Tara, watching as the next band—an eclectic mix of indie rock and folk—takes the stage. Their vibrant energy electrifies the crowd, and I feel a tremor of excitement ripple through my limbs, stirring something deep within me that I thought had gone dormant.

Tara leans in, her voice barely audible above the din. "This is where you belong, Lila. Let it all in. Let the music lift you." Her words feel like a lifeline, and I cling to them, willing myself to let go of the grief that has weighed me down for so long. The band launches into their first song, a catchy tune that invites the audience to sing along. I find myself joining in, my voice mingling with those around me, blending into the collective joy of the moment.

As the chorus swells, I feel a sense of freedom wash over me. The pain that has been my constant companion loosens its grip, if only for a moment. I glance at Tara, who is lost in the music, her head bobbing in time with the beat, her laughter spilling out like confetti. The sight is infectious, and I can't help but smile. There's something beautifully liberating about standing here, surrounded by strangers who feel like friends, all united by the power of music.

"Okay, but who is this band?" I shout to Tara, trying to keep my voice above the noise.

"They're called The Rhythm Seekers! Just wait until you hear their big song; it's a tear-jerker!" she responds, grinning. "You might cry. Just a warning."

"Great, so it's a tear-fest today!" I laugh, shaking my head. The light banter between us feels like the first step back to the surface, a break from the heavy current I've been swimming against. The music swells, wrapping around me, and I can't help but let go of my inhibitions, dancing like no one's watching. In this moment, I reclaim a piece of myself, the girl who thrived on the thrill of creativity and connection.

The performance ends, but the energy lingers, humming in the air like the fading notes of a favorite song. Tara and I make our way through the festival, navigating food stalls and merchandise tents, my heart pounding with a mixture of exhilaration and nostalgia. We stop at a booth selling handmade jewelry, and Tara picks up a delicate silver bracelet adorned with tiny musical notes. "You need this," she insists, clasping it around my wrist. "It'll be a reminder that music is always with you."

I admire the bracelet, its cool metal against my skin like a promise. "What if I can't create anymore?" The question slips out before I can stop it, vulnerability catching in my throat.

Tara's expression shifts, and she squeezes my hand. "You can. You just need to believe it. Music isn't just about the notes; it's about the feelings. You can feel, can't you? Let that guide you."

Her words echo in my mind as we wander, and I find myself absorbing the vibrancy around us, the smiles and laughter weaving together like an intricate tapestry. As the sun begins to dip toward the horizon, painting the sky in hues of orange and pink, I catch sight of a familiar figure standing near the main stage. My heart skips a beat.

"Is that—?" I start, squinting through the crowd.

"Jake?" Tara finishes, and I can hear the disbelief in her tone.

"No! It can't be!" My heart races, but I can't help but push through the crowd for a closer look. As I get nearer, the figure turns, revealing a tall man with tousled hair and a guitar slung over his shoulder. My breath catches in my throat. It's not Jake, but someone who looks uncannily like him, a mirror image with a smile that radiates warmth. I feel an inexplicable pull toward him, the resemblance both a comfort and a painful reminder.

"Who is that?" I murmur, my curiosity piqued.

"Let's find out!" Tara replies, her excitement infectious. She grabs my hand again, leading me through the throng of festival-goers. As we approach, I notice that he's surrounded by a small group of fans, each hanging on his every word. I can't shake the feeling that I'm meant to be here, that somehow, this moment holds significance.

"Excuse me," Tara says, stepping forward with a boldness that surprises me. "We're huge fans! What's your name?"

The man turns, his smile widening as he takes in our presence. "I'm Max, just here for the music like everyone else." His voice is smooth, rich like the finest whiskey, and my heart skips again, this time with an entirely different rhythm.

I step forward, intrigued. "You have an incredible stage presence, Max. Are you performing here?"

"Not today, but I might get onstage later for an impromptu jam. Nothing better than sharing music with strangers," he replies, his eyes sparkling with genuine enthusiasm.

"Impromptu? That sounds risky!" I tease, the spark of my old self flickering to life.

"Risky is where the best stories begin," he shoots back, a playful grin dancing on his lips.

Tara nudges me, her eyes gleaming with mischief. "And what's your story, Lila?"

Before I can formulate a response, the crowd begins to shift, excitement rippling through the air as the next act is introduced. Max turns to me, his expression softening. "You should come watch. It's going to be a wild ride."

As the music begins, the energy surges, and I find myself caught in the thrill of the moment. The band takes the stage, and the crowd erupts into cheers. I glance back at Max, who is already immersed in the music, his passion igniting something inside me. It's as if, in his presence, the ghost of Jake softens, allowing space for something new to bloom.

"Are you a producer?" he asks, his voice barely rising above the thrumming bass.

"Yeah," I respond, the words slipping out easily, "though it feels like it's been ages since I actually produced anything worth sharing."

"Then you're in the right place," he replies with a wink, and suddenly, I'm reminded that possibility exists. It's a reminder I desperately need.

As the band launches into a high-energy song, I let the music wash over me, feeling the rhythm thrumming through my veins. I close my eyes and sway, a smile breaking free as I lose myself in the moment. But beneath the surface, questions bubble up like an unresolved melody. Who is this man, this echo of my past? What is it about him that feels so familiar? The music envelops me, wrapping me in warmth, and for the first time in what feels like forever, I allow myself to imagine the future—one filled with notes yet to be played, stories yet to be told, and connections just waiting to be forged.

The energy of the festival crackles in the air as I immerse myself in the music, each beat resonating deep within my core. The band onstage is a whirlwind of sound and movement, their infectious enthusiasm drawing the crowd into a euphoric dance. I sway with abandon, letting the rhythm guide me, feeling every note as if it were a part of my very being. Max stands nearby, his presence warm and magnetic, an unspoken connection weaving itself between us.

"Isn't this incredible?" I shout over the music, my heart racing with a mix of excitement and nerves.

"It's like a giant therapy session, but with better outfits!" he laughs, gesturing to a woman twirling in a sequined dress that glimmers in the fading sunlight.

"Only if you don't mind sharing the therapist," I retort, a playful smile on my lips. There's an undeniable chemistry between us, a spark ignited by shared laughter and the heady atmosphere of the festival.

As the song winds down, I notice a small group forming near the edge of the stage, a mix of dedicated fans and curious festival-goers. They're all eagerly snapping photos, but something in the energy feels different—a tension that prickles at my skin. Max tilts his head, his expression shifting as he catches a glimpse of something in the crowd. "You okay?" he asks, his brow furrowing slightly.

"Yeah, just—there's something going on over there," I reply, my instincts kicking in. Curiosity pulls me closer to the gathering, a thread weaving me into the unfolding drama. I squeeze past the crowd, Max right behind me, his presence a steadying force as we navigate through.

As we draw closer, I see a commotion near the barricade, a figure flailing against the security staff. A girl, no older than twenty, her face streaked with tears and panic. "Let me go! I have to see him!" she screams, her voice breaking, desperation lacing her every word.

"Who?" I ask a nearby festival-goer, my pulse quickening.

"Max Parker!" they reply, eyes wide with intrigue. "She says she's his biggest fan or something."

Max's expression darkens, and I feel a shiver of unease. "That's... unexpected," he murmurs, tension creeping into his voice.

The girl manages to break free from the guards for a moment, charging toward the stage before they catch her again. "I need to talk to him! I have something important to tell him!" She writhes in their grip, a mix of fury and fear, and the crowd's murmurs grow louder, a ripple of unease flowing through the onlookers.

"What could she possibly want?" I whisper to Max, my curiosity morphing into concern.

"I don't know, but I've had my fair share of unexpected encounters lately," he replies, his eyes fixed on the scene, a mixture of sympathy and apprehension in his gaze.

Before I can respond, the girl's words cut through the chaos, clear as a bell. "I know the truth! You have to listen!" She looks directly at Max, her eyes wild with urgency.

"Truth? What truth?" I ask, a tight knot forming in my stomach.

"I... I think she knows something," Max replies, his voice low, his brow furrowing as he steps forward, instinctively drawn to the chaos.

Just then, the security team manages to restrain her more firmly, and she gasps for breath, her eyes darting around as if seeking an escape. "You have to believe me! It's about Jake!" Her voice rises, piercing through the crowd like a jagged shard of glass.

Time seems to freeze, and a chill runs down my spine. Jake? My Jake? The world around us fades into a muted blur as her words hang in the air like a specter. Max stiffens beside me, his gaze snapping to mine, the weight of the revelation pressing heavily between us.

"What does she mean?" I ask, my voice barely above a whisper.

"I have no idea," he replies, concern etched across his features. "But if it's about Jake..." His voice trails off, the gravity of the moment hanging thickly.

The girl manages to catch her breath, her gaze darting between Max and me, desperation etched in her features. "Please! You don't understand! I know what really happened!"

The crowd shifts, a wave of curiosity and tension building as everyone leans in closer, eager to catch the next revelation. I can feel my heart pounding in my chest, every beat echoing the tumult of emotions swirling within me. The music fades to a distant hum, replaced by the urgency of her plea.

"Just tell us!" someone from the crowd shouts, the frustration palpable.

"I can't say here!" she cries, her voice trembling. "It's too dangerous. But I swear I can prove it!"

Max looks at me, his eyes wide with alarm. "Lila, we can't let her go like this. If she knows something about Jake..." His voice trails off, the implication hanging in the air between us like a fragile thread.

"Wait!" I step forward, my instincts kicking in. "If you know something, you need to tell us. What happened to Jake?"

The girl's expression shifts, fear giving way to determination. "Meet me at the fountain behind the main stage after the last act. I'll tell you everything. But you have to promise me no one else will come!"

"What if it's a trap?" Max asks, his protective instincts flaring.

"It's our only chance," I reply, my heart racing with the possibilities swirling in my mind. The promise of answers, of closure, tinged with danger and uncertainty.

The girl nods fervently, and just as quickly, security manages to lead her away from the crowd, her cries fading into the distance. A thick silence envelops us, the weight of what's just transpired pressing heavily against my chest.

"Do you think we should?" Max asks, concern etched into his features. "What if it's a bad idea?"

"I don't know," I reply, my thoughts swirling with confusion. "But I can't walk away from this. If there's even a chance to understand what happened to Jake... I have to take it."

Max studies me for a moment, and I can see the resolve hardening in his expression. "Then we'll go together. Whatever this girl has to say, we'll face it as a team."

His words are like a lifeline, and for the first time since arriving at the festival, I feel a flicker of hope amidst the chaos. But as the last act begins, a sense of foreboding lingers in the air, a reminder that the past is never truly buried. The music swells around us, but the truth waits just beyond the notes, teasing us with the promise of revelations yet to come. I glance at Max, and our eyes lock, an unspoken agreement binding us together in this moment of uncertainty.

"Are you ready?" he asks, a mix of apprehension and determination in his voice.

"Ready as I'll ever be," I reply, steeling myself for the journey ahead. But as the final chords resonate through the crowd, a sudden shout pierces the air, and I turn just in time to see the girl break free once more, panic etched across her face. "You don't understand! You need to get out of here! It's not safe!"

Before I can react, the ground shakes beneath us, a tremor that sends the crowd into chaos. A low rumble reverberates through the air, drowning out the music, and my heart drops as I grasp Max's arm tightly.

"What's happening?" I yell, adrenaline coursing through me as confusion spreads among the festival-goers.

"Lila!" Max shouts over the noise, his voice urgent. "We need to move! Now!"

And as we turn to escape, the world around us erupts into chaos, the very foundation of everything I thought I knew trembling beneath my feet. The echoes of the past grow louder, crashing against the present in a wave of uncertainty, and I know one thing for certain: the night is far from over, and the answers I seek may come at a cost I'm not prepared to pay.

Chapter 2: Unscripted Melodies

The festival unfolds like a sprawling canvas, drenched in vibrant colors that dance under the late afternoon sun. Booths adorned with kaleidoscopic decorations line the winding paths, each pulsating with the rhythm of laughter and music that wafts through the air. Vendors hawk their artisanal wares, the scent of freshly baked bread mingling with the sweet notes of funnel cakes, creating a heady aroma that tickles my senses. My heart beats in sync with the thumping bass reverberating from the main stage, each pulse stirring an insatiable curiosity within me.

As I navigate the throngs of festival-goers, I feel a spark of exhilaration that I haven't experienced in what feels like an eternity. The heat of the sun kisses my skin, a reminder that life is still vibrant and alive, even amidst the chaos of my own internal storms. I pause, allowing the melody of laughter and music to wash over me, feeling like an intruder in a world that seems to revel in its own joy.

But then, the moment I've been waiting for arrives. Zane Hart steps onto the stage, and the world shrinks down to just him and me. He stands with an unassuming confidence, his tousled hair catching the light like spun gold. As he strums his guitar, the notes flutter through the air like butterflies, landing softly in my chest and awakening something long dormant. His voice, rough yet melodious, tells stories that curl around my heart, and I can't help but sway with the rhythm, completely entranced.

"Tell me," I whisper to myself, captivated, "is it possible to feel so connected to a stranger?"

Zane's lyrics are steeped in honesty, each word weaving tales of heartache and hope, loss and redemption. It feels like he's laying bare his soul, and in the process, I find pieces of my own story reflected in the shadows of his. The pain of loss—his mother, my father—seems to intertwine between us like a shared thread, binding us even though we've never met. I'm swept away, the crowd around me fading into a mere backdrop to this intimate revelation.

As his set draws to a close, an inexplicable urge propels me toward the backstage area, where I feel a mixture of exhilaration and trepidation. I'm just a fan, a random face in a sea of admirers, yet my heart thunders with the hope that our connection might linger beyond the stage.

Backstage, the air is thick with the afterglow of performance, and I'm caught in the riptide of adrenaline and anticipation. Zane is chatting with a few friends, a bright smile lighting up his face, but when his gaze lands on me, something shifts. It's like he sees past the festival-goer facade and into the depths of who I am. My heart skips, and suddenly I'm tongue-tied.

"Hey, you were amazing out there!" I blurt, my voice slightly breathless, betraying the calm facade I'd hoped to project.

"Thanks! Glad to know I didn't scare anyone off." He laughs, a warm, genuine sound that wraps around me like a cozy blanket. "What did you think? I was worried I'd lose the crowd halfway through."

"Are you kidding? You had everyone in the palm of your hand." I lean against the wall, attempting to appear relaxed, though my insides are a whirlpool of nerves and exhilaration. "The way you connect with the music... it's infectious. You're like a walking playlist of emotions."

He chuckles, running a hand through his hair, his eyes sparkling with amusement. "A walking playlist, huh? That's a new one. I'll have to add that to my bio."

Our conversation flows effortlessly, laughter punctuating the air between us, creating a rhythm that feels both exhilarating and terrifying. I learn that he's been on a long journey, a soul wandering through a landscape of grief and music, and with each revelation, I feel an undeniable pull toward him. The way he speaks of his mother—his voice thick with unprocessed emotion—resonates deeply within me, like a long-forgotten song finally finding its melody.

"I used to write songs with her," he confesses, his tone shifting to something softer, more vulnerable. "She was my biggest fan. Losing her felt like losing my compass." His words hang in the air, heavy with a shared understanding that shimmers like the evening light filtering through the trees.

"I get it," I respond, my voice barely above a whisper, fear and familiarity mingling in the depths of my chest. "I lost my dad a few years ago. It's like a part of you is just... gone. You keep trying to find your way back, but the map keeps changing."

The honesty between us creates a sacred space, one that is laden with unspoken promises and mutual understanding. The world around us blurs, the sounds of the festival fading into a distant hum. I catch a glimpse of Zane's vulnerability, a rare and precious thing that pulls me closer, igniting an inexplicable yearning to share my story, too.

"Do you think they'd be proud of us?" he asks suddenly, his eyes locking onto mine with an intensity that sends shivers down my spine.

"I'd like to think so," I reply, my heart racing. "I think they'd be proud of how we keep pushing through the pain."

There's a long pause, thick with the weight of our revelations. It's a moment suspended in time, and in that space, I realize I don't want this to end. I don't want our paths to diverge, leaving behind the possibility of something beautiful and raw.

"I know this is crazy," I say, my words tumbling out before I can second-guess myself. "But would you want to grab a coffee sometime? Or something stronger?"

Zane's grin is infectious, a spark of mischief dancing in his eyes. "You know what? I think I'd like that. Let's see if we can turn this festival magic into something a little less... scripted."

With those words, the air crackles with an unexpected promise, and as we exchange numbers, I can't shake the feeling that this is just the beginning of a duet I never saw coming.

The days following the festival are a blur of anticipation and self-reflection, each moment tinged with the excitement of possibility. I wake up each morning to sunlight spilling through my window, illuminating the dust motes dancing in the air like tiny, glittering stars. The world feels softer, more vivid, and as I sip my coffee—black, just like my sense of humor—I can't help but think about Zane. It's ridiculous, really. I mean, we had a connection, sure, but did I actually expect to hear from him?

Each time my phone buzzes, my heart leaps into my throat, only to settle back down in disappointment as it's just another message from my overly enthusiastic friend Lucy, who's trying to convince me to join her for karaoke. "Come on! What's more fun than belting out show tunes and embarrassing ourselves in public?" she'd text, complete with a barrage of enthusiastic emojis.

But I can't shake the memory of Zane's laugh or the way he looked at me when I opened up about my dad. It felt significant, a moment carved out from time, like we'd stumbled into our own little universe away from the noise of the festival.

Then, on the fourth day post-festival, as I'm elbow-deep in flour attempting to perfect my sourdough recipe—because apparently, artisanal baking will make me feel like I have my life together—my phone pings. My heart does that ridiculous leap again, and this time, it's not Lucy.

"Hey! It's Zane. I was wondering if you'd like to grab that coffee—or something stronger—this weekend?"

I blink at the screen, almost willing the words to rearrange themselves into something less exciting, less promising. But they don't. A grin stretches across my face, and suddenly the dough feels like a boulder I need to shove aside. I quickly type a reply, my fingers trembling with excitement. "I'd love to! How about Saturday?"

As the weekend approaches, I find myself oscillating between excitement and sheer panic. What am I supposed to wear? Do I go for cute and casual, or should I opt for something that screams "I have my life together"? My closet, a chaotic array of thrift store finds and the occasional impulse buy, offers little in the way of clarity. After a few rounds of trying on different outfits, I settle on a vintage floral dress, soft and breezy, with just enough personality to keep things interesting without shouting "date."

When Saturday arrives, the morning sun spills golden light across the streets, and the world seems to hum in tune with my racing heart. I make my way to the coffee shop—one of those quaint, indie places with mismatched furniture and the intoxicating aroma of freshly ground beans hanging thick in the air. As I walk through the door, a small bell jingles, announcing my arrival in a way that feels both welcoming and slightly intimidating.

I scan the room, and my heart does another leap when I spot Zane in the corner, casually leaning against a worn wooden table, his guitar case propped beside him. He's wearing a simple white tee and jeans, yet somehow he manages to look effortlessly cool. I can't help but admire how he seems so at ease, as if he belongs to this space, and maybe, just maybe, he belongs in my world too.

"Hey! You made it!" he greets, a smile breaking across his face that sets my nerves at ease.

"I wouldn't miss it for the world," I reply, trying to sound casual while internally berating myself for how breathless I feel.

We settle into conversation, the easy rapport from backstage seamlessly returning as we sip our drinks. Zane orders a black coffee, the kind that can wake the dead, while I opt for a matcha latte, the trendy drink I secretly hope makes me seem sophisticated.

"So, tell me about your life outside of the festival," he prompts, his gaze steady and curious, as if he's genuinely interested in peeling back the layers.

I take a deep breath, ready to share snippets of my world. "Well, I'm a graphic designer by day, which sounds fancier than it is. Mostly, I'm sitting in front of a screen trying to convince clients that pastel pink and mustard yellow can coexist peacefully. It's like a never-ending battle between creativity and practicality."

He laughs, and it's the kind of laugh that echoes and lingers in the air, drawing me in. "That sounds like a worthy challenge. How often do you win?"

"Let's just say my track record isn't stellar," I confess, "but I make a mean mood board. You know, just to add a splash of color to my otherwise monochrome existence."

Zane leans in, a conspiratorial glint in his eyes. "I feel that. My life is basically a soundtrack to the chaos. I write songs between gigs, which is sometimes cathartic and other times just a creative excuse to avoid laundry. So, you could say we're both artists in a battle against the mundane."

I chuckle at the mental image of Zane holed up in his apartment, surrounded by crumpled papers and dirty socks, frantically composing a ballad while contemplating the deeper meaning of laundry day. It's oddly endearing.

Our conversation flows effortlessly, filled with laughter and surprisingly deep insights that feel both intimate and safe. I discover that Zane's latest album, filled with songs about loss and healing, is inspired by his mother's love for music. "She used to dance around the kitchen while baking, and I swear, that's where I learned the magic of blending chaos with creativity," he shares, his eyes softening.

"Do you ever feel pressure to keep that legacy alive?" I ask, genuinely curious.

Zane's expression shifts, and for a moment, I see the weight of expectation behind his playful demeanor. "Every day. But it's a beautiful burden, you know? It drives me to keep writing and sharing, even when it's hard. Like I owe it to her to create something beautiful from the pain."

I nod, recognizing the shared struggle in our stories—the desire to turn grief into art, to transform our losses into something meaningful. The air between us crackles with understanding, a shared warmth that ignites a flicker of hope in my chest.

But just as I begin to think that maybe, just maybe, this could be something more, Zane's phone buzzes on the table, breaking the moment. He glances at it, and his expression shifts, just slightly.

"I should probably take this," he says, a hint of reluctance in his voice. "It's my manager. You know how it is—always a million things to juggle."

I smile, but it feels like a damper on the moment, the sudden intrusion of reality threatening to pull us apart. "Of course! Take your time."

As he answers the call, I can't help but feel the slightest pang of worry. The connection we've built feels fragile, teetering on the edge of something beautiful and uncertain. I watch him talk, his gestures animated as he tries to balance the conversation and maintain his signature charm. But I can't shake the feeling that whatever he's discussing is serious, pulling him away from the lightness we've shared.

When he hangs up, a cloud of tension lingers in the air. "Sorry about that. Just some last-minute arrangements for my tour. It's always something, right?" His smile doesn't quite reach his eyes this time.

"Of course," I reply, trying to mask my concern with a lighthearted tone. "Life waits for no musician."

"Exactly!" he says, returning to his playful demeanor. "And I can't let my socks win the battle for the throne of creativity."

Yet even as we continue our banter, a nagging feeling settles in my stomach, a whisper of uncertainty. I realize that the space we've carved out for ourselves is fragile, a delicate balance between shared dreams and the harsh reality of our lives.

As our playful banter drifts into a comfortable silence, I can't help but feel a flicker of anxiety in the space between us. Zane seems distracted, and while I want to believe it's just the chaos of the call that's clouding his thoughts, a nagging voice whispers otherwise. I take a sip of my matcha latte, letting the earthy bitterness ground me, and mentally review my own to-do list. Yet, the world outside this café feels suddenly distant, like a hazy backdrop against the vivid colors of our moment.

"So, what's next on your agenda?" I ask, trying to pull the conversation back to lighter ground, but my voice wobbles slightly. "More music? A revolution in laundry care?"

Zane chuckles, and for a second, the tension lifts. "A revolution in laundry care would be a game changer! But seriously, I'm gearing up for a mini-tour next month. Just a few local spots to start. Nothing too wild."

"Just a few local spots? Sounds like you're a rock star on the rise," I tease, leaning forward, genuinely curious. "Where are you headed first?"

"Mostly smaller venues, places where I can really connect with the audience," he replies, his enthusiasm sparking a warmth in my chest. "I like the intimate settings. Feels more genuine, you know? Last year, I played at this tiny coffee shop that had a cat wandering around. It was glorious."

"Sounds like a purr-fect gig."

Zane rolls his eyes but laughs nonetheless. "Okay, I see what you did there. I'm impressed."

Just as I'm about to share a story of my own, a shadow looms over our table. I look up, momentarily blinded by the sunlight filtering in, and squint at the silhouette. It's a tall figure, an imposing presence that instantly shifts the atmosphere around us. Zane's expression changes too; the spark in his eyes dims slightly, replaced by something harder to read.

"Zane," the figure says, a voice dripping with authority. "We need to talk."

I shift in my seat, confusion swirling inside me. This wasn't the "something stronger" I had anticipated. The man, dressed in a sharply tailored suit that screams of high expectations, stands with his arms crossed, a tight frown etched on his face. I can't help but feel like I'm intruding on something private, something delicate.

"Can it wait?" Zane replies, a hint of irritation creeping into his tone. "I'm in the middle of—"

"No, it can't," the man interrupts, his gaze flicking to me with barely concealed annoyance. "This is business."

I suddenly feel like an intruder in my own little bubble of connection, the warmth of our previous conversation dissipating into the cold, clinical air of obligation. Zane glances at me, his expression apologetic, and in that moment, my heart sinks. Whatever this is, it's urgent and important, and I don't want to be the reason he's pulled away from it.

"I'll just... I'll step outside for a moment," I say quickly, attempting to keep my tone light, but the words feel heavy as they leave my lips. I rise from my seat, a forced smile plastered on my face, even as my insides twist with disappointment.

"Wait," Zane says, standing too, the urgency of the situation flickering in his eyes. "I don't want you to go. I—"

But the suited man steps closer, cutting off whatever Zane was trying to say. "We don't have time for this. You need to focus on the tour."

With one last look that feels charged with unspoken words, Zane's shoulders sag, the fight in him dissipating like the last notes of a song fading away. I turn to leave, a mixture of hurt and confusion bubbling up inside me.

As I step outside, the warm sunlight envelops me like a comforting embrace, but it does little to soothe the rising tide of uncertainty. I lean against the cool brick wall of the café, taking a deep breath to steady myself, the sound of laughter and chatter from inside becoming a distant murmur. I can't shake the feeling that the moment had shifted, that the carefree atmosphere we'd created had been pierced by something sharp and unwelcome.

I glance down the street, my mind racing with thoughts. What kind of business did Zane have to attend to? Was it related to his music? Did it involve contracts, managers, perhaps the very tour he was excited about? It felt like I had glimpsed a hidden layer of his life—one filled with pressures and expectations—and it scared me more than I'd anticipated.

Just as I'm grappling with these thoughts, my phone buzzes in my pocket. I pull it out, half-expecting another enthusiastic message from Lucy, but my heart drops when I see the name on the screen. It's an unknown number, yet something inside me urges me to answer.

"Hello?" I say cautiously, half-wondering if this is a sign of bad news or perhaps just a wrong number.

"Is this Sofia?" The voice on the other end is smooth but clipped, with an undercurrent of urgency that sends a shiver down my spine.

"Yes? Who is this?"

"I need to speak with you about Zane Hart," the voice says, each word carefully measured. "It's important. Can you meet me?"

My stomach drops at the mention of Zane's name, alarm bells ringing in my mind. "Why? What's happened?"

"I can't discuss it over the phone. Meet me at the park, near the fountain. Ten minutes." The line goes dead before I can respond, leaving me clutching my phone in disbelief.

What could this possibly mean? My heart races as a thousand thoughts collide in my mind. Is Zane in trouble? Is there something I don't know about his life? A million questions swirl around me, each one demanding answers.

Taking a deep breath, I push off the wall and start walking toward the park, the sunlight fading as clouds gather overhead. Each step feels heavier, laden with an anticipation I can't shake. The idea of Zane facing something serious, something potentially dangerous, fills me with dread.

By the time I reach the park, the air feels electric, charged with tension. I scan the area for anyone who looks out of place, my heart pounding as I approach the fountain. The water cascades down in a soothing rhythm, but my nerves are anything but calm.

As I wait, the shadows lengthen, and the world around me blurs into a haze of uncertainty. My pulse quickens as I spot a figure emerging from the treeline—a woman with striking red hair, her expression intense and focused. She strides toward me with purpose, a look in her eyes that suggests she knows far more than she's letting on.

"Are you Sofia?" she asks, her tone leaving no room for pleasantries.

"Yes. What's going on? What do you know about Zane?"

Her eyes narrow slightly, and the weight of the moment settles heavily between us. "We don't have much time. You need to listen carefully..."

Before she can finish, a sharp noise shatters the air—a sound that sends a jolt of panic through my veins. I turn just in time to see a figure emerge from the shadows, and my heart drops as I recognize him. Zane stands there, his face pale and strained, and behind him, the tension in the air shifts abruptly.

"Get away from her!" he shouts, and in that moment, everything fractures, a world of secrets and truths ready to collide.

Chapter 3: Chords of Conflict

The studio felt like a ghost town without Jake, the silence hanging heavy like an overripe fruit, just waiting to drop and spoil everything. I settled into my chair, the familiar creak of wood beneath me resonating with an unsettling nostalgia. The walls were adorned with mementos of past projects: gold records gleaming like trophies, photos of artists laughing and dancing under bright lights, and the remnants of our late-night brainstorming sessions that often bled into dawn. But now, each piece seemed to mock me, a reminder of the magic that had once flowed freely through these walls and the brilliant partnership we had forged, now scattered like autumn leaves in the wind.

With my fingers hovering over the keyboard, I scanned the empty tracks before me, waiting for inspiration to strike. I pressed a few keys, producing an uninspired series of chords that echoed into the silence, a hollow sound that felt like my current state of being. I missed the lively banter, the teasing remarks about my inability to create a decent hook. I missed Jake's presence, that effortless energy that fueled my creativity. The truth was, I didn't just miss him as a collaborator; I missed him as a friend.

The walls of my sanctuary began to close in, and I could feel the weight of expectations settling on my shoulders like an unwelcome blanket. Just as I was ready to drown in my thoughts, my phone buzzed insistently on the desk, breaking the stifling quiet. I glanced at the screen: Nina.

"Hey, you," she chirped, her voice spilling over the line like a fresh brew of coffee. "I've got an opportunity for you."

"Nina, I'm not sure I'm ready to—"

"Listen, you're going to want to hear this. There's a rising star, Aliana Rivers. The girl is a whirlwind, and her debut album is set to drop soon. She's been causing quite the stir, and they need someone to produce it. I immediately thought of you."

Aliana Rivers. The name struck a chord. Her rise was meteoric, fueled by social media buzz and a penchant for theatricality. I had heard whispers of her antics—over-the-top performances, dramatic social media posts, and a talent that was both celebrated and critiqued. The thought of diving headfirst into the chaos of her world made my skin prickle with anxiety. "Nina, you know I'm not looking to chase drama right now."

"I get that, but this is a chance to reclaim your space in the industry. You're a producer, and you can't hide forever. Besides, think of it as a challenge—a way to channel your frustrations. I know how hard it's been since Jake...well, you know."

Her words stung like a cold wind. I didn't want to admit it, but she was right. I had been hiding, cocooned in the comfort of my solitude, avoiding the music scene that had once thrilled me. The fire of my passion was flickering low, and perhaps I needed this push to reignite it.

"Fine. I'll do it," I said, forcing enthusiasm into my voice.

"Great! I'll set it up. Just remember, Aliana thrives on chaos, so brace yourself."

After we hung up, I couldn't shake the sense of impending doom mixed with a flicker of hope. I needed this project to either renew my spirit or confirm my fears. I gathered my courage, threw on my favorite leather jacket—my armor, really—and headed out to meet this tempest of talent.

Arriving at the studio, I was greeted by an explosion of color and sound. The space was vibrant, brimming with youthful energy. Aliana was a vision of eclectic style, dressed in mismatched patterns that somehow worked together, her hair a cascade of wild curls that danced around her shoulders. She was flanked by a group of friends who were as flamboyant as she was, their laughter echoing off the walls like a song that couldn't quite find its melody.

"Welcome to the circus!" Aliana exclaimed, her eyes sparkling with mischief. "Are you ready to turn the world on its head?"

"Um, I think I'd settle for just a single track for now," I replied, struggling to keep my tone light as I scanned the room. The chaos was palpable, and the way her entourage buzzed around her felt like a live performance without any rehearsal.

Aliana shrugged, unfazed by my hesitation. "We'll see about that! I need you to bring your magic, and we'll create something that'll make everyone sit up and take notice."

As we began to discuss her vision, it became clear we were operating on entirely different wavelengths. Aliana was all about theatrics—grand gestures, dramatic storytelling, and an approach that felt almost reckless to me. I, on the other hand, thrived on structure, seeking clarity and depth in every note. The tension between us simmered like a pot about to boil over, each of us reluctant to bend in the name of collaboration.

"This is going to be fun," I said, my voice drenched in irony.

"Fun? Honey, this is going to be fabulous!" Aliana shot back, grinning widely.

As the first session unfolded, I realized just how much I yearned for the creative camaraderie I once had with Jake. Every attempt I made to guide Aliana towards a cohesive sound felt like I was pushing against a tidal wave of her exuberance. Her ego was as large as her ambitions, and every note I suggested was met with playful resistance or spirited debate. The experience was both exhilarating and exasperating, a constant tug-of-war that left me exhausted yet strangely invigorated.

With each passing day, I found myself entangled deeper in this whirlwind of artistry, longing for the familiar rhythm that Jake and I had once shared. Yet, within the chaos, I also felt the flicker of inspiration. Aliana's passion was infectious, and as she challenged me, I discovered glimmers of my own creativity reawakening, the first notes of a symphony waiting to be composed.

And as I navigated this tumultuous partnership, I realized that sometimes, in the most unexpected collaborations, the best music is born from the clash of differing visions.

The studio buzzed with a frenetic energy as Aliana and her entourage settled into our sessions. It felt like trying to choreograph a ballet in a mosh pit. On one hand, Aliana was an undeniable force; her voice possessed an electric quality that could pull at your heartstrings and ignite the dance floor simultaneously. On the other hand, her whims often left us teetering on the edge of chaos, where inspiration and frustration collided like two stubborn teenagers arguing over the last slice of pizza.

"Okay, let's take it from the top," I said, clenching my notes, half-hoping for a miracle. "This time, let's focus on the bridge. It needs to build the emotion, you know? Give it some heart."

"Heart? Darling, we're not trying to make a soup," Aliana replied, tossing her curls dramatically. "This is a masterpiece! We need fireworks, confetti, and maybe a live chicken!"

"A live chicken?" I blinked, unsure if she was serious or just messing with me.

"Of course! Have you ever heard of the 'Avenue Q' musical? You can't have a show without some unexpected flair! We could totally work with that!" She grinned, winking at her friends, who burst into laughter.

"Right, because when I think of chart-topping hits, my mind immediately goes to poultry." I attempted to maintain my composure, but the absurdity of it all was disarming.

"Just imagine! The critics would be raving! 'This song really took flight!'" she cackled, her laughter contagious.

I couldn't help but chuckle, albeit reluctantly. Her playful absurdity was a stark contrast to my usually meticulous approach. I decided to lean into the ridiculousness. "Alright, let's add 'live chicken' to the list of demands for our next rehearsal. But let's start with a solid melody first, yeah?"

The ensuing hours felt like a roller coaster of emotions, our dynamic veering between playful banter and tense disagreements. While Aliana thrived on spontaneity, I craved structure, wanting to cultivate something raw and real without straying too far into theatrical absurdity. As the days turned into weeks, I found myself grappling with an unsettling question: was this really what I wanted?

"Seriously, though, do we have to record with a live chicken?" I asked one afternoon, my voice laced with both amusement and exasperation.

"I mean, if you want a hit, we have to think outside the box!" she declared, tossing her head back dramatically.

"Right, because nothing screams 'award-winning single' quite like chicken sounds," I replied, rolling my eyes.

And yet, for every laugh we shared, I couldn't ignore the nagging sensation that our creative processes were at war. I started to wonder if Nina's idea of rekindling my passion was a bit misguided. There were moments when I glimpsed the potential in our collaboration—a melody would shimmer through the chaos, sparking excitement, but just as quickly, it would dissolve into the ether, drowned out by Aliana's grand ideas and wild gestures.

One evening, as I left the studio, the sky painted with the fading blush of sunset, I found myself weighed down by the conflicting rhythms of my heart and mind. The city hummed around me, and I felt oddly adrift in a sea of lights and sounds. I was pulled in two directions: the longing for the creative sanctuary I had once shared with Jake and the frenetic allure of Aliana's audacious spirit.

My phone buzzed again. This time it was a text from Jake. The mere sight of his name stirred something deep within me, a mix of fondness and unresolved tension.

Hey, how's the new project?

My fingers hesitated over the screen. How could I explain that the project was equal parts exhilarating and exhausting, that I was wrestling with my identity as a producer without him? After a moment, I typed back a simple reply: It's chaotic but fun. I miss our jams, though.

His response was swift, filled with that familiar warmth I'd grown to rely on. Maybe we can jam together again soon?

I couldn't help but smile, my heart swelling with the nostalgia of our late-night sessions filled with laughter, creativity, and the occasional bickering over which chord progression was better.

"Hey, you okay?" Aliana's voice broke through my reverie, pulling me back to reality.

"Just texting an old friend," I said, attempting to keep my tone light.

She raised an eyebrow, her curiosity piqued. "A friend or a 'friend'?"

"Just a friend," I assured her, though her playful skepticism made me wonder if I was trying to convince myself more than her.

"Right, sure. Just friends don't make each other smile like that. It's a sparkle."

I chuckled. "You know, for someone who loves chaos, you've got a knack for being perceptive."

"Oh, honey, I live for the chaos. But I also know a good connection when I see one. Speaking of which, you should totally invite him to the studio. I need to meet this 'friend' of yours. We could use some extra creative vibes."

The idea sent a jolt of unease through me. Could I introduce Jake to this world of vibrant chaos, the complete opposite of our harmonious melodies? But as I contemplated the notion, a part of me felt that maybe it could work, perhaps even add a spark of stability to our whirlwind sessions.

And so, with a mix of trepidation and excitement, I decided to take the plunge. I texted Jake, inviting him to join us at the studio. Would it lead to laughter and inspiration, or would it ignite a tension I had been desperately trying to avoid? Only time would tell, and as I prepared for our next session with Aliana, I couldn't shake the feeling that I was on the cusp of a pivotal moment.

With a renewed sense of purpose, I stepped into the studio, ready to face whatever chaos Aliana and the universe would throw my way. It was time to embrace the unexpected, to blend our sounds, even if it meant trading a quiet heart for the raucous symphony of life.

The studio felt electric as I prepared for Jake's arrival. Aliana flitted around, like a hummingbird on caffeine, adjusting the lighting and fluffing her extravagant cushions as if they were props for a Broadway show. "This place needs more drama, don't you think?" she mused, draping a sparkly shawl over the back of a chair. "I mean, we're making magic here!"

"Right, because nothing says 'music production' quite like sequins," I replied, arching an eyebrow.

"Exactly! It's all about the atmosphere. If we're going to create hits, we need to feel them." She twirled, the shawl catching the light, and for a fleeting moment, I almost understood her logic.

As the minutes ticked by, anticipation curled in my stomach, and I found myself torn between excitement and anxiety. What would happen when Jake entered this vibrant, chaotic sphere? Would he fit in, or would the contrast highlight the absence of the easy rhythm we once shared? Just as the clock struck six, the door swung open, and in walked Jake, looking as effortlessly cool as ever, with his signature half-smile and tousled hair.

"Hey, stranger!" he greeted, his eyes brightening at the sight of me.

"Stranger? I'm pretty sure I'm the one who sent you an invitation," I teased, stepping forward to embrace him.

"It's good to be here," he replied, scanning the room, his expression shifting from casual to curious. "What's going on? Did you join a circus?"

"Oh, this is just a taste of my new project." I gestured towards Aliana, who was now posing dramatically with a sparkling microphone. "Meet Aliana Rivers, the force of nature I've been telling you about."

"Ah, the whirlwind!" Jake said, extending a hand. "Nice to meet you. I've heard stories."

"Nice to meet you too, Jake! I'm thrilled you're here. We're about to embark on an adventure!" Aliana exclaimed, her excitement infectious.

As they exchanged pleasantries, I couldn't help but watch the dynamic unfold. Jake seemed at ease with Aliana's theatricality, his natural charm drawing her in, while I felt a twinge of anxiety about how our collaboration would morph with his presence.

"So, what's the plan?" Jake asked, glancing at the instruments scattered around the studio.

"Today, we're diving into the heart of the first track," I said, gesturing towards my notes. "It needs some structure, but Aliana has some interesting ideas about how to approach it."

"Interesting, huh?" Jake shot me a knowing look, a smirk playing on his lips.

"Try chaotic," I corrected, rolling my eyes. "Aliana believes that every hit needs at least a sprinkle of confetti and possibly a live chicken."

"Definitely a new approach," he chuckled, leaning back in his chair. "Alright, I'm intrigued. Let's see what we can make of it."

The session unfolded like a Broadway play gone slightly off-script. Jake settled into the producer's chair, easily weaving his influence into the fabric of our work. Aliana thrived under his direction, her ideas flowing freely, and I could see the glimmer of genuine creativity igniting between them.

"Let's try this," Jake said, tapping out a rhythm on the tabletop. "How about we build from a classic chord progression, then layer in Aliana's flair?"

Aliana clapped her hands excitedly. "Yes! But let's add some tempo shifts and maybe a bridge that hits harder than a freight train! And if we can manage a key change in there, even better!"

"Alright, let's not blow the entire sound system in one go," I interjected, trying to rein in the escalating ideas while feeling a twinge of exhilaration. "We need to ground it somehow. Remember, it has to resonate with listeners, not just make them wonder if they walked into a festival."

As the hours passed, the studio became a hive of creativity. The blend of Jake's methodical approach and Aliana's instinctual artistry formed a surprisingly harmonious chaos. I felt a thrill coursing through me as we bounced ideas back and forth, laughter mingling with the sound of our music taking shape.

But just as the atmosphere shifted into a comforting rhythm, a sudden crash shattered the moment. One of Aliana's friends, a lanky guy with an unkempt mop of hair, had accidentally knocked over a stack of equipment, sending cables and microphones cascading to the floor like a tangle of snakes.

"Oops! My bad!" he exclaimed, scrambling to help.

"Careful!" I shouted, my heart racing. "That's expensive!"

"Is everything alright?" Jake asked, rising to assess the chaos.

"Yes, just the sound of creative genius at work," I replied dryly, my eyes darting to Aliana, who was biting back laughter.

With the distraction cleared, we resumed our session, but I noticed Jake and Aliana exchanging glances, a subtle connection sparking between them that made my heart flutter with a tinge of jealousy.

As we delved deeper into the song, the vibe shifted again, and soon we were all caught in the euphoria of creation. I found myself surprised by how seamlessly Jake fit into this world, weaving Aliana's ideas with my structure into something beautiful. Yet, somewhere in the back of my mind, doubt lingered, whispering that I was losing my hold on this collaboration.

"Okay, let's take it from the top!" I announced, trying to rally everyone's focus.

Aliana took a deep breath, and just as she began to sing, the power flickered, then went out completely, plunging the studio into darkness.

"What the—?" I exclaimed, fumbling for my phone to illuminate the space.

"Maybe the music gods are trying to tell us something," Jake quipped, attempting to lighten the mood, but I could hear the undercurrent of uncertainty in his voice.

"Do you think we blew a fuse?" I wondered aloud, feeling the tension thicken in the air.

"Or maybe it's a sign that we need to take a break," Aliana suggested, her tone suddenly serious.

Just then, the emergency lights flickered on, casting an eerie glow over the room. Shadows danced along the walls, and a thick silence enveloped us, broken only by the soft hum of the backup generators struggling to kick in.

"I'll check the panel," I said, pushing through the sudden chill creeping down my spine.

As I made my way toward the control room, I sensed a shift in the atmosphere—a weight, an inexplicable tension. Something wasn't right. I opened the door, ready to face the technical chaos, but what greeted me was a sight that sent chills racing up my arms.

The control panel had been tampered with; wires were frayed and exposed, and a small device, one I didn't recognize, blinked ominously in the dim light.

"Guys!" I shouted, panic rising in my chest. "You need to see this!"

Jake and Aliana hurried in, their expressions shifting from curiosity to concern as they took in the scene.

"What the hell is that?" Jake murmured, stepping closer.

"I don't know, but it looks like someone messed with the wiring. This isn't just a blown fuse."

Before I could utter another word, the device emitted a high-pitched beep, and the lights flickered ominously again. A sinking feeling filled the pit of my stomach as the power surged back on, but the atmosphere in the studio was charged, electric with something darker than mere technical difficulties.

"Who would do this?" Aliana whispered, her earlier bravado stripped away, leaving only a palpable fear.

The air was thick with uncertainty, and as I turned to face them, my heart raced at the realization that the chaos we had embraced might just be the beginning of something far more sinister.

Chapter 4: Harmony in the Chaos

The dim lights of the venue cast a warm glow over the crowd, wrapping us in a cocoon of anticipation. The air buzzed with chatter and laughter, thick with the scent of spilled beer and popcorn. It was the kind of place where the floor felt alive beneath your feet, a patchwork of worn wooden boards that had absorbed countless stories whispered over drinks and promises made under the influence of good music. I slipped through the crowd, letting the rhythm of the night pulse through me, a soundtrack to the chaos swirling in my mind.

And then, there he was—Zane. Leaning into the mic like he was born to command it, his tousled hair catching the light in a way that made him look almost ethereal. The crowd erupted into cheers as he strummed the first chords of his set, the sound piercing through the haze of my thoughts. There was something magnetic about him, an unfiltered authenticity that wrapped around me like a familiar melody. I couldn't help but sway, a helpless marionette to the strings of his voice, which danced through the room, mingling with the laughter and the clinking of glasses.

With every note, I felt my heart race. Zane's songs unfolded stories that felt deeply personal yet universally relatable, weaving tales of love and loss, chaos and serenity. The lyrics spilled out like secrets shared between friends, full of vivid imagery that painted a world I could almost touch. He sang with such intensity, his blue eyes shining with passion as if each word were a spark igniting something dormant within me. My admiration morphed into yearning, a bittersweet ache that stirred memories of late-night writing sessions and pages filled with half-formed thoughts.

As he wrapped up his set, the crowd erupted into applause, a thunderous roar that echoed through the venue like a crashing wave. Zane stepped down, a boyish grin splitting his face, and our eyes met for just a heartbeat. I felt something electric in that moment—a recognition that surpassed mere attraction, something raw and vibrant. I couldn't help but follow him to the bar, my heart racing in a way that felt both thrilling and terrifying.

"Did you like it?" he asked, leaning against the counter, his casual demeanor a stark contrast to the storm of feelings brewing inside me.

"I loved it," I said, my voice steady despite the flutter in my chest. "You have a way with words. It's like you pull them from some hidden place and make them feel so real."

He chuckled, the sound rich and warm, wrapping around me like a blanket on a chilly night. "Thanks. I try not to overthink it. Just let it flow. You know?"

As we shared a round of drinks, the conversation flowed as easily as the music that had just filled the room. I found myself revealing more than I intended—the struggles I faced as I tried to carve out my own creative space, my doubts clawing at my confidence like a persistent shadow. Zane listened intently, his expression a mix of understanding and encouragement. "You're overthinking it," he said, his tone light yet piercing. "You're trying to fit into some mold that doesn't even exist. Just create. Embrace the chaos."

His words sank into me, the truth resonating like a forgotten melody returning to the forefront of my mind. "But what if it's not good enough? What if I'm just chasing shadows?"

"Good enough for whom? The critics? Your family? Yourself?" Zane's eyes sparkled with mischief. "The only person who needs to be satisfied with your work is you. And trust me, there's beauty in the mess. It's where the magic happens."

I raised an eyebrow, half-amused. "You make it sound so simple."

"Simple doesn't mean easy. But it's all about perspective. You're creating art, not curing diseases. So why not have fun with it?" He leaned in closer, and the warmth of his presence sent an unexpected shiver down my spine. "Think of it like this: every mistake is just a stepping stone to something greater. Embrace it, and you'll find your voice. You'll see."

The atmosphere shifted as we shared more stories, laughter bubbling up between us, a delightful concoction of words and whiskey. I could feel the connection solidifying, something electric dancing in the air, charged with possibilities. He was charismatic, and as he talked about his own creative struggles, I couldn't help but admire the vulnerability that lurked beneath his confident exterior. It was in those moments that I recognized a shared longing, an unspoken understanding that bound us together like the chords of his songs.

"Have you ever felt like you were standing on the edge of something big?" I asked, my voice barely above a whisper, the weight of my question hanging in the air. "Like you're just waiting for the right moment to leap?"

Zane nodded, his gaze piercing into mine. "Every time I step on stage. Every time I write a song. It's terrifying and exhilarating all at once. But you have to trust yourself enough to jump. Otherwise, you'll never know what you're capable of."

His words hung in the air like a promise, igniting a flicker of courage in my chest. In that crowded bar, surrounded by the echoes of laughter and music, something deep within me began to awaken—a fierce determination to reclaim my creative voice, to embrace the chaos and create something authentic.

The hours slipped by, entwined with laughter and the soft clinking of glasses, as if time itself had surrendered to the rhythm of our conversation. The bar pulsed around us, a heartbeat fueled by the ebb and flow of patrons lost in their own stories. Zane leaned in, the warmth of his shoulder brushing against mine, and I could feel the tension in the air shift, becoming something more—something that crackled with unspoken possibilities.

"I mean, how do you even know when you've found your voice?" I asked, swirling the remnants of my drink, the ice clinking against the glass as if to punctuate my doubts. "It feels like a never-ending search for a treasure that might not even exist."

Zane chuckled, his laughter resonating deep within my chest, an infectious sound that drew me closer. "Think of it this way: finding your voice is like trying to catch a fish in a sea of thoughts. Sometimes, you just have to throw the line in and hope for the best. You might reel in a tiny sardine, but that's okay. Every catch is part of the journey."

"Now you're just mixing metaphors. Are we fishing or writing?" I teased, a grin breaking across my face despite the weight of my earlier frustration. His lightness was infectious, pulling me away from my self-imposed worries.

"Why not both? Art and fishing require patience, a bit of skill, and a whole lot of hope," he replied, raising his glass in a mock toast. "To sardines and stories!"

I laughed, the sound bubbling up from somewhere deep inside me. It felt good, like a much-needed rain on a parched landscape. Our banter flowed effortlessly, as if we were old friends reunited after years apart. Zane spoke of his latest projects, the struggles he faced in finding the right words to accompany his melodies, and how sometimes he just had to let go of the reins and let the music guide him. I hung on every word, captivated by the way he navigated through the chaos of his thoughts, unearthing gems that sparkled under the dim lights.

"Tell me," he said, suddenly serious, "what's the one thing you're afraid of creating?"

The question struck me like a chord struck too hard on a guitar, vibrating through the air and landing squarely in my chest. I hesitated, caught off guard by his sincerity. "I guess... I'm afraid of making something that's just noise. Something no one wants to hear," I confessed, the words slipping out before I could rein them in.

Zane tilted his head, his eyes narrowing slightly as he considered my response. "But what if noise is exactly what you need to embrace? Not every sound is music, but every sound can be part of a symphony. Your job is to compose it."

There was a weight to his words, a grounding force that made me reconsider everything I'd been holding onto. I'd spent so much time trying to mold myself into what I thought was expected of me—perfectly polished, carefully curated. The idea of embracing noise, of allowing imperfections to dance freely across the page, ignited a flicker of excitement within me.

"Maybe you're onto something," I mused, stirring my drink as I pondered his perspective. "But how do I start? It feels so daunting."

Zane leaned closer, his voice dropping to a conspiratorial whisper, "You start by just doing it. Put pen to paper, or fingers to keys, and let it flow. You don't have to show anyone. Just create for the sake of creating. You might surprise yourself."

Our conversation veered into deeper territory, filled with shared vulnerabilities and dreams that lingered on the edges of reality. Zane spoke of his childhood, the pressure to succeed echoing through the halls of his home like a haunting refrain. "I think that's why I put my heart into every song," he said, a shadow flickering across his expression. "Music is my rebellion, my way of claiming my space in the world."

"Rebellion, huh? Sounds romantic," I quipped, unable to resist the urge to lighten the mood. "I thought art was supposed to be all about flowers and sunsets."

He chuckled, the tension between us dissolving momentarily. "Only if you're painting them in a sterile gallery. I prefer my art a little messy, a little wild."

Just then, the atmosphere shifted, the bar door swinging open to let in a gust of chilly night air that cut through our warmth. I glanced back, and my heart sank when I saw a familiar figure step inside—my ex-boyfriend, Jamie, with that infuriatingly charming smile plastered across his face. He scanned the room, his gaze landing on me like a spotlight.

"Is this a bad time?" Zane asked, sensing my shift in mood.

"Not for me," I replied, forcing a smile that felt more like a mask than a genuine expression. "But I think my past just walked in."

Jamie approached, his presence a blend of nostalgia and irritation. "Fancy seeing you here. I didn't know you were into live music," he said, his tone light but laced with an undertone of something I couldn't quite place.

"Surprise, surprise," I replied, trying to keep my voice steady. "I have layers, you know."

Zane stiffened slightly beside me, his earlier warmth dissipating into the chill that Jamie seemed to bring with him. "Nice to meet you," he said, extending a hand in a casual yet deliberate manner.

Jamie hesitated for a moment, then took Zane's hand, a flicker of confusion crossing his face as if he couldn't quite place this unexpected encounter. "And you are?"

"Just a friend," Zane replied smoothly, his gaze steady as if trying to gauge the dynamic unfolding before him. "We were just talking about how important it is to create art without fear."

Jamie smirked, his expression shifting. "Sounds deep. Are you a musician too?"

"More of a storyteller," Zane replied, his confidence unshaken. "What brings you here?"

The tension thickened, a palpable energy crackling between the three of us. Jamie shifted his focus back to me, and I could see the wheels turning in his mind, analyzing the unexpected scenario before him. "I was just grabbing a drink with some friends. Didn't think I'd run into you... or him."

The night was no longer just about the music or the drinks; it had morphed into something else entirely—a collision of past and present, of dreams and disappointments. As I stood between the two men, the path forward seemed both daunting and exhilarating, and I couldn't shake the feeling that the choices I made in this moment might echo far beyond the confines of the bar.

The moment hung in the air like the last note of a song, vibrating with unspoken tension. Jamie stood there, his presence a jarring reminder of the past, while Zane's eyes flicked back and forth between us, assessing the unfolding drama as if he were part of a play. I could feel my heart racing, a wild drumbeat echoing the uncertainty of the situation.

"Didn't expect to find you here, especially not with... friends," Jamie said, his tone dripping with a mix of sarcasm and something that felt far more complicated. He raised an eyebrow, a smirk dancing on his lips as if he were trying to claim some kind of superiority.

I crossed my arms, determined not to let his attitude rattle me. "Surprises seem to be the theme of the night," I shot back, my voice firm. "But let's not make this weird."

Zane shifted slightly, leaning against the bar with a casual ease that belied the tension tightening around us. "We were just discussing the importance of finding your own voice," he interjected, his expression calm yet firm. "Maybe you could share your thoughts on that."

Jamie's smirk faltered, and for a moment, I saw genuine confusion cloud his features. "Finding your voice? Is that what this is all about?" He glanced at me, his gaze sharp as if searching for something that wasn't there. "I thought you were just looking for a way to fill the silence."

My pulse quickened, a mix of frustration and something else—something like fear. "Maybe silence isn't what I want to fill," I said, pushing back against the rising tide of anxiety. "Maybe I'm looking for more than just the easy words."

The bar around us faded as Jamie stepped closer, lowering his voice as if we were in a bubble, insulated from the noise of the world outside. "You've always been good at talking a big game. But what about following through?" The challenge hung between us, and I could feel Zane's presence beside me, a steady anchor in the shifting waters of my emotions.

"Maybe it's time I stopped talking and started creating," I replied, surprised at my own resolve. "What would you know about it anyway? You're the one who left without a backward glance."

The sharpness of my words cut through the haze, and for a heartbeat, Jamie seemed taken aback. He opened his mouth to respond, but the familiar sound of laughter from a nearby table momentarily distracted him. His eyes flickered, then returned to me, a flash of something—regret, perhaps?—crossing his face before his mask slipped back into place.

"I didn't think you'd be so emotional about it," he said, an edge creeping back into his tone. "I thought you were better than that."

"Better than what? Better than feeling?" I shot back, my own frustrations boiling to the surface. "Or maybe you just don't want me to get too comfortable finding my voice. It's a little inconvenient, isn't it?"

Zane cleared his throat, his presence at my side grounding me. "Look, maybe this isn't the best place to hash out old wounds," he said, his voice calm yet firm. "We're all here to enjoy the night. Why not let it be that?"

Jamie's gaze narrowed as he considered Zane, a hint of defensiveness creeping into his posture. "And you are?" he asked, his tone dripping with skepticism.

"Someone who believes in honesty," Zane replied smoothly, unfazed by Jamie's challenge. "And someone who believes that art is best when it's authentic."

"Authentic?" Jamie laughed, a harsh sound that echoed in the crowded bar. "That's rich coming from a guy trying to impress a girl with some half-baked philosophy."

Before I could respond, Zane leaned in, his intensity sharpening. "You're right about one thing—she is worth impressing. But the difference is, I'm here to support her, not to stifle her creativity."

The tension escalated, wrapping around us like a coiled spring ready to snap. I could feel my heart pounding in my chest, caught between the past and the present, torn between the familiarity of Jamie's presence and the magnetic pull of Zane's authenticity.

"Support?" Jamie scoffed. "What do you know about support? You just met her tonight. You're a fleeting distraction. I'm the one who really knows her."

"Knowing someone isn't the same as understanding them," Zane shot back, his voice steady, cutting through the simmering hostility. "You don't get to claim ownership over her experiences just because you've shared a history."

I stood there, caught in the crossfire, feeling both exhilarated and terrified by the heat of the moment. The world around us faded into a blur, the laughter and music becoming distant echoes as I felt the weight of their words pressing down on me.

"Why do you care so much?" I finally interjected, my voice shaking slightly but determined. "What does it matter to you, Jamie? You've moved on, and I've been trying to do the same."

Jamie opened his mouth, but before he could respond, the bar's door swung open again, and a new wave of patrons flooded in, laughter and chatter washing over us like a tide. Among them, I caught sight of a familiar face—a woman I had once considered a friend, a burst of brightness in the shadows of my uncertainty.

"Look who decided to show up!" she exclaimed, her voice ringing with excitement. She approached, her presence an unexpected jolt. "I heard there was a surprise performance, and I had to come see for myself."

Jamie's demeanor shifted, his attention diverting toward her, and I seized the moment, a flicker of hope igniting within me. Maybe this was the chaos I needed—a distraction to break the tension that threatened to engulf us.

"Great to see you!" I forced a smile, trying to pull myself together as I greeted her. "This night just keeps getting more interesting."

But as she joined the conversation, I couldn't shake the feeling that the real storm was still brewing beneath the surface. Jamie's eyes lingered on me, and Zane's presence felt like a protective shield against the turbulence that threatened to rise.

"Let's take this party to the stage!" the woman declared, her enthusiasm infectious. "I want to hear more of Zane's music!"

With a shared glance, Zane and I exchanged a moment of understanding. Maybe this was the break I needed, a chance to step away from the tension and reclaim my voice, even if it meant confronting my past head-on.

As the crowd surged toward the stage, I felt the warmth of Zane's presence beside me, a steady reminder of the path I was choosing to embrace. Just as I was about to take a step forward, Jamie grabbed my wrist, his grip firm and unyielding.

"Don't think this changes anything," he warned, his voice low, laced with an urgency that sent a shiver down my spine.

The sudden intensity of his words made my heart race. I looked into his eyes, searching for the flicker of something—remorse, anger, or maybe just a desperate plea for understanding.

And then, before I could react, Zane stepped in between us, his expression a mix of determination and protectiveness. "She's not yours to hold onto," he said firmly, his voice a barrier against the chaos. "Let her go."

The tension escalated, the air crackling with unspoken words as I stood caught in the middle of their conflict, the very ground beneath me feeling unstable, a precarious balance that threatened to tip at any moment. The music swelled around us, but all I could hear was the pounding of my heart, and I knew that no matter what happened next, I was on the brink of something transformative—a choice that would echo through my life long after the music faded away.

Chapter 5: The Weight of Expectations

The city shimmered like a mirage under the twilight, the vibrant pulse of nightlife throbbing against the backdrop of a sky slowly deepening into indigo. I walked beside Zane, the sharp lines of his jaw softened by the glow of street lamps, casting our shadows long and intertwined. Each step felt both exhilarating and treacherous, a balance between liberation and a tightening grip of guilt that threatened to shatter my newfound peace.

"Here's the plan," Zane declared, his voice cutting through the din of laughter and clinking glasses spilling out from the bars lining the street. He had this way of framing his ideas that felt theatrical, as if he were auditioning for the lead role in a play where I was the reluctant star. "We'll start at that dive with the ridiculous neon sign. They serve the best wings in the city, and I swear, the place is like a hidden treasure chest."

I smirked, allowing myself a moment of levity as I pictured the gaudy sign, a relic from an era when taste had taken a backseat to exuberance. "You mean the one that looks like it was designed by a toddler with a crayon?"

"Exactly! You're catching on." He shot me a grin, one that lit up his whole face. It was infectious, a spark in the darkness that made the edges of my worries blur. For the first time in what felt like forever, I wasn't just going through the motions of living; I was starting to feel alive.

The scent of fried food wafted towards us as we approached the dive, thick and greasy, making my stomach growl in anticipation. Inside, the ambiance was a chaotic blend of laughter, clinking glasses, and an overzealous jukebox belting out classic rock tunes that made me want to sway, but I kept my feet planted firmly on the ground. This was Zane's realm, and I was just an intruder in his world of spontaneity.

After securing a rickety table in a dim corner, we ordered a mountain of wings and a couple of beers. As we sat, I felt the weight of my responsibilities slip away, if only for a little while. Zane was a whirlwind, spinning tales of his latest artistic exploits and misadventures with such flair that I couldn't help but hang onto every word. His passion was contagious, a reminder of the fervor I once felt about my own work before the shadow of expectations loomed so large that it nearly suffocated me.

"You should see the way the critics lose their minds over my pieces," he said, leaning forward, his eyes gleaming. "I mean, they don't know what to make of my new abstract series. I'm turning the art world upside down, one brushstroke at a time."

I raised an eyebrow, unable to resist a playful jab. "Is that what you call it? I thought you were just splattering paint and calling it genius."

His laughter rang out, a genuine sound that made the edges of my worries blur once more. "Hey, it's a fine line between chaos and brilliance. You should try it sometime—let the madness take over!"

As the wings arrived, slathered in a tangy sauce that glistened under the low lights, I took a moment to appreciate the messy feast laid out before us. The first bite was a revelation, the flavors exploding like fireworks, and for a second, I forgot all about my looming deadlines and the difficult artist who could turn a simple collaboration into an Olympic sport of frustration.

We bantered back and forth, our conversations punctuated by bites and sips, laughter mixing with the surrounding noise like a private symphony. With every shared joke, every teasing comment, I could feel the barriers I had built around my heart starting to crack. I was not just a ghost of my former self; I was a person capable of joy, of laughter, of spontaneity.

Yet beneath that surface, a storm brewed—a tempest of guilt and confusion. As Zane talked animatedly about his upcoming gallery showing, I couldn't shake the feeling that my laughter echoed like a betrayal in the silence left by Jake's absence. Would he have wanted me to enjoy life again? The thought twisted in my gut, an anchor pulling me down into darker waters.

As if sensing my internal struggle, Zane leaned back, studying me with an intensity that made me squirm. "You okay? You've gone quiet on me."

I forced a smile, shaking my head as I poked at the remaining wings. "Just enjoying the food, I guess. Who knew this place would be so good?" My voice sounded false even to my ears, a brittle veneer over a tumult of emotions.

"Sure," he said, his tone teasing but his eyes searching. "But if you want to share, I'm all ears. I'm pretty good at listening."

The sincerity in his words cracked through my defenses, and I took a sip of my beer, steeling myself against the wave of vulnerability that threatened to wash over me. "It's just... I've had a rough couple of months," I admitted, the words slipping out before I could call them back. "I'm not used to... this." I gestured around us, encompassing the laughter, the joy, the momentary escape from reality.

"Life has a way of sneaking up on us, doesn't it?" he said softly, his gaze steady and understanding. "But that doesn't mean you don't deserve to feel good. We're not programmed to live in sorrow."

His words wrapped around me, warm and comforting, but the shadow of guilt remained, lurking just beneath the surface. As the evening wore on and the laughter grew, I began to wonder if maybe, just maybe, it was possible to feel both joy and sorrow simultaneously. Would Jake want me to linger in the shadows forever, or would he encourage me to step into the light?

The night deepened around us, wrapping us in its embrace, and I found myself caught in a delicate dance of emotions, one step forward into joy and another back into the darkness.

The laughter of the night wrapped around me like a well-worn blanket, warm and familiar, but beneath its comfort lay a fraying thread of uncertainty. I could feel Zane's energy, a vibrant spark, igniting something dormant within me. The restaurant had morphed from a mere stop on our evening tour into a moment suspended in time, a haven where my worries drifted away with the sweet scent of barbecue sauce. Yet, with every chuckle that escaped my lips, a nagging thought tugged at the corners of my mind, whispering that this joy might come with a price.

As we stepped out onto the bustling street again, the cool air brushed against my flushed cheeks, reminding me of the reality waiting just beyond the veil of this carefree night. Zane turned to me, eyes glinting mischievously. "What's next on our grand adventure? Dance-offs? Karaoke? An impromptu art show?" His voice carried the hint of mischief, and I couldn't help but smile.

"Art show? Are you sure you want to put your masterpieces on display? I hear they attract quite a crowd, and not all of them have good taste." I raised an eyebrow, my tone light, but I felt the tightening knot in my stomach.

"Ha! Taste is subjective, my dear." He waved his hand dismissively, a grand gesture that nearly knocked over a passerby. "But I do have a killer karaoke rendition of 'Livin' on a Prayer' that I've been dying to unleash on an unsuspecting public."

"You'd subject innocent bystanders to that? That's a crime against humanity," I replied, laughing, but a part of me felt the urge to keep this lightness alive. I couldn't help but picture him belting out Bon Jovi, his charming bravado drawing an audience, and I let out a breath I didn't know I was holding.

As we strolled further, Zane paused, looking contemplative as the colorful glow of a bar caught his attention. "How about we grab a drink at that place? They have a rooftop patio, and the view is spectacular. Trust me, it's not just about the alcohol." He tilted his head, a playful glimmer dancing in his eyes. "Although that is a bonus."

Curiosity piqued, I nodded, feeling an eagerness replace the anxiety that had gripped me since I stepped away from my usual routine. We ascended the narrow staircase to the rooftop, where the city sprawled beneath us like a glittering tapestry of lights and life. The atmosphere was electric, the sounds of laughter and music floating upward as if the night itself was putting on a show.

Zane ordered two drinks—a vibrant cocktail for me, and a dark beer that looked as if it could fuel a small car for him. As we settled into our seats, the world around us buzzed with a life of its own. I took a sip of my drink, the sweetness mingling with the tartness of lime, invigorating my senses.

"Cheers to spontaneous adventures!" Zane raised his glass, his eyes shining with enthusiasm. "And to letting go of the past, if only for a night."

"Are you my therapist now?" I joked, raising my glass to clink against his, but the sincerity behind his words echoed in my mind. I felt a knot of tension loosening in my chest. The rooftop view was breathtaking—skyscrapers reaching for the stars, illuminated by a thousand tiny lights, like fireflies trapped in glass.

"I can be if you pay me in wings," he quipped, a teasing grin spreading across his face. "But seriously, it's easy to get trapped in the past. Sometimes you need a nudge to remind you there's a world beyond the pain."

I nodded slowly, caught in the sincerity of his gaze. "You make it sound so simple," I said, my voice barely above a whisper. "Like I can just decide to let it all go."

"Why not? You're not a statue carved from stone. You're a work in progress, a masterpiece that's still being painted," he replied, his tone earnest. "Life is too short to wear the weight of expectations like a heavy coat."

I took another sip, the alcohol warming me from the inside. "And what if I'm afraid to take that coat off? What if I forget how to put it back on?"

"Then I'll be right here, with an arsenal of bad jokes and karaoke suggestions, ready to remind you what laughter feels like." He leaned back, a casual air about him that made me want to let my guard down.

As the night wore on, we exchanged stories, each revelation drawing us closer together. Zane spoke of his childhood adventures, a wild mix of mischief and creativity that painted a picture of a boy unafraid to embrace life. In turn, I shared snippets of my own past, carefully selecting the lighter moments, even as the darker shadows lurked in the corners of my memory.

"Okay, but tell me, what's the craziest thing you've ever done?" Zane asked, leaning closer, eyes sparkling with curiosity.

"Hmm, let's see... I once tried to learn how to surf on a whim," I started, rolling my eyes at the memory. "Spoiler alert: I spent more time tumbling into the waves than actually riding them. The lifeguard had to save me. Twice."

He threw his head back and laughed, the sound rich and genuine. "That's epic! I can't believe you tried it twice! The ocean clearly had it out for you."

"Tell me about it! It was like trying to dance with a very angry partner who had no intention of letting me lead."

Our laughter echoed into the night, intertwining with the city sounds, creating a symphony of joy that pushed my worries further away. I could feel my heart slowly starting to open, just a fraction, to the idea that perhaps I could let go, if only for a moment.

Then Zane turned serious, the humor fading from his expression. "But what about now? What's holding you back?"

The question hung between us, heavy and palpable. I felt the weight of his gaze, as if he were peeling back layers I had meticulously woven to shield myself from vulnerability. It was unsettling, the way he saw right through my façade.

"I guess... I just don't want to forget. Jake meant everything to me," I confessed, my voice catching slightly. "I'm scared that if I let go of this grief, it means I'm letting go of him."

Zane nodded, understanding flickering across his face. "You can cherish his memory without being trapped by it. It's like carrying a piece of art with you; it can inspire you without suffocating you."

His analogy was simple yet powerful, and for a moment, I felt a wave of clarity wash over me. Maybe he was right; maybe I could find a way to navigate this delicate balance. The night felt charged with possibilities, an electric pulse urging me to take a step forward, to redefine what it meant to live in this world without losing the essence of what had shaped me.

Just then, the rooftop began to fill with more patrons, laughter rising like bubbles in a fizzy drink, and the ambiance shifted once again. Zane stood, his demeanor shifting from contemplative to playful. "Come on, let's show these people how to really have a good time. I think we're ready for karaoke."

Before I could protest, he grabbed my hand, leading me to the small stage at the edge of the patio. My heart raced, a mix of excitement and fear. What had begun as a night to unwind had morphed into something entirely unexpected—a challenge that forced me to confront my feelings head-on.

As the microphone hovered in front of me, Zane flashed me a confident grin. "Together, we're unstoppable. Just follow my lead, and if we fall flat, we'll do it in style."

With my heart pounding, I took a deep breath, feeling the night embrace me as I stepped into the spotlight, ready to face whatever came next.

The microphone felt heavier than it looked, almost like it had absorbed the weight of every soul who had ever dared to step onto that tiny stage. Zane had a confident gleam in his eyes, his infectious energy igniting something deep within me. I could hear the chatter of the bar fading into the background, replaced by the pounding of my heart, each beat synchronized with the pulsing bass of the music from below.

"Just remember," Zane said, leaning in close so only I could hear. "It's not about the singing. It's about the performance. Channel your inner diva!" His playful wink pushed my anxiety aside, and I couldn't help but smile.

"Right. Because what every diva needs is a sidekick who thinks he's auditioning for a boy band," I teased, nudging him playfully.

As the crowd quieted, I took a deep breath, letting the moment wash over me like the rhythm of the city outside. Zane stepped back, his anticipation evident. "You know what? I believe in you. Let's show them what real talent looks like. And if it goes horribly wrong, well, at least we'll have a great story."

The music began to play, a familiar tune that made my stomach flutter. The lyrics sprang to life, and before I could second-guess myself, I found my voice emerging, shaky yet bold. "Tonight's gonna be a good night..." I sang, feeling the thrill of the spotlight wash over me.

Zane joined in, his voice harmonizing with mine, lifting the moment to a different level. The energy in the room shifted, laughter and cheers bubbling up around us, enveloping me like a warm embrace. As we belted out the chorus together, the initial nerves melted away, replaced by an exhilarating sense of freedom.

With each line, I could feel the tension of the last few months dissipating, like the steam rising from the city streets on a warm summer evening. There was something liberating about standing there, vulnerable yet empowered, sharing a piece of myself with strangers who were now allies in this moment. I glanced at Zane, and in that shared smile, I found a glimmer of understanding.

But just as I was starting to enjoy the exhilarating high of the performance, the song faded into a crescendo, and the realization hit me like a splash of cold water. What was I doing? Jake's face flickered in my mind like a photograph in a flickering frame, reminding me of the laughter we had shared, the music we had loved. Could I really allow myself to feel this alive, to embrace this joy, when he was gone?

In a moment of panic, I stumbled on the lyrics, the notes twisting into a confusing jumble that turned my triumphant performance into a comedic spectacle. Laughter erupted around us, not in a cruel way but in shared delight. Zane winked, unfazed, and plowed through, carrying us back on track like a true partner-in-crime.

As the song wrapped up, the room erupted into applause. My cheeks burned with a mix of embarrassment and exhilaration, and as I stepped off the stage, Zane was there to catch me. "See? I told you it would be amazing!" he exclaimed, his voice laced with genuine excitement.

"Yeah, amazing at nearly ruining a classic!" I shot back, laughing as I brushed my hair back from my face. "But you were right. That was kind of fun."

"Kind of fun? You were a rockstar! I fully expect a fan club to form overnight." He took my hand and twirled me around playfully, and for a fleeting moment, I let the music carry me away, losing myself in the rhythm of laughter and companionship.

As we sank into a booth, drinks in hand, the atmosphere felt electric, charged with possibility. "You're lucky to have me as your duet partner," he quipped, taking a sip of his beer. "Otherwise, you'd still be stuck in that shadowy place."

"Lucky? More like crazy. What kind of fool drags someone into a karaoke bar in the middle of the night?" I chuckled, but the laughter quickly faded as a shadow crossed my mind again. "But seriously, I didn't know I needed that. It felt good... freeing."

"Exactly! You have to embrace it. Life is too unpredictable to hide away. You can still honor Jake while letting yourself feel happiness. They're not mutually exclusive," he said, his tone shifting to something deeper, more sincere.

"Maybe. But what if it feels wrong?" The words slipped out, heavy with meaning. I leaned back against the booth, feeling the warmth of the night seep into my bones, yet grappling with the pang of guilt that gnawed at me.

Zane watched me with a steady gaze, as if he were searching for a way to break through the layers of my hesitation. "Then think of it this way: every time you laugh or enjoy life, you're keeping his memory alive. You're honoring him by living fully."

A silence fell between us, filled with the clinking of glasses and the hum of conversation, and for a brief moment, I allowed myself to contemplate his words. Perhaps there was wisdom in his perspective. Perhaps laughter didn't erase the memories; perhaps it added new colors to the canvas of my life, allowing me to paint a future that could coexist with the past.

As I pondered this, the atmosphere shifted again, like a sudden gust of wind. The door to the rooftop patio swung open, and a group of rowdy patrons spilled in, the sound of their boisterous laughter cutting through the soft murmur around us. Among them, one figure caught my eye—a familiar face that sent a shockwave through my chest.

"Is that...?" I stammered, staring wide-eyed at the intruder who had stepped into my moment of reprieve. There he was, framed by the neon glow, an unwelcome ghost from the past. It felt like time had reversed, the past rushing forward to collide with the present, and the laughter faded into a nervous hush.

"Who?" Zane followed my gaze, and the playful demeanor that had characterized the evening shifted into something more serious.

Before I could answer, the figure approached our booth, a slow smirk spreading across his face as recognition flickered in his eyes. "Well, well, if it isn't my favorite art critic," he said, his voice dripping with sarcasm. "I thought I'd find you here, mixing with the locals."

I felt Zane tense beside me, his protective nature emerging as he leaned slightly forward, ready to intercept any potential confrontation. "You know this guy?" he asked, keeping his tone low, like a predator ready to defend its territory.

"Unfortunately," I managed to reply, my heart racing as the laughter from earlier seemed to echo mockingly in my ears. "He's... someone from my past."

The man grinned, his presence suddenly overshadowing the laughter around us, threatening to pull me back into the emotional quicksand I'd fought so hard to escape. Zane's hand found mine beneath the table, a silent promise of support, but as I looked up, all I could see was the storm brewing in the eyes of the one person I hadn't expected to see tonight.

"Miss me?" he said, and I felt the weight of his gaze like a heavy anchor, dragging me down into a whirlpool of memories I wasn't ready to confront.

Chapter 6: Notes of Betrayal

The lights of the gallery flickered softly, casting a warm glow on the sprawling canvases that leaned precariously against the white walls, each one a chaotic dance of color and emotion. I was lost in my thoughts, sifting through the day's disappointments, when I heard the low murmur of voices drifting in from the adjoining room. A twinge of curiosity pulled me from my reverie, nudging me toward the slightly ajar door. Peering through the narrow crack, I caught sight of my difficult artist, Clara, engaged in what appeared to be an earnest discussion with a man whose presence seemed to drain the room of light—a music critic, of all people, with a reputation for savaging anyone who dared to step out of line.

My heart raced. I pressed my ear against the cool wood, straining to catch snippets of their conversation.

"...a collaboration with him could ruin everything we've built," Clara hissed, her voice laced with an edge I had never heard before. "She's been enamored with Zane since day one. If she puts him on a pedestal, we're all done for."

The critic's response was a low, almost conspiratorial whisper, sending chills down my spine. "It's not just about the art, Clara. It's about the narrative. If she showcases his talent without us in the picture, we risk losing control of the story."

I felt a sharp intake of breath; betrayal seeped through the cracks of their words like a poison. The room felt smaller, the air thicker. I wanted to retreat, to hide from the swirling emotions that threatened to pull me under. But this was my gallery, my vision at stake. I couldn't let them undermine everything I had fought for.

In a sudden surge of determination, I swung the door open. Clara and the critic froze, their expressions shifting from surprise to something more guarded.

"Respect," I demanded, the word cutting through the tension like a knife. "I deserve that much for the work I've done, especially from you, Clara."

She crossed her arms, her lips pressed into a thin line, a habit she had when bracing for conflict. "You don't understand the stakes. You're too caught up in your little fantasy with Zane to see what's really happening here."

"Fantasy?" I spat, feeling the heat of anger rise in my chest. "Zane is a genuine talent, and I'm trying to help him. Not that it's any of your business, but he deserves a chance."

"Is that what you call it? A chance?" Clara shot back, her eyes narrowing. "You're not just putting him on display. You're putting your reputation on the line. This isn't just some hobby for you. It's a career, and you're about to throw it all away."

The critic leaned back, a small smirk playing on his lips as he observed our exchange. It felt like I was performing in a twisted play where the script had been written by someone else entirely. "Perhaps it's time to reconsider your priorities," he interjected smoothly, the condescension dripping from his tone. "Art isn't just about raw talent; it's about refinement, vision—something that seems to elude both of you."

I clenched my fists, wanting to wipe that smirk off his face with a single swing. Instead, I turned to Clara, desperate to salvage the fraying threads of our professional relationship. "You're better than this, Clara. Don't let fear dictate your choices. This could be an opportunity for both of us."

She glanced away, her features softening ever so slightly before hardening once more. "You think this is just about you and Zane? You're in over your head. If you want to keep this gallery thriving, you'll have to make sacrifices. Think about what you really want."

In that moment, it felt like the ground beneath me had shifted. I was caught between my burgeoning friendship with Zane and the crumbling facade of my collaboration with Clara. I could sense the looming shadows of betrayal, yet the prospect of losing Zane felt like a heavier weight.

The argument spiraled, words flying like arrows, each one finding its mark. Clara's passion morphed into resentment, and mine into frustration as I fought to articulate my vision, my belief that art should be a reflection of the artist, unfiltered and true. Finally, when I could no longer withstand the strain, I stormed out of the gallery, the air outside fresh yet tinged with the sharp edge of confrontation.

I paced the empty street, the cool breeze tugging at my hair as I fought to catch my breath. My phone buzzed in my pocket, and I fished it out, hoping it would be Zane, the sound of his voice a balm for my frayed nerves.

"Hey," he said, his voice laced with concern. "You okay?"

I wanted to break down, to spill everything—the conversation, the betrayal, the disillusionment. Instead, I forced a laugh, though it sounded hollow even to my ears. "Just had a little disagreement with Clara. Nothing I can't handle."

He paused, and I could hear him shift on the other end, his hesitation palpable. "You know, you can talk to me about it. I'm here."

A lump formed in my throat as I leaned against a nearby lamppost, its light bathing me in a soft glow. "It's just... I thought we were on the same team. Now I'm not so sure."

"People can be... unpredictable," he said, his voice gentle yet firm, like the steady pull of the tide. "But that doesn't mean you have to lose sight of your own vision. You've got talent, and it's time others saw that, too."

As we shared our fears and frustrations, the distance between us began to dissolve. The warm glow of his encouragement ignited something deep within me, a sense of belonging I hadn't realized I craved. I felt the weight of our connection shifting, transforming the foundation of our friendship into something much more complex.

"Zane, I..." I started, unsure of how to articulate the growing feelings I couldn't ignore. "I think—"

"Wait," he interrupted, his tone suddenly serious. "Before we dive deeper, there's something I need to tell you."

The air crackled with anticipation, and my heart raced, unsure of whether to brace for impact or leap into the unknown.

The streetlight flickered like a bad romance novel, casting shadows that danced across the pavement as I stood outside, the weight of my earlier confrontation still heavy on my shoulders. Zane's voice lingered in my mind, a soothing balm amidst the chaos. "There's something I need to tell you."

I wanted to ask him what was so urgent, but instead, I swallowed hard, grappling with the surge of emotions that accompanied the uncertainty. My fingers danced over the cool metal of my phone, debating whether to press him further. In that moment, the world around me faded, and it was just the two of us, tethered by something that felt both exciting and terrifying.

"Okay," I said, drawing in a deep breath. "What is it?"

"Not here," he replied, his voice low, almost conspiratorial. "Meet me at the café around the corner in twenty minutes."

With that, he hung up, leaving me suspended in a mix of anticipation and anxiety. I stuffed my phone back into my pocket, the warmth of his words still lingering like the last rays of sun on a summer day. The café was a haven, its windows glowing with a warm, inviting light that felt like a promise. As I made my way there, the familiar scents of freshly brewed coffee and baked goods wrapped around me like a comforting hug.

Inside, the café buzzed with the hum of conversation and the clinking of cups, but I barely registered the surrounding chaos. My focus narrowed to Zane, seated at a corner table, his gaze fixed on the door as if he were waiting for the world to shift. When our eyes met, a spark ignited between us, igniting the shadows of doubt swirling in my mind.

"Hey," I greeted, sliding into the seat opposite him. "You seemed serious on the phone."

His brow furrowed, and for a fleeting moment, I could see the weight of his thoughts pressing down on him. "I wanted to talk about Clara," he said, leaning forward, his voice barely above a whisper. "And the plans for the showcase."

"Plans? What plans?" I raised an eyebrow, my heart pounding. "Is there something going on that I don't know about?"

Zane ran a hand through his unruly hair, a gesture that revealed his own frustration. "Clara is worried about the direction of the showcase, but she's not the only one. There are people in the background—critics, artists—who are not happy with what we're doing. They see you and me as a threat to their vision."

A wave of anger surged within me, but I forced myself to take a deep breath. "So, this is about them, not us? They want to dictate how we create?"

He nodded, his expression earnest. "Exactly. And I don't want you to be caught in the crossfire. You're too talented for that."

The sincerity in his eyes warmed me, but it also sent shivers down my spine. I felt a sudden urge to grab his hand, to tether myself to him and pull him closer, but I resisted the impulse, afraid of what it might reveal. "What are we going to do?"

"We fight back," he said, his voice rising with confidence. "We show them that we're serious about this, that we're not afraid to push boundaries."

I nodded, a flicker of determination igniting within me. "And how do we do that?"

Zane leaned back in his chair, a mischievous grin creeping across his face. "We throw the best showcase this city has ever seen. We put you and me front and center, and we make it clear that our collaboration is not just a fluke. It's a force to be reckoned with."

The idea was thrilling. The thought of stepping into the limelight with Zane, showcasing our vision against the backdrop of Clara's objections, sent a rush of adrenaline coursing through me. "But what if they try to sabotage us?"

"Then we outsmart them," he replied, leaning forward again, his eyes bright with excitement. "We'll invite the right people—the ones who will see the potential in our work. We won't let Clara or the critics dictate our success."

The fire in his voice ignited something deep within me, an unwavering resolve. "Alright, let's do it. We'll make this showcase something they won't forget."

"Now you're talking," he said, grinning. "But first, we need to strategize. We should start by revamping the artwork you want to feature. What do you have in mind?"

"I want to capture the raw emotion behind the art," I said, my voice gaining strength. "I want people to feel something when they see it—not just appreciate it, but connect with it."

Zane nodded thoughtfully. "Good. We should also include some interactive elements. Let the audience participate in the experience. It'll set us apart from everything else happening in the art scene right now."

As we brainstormed, the ideas flowed effortlessly between us, each suggestion sparking another until we had an entire vision laid out in front of us. The more we talked, the more the café around us faded into the background, our world shrinking to just the two of us and the exhilarating possibilities we were creating.

The conversation soon drifted toward our personal lives, the walls between our friendship and something deeper beginning to crumble. "So, what about you?" I asked, a playful smile dancing on my lips. "Do you have any secrets you've been hiding?"

Zane chuckled, leaning back in his chair, his posture relaxed yet somehow still charged. "Me? Secrets? I'm an open book."

"Right, like a really complicated novel that's been heavily edited," I teased. "There's no way you don't have some juicy tidbit hidden away."

"Okay, you got me," he said, his expression shifting. "I used to play in a band. We thought we were going to make it big. But life happened, and I ended up here instead."

I raised an eyebrow, intrigued. "A band? Why didn't you tell me?"

He shrugged, a flicker of vulnerability in his eyes. "It was a long time ago. I didn't want it to define me. But it did shape my view of the art world. It made me realize how important it is to stay true to your vision, no matter the noise around you."

"Do you miss it?" I asked softly, genuinely curious.

"Sometimes," he admitted, his gaze distant. "But I think I found something more fulfilling here."

My heart swelled at his words, the air between us thick with unspoken feelings. Just as I opened my mouth to respond, the café door swung open, drawing our attention. A gust of wind swept in, carrying with it the vibrant energy of the street outside. In walked a group of familiar faces—critics, artists, and influencers—all laughing and chatting, their presence a stark reminder of the world we were up against.

"Great," I muttered, my heart sinking. "Just what we need."

Zane looked at me, a mischievous glint in his eye. "Let's show them what we've got."

I felt a surge of courage rush through me. "Alright, let's make a statement."

We stood together, two forces ready to challenge the norms, the lines of our friendship blurring further as the stakes grew higher. The tension in the air crackled with possibility, and as we stepped out from the shadows of the café, I knew one thing for certain: whatever was about to unfold, we would face it together.

The atmosphere outside the café had shifted dramatically as we stepped into the bustling street, a vibrant tapestry of life humming around us. The air was thick with the scent of freshly baked pastries and rich coffee, but the underlying tension from earlier lingered like a storm cloud. Zane walked beside me, our shoulders brushing occasionally, igniting sparks of electricity that sent my thoughts racing.

As we moved deeper into the throng, I could hear snippets of conversations drifting around us—names of critics and artists exchanged like currency, each one a reminder of the world we were trying to penetrate. I glanced sideways at Zane, who seemed unbothered by the storm brewing in the art scene.

"You're unusually calm," I remarked, my tone teasing.

He chuckled, a low, melodious sound that made my heart flutter. "I'm just enjoying the chaos. It's kind of beautiful, isn't it? Everyone fighting for their moment."

"Beautiful? It feels more like a battlefield to me," I replied, the gravity of our situation weighing heavily on my shoulders.

"Battlefields are where heroes are made," he shot back, winking at me.

I rolled my eyes but couldn't help the smile tugging at my lips. "So, we're heroes now? What's our superpower? Making really awkward art together?"

"Actually," he said, his expression shifting to something more serious, "I think our superpower is turning the tables on the critics. We're not going to let them dictate how we create."

His conviction was infectious, and I felt a surge of determination swell within me. "Alright, then. Let's give them a show they won't forget."

As we walked, ideas tumbled between us like leaves caught in the wind—bold concepts, daring installations, and the thrill of using our art to make a statement. With each passing minute, I felt the weight of Clara's skepticism lift, replaced by the buoyant energy of possibility. I could hardly believe that just hours before, I had been questioning everything.

We decided to head to the studio to flesh out our plans. The moment we stepped inside, the familiar scent of paint and varnish washed over me, grounding me. Zane picked up a brush, swirling it in the air like a wand, his eyes twinkling with mischief. "What do you say we start with a little brainstorming session? I'll cover the wild ideas, and you handle the practical side."

"Wild ideas, huh?" I grinned, leaning against the doorframe. "Should I prepare for chaos?"

"Chaos is just another form of creativity," he retorted, his tone playful as he began to paint abstract shapes on the canvas. The vibrant strokes danced across the surface, each flicker of the brush echoing the excitement in his eyes.

Watching him work was mesmerizing, and for a moment, I let myself forget the external pressures bearing down on us. It was just Zane and me, a shared passion connecting us in this vibrant space. "You really have a knack for this," I said, genuine admiration lacing my words.

He paused, looking up at me with an intensity that made my stomach flutter. "It's not just the paint. It's the connection we're creating—this is what I want people to feel when they walk into the showcase."

I nodded, but unease began to creep back in. "And if they don't feel it? If Clara and the critics succeed in tearing us apart before we even begin?"

Zane stepped closer, his eyes unwavering. "Then we show them what we're made of. Together."

The strength in his voice sent a shiver down my spine, a reminder that I wasn't alone in this. "Alright. Together it is."

We spent the next few hours lost in our creations, laughter mingling with the sound of brushes against canvas. The vibrant colors came alive under our hands, each stroke a declaration of our resolve. Yet, as the sun dipped below the horizon, casting the studio in a soft golden hue, the reality of our situation crept back in, the shadows lengthening like the doubt in my heart.

As we put the final touches on our piece, the tension in the air shifted. My phone buzzed on the table, interrupting our creative flow. I glanced at the screen, and my stomach dropped. Clara's name loomed large. "It's her," I said, hesitating before answering.

"Take it," Zane urged, the warmth of his encouragement a comforting presence as I swiped to answer.

"Clara," I said, forcing a calmness into my voice that I didn't feel. "What's up?"

"We need to talk," she said, her tone sharp and unforgiving. "I've heard whispers around town about your little collaboration. It's causing quite a stir."

"Good or bad?" I asked, bracing myself for the fallout.

"Let's just say people are concerned about the direction this is heading. You're risking everything, and I can't just stand by and watch."

"Are you concerned for me or for yourself?" I shot back, the words escaping before I could temper my frustration.

"Both," she snapped. "If you crash and burn, it takes us all down. You think I care about my reputation less than yours? You need to reconsider this partnership."

I felt my blood boil, a potent mixture of anger and hurt. "This isn't just a partnership. It's an opportunity for both of us to grow, to break out of the mold you want to keep us in."

Silence stretched between us, a taut line threatening to snap. "You're making a mistake, and I don't know how to help you if you won't listen," she finally said, her voice softer but still edged with concern.

Before I could respond, Zane reached out, placing a reassuring hand on my arm. "You have to stand your ground," he murmured. "Show her you mean business."

"Clara, I appreciate your concern, but I have to do this," I said, feeling the weight of my words settle into the silence. "I'm taking a risk, yes, but it's mine to take. You've had your chance to shape things; now it's my turn."

"Just think about what you're throwing away," she warned, the underlying threat palpable even through the phone.

With that, I hung up, my heart racing. Zane's gaze met mine, filled with a mix of admiration and concern. "You handled that well."

"Did I?" I replied, pacing the floor as frustration bubbled inside me. "What if she's right? What if I am risking everything?"

"Then we make sure it's worth the risk," he said, determination etched into his features.

I nodded, but uncertainty gnawed at me. The pressure of the upcoming showcase loomed large, the critics' whispers echoing in my mind. The very foundation of my collaboration with Zane felt precarious, like a house built on sand.

"Let's take a break," I suggested, trying to clear my head. "I need some air."

We stepped outside, the cool night wrapping around us like a comforting blanket. The stars twinkled above, distant and indifferent, as I took a deep breath, trying to steady my racing heart.

As we stood in silence, the weight of unspoken words hung in the air. I turned to Zane, catching him watching me with an intensity that sent my heart fluttering. "What if Clara really does try to undermine us?"

"Then we'll outsmart her," he said confidently, but the slight tremor in his voice betrayed his own concerns.

Just then, the sound of a nearby crowd erupted into cheers, drawing our attention. I turned my head toward the commotion and felt a knot tighten in my stomach as I spotted Clara in the midst of it, her face a mask of determination as she addressed a group of eager critics.

"Looks like she's already at work," I whispered, dread pooling in my stomach.

Zane's expression hardened, and I felt the air thicken with the reality of our situation. "We can't let her take the narrative," he said, his voice resolute. "We need to act fast."

Before I could respond, a figure emerged from the crowd—a tall man with dark hair, a familiar face that made my breath hitch. It was the critic I had overheard earlier, the one who had made it clear he had no intention of letting our collaboration go unnoticed.

"Zane, we need to—" I started, but my words faltered as the critic locked eyes with me, a predatory smile spreading across his face.

"Looks like the show is just getting started," he called out, his voice dripping with disdain. "I hope you're ready for the fallout."

Zane stepped protectively in front of me, his body tense with urgency. "What do you want?"

"Just here to see how the little artist and her muse plan to unravel the carefully crafted narrative," the critic taunted, his gaze piercing.

As my heart raced, the weight of the situation crashed down on me. I glanced at Zane, our resolve intermingling with a rising tide of uncertainty.

"What if this is it?" I whispered, the reality of our impending showcase looming larger than life.

"Then we fight," he replied, his voice steady despite the storm swirling around us.

And in that moment, as the crowd around us surged with anticipation, I felt the threads of fate tightening, each one woven into a fabric of impending confrontation. With Clara and the critic on one side and Zane and me on the other, the stage was set for a

Chapter 7: Crescendo of Emotions

The evening light spilled into my studio like melted gold, casting a warm glow over the scattered sheets of music and the cluttered shelves filled with instruments I had collected over the years. Each corner bore witness to my journey—the battered guitar from my first heartbreak, the piano my grandmother used to play, and the ukulele I'd bought on a whim, hoping to recreate the carefree days of summer. I looked over at Zane, his fingers dancing over the keys, effortlessly coaxing a melody from the piano that resonated through the air like a soft caress.

His concentration was palpable, a deep furrow creasing his brow, and I couldn't help but admire how music seemed to transform him. It was as if the notes were weaving a spell, pulling him deeper into a world where nothing else mattered. I found myself drawn to the way his hands moved, the way he poured himself into each note. There was a rawness to him, a passion that ignited something inside me, a flicker of warmth that spread through my chest, awakening desires I had long buried.

"What do you think?" he asked, breaking the spell. His voice was low, almost a whisper, as if he feared shattering the moment.

I leaned against the doorframe, crossing my arms, trying to suppress the smile tugging at my lips. "It's beautiful. Like a lullaby for the soul," I said, my words wrapping around the truth of my heart.

He met my gaze, and for a heartbeat, the world outside faded into nothingness. In that instant, the weight of our unspoken connection hung in the air between us, thick and electric. Zane's eyes were a storm of emotion, swirling depths that promised adventure and heartbreak in equal measure. It was terrifying and exhilarating, a dance on the edge of a precipice, and I was teetering dangerously close.

"What if we took it further?" he suggested, his voice barely above a whisper. The casual question felt loaded, thick with possibility, yet it sent a tremor of panic racing through me. I wanted to say yes, to leap into the unknown with him, but my heart was anchored by the ghosts of my past.

I was no stranger to desire, yet the shadows of Jake loomed large in my mind, dark tendrils creeping in, reminding me of the vows I had never truly abandoned. The laughter we had shared, the dreams we had built together—they were still fresh, alive in my memory. It felt wrong, so very wrong, to even consider the thought of Zane filling that space, of him carving a place in my heart that I still reserved for someone else. I felt like a traitor, betraying the love I had cherished, even as it spiraled into something I could no longer recognize.

Before I could respond, Zane shifted closer, the warmth of his body radiating like the summer sun. "You're thinking too much," he teased, a playful grin breaking through his earlier intensity. "You know what they say—overthinking is the enemy of creativity."

I chuckled lightly, a nervous sound that barely filled the silence. "And yet here I am, an expert at overthinking." The air around us crackled with unspoken words, our chemistry simmering beneath the surface, ready to boil over at any moment.

"Maybe we need to stop thinking," he suggested, his voice dropping an octave, the tension between us building like a well-tuned string about to snap.

In that charged moment, I leaned in, my heart racing in anticipation. The distance between us melted away, and I felt the world slip into a blissful oblivion as our lips met. It was tentative at first, a gentle exploration that ignited a wildfire within me, awakening every nerve ending and flooding my senses with a dizzying thrill. I lost myself in the taste of him—warmth, sweetness, and a hint of something more, something daring.

But just as I began to melt into the kiss, a cold splash of reality crashed over me like icy water. The moment stretched, pulled taut by the weight of what I was doing, and I panicked. I pulled away, gasping for air, my heart pounding like a drum in my chest. The warmth faded, replaced by a frigid rush of guilt that wrapped around me like a shroud.

"What just happened?" Zane asked, confusion flickering in his eyes. He leaned back, a vulnerable edge to his expression that tugged at my heart.

"I can't," I whispered, the words barely escaping my lips. "I'm sorry, I just... I can't." The rejection tasted bitter, a lump of regret lodged in my throat. I felt the weight of my past hanging heavy in the air, as if it had materialized into a ghostly presence, haunting us both.

Zane's gaze sharpened, a mix of hurt and understanding etched across his face. "Is it Jake?" The name hung in the air like a delicate thread, the unspoken tether that tied me to my past.

"It's complicated," I murmured, the truth a tangled mess of emotions I couldn't unravel in that moment. I wanted to explain, to share the depth of my fears, but every word felt like a betrayal. Zane, with all his kindness and charm, deserved better than my haunted heart.

"Complicated doesn't mean impossible," he replied, a note of stubbornness lacing his tone. "You can't just keep holding onto the past, you know. It'll weigh you down."

He had no idea how true that was. Each word he spoke was a nail digging deeper into my conscience, and the rift between us widened, palpable and painful. I had thought I could dance around the truth, but it was demanding to be acknowledged, looming larger than I had dared to admit.

"I'm not ready to let go," I confessed, my voice trembling as the admission escaped. "And I don't want to hurt you in the process."

Zane's shoulders slumped, the fire in his eyes dimming. "You're not hurting me. I just wish you could see what's right in front of you."

I closed my eyes, breathing in the familiar scent of wood and music, fighting against the emotions swirling inside me. I had thought I could build a bridge to something new, but the ghosts of my past had made it clear: the path was littered with thorns, and I wasn't ready to walk it.

The silence that followed felt heavy, like a thick fog settling in, muffling the sound of our dreams and hopes. I stared at Zane, who was now a landscape of shadows and uncertainty. The warmth of our kiss lingered in the air, but my heart thudded loudly, a frantic drumbeat that matched my rising panic. I wanted to explain, to unravel the tapestry of my emotions, but words danced just out of reach, tantalizingly close yet frustratingly elusive.

Zane turned away, his fingers brushing against the piano keys, but the music felt muted now, as if even the notes were mourning the moment we had just shared. "I get it," he said, his voice a mix of resignation and understanding. "But you can't live in the past forever. It's exhausting, isn't it?"

I hated how much sense he made. The truth was like a sharp knife, cutting through the fog, revealing the jagged edges of my reality. "I just don't know how to let go," I admitted, the words spilling out before I could catch them. "Jake and I... we had plans, dreams. And now..."

"Now you're afraid," he interrupted gently, turning to meet my gaze, his eyes a mirror reflecting my own insecurities. "You're afraid of starting over, of what it means to step into something new. Trust me, I get it."

The way he looked at me made my heart ache with both longing and frustration. "You don't understand," I snapped, the words tumbling out with a bitterness I didn't fully mean. "You've never been in my position."

He raised an eyebrow, a flicker of amusement cutting through the tension. "Well, I haven't been in your shoes, but I've had my fair share of complications." His voice held a playful lilt, teasing yet somehow comforting, like a warm blanket on a chilly night.

I folded my arms across my chest, unwilling to let the warmth seep through my defenses. "Is that supposed to make me feel better?" I shot back, half-smiling despite myself.

"Honestly? Not really," he replied, a playful smirk gracing his lips. "But it's true. We all have our baggage, our scars. It's what makes us human."

I couldn't help but chuckle at his candor. "Wow, Zane. Your insight is almost poetically profound," I replied, rolling my eyes in mock annoyance. "Next thing I know, you'll be handing me a self-help book."

"Only if it's an uplifting one," he shot back, laughter dancing in his eyes. The banter felt like a lifeline, pulling me away from the edge of despair, if only for a moment.

But the smile faded as the weight of my emotions returned, heavier than before. "What if I make the wrong choice? What if I hurt you, or worse, hurt myself?" I could hear the tremor in my voice, the doubt clawing at my insides.

Zane's expression shifted, the lightness dimming. "Life is all about choices. Sometimes, you just have to take the leap and hope the net appears."

The thought felt terrifying. "You make it sound so simple," I murmured, looking down at my hands, which were fidgeting nervously.

"It's not simple," he replied, his voice softening. "It's complicated and messy. But you're stronger than you think. You've survived a lot, and it's okay to be scared. Just don't let that fear keep you from what could be beautiful."

His words wrapped around me like a warm embrace, igniting a flicker of hope within me. Could it be that simple? To let go of the past and allow myself to be swept away by something new? My heart raced at the thought, but doubt pulled me back.

The studio felt like a sanctuary, but it was also a cage, the walls closing in around me. I needed to escape the weight of my thoughts, to clear the fog that clouded my heart. "Can we just... play?" I suggested, the words barely above a whisper, desperate for the familiar comfort of music to soothe my restless soul.

"Play?" he asked, a spark of excitement lighting up his features. "What do you have in mind?"

"Something spontaneous," I said, a grin creeping back onto my face. "Let's not overthink it. Let's just create."

Zane's eyes sparkled as he nodded, his fingers hovering above the keys like a conductor ready to unleash an orchestra. "Alright, I'm in. Let's see where this takes us."

The moment I began to strum my guitar, a sense of liberation washed over me. The strings vibrated under my fingers, resonating with a familiar rhythm that eased my troubled mind. Zane joined in, layering melodies over the chords, our sounds intertwining like vines in a summer garden, wild and untamed.

As we played, the music swelled, wrapping around us like a warm hug. It was a conversation without words, a dance of notes and rhythms that expressed everything we hadn't said. The chaos of my thoughts began to quiet, the layers of tension melting away with each chord, each note that echoed off the studio walls.

"See? This is what it's about," Zane said, grinning at me as we navigated the melody, his passion infectious. "Letting go. Finding freedom in the music."

With each strum, I felt a weight lifting, a connection blossoming between us that was pure and invigorating. It was as if the music had given us a secret language, a place where vulnerability was a strength, not a weakness.

The song morphed into something beautiful, filled with soaring highs and tender lows, a testament to the emotions swirling between us. It became our shared catharsis, a declaration of all the things we couldn't say out loud. We played on, caught in a rhythm that felt almost magical, as if we were crafting something greater than ourselves.

But just as the crescendo reached its peak, the door swung open, and my heart dropped like a stone. There stood Jake, framed in the doorway, his expression a mix of surprise and confusion. The air thickened with unspoken tension, the music faltering, as if it too had sensed the shift in the atmosphere.

"Am I interrupting something?" Jake's voice was steady, but the question hung heavy, the weight of my past crashing back down on me, relentless and unyielding. I felt Zane's tension spike beside me, the camaraderie we had built moments ago now shattered like glass.

"Jake," I stammered, caught between two worlds, the weight of choices pressing down on me as the lines of my heart blurred further.

The air turned dense with the weight of unspoken words, and I felt the familiar rush of panic as Jake stood in the doorway, his eyes flickering between me and Zane. It was as if time itself had ground to a halt, the vibrant world we had created through music collapsing into a silent void. The notes that had danced in the air moments before now faded into an uncomfortable quiet, leaving an echo that felt almost haunting.

"Jake," I managed, my voice thin and shaky, each syllable weighted with the gravity of the moment. He looked so different from the last time I'd seen him—tired, maybe, or perhaps just burdened by whatever secrets lay between us. His usual confident demeanor faltered as he processed the scene before him, the remnants of our music hanging like invisible threads, stretching taut between us.

"Didn't mean to barge in," he said, attempting a lighthearted tone that felt forced. "I just... I heard you playing. It sounded great." The compliment hung awkwardly in the air, a lifeline thrown into turbulent waters, but it barely broke the tension.

Zane shifted beside me, his expression a mix of irritation and discomfort. The camaraderie we had just shared felt fragile now, as if it might shatter with the slightest breeze. "We were just jamming," he replied, his voice steady yet clipped. "No big deal."

"Right," Jake said, his gaze narrowing slightly as he studied us. There was a flicker of something in his eyes, a protective instinct perhaps, or maybe a hint of jealousy. It sent a shiver down my spine. "I just didn't realize you were busy."

"Busy creating something new," I interjected, trying to fill the space between us with positivity. "You know, sometimes it helps to have a fresh perspective."

Jake raised an eyebrow, his expression shifting. "Is that what this is? A fresh perspective?" The sarcasm dripped from his words, and I bristled at the accusation woven into them.

Zane met my gaze, and I could see the question in his eyes: Should we address the elephant in the room, or let it trample us underfoot? I could feel my heart racing, a chaotic drum in my chest, desperate for clarity amidst the confusion.

"Listen," I said, taking a step toward Jake, the space between us a chasm I desperately wanted to bridge. "We were just having fun. Music has always been our thing, remember?"

He hesitated, his features softening slightly, but the edge in his voice remained. "Yeah, but it seems like things have changed. Maybe it's time to acknowledge that."

There it was—the uninvited truth that danced around us like a specter, haunting and unavoidable. I opened my mouth to respond, but Zane interjected, his voice firm. "What do you want, Jake? Are you here to talk, or just to drop in and make accusations?"

Jake's gaze darted between us, the uncertainty palpable. "I didn't come to make accusations. I came to see you," he said, his tone dropping slightly, revealing a hint of vulnerability. "I wanted to check in, to see how you're doing."

The sincerity of his words struck a chord within me. I wanted to respond, to tell him how I'd been feeling, the turmoil of emotions raging inside me like a tempest. But as I looked at Zane, his face a mask of tension, I felt trapped between two worlds, each one pulling me in opposite directions.

"I'm fine," I said, forcing a smile that felt more like a grimace. "Really, just busy with music and... things."

Jake's eyes searched mine, and I could feel the weight of his concern pressing down on me. "Things? Like what?"

"Like life," I replied, deflecting the question with a lightness I didn't feel. "You know how it is."

"I do," he said, crossing his arms over his chest, a defensive gesture that sent a ripple of frustration through me. "And I know that avoiding the conversation isn't going to help either of us."

Zane's presence beside me felt suddenly burdensome, as if I were carrying the weight of both our emotions. "Look, Jake," I began, my heart racing as I struggled to find the right words, "I appreciate you coming by, but—"

"But what?" he interrupted, his voice rising slightly. "You're just going to pretend everything's okay when it's not? You've been distant, and I can't ignore that. I deserve to know what's going on."

The air crackled with tension, and I felt like a pendulum swinging between them. Zane opened his mouth to speak, but I raised a hand, halting him. "You're right," I said, my voice stronger than I felt. "I've been avoiding things. I just... I don't know how to navigate this."

A flicker of understanding passed over Jake's face, but it was quickly overshadowed by a flicker of annoyance. "Navigate what? Your feelings for Zane? Because it sure looks like you're having a grand time here."

The accusation hung heavy in the air, and I could see Zane tense beside me, his jaw clenched as he fought to keep his composure. "This isn't about us, Jake," he said, his voice low but firm. "It's about her. She deserves to choose her path without pressure from you."

"Pressure? I'm not pressuring her! I'm trying to understand!" Jake shot back, the heat rising between them, creating a wall of tension that felt insurmountable.

I rubbed my temples, the mounting stress threatening to spill over. "Enough! This isn't helping."

Both men fell silent, their expressions a mix of frustration and hurt. I stood between them, feeling like a fragile glass vase caught in a storm, afraid to shatter under the weight of their expectations.

"Maybe it's time for me to be honest," I said, my voice steady despite the chaos inside. "I'm confused. I care about both of you in different ways, and I don't want to hurt either of you. But I can't keep pretending everything is fine when it's not."

Jake's face softened, his eyes searching mine for sincerity. "I just want you to be happy," he said quietly. "I don't want to lose you."

Zane stepped closer, his presence grounding me. "You won't lose her by giving her space to breathe, Jake. This isn't about you or me; it's about her finding what she truly wants."

The truth of his words hung in the air, a delicate thread connecting us all. My heart raced, torn between the familiarity of Jake and the thrill of the unknown that Zane represented. I could feel the tension rising like a tidal wave, threatening to pull me under.

"Look," I said, my voice wavering as I tried to navigate the tumultuous waters of my emotions. "I need time to think. Time to figure out what I want. Please, just give me that."

"Time?" Jake echoed, incredulous. "You think time will solve this?"

"Sometimes, it's the only thing that can," I replied, the strength in my voice faltering as uncertainty clawed at my insides.

As I turned to face Zane, the intensity in his eyes mirrored my own fears and desires. "I don't want to make this harder for you, but I also can't stand by and watch you wrestle with these feelings alone," he said, his voice steady.

Just then, the ringing of my phone shattered the tension, an insistent sound that pulled me back to reality. I glanced at the screen, my stomach dropping as I saw the name flashing back at me. It was my mother.

"Sorry, I need to take this," I said quickly, stepping away, relief and anxiety battling inside me. The last thing I wanted was to add another layer of chaos to the already turbulent moment, but I couldn't ignore her call.

As I answered, the voices of the two men behind me faded into the background. "Hello?" I said, forcing cheerfulness into my voice, but the air felt thick with unaddressed emotions.

But the moment I heard her voice, the cheerful facade crumbled. "Honey, I need to talk to you," she said, her tone serious.

"What's wrong?" My heart raced, an uneasy knot forming in my stomach.

"It's about your father," she began, and I felt the ground shift beneath my feet. The world around me blurred, and I was suddenly acutely aware of the tension lingering in the studio, the two men standing silent witnesses to my unraveling reality.

"Mom, what do you mean?"

But before she could answer, the sound of a door slamming echoed through the house, followed by raised voices just outside. Panic gripped me as I turned to see Zane and Jake, both poised at the edge of an invisible cliff, caught between the tumult of my life and their own feelings.

"Mom?" I breathed, fear creeping into my voice as the world around me felt like it was collapsing. I turned back to the phone, desperate for answers, my heart racing as uncertainty settled in the pit of my stomach.

"Mom?"

"Julia, please listen—" she said, but the words were lost as the door burst open, and the shadows of my past threatened to engulf us all.

Chapter 8: Silence in the Sound

The hum of my computer was the only sound filling the air, a steady thrum that mirrored the relentless tempo of my racing thoughts. I sat at my cluttered desk, surrounded by hastily scribbled notes and sketches of designs I hoped would finally impress the clients who seemed perpetually dissatisfied. Each keystroke felt like a tiny rebellion against the silence that stretched between Zane and me, a silence heavier than a storm cloud, thick with unspoken words and unresolved tension. I could almost hear the echoes of our last conversation ricocheting off the walls, but I didn't dare delve too deeply into that mess. Instead, I focused on work as though it were a life raft thrown into turbulent waters.

The project had begun as an exciting challenge, a chance to flex my creative muscles and prove myself. Yet, as the days dragged on, it morphed into a double-edged sword. Each design I created felt both exhilarating and crushing, the expectations looming larger with every stroke of my stylus. I could almost feel the weight of my boss's gaze, burning into my back with the intensity of a thousand suns, while the clock ticked down the minutes until my deadline.

In this unyielding quiet, the past had a way of creeping in, curling around my mind like tendrils of smoke. It was during one of these restless evenings, when the shadows grew long and the world outside dimmed, that I stumbled upon a relic of another time. The moment I saw the old recording nestled among my dusty belongings, a knot tightened in my chest. It had been years since I heard Jake's voice, yet it felt like yesterday. I hesitated, fingers hovering over the play button, uncertainty prickling at my skin. What was I hoping to find in that faded melody?

With a deep breath, I pressed play, and the room filled with the sound of strummed guitar and raw, aching lyrics that pulled me back to a different life. Jake's voice had always held a warmth, a softness that could wrap around you like a favorite blanket. But now, it felt like a fragile thread, tugging at the seams of my heart, unraveling everything I had carefully stitched together since he left. The words washed over me, each note a reminder of love and loss, of dreams deferred and the sharp pang of memories best left buried.

As the final chord echoed and faded, I found myself staring at the screen, the corners of my eyes prickling with tears I hadn't realized were there. The floodgates opened, and emotions I had suppressed for so long surged to the surface, crashing against the walls of my carefully crafted composure. I hadn't just lost Jake; I had lost a part of myself in the process. The pain of his absence was an ever-present ghost, lingering just beyond the edges of my daily life, waiting for moments of vulnerability to remind me of the void he left behind.

It was in that moment of emotional upheaval that I recognized the pressing need to confront my feelings, not only about Jake but also about Zane. Zane, with his easy smile and laughter that felt like sunshine breaking through a clouded sky, had become a fixture in my life. But where did that leave me? Confusion swirled in my mind like leaves caught in a gust of wind, threatening to sweep me away if I didn't find solid ground.

I pulled out my journal, the pages filled with my hopes, fears, and everything in between. I had always used it as a sounding board, a place to lay bare my heart without judgment. Tonight, it felt like a lifeline. I scribbled furiously, pouring out the chaos within, letting the ink bleed into the paper, creating a messy tapestry of my thoughts.

"I miss him," I wrote, the words flowing as easily as the tears. "But Zane makes me feel alive again. Why does it have to be so complicated?" Each line felt like an admission, a revelation, as I explored the tangled web of my emotions. The more I wrote, the clearer it became: I had to face the truth, to acknowledge what I was feeling.

The following morning, the sun peeked through my curtains, casting a golden glow across my cluttered desk. I felt a flicker of determination ignite within me, a resolve to take control of the chaos. Zane's absence had been suffocating, and it was time to break the silence that had stretched between us like an unbridgeable chasm. We were two stars in the same galaxy, but we had drifted too far apart. I needed to find a way back.

I spent the day reorganizing my workspace, clearing out old notes and sketches, making room for fresh ideas and renewed energy. It felt cathartic, like shedding an old skin. Each discarded paper was a step toward liberation, a move away from the shadows that had clouded my mind. Yet, despite the optimism pulsing through me, a nagging doubt lingered at the edges of my thoughts.

What if Zane didn't feel the same? What if he had retreated behind his own walls, just as I had? The thought was a chill that crept into my heart, but I shoved it aside, unwilling to let fear dictate my actions any longer. I needed to talk to him, to lay everything bare, to strip away the pretense and find a way to bridge the silence.

As I readied myself for the encounter, my heart raced, a frantic drumbeat echoing in my ears. I knew what I had to do, and it terrified me. But the thought of remaining in this limbo, stuck between my past and a future I craved, was even more daunting. I glanced in the mirror, searching for the courage I hoped would shine through my reflection.

"Alright, girl," I muttered under my breath, squaring my shoulders. "It's now or never." With a final deep breath, I stepped out into the world, ready to confront the silence and whatever it held.

The coffee shop had never felt so vibrant as it did that afternoon, each table filled with the soothing murmur of conversation and the clinking of mugs against saucers. I perched at the corner table, a fortress of notebooks and half-empty cups surrounding me like a protective barrier. I hoped this would be the place to summon the courage to finally reach out to Zane. My fingers tapped nervously on the table, a staccato rhythm that mirrored the fluttering in my stomach.

Outside, the world moved with a lively cadence. The sun filtered through the large windows, illuminating the golden flecks in the wood and warming the faces of the patrons lost in their own worlds. I had always adored this place, where the scent of freshly brewed coffee mingled with the sweetness of pastries, but today it felt charged with an energy that both thrilled and terrified me. Every laugh that erupted around me was a reminder of the joy I craved yet felt so distant from.

In that moment, I caught sight of Zane through the glass door, his silhouette framed against the light. He stepped in, shaking off the chill of the outside air, his smile brightening the room as he scanned the café. The way his eyes lit up when he spotted me sent an involuntary thrill through my veins, a mix of excitement and anxiety as he made his way over.

"Hey there, fortress of solitude," he quipped, a teasing lilt in his voice. "Did you summon me with the aroma of caffeinated bravery?" He slid into the seat opposite me, and I could feel the weight of his gaze, steady and warm. It was both a comfort and a challenge.

"Something like that," I replied, forcing a casual smile, my heart pounding in time with the buzz of the espresso machine. "Just trying to figure out how to keep my head above water in this project. You know, typical existential crisis stuff."

"Ah, the joys of adulting," he said, leaning back, arms crossed casually. "The only thing I've figured out is that coffee is the answer to all of life's questions." He gestured toward my cup, half-empty and lukewarm. "I'd say you're doing it all wrong."

I laughed, but beneath the humor was an undercurrent of tension. We danced around the real issue, the silence that had built a fortress between us. "And if coffee doesn't work?" I ventured, my voice softer now, more earnest.

Zane's expression shifted slightly, the teasing glint fading as he leaned forward, elbows resting on the table. "Then we dive into the existential dread together. I'll bring the snacks, you bring the angst." He flashed a grin, but his eyes were searching, as if he were trying to peel back the layers I had carefully wrapped around my heart.

"I'm not sure snacks can help with everything," I replied, my voice barely above a whisper, but the words hung heavy in the air between us.

"Maybe not, but they help. And I've got a killer recipe for distraction if you're interested." His smile returned, but I sensed the subtle shift, a deeper understanding lurking just beneath the surface. "Look, I know things have been... tense. We don't have to talk about it if you're not ready, but I'm here. Just say the word."

It was as if a dam within me broke. The facade I had been maintaining, the careful separation between my heart and my head, crumbled with the simplicity of his words. "I need to talk about it," I admitted, my throat dry, as the weight of my unspoken fears threatened to spill over. "About Jake. About us."

His expression softened, and for a moment, I saw vulnerability in his eyes, a glimpse of the man behind the confident exterior. "I'm listening," he said, his tone steady, inviting me to share my truth.

I took a deep breath, glancing around to ensure we were cocooned in our own little world amidst the bustling café. "I found an old recording of Jake's music. It just... hit me hard." My voice trembled slightly, and I clenched my hands, feeling the warmth of my coffee mug seep into my palms. "I thought I had moved past it, but it's like the past came rushing back, and I realized I haven't really processed any of it."

Zane's eyes didn't waver; he held my gaze, allowing the weight of my confession to settle between us. "Jake was a part of your life. He meant something to you. There's no timeline for grief or healing."

"It's complicated," I continued, my voice thick with emotion. "I loved him, but I also love this... whatever it is between us. And it feels wrong to feel both things at once. Like I'm being disloyal to his memory."

Zane nodded slowly, taking in my words. "You don't have to choose. Love isn't a zero-sum game. Just because you have feelings for someone else doesn't erase what you had. It's okay to let both exist."

His insight struck a chord within me, and I felt the tension in my chest loosen ever so slightly. "But what if it makes me a bad person? What if I'm just trying to fill a void?"

"Then at least you're honest about it," he replied, his voice low and earnest. "People are messy. Emotions are messy. I mean, look at me." He gestured dramatically to himself, earning a soft laugh from me. "I can barely keep my life organized; you should see my sock drawer. Just ask my roommate."

"Maybe you're right," I said, a tentative smile forming. "You're a disaster in a charming way."

"Exactly! It's my brand." He leaned closer, eyes sparkling. "But seriously, I'm here. I'm not going anywhere. Just because you're dealing with your past doesn't mean you have to face it alone."

A warmth blossomed in my chest, the weight of my solitude lifting slightly. "You make it sound so easy."

"Trust me, it's not," he admitted, his tone turning serious. "But I'd rather walk through the chaos with you than stand on the sidelines. I like you, and I want to be part of your journey, even the messy bits."

His words wrapped around me like a warm blanket, soothing the sharp edges of my worries. It was as if he was giving me permission to feel, to explore this new connection without guilt. I opened my mouth to respond, but before I could find the words, a sudden commotion erupted from across the café. A group of people burst through the door, laughter trailing in their wake, and my attention shifted momentarily.

Among them, a familiar figure caught my eye. Jake's sister, Claire, stepped into the café, her vibrant energy lighting up the room. She spotted me instantly and waved, her smile bright and genuine. I felt a rush of affection mixed with anxiety.

"Hey!" she called out, her voice cutting through the din. "I didn't know you came here! Come join us!"

I glanced back at Zane, uncertainty flickering in my chest. This was the last thing I needed right now, a reminder of the past crashing into my present. But there was no backing out now, no escaping the intertwining threads of our lives.

"Looks like we're invited to the party," Zane said, his tone playful but his eyes focused on me, gauging my reaction.

"Guess we can't turn down an invitation," I replied, my heart racing in anticipation. I stood up, feeling a mix of trepidation and resolve as we joined the lively group. Whatever lay ahead, I was determined to navigate it with Zane by my side, ready to embrace whatever chaos awaited us.

The laughter from Claire and her friends swirled around me like a whirlwind, pulling me out of my introspective cocoon. As we joined their table, the vibrant energy was palpable. The group was alive with stories and jokes, their voices layering over each other like an intricate melody. I caught Claire's eye, and she beamed, her enthusiasm infectious.

"Zane! You made it!" she exclaimed, pulling him into a brief hug. "I was hoping you'd join us. You're just in time for the 'most embarrassing college stories' round."

Zane raised an eyebrow, his expression playfully skeptical. "You've got me intrigued. Does this come with a disclaimer or a warning?"

"Oh, only if you want to keep your dignity intact," Claire shot back, laughter twinkling in her eyes. The rest of the group joined in, urging Zane to start the tales, their anticipation thick in the air. It was a beautiful distraction, the way the light danced on their faces and the camaraderie wrapped around us like a warm embrace.

"Alright, alright, but I'm not responsible for any reputational damage that ensues," Zane replied, leaning back with mock seriousness. He glanced at me, the corner of his mouth twitching, and I felt a warmth spreading in my chest. The ease with which he slipped back into playful banter was a welcome contrast to the weight I had carried just moments before.

As Zane regaled the group with a hilarious, albeit mortifying story about an ill-fated karaoke night, I found myself leaning in, genuinely captivated. His animated gestures and exaggerated expressions had everyone in stitches, laughter bubbling up around the table like effervescent champagne. I couldn't help but notice the way his confidence lit up the room, and for the first time in days, I felt the knot in my stomach begin to unravel.

After a series of uproarious anecdotes, the atmosphere shifted slightly. Claire turned to me, her expression softening, as if she could sense the undercurrent of tension still lingering beneath my smile. "So, how have you been?" she asked, her tone sincere, cutting through the laughter like a gentle breeze.

The weight of her question hung in the air, and I hesitated, torn between the desire to confide and the instinct to protect my heart. Zane caught my eye, a knowing look passing between us. He nodded slightly, an unspoken encouragement urging me to speak my truth.

"I've been... navigating," I finally said, the words feeling inadequate but authentic nonetheless. "It's been a bit of a whirlwind, you know?"

"Yeah, I get that. Life has a way of throwing curveballs," Claire replied, her voice empathetic. "If you ever need to talk, I'm here."

Her words felt like an anchor, grounding me in the chaotic sea of emotions swirling around. I nodded, grateful for her support, but before I could delve deeper, a sudden voice broke through the conversation, slicing through the lightheartedness.

"Look who decided to show up!" The playful tone dripped with sarcasm as Jake's best friend, Ryan, sauntered over. His eyes landed on me, and I braced myself for the inevitable. "I didn't think you'd ever leave your cave of nostalgia."

My heart dropped, and I felt Zane tense beside me. Ryan's presence felt like an unwelcome reminder of the past I was trying to navigate, a specter lurking at the edge of my newfound connection with Zane. "Nice to see you too, Ryan," I replied, forcing a smile that didn't quite reach my eyes.

"Hey, I'm just saying, I was worried we'd have to send out a search party," Ryan continued, a smirk playing at his lips. "You were getting all moody with the memories. Maybe you should have joined Zane for karaoke."

Before I could respond, Zane's arm brushed against mine, a subtle yet reassuring gesture. "Maybe you should keep your comments to yourself, Ryan," he said coolly, his tone shifting to something more protective. The warmth of his presence shielded me from the biting remarks that threatened to unravel my composure.

"Relax, man," Ryan shot back, his bravado not wavering. "I'm just teasing her. It's not my fault she's still stuck on the past."

I felt the heat of embarrassment flood my cheeks, the weight of their words pressing down on me. It was as if Ryan's comment opened a floodgate, letting all my insecurities rush in. "I'm not stuck," I retorted, more sharply than I intended. "Just figuring things out."

Ryan held up his hands in mock surrender, but the smirk never left his face. "Alright, alright. Just don't drown in your own nostalgia, okay?"

The atmosphere shifted again, a subtle tension threading through the group. I could see Zane's jaw tighten, his frustration palpable, but I held up a hand to defuse the situation. "Let's not make this a thing," I said, forcing a lighthearted tone. "We're all here to have fun, right?"

"Right," Claire chimed in, trying to steer the conversation back to safer waters. "How about we share our favorite moments from college? I'll start!"

As she launched into a story, I could feel the tension begin to dissipate, the laughter returning to our table, but I remained aware of Ryan's lingering gaze, a shadow lurking in the back of my mind. Zane caught my eye again, and for a moment, I saw concern etched on his features.

The rest of the evening passed in a blur of laughter and stories, each moment feeling both cathartic and bittersweet. I enjoyed the camaraderie, but the undercurrent of uncertainty lingered, a constant reminder of the complexities of my emotions.

As the night wore on and the group began to disperse, Zane and I lingered behind, exchanging knowing glances that spoke volumes. "You okay?" he asked, his voice low and genuine, a cocoon of warmth enveloping us as we stepped outside into the cool night air.

"I think so," I replied, though uncertainty threaded through my voice. "It's just... complicated."

Zane nodded, his expression contemplative. "You don't have to have it all figured out. It's okay to take your time."

"Thanks," I said, grateful for his understanding. "It's nice having you here. It makes the noise a little easier to handle."

He grinned, a flicker of mischief in his eyes. "You mean I'm your noise buffer? I'll take it."

As we walked side by side, the moon hung low, casting a silver glow over the path. Just as I thought the moment couldn't get any more perfect, I heard it—a sudden rustle in the bushes nearby.

Startled, I turned, my heart racing. "Did you hear that?"

Zane paused, his expression shifting from playful to alert. "Yeah, I did."

Before we could react further, the underbrush parted, and a figure emerged, cloaked in shadow but unmistakably familiar. My heart plummeted as recognition dawned, and I felt the ground shift beneath me.

"Hello, stranger," Jake's voice rang out, smooth yet laced with something darker. The world seemed to tilt on its axis as I stood frozen, caught between the past I was trying to escape and the present I was desperate to embrace.

Chapter 9: The Choice Between Past and Present

The air was electric with the pulse of bass-heavy beats reverberating through the brick-walled venue, where time seemed to suspend itself in the flickering glow of neon lights. I pushed through the throng of bodies, each one swaying to the rhythm of the music, laughter and the clinking of glasses creating a symphony of life that was both intoxicating and daunting. It was here, amidst the vibrant chaos, that I hoped to find Zane, my anchor in the tempest of emotions that had swept through my heart like a summer storm.

I spotted him by the bar, leaning casually against the counter, a half-full glass in his hand. He looked effortlessly handsome, the dark waves of his hair catching the light as he tossed back his head in laughter at something a friend had said. There was an ease about him, a warmth that radiated like the soft glow of the nearby neon sign, and it pulled me closer. With each step, the weight of my uncertainty seemed to lighten, the fears that had gripped me loosening their hold just enough to let a sliver of hope shine through.

As I approached, Zane's laughter faded, replaced by a soft smile that spread across his face like the dawn after a long night. He had this uncanny ability to make the world around him fade away, leaving only the two of us in our own little bubble. I felt my heart flutter, a familiar ache reminding me of the reasons I had come here tonight.

"Hey," I said, my voice a blend of nerves and longing, the music washing over us like a gentle wave.

"Hey yourself," he replied, his tone warm and inviting. He set his drink down, giving me his full attention, and I felt a surge of courage bubble up inside me. "What's on your mind?"

In that moment, I realized I was standing at the precipice of something monumental, my past and present colliding in a dizzying whirl of memories and emotions. Taking a deep breath, I plunged into the depths of my fears. "I don't know how to do this," I confessed, my words tumbling out in a rush. "I mean, after everything with Jake, it feels wrong to even think about moving forward. I'm scared that I'm betraying him by letting someone else in."

Zane's expression softened, his brow furrowing slightly as if he were processing my words like a delicate melody. "You're not betraying anyone," he said, his voice steady and reassuring. "Jake was a part of your life, and he always will be. But that doesn't mean you can't create new memories or find joy again. It's not about replacing what you had; it's about honoring it while still allowing yourself to feel happiness."

I leaned against the bar, my heart racing at the thought of letting go, even just a little. "It's just so hard. Some days, I feel like I'm drowning in my grief, and other days, I catch myself smiling at the silliest things, like a song on the radio or a funny meme. I don't know if I'm allowed to feel both things at once."

Zane reached out, brushing his fingers against mine, sending a jolt of warmth through me. "You're allowed to feel whatever you need to feel. Life is messy and complicated, and love—love is even messier. You can remember Jake and still want to be happy. You deserve that."

His words wrapped around me like a soft blanket, and for the first time in a long time, I felt the tightness in my chest ease, even if just slightly. "But what if I can't? What if I mess it all up?" I looked into his eyes, searching for answers, and found only understanding reflected back at me.

"Then you mess it up," he said with a half-smile, his eyes glinting with mischief. "And we laugh about it later over drinks, like this. Life isn't about getting it right; it's about the experience. Besides," he added, a playful glint in his eye, "I have faith in your ability to charm the pants off me, even if you do stumble a bit along the way."

I laughed, a genuine sound that surprised me. "Is that your way of saying you'd be willing to pick up the pieces if I fall?"

"Absolutely," he said, his smile widening. "And I promise to make it worth your while. Just imagine all the awful karaoke we could do together. It'll be a sight to behold."

I could picture it vividly: the two of us, lost in the music, singing off-key yet blissfully unaware of the world around us. A thrill ran through me at the thought, and I found myself yearning for that kind of connection, a bond that felt as vibrant as the neon lights casting a glow over our conversation.

"I guess I've always loved a bit of chaos," I admitted, feeling a flutter of something warm and bright bloom in my chest. "It keeps life interesting."

Zane leaned closer, his voice dropping to a conspiratorial whisper. "Then let's make some chaos together. What's the worst that could happen? We trip over our own feet and end up creating the most legendary dance floor fail of all time?"

The laughter spilled out of me, unrestrained and liberating. For the first time in what felt like forever, I felt lighter, like a veil had been lifted. The prospect of letting love in again was daunting, yet it no longer felt insurmountable. Perhaps I could find a way to honor my past while also embracing the possibility of something new.

As we stood there, a whirlwind of music and laughter surrounding us, the choice between my past and present felt less like a burden and more like an opportunity. Maybe, just maybe, love and music could intertwine once more, creating a melody all its own, rich with complexity and unexpected beauty.

The music pulsed around us, a vibrant heartbeat that matched the racing of my thoughts. I could feel the energy of the crowd ebbing and flowing, drawing me in like a tide while Zane remained my steadfast anchor. The world beyond our little bubble faded into a hazy blur, the neon lights painting everything in electric hues. In that moment, laughter bubbled between us like a shared secret, weaving a connection that felt both exhilarating and terrifying.

"Okay," Zane said, his voice cutting through the din, "if we're going to create chaos together, we need to do it right. First order of business: we need a plan. What kind of chaos are we talking about here? Mild mischief or full-on revelry?"

I raised an eyebrow, leaning closer. "Are you suggesting we need a strategy for mayhem? Because I thought the whole point of chaos was that it's spontaneous."

"True," he replied, his eyes glinting with mischief, "but every good adventure needs a little bit of structure. You know, to avoid being chased out of a bar or accidentally crashing a wedding."

A playful smile crept onto my lips. "So, you're saying you have experience in avoiding wedding crashes? I might need to take notes."

"Let's just say I've learned to keep my distance from the bouquet toss," he quipped, then leaned in conspiratorially. "But in all seriousness, what's something you've always wanted to do but never had the courage to try?"

The question hung in the air, swirling with the energy of the crowd. My mind raced, rifling through a mental catalog of aspirations that had somehow been pushed aside in the wake of loss. I wanted to feel alive again, to embrace the thrill of the unknown without fear chaining me down. "I've always wanted to take a spontaneous road trip. Just pack a bag, jump in the car, and see where the road takes me."

Zane's eyes sparkled with intrigue. "Now that sounds like the perfect recipe for chaos. Imagine it: two people with no destination, armed with nothing but snacks and questionable playlists."

Laughter bubbled up inside me. "And a map that we probably wouldn't use. We'd be hopelessly lost before we even hit the highway."

"Exactly!" he said, his enthusiasm infectious. "But that's where the magic happens. You discover places you never would have found otherwise—quirky diners, roadside attractions, maybe even the world's largest rubber band ball."

The mere thought of it was enough to stir something deep within me—a yearning that had been dormant for far too long. "Okay, but what if we run out of gas in the middle of nowhere? Or worse, what if we end up in a horror movie situation? You know, stranded with only each other for company?"

Zane smirked, clearly enjoying my playful paranoia. "I'll protect you from the crazed ax murderer lurking behind the bushes. And if we do run out of gas, I'll fashion a makeshift slingshot from the car's spare parts to shoot for help."

"I can't wait to see that," I chuckled, imagining Zane fashioning a slingshot like some kind of rugged MacGyver. The idea sent a wave of warmth through me, a gentle push against the walls I had built around my heart. "You're on."

His grin widened, and for a moment, the world outside faded into oblivion. The thought of embarking on an adventure—however reckless—was like a breath of fresh air, a glimpse into a future that felt increasingly possible. Yet, the whisper of caution lingered, reminding me that diving headfirst into the unknown was a risk.

As if sensing the shift in my demeanor, Zane gently squeezed my hand. "Hey, I know it's not easy to let go of the past. But what if this is the first step? An adventure to help you rediscover the parts of yourself that you've tucked away?"

His words wrapped around me like a soothing balm, melting away some of my anxiety. "You really think I could just... move forward? Like it's that simple?"

"Not simple," he corrected, his voice softening. "But it can be transformative. Every step you take into the future doesn't erase the past; it honors it. Jake will always be a part of you, but he wouldn't want you to be stuck. You deserve to find joy again."

With those words, a spark ignited within me—a flicker of determination that felt foreign yet exhilarating. Maybe I could take that leap. Maybe I could be brave enough to let go, if only just a little. "Okay, let's do it. Let's go on that road trip."

Zane's face lit up, a mix of surprise and delight. "Really? You're in?"

"Absolutely. But I have to warn you, I'm prone to spontaneous singing and very bad dance moves, so prepare yourself."

"Bring it on," he laughed, a rich sound that filled the space between us. "We'll make a grand spectacle out of it. And if we get lost, I promise to keep the snacks stocked."

"Deal," I said, feeling a surge of excitement flutter in my chest. The thought of hitting the road with Zane—a man who could make me laugh and who seemed genuinely invested in my happiness—was intoxicating.

As we stood there, caught in our own little world, a woman with wild red hair and a sparkly outfit pushed her way to the bar. She glanced at us, her eyes narrowing playfully as she leaned over the counter, obviously eavesdropping. "You two look like trouble," she said, a sly grin spreading across her face.

Zane raised an eyebrow, his voice dripping with charm. "We prefer to think of ourselves as adventurers. Care to join?"

"Only if you promise to keep the slingshots to a minimum," she shot back, clearly unimpressed. "I've had enough of that nonsense tonight."

With laughter spilling from us, we fell into easy conversation with her, sharing snippets of our lives and our spontaneous road trip plans. Each story exchanged added another thread to the tapestry of the night, weaving our laughter into the fabric of the music that pulsed around us. It felt effortless, as if the universe was conspiring to remind me that connection, even amid uncertainty, was not only possible but also exhilarating.

The night wore on, filled with unexpected camaraderie and the kind of laughter that made my heart feel light. Yet beneath the surface of the merriment, an undercurrent of something deeper stirred—a sense of possibility that left me both exhilarated and slightly terrified. Each moment spent with Zane blurred the lines between past and present, inviting me to embrace the idea of love again without erasing the memory of what I had lost.

The evening stretched on like a lazy river, winding through laughter and music, each moment building a bridge from the past to a hopeful present. As I stood shoulder to shoulder with Zane, our easy camaraderie unfurling like a vibrant banner, I felt a shift inside me—a tentative yet exhilarating embrace of what might lie ahead. The woman with the wild red hair, having quickly turned into our impromptu ally, regaled us with tales of her own questionable adventures.

"Last summer, I tried to start a llama petting zoo in my backyard," she declared, her eyes sparkling with mischief. "Turns out, llamas have a way of leaving little surprises everywhere, and my HOA was not amused."

I choked on my drink, laughter spilling out of me like confetti. "That sounds like a disaster waiting to happen!"

"Disaster? Please," she said, waving a dismissive hand. "It was more of a... learning experience. And I've now officially been banned from any future petting zoo endeavors. So I'm all in for your road trip chaos."

"Welcome aboard," Zane said, his voice dripping with charm. "We'll make sure to steer clear of any llamas. At least until you get your backyard cleaned up."

The night felt alive, charged with energy, and I couldn't shake the feeling that something monumental was brewing just beneath the surface. The drinks flowed, stories unfolded, and the atmosphere was charged with a mix of nostalgia and the thrill of new beginnings. Each laugh echoed in my chest, coaxing out the shadows of my grief, making room for the light that Zane brought into my life.

"Alright, what's the first stop on this infamous road trip?" Zane asked, glancing between me and our new friend, his excitement palpable.

"Somewhere that serves excellent breakfast tacos," I declared, thinking about how my stomach always seemed to rumble for adventure, much like my heart. "And maybe a quirky roadside attraction? I've always wanted to see the world's largest ball of yarn."

"Of course," Zane chuckled, his laughter rich and infectious. "Because nothing says 'life-changing journey' like an oversized ball of yarn."

"Don't knock it until you see it," I shot back, smirking. "It's all about embracing the absurd. And who knows? Maybe I'll knit a sweater while I'm there."

He leaned closer, his voice dropping conspiratorially. "If you knit me a sweater, I'll wear it proudly, regardless of how it looks. Deal?"

"Deal," I replied, feeling the warmth spread through me, an ember of something new igniting in the space between us.

As the night wore on, the energy shifted, a gentle undercurrent of tension weaving its way through our laughter. There was something exhilarating about sharing our dreams, our ridiculous aspirations, and for a moment, it felt as if we were standing on the precipice of something great. Yet, in the back of my mind, a whisper of doubt curled its fingers around my heart, reminding me of what was at stake.

The venue began to wind down, the music fading into a soft hum as patrons trickled toward the exit. Zane and I lingered, reluctant to part ways. The last remnants of the night clung to us, and the neon lights painted our faces in a kaleidoscope of colors that felt almost magical.

"Hey, can we talk?" Zane asked, his tone shifting to something more serious.

"Of course," I replied, my heart thudding in my chest.

We stepped outside into the cool night air, the world around us quieting, the stars overhead twinkling like tiny, distant beacons. Zane leaned against the wall, his expression contemplative, a hint of vulnerability surfacing in his gaze. "I know we're having fun planning this adventure, but I want you to know that I'm here for you—no matter what you need."

A wave of emotion surged through me. "You're making it really hard not to fall for you, you know that?" I said, my voice barely above a whisper.

He chuckled softly, a hint of a blush creeping onto his cheeks. "Is that so terrible?"

"I mean, no. But it complicates things."

His expression turned earnest, his gaze steady on mine. "Complications are what make life interesting. I don't want you to feel pressured to choose between your past and whatever this is," he gestured between us, "but I also don't want to be a rebound or a distraction from your healing. That wouldn't be fair to either of us."

My heart sank a little, the weight of his words settling in the pit of my stomach. I had no desire to hurt him or to move too quickly, yet the connection we shared felt like a flame, flickering just out of reach. "I don't want you to feel like I'm holding back because I'm scared. It's just—"

"—a process," he finished, nodding as if he understood the unspoken fears swirling in my mind. "I get it. But I want you to know that I'm willing to wait. And maybe, just maybe, we can figure this out together."

A soft breeze brushed past us, carrying the scent of rain-soaked earth and wildflowers. I longed to close the distance between us, to explore the warmth blooming in my chest, but a flicker of uncertainty held me back. "I don't want to hurt you, Zane."

He stepped closer, his voice low and sincere. "You won't. Just be honest with me, okay? Whatever you're feeling, share it. I can handle the truth."

Before I could respond, a sudden commotion erupted from the street, drawing our attention. A group of rowdy patrons stumbled out of a nearby bar, their laughter punctuated by shouts. It was all so sudden, and for a moment, the atmosphere felt charged with anticipation.

I glanced back at Zane, his expression shifting as he focused on the group. "What's going on over there?"

But before I could finish my question, a figure darted past us, clearly in distress, shoving through the crowd with an urgency that sent a jolt of adrenaline through my veins. My instincts kicked in, and without thinking, I stepped forward.

"Hey, are you okay?" I called out, but the figure barely glanced back, their face shadowed beneath the flickering streetlights.

Zane's hand wrapped around my wrist, holding me back as the chaos unfolded. "Wait, don't—"

But it was too late. The figure stumbled, and I caught a glimpse of a panicked expression—a familiar face, one I had thought I'd left behind. My heart dropped into my stomach as recognition hit me like a punch. "Jake?"

The name escaped my lips before I could stop it, a whisper of disbelief mixed with the rush of emotions that swirled through me.

The figure turned, eyes wide, and for a fleeting moment, our gazes locked in a collision of past and present, uncertainty and unearthing. Time froze as everything around us blurred into insignificance, leaving only the question that hung heavily in the air:

Had I really been ready to embrace a new beginning, or had the past come roaring back with the force of a tidal wave, intent on pulling me under?

Chapter 10: A Chorus of Doubts

Each day, the sun spills its golden rays through the sprawling windows of the studio, illuminating the myriad of colors splattered across the walls and the wooden floorboards that creak underfoot. It's a creative haven, alive with the hum of art in progress. Yet, beneath the vibrant hues and artistic chaos, a storm brews within me, swirling with uncertainty and apprehension. As I set my easel in place and prepare to dive into another long evening of work, I can feel the electric charge in the air—the palpable tension that always accompanies my artist, Faye.

Faye is a tempest wrapped in a silk scarf, a genius plagued by demons of her own making. She drifts from canvas to canvas like a restless ghost, her sharp tongue and sharper gaze cutting through any sense of calm that might linger. Today is no different. I can hear her voice rising above the chatter of the team, each word laced with doubt. "This color is all wrong!" she snaps, slamming a brush down as if it had betrayed her in the midst of a heated affair. "It's lifeless. It's—"

"Just like your last piece, apparently," I mutter under my breath, my heart racing as I fight to keep my composure. It's a petty retort, but the frustration bubbles to the surface after hours of her relentless critique. The moment the words escape, I glance around the studio, half-expecting to see the others stifling laughter or exchanging knowing looks. Instead, they seem to shrink away, eyes glued to their workstations, acutely aware of the simmering tension.

Faye's gaze swings towards me, and for a heartbeat, the world narrows down to just us. "What did you say?" she demands, her tone cold and cutting. The way she leans into my space feels like a challenge, her presence a weight on my chest. I can't help but feel cornered by her ferocity and artistry, caught in a tug-of-war between admiration and resentment.

"Nothing," I reply, forcing a smile that feels more like a grimace. "Just thought I'd try out a new shade. You know, the 'dead fish' technique."

Her eyes narrow, but a flicker of surprise passes over her face. Maybe she didn't expect me to bite back. The studio goes silent, tension thick enough to cut with a knife. I can feel the collective breath of the team as they hold their focus on their projects, daring not to step into the fray.

"Perhaps if you put as much effort into your painting as you do into your snark, we wouldn't be in this mess," she replies, voice low and dangerous, and I can feel the heat rising in my cheeks.

In that moment, I catch Zane's gaze through the studio's expansive glass walls. He's standing there, arms crossed, an anchor amidst the chaos. The corners of his mouth twitch upwards, and I feel the warmth of his encouragement seep into my bones. It's an unspoken reassurance, a reminder that I'm not in this battle alone, even if Faye's storm rages fiercely. I return my focus to the canvas, determined to prove that I belong here, that I am more than a mere footnote in someone else's story.

Yet, as the hours slip by, that resolve begins to falter under the weight of self-doubt. I mix colors, my mind swirling with insecurities. What if I'm not cut out for this? What if my artistic vision is merely a shadow of Faye's brilliance? My brush glides across the canvas, each stroke a whisper of fear. The paint blends in a chaotic array, neither cohesive nor compelling, much like my thoughts.

"Are you sure you're ready for this?" Faye's voice cuts through my introspection, laced with a condescending edge. "It seems like you're struggling. Maybe you'd be better off handling the logistics than attempting to paint."

I feel the heat rise in my chest, a mix of anger and embarrassment. "I'm fine, Faye. Just exploring new techniques," I manage, though I can feel the tremor in my voice. The truth hangs heavy between us, suffocating; the uncertainty I try to hide from her is palpable.

Zane, who has been observing silently, steps closer, the warmth of his presence a welcome balm. "Everyone has their off days, Faye. Perhaps you could give them some space to experiment instead of shutting them down," he interjects, his tone steady, like a gentle wave pushing against the tide.

Faye scoffs but doesn't reply, her expression unreadable as she turns back to her work. The moment feels like a breath held too long, the tension thick and suffocating. I force myself to breathe, focusing on the rhythm of my brush against the canvas, the tactile satisfaction of paint squishing beneath my fingers.

But as the night stretches on, the gnawing doubts creep back in. Despite the camaraderie and the vibrant energy that buzzes through the studio, I'm trapped in my own head. Zane's presence, once a source of comfort, now feels like a lighthouse flickering in a storm—bright and promising, yet impossibly distant. Am I strong enough to carry the weight of my dreams, to protect my heart against the criticisms that seem to come from every angle?

The answer eludes me like a wisp of smoke, and the realization settles in my gut, heavy and unsettling. Maybe I'm not as resilient as I once thought. I pause, brush poised above the canvas, and the uncertainty fills the air, a chorus of doubts threatening to drown out my resolve.

The cacophony of brushes clattering against palettes and paint tubes rolling across tables filled the studio, yet I felt oddly isolated, wrapped in a cocoon of uncertainty. As I looked at my canvas, splashes of color seemed to mock me, a swirling storm of potential turned muddled and chaotic. The light from the overhead fixtures flickered, casting odd shadows that danced across the walls, reflecting my disarray. Every time I attempted to focus, Faye's criticisms echoed in my mind like a relentless drumbeat, threatening to drown out any flicker of creativity.

I took a deep breath, determined to push through. It was just paint. Just colors. I was not going to let her suffocating presence snuff out the spark I had fought so hard to ignite. Zane's supportive smile floated back into my thoughts, a beacon of warmth in the frigid air of doubt. Gathering my resolve, I began to layer my colors again, allowing the brush to glide with more intention. With every stroke, I visualized Zane's encouraging nod, urging me to keep going, to keep creating.

"Is that how we're going to do it today?" Faye's voice cut through my concentration, sharp and biting. I turned to find her observing me, arms crossed, a familiar look of disapproval painted across her features. "Just smearing colors around like you're in kindergarten?"

The irritation flared inside me, bubbling up like an old soda bottle shaken one too many times. "It's called abstract expressionism, Faye. Ever heard of it?" I shot back, unable to help the sharpness in my tone. A few heads turned, surprised by my sudden boldness, but I refused to let her diminish my spirit.

"Maybe you should spend less time worrying about what I've heard and more time actually mastering the technique." Her eyes glinted with a challenging spark, and I could feel the air shift, the rest of the team bracing for impact like spectators at a boxing match.

"Technique? Right. I forgot that your definition of 'technique' means letting your insecurities bleed into every canvas. My mistake!" I didn't mean for it to slip out, but the words poured from me, fueled by a mixture of frustration and an insatiable desire for validation.

The silence that followed felt monumental, stretching across the studio as tension thickened. A heartbeat passed, and then Zane stepped forward, a calming presence amidst the brewing storm. "Faye, maybe we should all take a breather," he suggested, his voice steady and soothing, like a gentle hand on a fevered brow.

I shot him a grateful look, and for a fleeting moment, the storm inside me quieted. Faye, however, merely waved a dismissive hand. "Breather? We're not here to relax. We're here to create." Her voice dripped with disdain, and my heart sank.

Zane's brows knitted together, and he took a step closer to her, his voice low yet firm. "Creation doesn't flourish in hostility. It needs room to breathe, just like our team."

Faye's jaw clenched, and I could see her weighing his words, the fire in her eyes flickering just slightly. She turned away, the tension deflating but not quite dissipating. I could feel the collective sigh of relief ripple through the team, but my heart was still racing, adrenaline coursing through my veins.

"Thanks," I whispered to Zane as he returned to my side, his presence grounding me once more.

"Anytime," he replied with a playful grin, the corners of his mouth curving up in a way that made the chaos of the studio feel a little less overwhelming. "Besides, I wouldn't want to see you turn into a walking paintbrush."

I laughed, the sound light and airy, a welcome reprieve from the heaviness that had settled in the studio. "A walking paintbrush would be quite the sight, wouldn't it? Perhaps I'd even start a new trend in abstract art."

"Trend or not, I'd pay to see that performance." His eyes sparkled with mischief, and I could feel my spirits lifting. Zane had this uncanny ability to peel away the layers of my anxiety, exposing the potential for laughter and lightness beneath.

Just then, the sound of my phone buzzing against the table disrupted the moment. I glanced down, my heart dropping as I saw the name on the screen. My mother. The thought of answering her made my stomach twist, a reminder of the expectations and pressures waiting to creep back into my life. I hesitated, torn between wanting to engage with Zane and the growing need to face whatever my mother wanted to discuss.

"Go ahead, I'll be right here," Zane said, a knowing look in his eyes, as if he could sense the struggle coiling within me.

With a deep breath, I picked up the phone, my pulse racing as I swiped to answer. "Hi, Mom," I managed, trying to keep my voice steady.

"Are you still in that studio?" Her voice was sharp, cutting through the air like glass. "You need to focus on something practical, dear. Art isn't going to pay the bills."

"Mom, I'm working on a project right now. I can't talk." My voice faltered, but I pressed on. "I'm really happy here."

"Happiness doesn't pay the rent, and you can't keep living in this fantasy. You should come home and—"

"Home?" I interrupted, the heat of frustration spilling over. "You mean back to a place where every corner reminds me of everything I'm trying to escape? I can't do that, Mom."

A silence enveloped the line, thick and suffocating, just like the atmosphere in the studio moments ago. "You know I only want what's best for you," she finally said, but the words felt hollow, lacking the warmth I craved.

"I know," I whispered, feeling the weight of disappointment settle on my shoulders like a heavy cloak. "But what's best for me isn't the same as what you think is best."

The conversation ended with a tense goodbye, and as I hung up, I felt like I was suffocating all over again. Zane stood close, his brow furrowed with concern, and I forced a smile, even though it felt like a mask slipping over a gaping wound. "Just family stuff," I said, though the tightness in my chest told me it was more than that.

"Want to talk about it?" he asked gently, his voice a warm balm against my fraying nerves.

I shook my head, grateful for the offer but feeling the need to process this on my own. "No, it's fine. I just... I need to paint."

"Then let's paint," he said, and just like that, the tension started to ease. As we both turned back to our canvases, I felt a glimmer of hope, a flicker of possibility that perhaps—just perhaps—this was where I belonged.

The brush glided across the canvas as I lost myself in the rhythm of color mixing, the world around me blurring into the background. The studio transformed into a cocoon of creativity, a vibrant sanctuary where paint fumes mingled with the electric pulse of inspiration. Zane stood nearby, his presence a steady anchor as I wielded my brush like a sword, battling against the shadows of doubt that loomed over me. I layered the colors, each stroke a defiance against Faye's scathing remarks, an assertion that my artistic voice mattered just as much as hers.

"Looks like you're channeling your inner Picasso," Zane remarked, stepping closer to observe the chaotic swirl of colors I had created. His voice was light, teasing, but there was an undertone of sincerity that made my heart flutter. "Or maybe a toddler on a sugar high."

"Hey, that's my artistic process you're mocking," I shot back, grinning as I wiped a smudge of paint across his cheek. He feigned shock, eyes widening comically.

"Now we're both going to be art installations," he quipped, dabbing a finger on the canvas and smearing the paint like it was an extravagant gesture of rebellion. "Abstracts that symbolize the chaos of our lives."

We exchanged playful banter, the kind that felt effortless and illuminating, chasing away the lingering tension that had wrapped around me like a heavy fog. Each laugh echoed off the studio walls, pulling the team back into the lightness we had almost lost. I could see them relax, their own smiles breaking through the seriousness that Faye's critiques had imposed.

"Alright, everyone, let's refocus," Faye called from her station, her tone still clipped but less biting. "We need to pull this together before the deadline."

The moment shifted, tension rising once more like a thick soup on the verge of boiling over. I felt a flicker of panic surge within me. The deadline loomed like a storm cloud, and the fear of failure clawed at my insides. Would I truly be able to contribute anything meaningful? My brush hesitated above the canvas, colors swirling in indecision, while Faye continued her relentless march toward perfection.

"Hey," Zane said softly, breaking through my spiraling thoughts. He stepped closer, his presence radiating calm. "You've got this. Just paint. Don't think about her."

With a small nod, I took a breath, inhaling the scent of linseed oil and turpentine that filled the air, grounding myself in the moment. Zane's encouragement wrapped around me like a warm blanket, and I returned to my canvas, pushing through the fear. I dipped my brush into a bold crimson, allowing it to bloom across the surface like a wild flower breaking through concrete.

Time faded as I painted, lost in the flow of creativity, each stroke igniting a sense of liberation that I desperately craved. Zane watched silently, his presence a reassuring backdrop as I surrendered to the colors. Every flick of my wrist felt like a step toward reclaiming my artistic identity, a step away from the confines of someone else's expectations.

As the evening wore on, the studio began to empty, the team drifting away one by one, each immersed in their own world of creativity or fatigue. Faye finally retreated to her corner, her silhouette tense but quiet. Just as I felt the last echoes of anxiety dissolve, Zane leaned against the wall, arms crossed, observing me with an intensity that sent a pleasant shiver down my spine.

"Are you really okay?" he asked, his voice low and sincere, a whisper that felt like an invitation to open up.

I hesitated, the weight of my emotions pressing against my chest. "I think so," I replied, though doubt lingered in the corners of my mind. "Just... family stuff. You know how it is."

"I do," he replied, a hint of understanding flashing in his eyes. "But you can't just brush it off. You're allowed to feel whatever you're feeling."

His words settled in the air between us, heavy with the kind of understanding that only someone who has experienced their own struggles can offer. I could see a flicker of vulnerability in his gaze, as if he was waiting for me to open up in return.

"What about you?" I asked, shifting the focus, eager to deflect the weight of my own burdens. "What do you do when life gets overwhelming?"

A shadow crossed his face, an emotion I couldn't quite read. "I paint," he admitted softly. "Or I escape into my music. It's how I process everything. But sometimes... sometimes, even that isn't enough."

I felt the urge to reach out, to bridge the space between us, but before I could say anything, a crash interrupted the moment, echoing through the studio like an unwelcome ghost. Faye's voice cut through the tension, shrill and accusatory. "What have you done? This is ruined!"

I turned, heart racing, to see Faye standing over a canvas that had slipped from its easel, its vibrant colors splattered across the floor like an accidental masterpiece. Her frustration radiated through the room, and for a moment, I felt the familiar pang of fear creep back in, the instinct to shrink away from confrontation.

"Faye, it's just paint," I said, trying to infuse my voice with calm. "We can clean it up."

"Just paint?" she spat, her voice rising. "You have no idea how much work went into that! And you're too busy playing at being an artist to notice!"

The accusation hit like a physical blow, each word laced with venom, and I could feel the heat of embarrassment rushing to my cheeks. Zane shifted beside me, tension coiling in the air like a tightly wound spring, but before he could say anything, I stepped forward, my voice steadier than I felt.

"Faye, we're all trying our best here. Everyone has their process, and yes, things can get messy. But art isn't always neat and tidy," I said, the words flowing with unexpected confidence. "Maybe if you let go a little, you'd see that."

The room fell silent, the team frozen in place, eyes darting between us as if waiting for the inevitable explosion. Faye's gaze flickered, surprise momentarily eclipsing her fury. I held my ground, heart racing, waiting for her retort, and for a moment, it felt as if the world had shifted beneath us, the foundations of our dynamic cracking.

But then, just as I thought I'd broken through, Faye's expression hardened. "You think you can challenge me?" she hissed, her voice low and dangerous. "You're nothing but a—"

"Enough!" Zane stepped in, his voice a firm barrier between us, his presence expanding in the charged air. "We're here to create, not to tear each other down. We can figure this out. Together."

The room was thick with tension, and I could feel the energy vibrating, a taut string ready to snap. I glanced at Zane, searching for an ally in this whirlwind, only to find him looking back at me with an intensity that sent my heart racing.

Before I could process the moment, Faye's phone buzzed loudly, breaking the silence. She glanced at the screen, the color draining from her face, a stark contrast to the vibrant chaos of paint around us. "What?" she breathed, her voice suddenly hollow.

"What is it?" I asked, curiosity sparking through the remnants of the confrontation, but her gaze had turned distant, as if she were grappling with something far beyond the studio's walls.

"It can't be..." she whispered, stepping back as if the phone had burned her. "No. No, no, no."

I could feel the tension shift once more, a new layer unfurling beneath the chaos. "Faye, what's going on?" I pressed, unease creeping in, gnawing at the edges of my mind.

But she only stared at the screen, mouth opening and closing as if she were struggling to form words. "This changes everything," she finally murmured, a shadow of something unnameable flickering in her eyes.

And just like that, the storm of paint, doubt, and confrontation faded into the background, leaving behind a silence so heavy, it felt like a weight pressing against my chest. A new, unwelcome tension unfurled in the air, palpable and raw, as the gravity of Faye's words settled between us, a storm brewing that none of us were prepared for.

Chapter 11: Heartbeats in the Silence

The sun hung low in the sky, casting a golden glow over the beach, painting the world in shades of amber and honey. I strolled along the water's edge, each step sinking into the warm, forgiving sand. The waves whispered their secrets as they rolled in and out, a rhythmic pulse that mirrored the turmoil within me. It had been too long since I allowed myself the luxury of stillness, too long since I heard my own heartbeat against the world's cacophony. With every crash of the surf, I hoped to wash away the remnants of my chaotic studio life, the noise of deadlines and expectations fading into the salty breeze.

I closed my eyes, tilting my face up to the sun, soaking in its warmth. The familiar scent of saltwater mixed with a hint of coconut sunscreen wafted through the air, and I could almost taste the freedom of my surroundings. The beach was a sanctuary, where the horizon met the sky in a blurred line of infinite possibility. I took a deep breath, letting the salty air fill my lungs as I let my thoughts drift like the clouds above.

Jake's laughter echoed in my mind, a sweet, haunting melody I couldn't shake off. Our time together had been a whirlwind of passion and dreams, and while I cherished those memories, they weighed on me like an anchor. I felt a tug in my chest, a familiar ache that had become a part of my existence. Jake had been my first real love, and though we had parted ways, his essence lingered in every note I played, every lyric I wrote. I couldn't help but wonder if I'd ever be able to untangle myself from the web of our shared history.

But then there was Zane. His presence was like a sudden gust of fresh air, sweeping in with an energy that was both exhilarating and terrifying. He had a way of making the world seem brighter, infusing life into every song we created together. It was as if he could see the pieces of me that had been buried beneath the noise. Yet, I hesitated, caught between the past and the uncertain promise of the future. Could I really open my heart again?

Just as I was beginning to settle into my thoughts, my phone buzzed in my pocket, pulling me back to reality. Zane's name lit up the screen, and for a moment, I felt the familiar flutter of nerves. His voice, warm and inviting, spilled through the receiver, wrapping around me like a favorite blanket. "Hey, you! What's the beach like today?"

I chuckled, the sound of my own laughter surprising me. "You know, pretty standard—sand, sea, and a very contemplative girl trying to figure out life."

"Sounds like a perfect opportunity for a spontaneous jam session. What do you say? I'll bring the guitar, you bring the magic?"

I could almost picture his mischievous grin through the phone, and the invitation tugged at something deep within me. The thought of creating music with him, of sharing this sacred space, sent butterflies dancing in my stomach. "I'm in. Where should we meet?"

"Let's do it right by the water. I'll be there in fifteen."

As I hung up, excitement bubbled up inside me, mixing with the remnants of my lingering anxiety. The waves became my metronome, setting the rhythm for my thoughts as I walked toward our meeting spot. Each footfall ignited a spark of anticipation, a sense of freedom tinged with the sweetness of possibility. This wasn't just about the music; it was about finding a connection that felt raw and genuine, something I had been yearning for without even realizing it.

When Zane arrived, he was a vision against the backdrop of the setting sun, his silhouette framed by the golden light. He approached with an easy confidence, his guitar slung casually over his shoulder. "Hey there, sunshine," he greeted, his smile infectious. "You look like you could use some music in your life."

"Let's hope I can keep up with you," I teased, gesturing toward the waves crashing rhythmically behind us.

As we settled into the sand, the world around us faded, leaving only the sound of the ocean and the strumming of his guitar. The first chords floated through the air, mingling with the salty breeze, and suddenly, I felt the tension in my shoulders begin to melt away. I picked up my own instrument, fingers trembling slightly as I found the right notes.

"Just follow my lead," Zane said, his voice smooth as the sea glass scattered along the shore. "And remember, there are no wrong notes—just the ones waiting to find their place."

With those words, I let myself surrender to the moment, allowing the music to wash over me like the waves lapping at my feet. We played, weaving our melodies together, laughter punctuating the space between notes. It felt effortless, like we had been doing this forever. For the first time in what felt like ages, I was lost in the music, heart soaring with each strum and pluck.

Time ceased to exist as we lost ourselves in the melodies, the lyrics spilling out as effortlessly as the tide. I found myself sharing snippets of my journey, the highs and lows, and Zane listened, nodding with understanding, his eyes reflecting the warmth of the setting sun. "You've got a story worth telling," he said, the sincerity in his voice wrapping around me like a warm embrace.

As the sun dipped below the horizon, the sky transformed into a canvas of vibrant colors, mirroring the explosion of emotions within me. With each chord, I felt a deeper connection forming, an understanding that transcended the surface. Zane was different, his energy grounding yet liberating. With him, I felt the thrill of new beginnings, a flicker of hope igniting in the quiet corners of my heart.

As night fell, the stars twinkled overhead like distant promises, and I realized that maybe, just maybe, it was time to let go of the past and embrace the music of the present. Zane had a way of making the world feel alive, and I wanted to be part of that symphony, to dance through the uncertainties with him by my side.

The music floated on the evening breeze, each note entwining with the sound of the surf, creating a harmony that felt both intimate and expansive. With every chord I played, I felt layers of my heart unravel, revealing a vulnerability that had been tucked away for far too long. Zane, with his effortless charm and the way he drew melodies from his guitar as if they were hidden treasures, filled the air with laughter and encouragement. Our shared songs became a tapestry of unspoken feelings, woven with threads of hope and a hint of uncertainty.

"So, what's the story behind this song?" Zane asked, strumming a playful riff that danced on the edge of mischief. He had a knack for pulling me into conversations that were as engaging as our music, and I found myself leaning into the connection we were building.

I chuckled, shaking my head slightly. "Oh, you know, just the classic tale of love lost, found, and lost again. A real tear-jerker."

"Ah, a true ballad of the heart," he replied, raising an eyebrow. "Very original. But seriously, there's something about your lyrics that feels... personal. Like you've lived them."

I paused, contemplating the weight of his words. It was true; my songs often drew from my experiences, but sharing that depth felt like peeling back layers I'd long guarded. "Let's just say I've had my fair share of heartbreaks. Each one a lesson wrapped in a little bit of sorrow."

"Is that your way of saying I should prepare for emotional whiplash if we ever record together?" He grinned, his playful banter lighting up the dimming sky.

"Only if you promise to keep your guitar handy for a good cry," I quipped back, feeling a surge of camaraderie that was as refreshing as the ocean breeze.

As the sun dipped lower, painting the horizon in deep purples and oranges, we transitioned to a more upbeat tune, the tempo rising in sync with the invigorating swell of excitement in my chest. The music seemed to pulse with life, filling the spaces between us with an electric energy. I couldn't remember the last time I had felt this alive—every note was a celebration, every laugh a reminder of the lightness I had almost forgotten.

"Okay, but what's the real story?" Zane pressed, his curiosity palpable, as he leaned closer, his guitar resting against his knee. "You can't just leave me hanging like that. What happened with Jake?"

Ah, the million-dollar question. My heart stuttered at the mention of his name, a delicate dance of vulnerability and guardedness. "Jake and I... we had something special," I began cautiously, feeling the warmth of nostalgia tugging at my heart. "He was my first love, you know? A whirlwind romance filled with late-night adventures and songs under the stars. But like most things that burn too brightly, it ended in flames."

"Flames?" he echoed, raising his eyebrows. "Now that sounds dramatic. Do tell."

"Let's just say we were young and reckless," I replied, allowing a bittersweet smile to escape. "We thought we could conquer the world, but reality had other plans. Miscommunication, career aspirations, a mutual friend who didn't know when to keep his mouth shut... you get the picture."

"Ah, the classic trifecta of relationship ruin," he laughed, the sound rich and warm. "So, you're saying you've got a history of turning heartbreak into song?"

"Guilty as charged." I let the laughter roll over me, a welcome release. "But I'm trying to break that cycle. Zane, I don't want my life to be just a series of ballads about what went wrong."

"Then let's write one about what could go right." His voice was earnest, and the sincerity in his eyes struck a chord within me. "How about we give that a shot right now?"

With a quick nod, I felt a thrill of excitement ignite as he launched into a soft, rhythmic strumming pattern. I let the music guide me, words flowing freely as I explored the idea of new beginnings. We traded verses back and forth, creating something fresh and exhilarating, a song built on possibility instead of pain.

As the notes filled the air, I couldn't help but glance at Zane, his expression a mixture of concentration and joy. There was something undeniably magnetic about him—a kindred spirit wrapped in an aura of creativity that beckoned me to open up. I felt like I was at the edge of something beautiful and terrifying, the gentle push of hope urging me forward.

When the last chord hung in the air, a comfortable silence enveloped us, punctuated only by the sound of waves rolling softly onto the shore. I could see the stars beginning to peek out, timidly at first, then with increasing confidence, as if they were joining our celebration.

"That was incredible," I breathed, a smile stretching across my face. "I didn't know I needed that until just now."

Zane returned my smile with a playful glint in his eyes. "I'm just getting started. How about a beach bonfire? I'll provide the marshmallows; you bring the storytelling."

"Marshmallows? What am I, a kid at camp?" I shot back, feigning indignation, but I couldn't help the grin that broke free.

"Hey, don't knock it till you try it! Besides, nothing pairs better with music than gooey marshmallows and slightly burnt graham crackers. It's practically a rite of passage."

"Fine," I conceded, my laughter bubbling over. "But only if you promise to serenade me while I roast them."

"Deal." He stood up, brushing the sand off his jeans, and I followed suit, my heart racing at the prospect of continuing our evening under the stars. We gathered driftwood and small logs, our laughter mingling with the crackling of the fire as it began to flicker to life.

As the flames danced and crackled, I caught sight of the warmth in Zane's gaze, a light that seemed to illuminate the shadows of my past. I felt a shift, as if the universe was whispering its secrets, urging me to lean into this moment. Here, in this cocoon of music and firelight, I was ready to embrace whatever came next, ready to face the unknown with a heart that, for the first time in ages, felt full of promise.

The bonfire crackled to life, casting flickering shadows that danced across the beach, igniting the night with a warmth that matched the growing chemistry between Zane and me. The air was rich with the smell of wood smoke and the promise of adventure, and I couldn't help but feel giddy as I settled onto the sand, pulling my knees to my chest. Zane, the ever-charming firestarter, tossed a few marshmallows onto a skewer, holding it over the flames with a practiced ease that made me wonder how many bonfires he'd hosted before.

"Watch closely," he said, leaning in closer, a mischievous grin stretching across his face. "The secret to the perfect marshmallow is a slow roast. You want it golden brown, not charred to oblivion."

"Golden brown? You mean like the perfect tan?" I teased, lifting an eyebrow. "I think I'm more of a sunburn red kind of girl."

"Hey, we all have our colors," he shot back, smirking. "Besides, there's a fine line between that and charcoal, and I'm not trying to make s'mores with someone who looks like they just crawled out of a barbecue pit."

As the flames flickered, the conversation flowed easily between us, punctuated by laughter and the occasional crackle of the fire. With every roasted marshmallow, I felt a sense of camaraderie forming, a bond strengthened by shared stories and a growing trust. I tossed him a perfectly golden marshmallow, and he caught it with a flourish. "I see you've mastered the art of the toss," he said, taking a dramatic bite.

"I aim to impress," I replied, a teasing light in my eyes. "Maybe I should add 'Marshmallow Throwing Champion' to my résumé."

"I'll make sure to recommend you for the next s'mores Olympics."

With a soft chuckle, I turned my gaze back to the sea, watching the waves as they danced under the moonlight. "You know," I said softly, the playful banter giving way to a more serious tone, "I've been running from my past for a while now. It's nice to just... be here."

Zane shifted slightly, his gaze focused intently on me. "What do you mean by 'running'?"

I took a moment, weighing my words like stones in my pocket. "Jake was my everything for a long time. When we ended, it felt like I lost a part of myself. I thought stepping away from it all would help, but it only created this giant hole. Music is my way of filling it, but it's not always easy."

"Music is the best therapy," Zane said, his voice steady. "But you have to let it be cathartic, not just a distraction. If you don't face it, it'll keep haunting you."

I nodded, contemplating his words as the fire crackled, embers rising like unspoken dreams. "You're right. I guess I've been scared to dive into those feelings, to really confront what I've lost."

"Maybe instead of running, it's time to face it head-on," he suggested gently. "Find a way to turn that pain into something beautiful. You've already started with your songs. It's just the next step."

I took a deep breath, absorbing his encouragement. "You make it sound so easy."

"Hey, I'm just a guy with a guitar and a fondness for marshmallows," he laughed. "But seriously, it's all about perspective. Sometimes the hardest battles lead to the best outcomes."

A comfortable silence enveloped us as the waves whispered their agreement, and I stole a glance at Zane, noticing the way the firelight flickered against his features, casting a soft glow on his face. There was something undeniably magnetic about him, a spark of creativity that ignited my own.

"Okay, let's write something together," I suggested, feeling emboldened by the intimacy of the moment. "Something that tells the story of letting go and moving forward."

Zane nodded, his expression brightening. "I'm in. How about we start with that feeling of the waves? They're always moving, never stagnant."

As we began to craft our new song, the lyrics flowed freely, weaving together metaphors of the ocean and the tides, capturing the essence of change and resilience. I could feel the energy shifting between us, the connection deepening as we shared our thoughts and dreams, stitching our vulnerabilities into the fabric of our creation.

Just then, a distant sound broke through the serenity of the night—a series of sharp yells echoed from the direction of the beach's rocky outcrop. Zane and I paused mid-lyric, exchanging puzzled glances. "What was that?" I asked, my heart quickening.

"Sounded like someone shouting," he replied, his brow furrowing in concern. "Should we check it out?"

"Definitely," I said, rising to my feet, the thrill of uncertainty sparking in my chest.

We approached the rocky edge cautiously, the sound of crashing waves underscoring our footsteps. As we neared the outcrop, the moonlight illuminated a group of people gathered around a small campfire, their animated gestures and raised voices hinting at a heated discussion.

"What's going on?" Zane called out, stepping closer.

One of the figures turned to us, a young woman with wild, tangled hair. "You need to leave! It's not safe here!" Her voice trembled, urgency lacing her words.

"Why? What happened?" I asked, feeling a jolt of alarm surge through me.

"There's someone out there," she said, pointing toward the water, where the waves crashed violently against the rocks. "We saw someone struggling. It looks like they're in trouble."

My heart raced as I peered into the darkness of the ocean, the shadows of the waves concealing whatever peril lurked beneath. Zane's expression shifted from confusion to determination, and I could see the resolve settling in his eyes.

"We need to help," he said, taking a step forward.

"No!" the woman shouted, grabbing his arm. "You don't understand. It's dangerous! You can't go out there!"

I felt the adrenaline pumping through my veins, a mix of fear and urgency. "We can't just leave them!"

"Think about it!" Zane urged, glancing between me and the group. "If someone is drowning, we have to try. It's what we're meant to do."

In that moment, the weight of the choice loomed over us, the crashing waves echoing like a heartbeat, urging us toward action. Would we brave the unknown? Would we dive into the chaos of the night, risking everything for a stranger?

The decision hung heavy in the air, and just as we prepared to step forward, a flash of light illuminated the water—a beacon cutting through the darkness, revealing the desperate figure struggling against the tide.

"Help!" they cried, their voice barely audible above the roar of the waves.

I looked at Zane, his expression set with determination, and I knew that whatever lay ahead, we were ready to face it together. But as we took our first steps toward the edge, the tide surged, pulling us back into uncertainty. The waves crashed harder, and the night thickened with an intensity that left me breathless.

Chapter 12: Secrets and Shadows

The rooftop was my sanctuary, a little slice of heaven perched above the city's chaotic pulse. Each evening, the sun dipped below the skyline like a cautious child, painting the horizon in brilliant hues of orange and lavender. The city twinkled to life, each light a whisper of a story, and I loved this time, when the world felt like it was holding its breath. On those warm nights, Zane and I would sit side by side, our legs dangling over the edge, our hearts laid bare under the expansive sky.

"Do you ever wonder what's up there?" he asked one night, tilting his head back, eyes tracing the stars. His voice was soft, almost wistful. I could see it—a flicker of hope against a backdrop of fear, as if he were trying to catch a glimpse of something brighter than the life he'd known.

"Sometimes," I replied, taking a deep breath, the cool breeze ruffling my hair. "But I've always been more curious about what's down here. The stories we carry, the ones that shape us." I let the words hang in the air, wishing I could draw out his secrets as easily as he did mine.

Zane turned to me, his expression unreadable. "You make it sound so poetic. But down here... it's messy. Life is full of shadows."

"Shadows can't exist without light," I countered, a grin dancing on my lips. "You have to embrace both, right?" I was trying to lighten the moment, but his gaze remained distant, almost lost in thought.

"Maybe," he murmured, but I could see the storm brewing in his eyes, a whirlwind of past hurts and memories unshared. "But sometimes, the shadows are just... too heavy."

A silence settled between us, thick and charged. I felt the weight of his unspoken story pressing against my chest, a palpable ache. I wanted to shake the shadows away, to wrap him in the warmth of my understanding, but I knew it wasn't that simple. Each moment he spent away from me, lost in his own turmoil, felt like a thief stealing pieces of our connection. I wanted to reach out, to touch him, to bridge the growing chasm, but a part of me hesitated, afraid of what lay beneath the surface.

"Zane, you don't have to tell me everything," I said, trying to keep my tone light, "but it's okay to share some of it. You know I'm here for you." The sincerity in my voice surprised me. I'd never been this open with anyone, yet with him, it felt natural, like peeling layers off an onion to reveal the sweet core inside.

He let out a sigh, deep and shuddering. "I suppose I've always thought I should carry it alone. It's easier that way." His fingers fidgeted with the hem of his shirt, and I could see the conflict in his eyes—desire for connection battling against years of solitude.

"Easier, maybe. But it can get lonely," I replied gently. "Trust me, I know what that feels like."

Finally, he turned to face me, the vulnerability in his gaze unraveling the tightly wound threads of my own defenses. "It's just... I had a pretty rough childhood. My mom left when I was young, and my dad... well, he wasn't the kind of guy you'd want around." His voice dropped, each word a weighty confession. "I learned early on that I couldn't rely on anyone. People leave, or they hurt you, and it's better to keep your distance."

His admission hung in the air like an unwelcome guest. My heart ached for him, for the little boy who must have felt so abandoned, adrift in a world that felt more like a storm than a shelter. I reached out, brushing my fingers against his, a spark of connection in the darkness. "I can't imagine how hard that must have been," I said softly, meaning every word. "But you're not alone anymore. You have me."

He hesitated, and for a heartbeat, I feared I'd misstepped. But then he met my gaze, and I saw something shift—a glimmer of hope, perhaps. "You make it sound easy, but I've built these walls for a reason. It's not just about letting you in; it's about keeping the pain out."

"I get that," I said, squeezing his hand gently. "But sometimes, those walls can feel like a prison, keeping out the good along with the bad."

His laughter came as a breath of fresh air, a rare smile breaking through the storm clouds. "You should be a therapist or something. You've got all the right lines."

I chuckled, shaking my head. "Nah, I'd probably just make people cry." There was something soothing in our banter, a lightness amidst the heaviness of our truths.

But then, as quickly as the laughter came, it faded, leaving behind a poignant silence that wrapped around us like a comforting blanket. I longed to press further, to peel back the layers of his heart and mind, but I could sense his hesitation, a ghost lingering just beyond the threshold of his walls.

"Zane," I said, my voice soft but firm, "if I'm going to stand beside you, I need to know the real you. The good, the bad, the shadowy bits in between. I promise I won't run."

His eyes locked onto mine, searching for sincerity. "And if I told you everything?" he whispered, vulnerability spilling from him like water from a cracked vessel.

"Then I'll hold it with you, every last drop," I assured him, my heart racing as I watched his resolve begin to waver. The shadows were still there, lurking just out of sight, but I could feel the warmth of our connection growing, each shared secret a brick pulled from the wall.

"I'll try," he finally said, the words spilling forth like a long-held breath. "But it's going to be messy."

"Messy can be beautiful," I replied, smiling to lighten the weight of his admission. "Just like this city at night."

And in that moment, beneath the stars, I felt a spark ignite—a fragile flame flickering against the shadows of our pasts, each promise a stepping stone toward the light.

Days passed like the slow turning of pages in a book, each one revealing a little more of Zane's world while peeling back the layers of my own. We had slipped into a comfortable rhythm, our rooftop evenings punctuated by shared laughter and vulnerable confessions, the city skyline standing sentinel over our unfolding narrative. Yet, despite the warmth of our connection, a question lingered, a stubborn itch at the back of my mind. I couldn't ignore the deeper shadows that flitted behind his laughter, nor the way his smile sometimes faltered, hinting at stories left untold.

On a particularly sultry evening, the air thick with the scent of blooming jasmine, I watched Zane as he leaned against the rooftop railing, his silhouette outlined against the deepening indigo of the sky. The stars twinkled like tiny diamonds scattered across velvet, but Zane's gaze remained fixed on the horizon, a troubled frown creasing his brow. It was as if he were searching for something just out of reach, an unclaimed treasure buried beneath the weight of his past.

"What are you thinking about?" I asked, a playful lilt in my voice, hoping to draw him back from whatever distant place had captured his mind. "Let me guess—an escape plan for the apocalypse?"

He turned, a flicker of amusement lighting his features, but the spark quickly faded. "More like wondering if I'll ever really belong anywhere," he replied, his voice barely above a whisper, heavy with unshared burdens.

"Belonging is overrated," I teased lightly, hoping to coax out the shadows lurking behind his bravado. "I mean, look at all the cool things we can do as free agents. No one telling us how to live, no responsibilities—just us against the world."

He chuckled softly, but it lacked the usual warmth. "Yeah, but freedom can be isolating, too. It's like being adrift in a vast ocean with no land in sight."

There was an honesty in his words that struck a chord within me. I leaned closer, letting the intimacy of our shared space wrap around us like a comforting blanket. "You know, sometimes I think we're all just lost souls looking for a harbor. It's the journey that defines us, not just the destination."

His eyes locked onto mine, searching for something—understanding, perhaps, or an affirmation that he wasn't alone in his struggles. "What if the journey leads you right back to the same storm you've always known?" he asked, vulnerability threading through his words.

"Then you bring an umbrella," I replied, attempting to keep the mood light, but I felt the seriousness beneath the surface. "And a boat. And snacks. I mean, what's a storm without snacks, right?"

A genuine laugh escaped him this time, a soft melody that mingled with the distant hum of the city below. "You're impossible, you know that?"

"Impossible? Or incredibly wise?" I grinned, leaning back on my hands. "You tell me."

As the laughter faded, I felt a shift in the atmosphere, a thickening of tension as if the very air around us had grown heavy with unspoken truths. I could sense he was teetering on the brink of confession, the kind of revelation that could either pull us closer or send us spiraling apart.

"Maybe I'm just scared," he said finally, his voice barely audible above the city's background murmur. "Scared that if I let you see the whole picture, you'll want to escape."

"Why would I want to escape?" I countered, my heart pounding in anticipation. "You've already let me in. I'm not going anywhere, Zane. We've been through too much together."

His expression shifted, a flicker of hope battling against a familiar darkness. "What if I told you I'm not worth the effort? That my baggage is heavier than you realize?"

"Then I'd tell you that every good story comes with baggage," I shot back, the words tumbling from my lips with surprising conviction. "And honestly? I'm a walking suitcase myself. We all have something that makes us human, Zane."

There was a moment of silence as he absorbed my words, his gaze drifting back to the skyline, lost in contemplation. I could feel the pull of his emotions, raw and tumultuous, a tempest brewing just beneath the surface.

"I had this... friend," he finally began, his voice steady yet laced with emotion. "She was my anchor. When my mom left, she was there. When my dad..." His voice faltered, the pain of remembrance etched across his face. "When he would lash out, she was the only one who kept me grounded. But one day, she just disappeared. No explanation. No goodbye."

The weight of his story settled over us, thickening the air with palpable grief. I could see the little boy he'd been, the one who had clung to hope amidst chaos, and the man before me, trying to reconcile his past with the future he longed for. "I never knew what happened to her. It's like I lost my way that day. She was my lifeline, and when she cut the cord, I was left adrift again."

"I'm so sorry," I said, my heart aching for him. "That must have been so hard."

He nodded, swallowing hard. "After that, I built these walls, thinking it would protect me from pain. But they just ended up isolating me. I figured if I couldn't rely on anyone, then I wouldn't have to deal with the loss."

"But what about trust?" I ventured, my voice steady, holding his gaze. "What's the point of living if you can't take a chance on someone? It's like watching a movie without the climax—it just falls flat."

Zane looked at me, and for a moment, it felt like I was standing on the precipice of something monumental. "You make it sound so easy," he said softly, a hint of admiration threading through his tone.

"Maybe because I've done it the hard way," I admitted. "I've faced my share of storms, and they're not pretty. But I've also learned that sometimes, the best thing we can do is let someone in, even when it terrifies us."

His eyes searched mine, a storm of emotions playing across his face—fear, hope, longing, and the raw truth of his past. "What if it doesn't work out?"

"Then we pick up the pieces and laugh about it over coffee," I replied, an easy smile spreading across my face. "Or maybe we cry over ice cream. Either way, we don't do it alone."

He was silent for a heartbeat, and I felt the tension ebb and flow, like the tide against the shore. Then, with a slow, deliberate motion, he reached out, wrapping his fingers around mine, grounding us both in that moment. "Okay. Let's see where this goes. Together."

My heart soared as I squeezed his hand, a promise forged between us under the blanket of stars. The shadows lingered, but so did the light—flickering, persistent, and alive.

The days that followed felt like stepping onto a tightrope, a delicate balance between the thrill of discovery and the fear of falling. Zane and I had entered a dance of sorts, each encounter layered with unspoken words and tentative steps toward a deeper connection. We spent evenings on the rooftop, where the stars bore witness to our unfolding story, and I reveled in every shared laugh, every tentative touch that felt like a promise hanging in the air.

Yet, amid the sweet moments, I could sense the weight of his past still shadowing him. There was a flicker of fear behind his eyes whenever he shared too much, as if he worried that opening up would mean losing everything he had just begun to trust. I felt the edges of my own insecurities prickling at the surface, reminding me that I wasn't just a bystander in this emotional journey. I had my own scars, my own history of heartbreak and loss.

One evening, as we sat on the rooftop, I leaned back against the cool concrete, contemplating the vast expanse of sky above us. Zane was unusually quiet, his gaze lost in the city lights that twinkled like distant galaxies. I turned to him, hoping to coax him out of whatever reverie held him captive. "You know," I began, "I've always thought rooftops are like the stage for our lives. We have the best views up here, but we're still so far from the ground, from the reality of it all."

He turned to me, a hint of a smile playing at the corners of his mouth. "Are you saying we're living in a theatrical performance?"

"Only if you want it to be," I replied, matching his teasing tone. "I mean, I wouldn't mind being the star, but the lead always has the biggest baggage."

He chuckled, but his laughter was brief, fading quickly into silence. "You might be right about that."

"Seriously, though," I said, my tone shifting, "what's stopping you from letting me in? We can carry each other's baggage, you know? It's like a really awkward three-legged race—messy but kind of fun if you embrace the chaos."

His expression turned serious, and he took a deep breath as if preparing to dive into deep waters. "It's just... I've learned that opening up can lead to hurt. And I don't know if I'm ready for that."

"Every relationship comes with risks," I countered gently, my heart racing. "But the real question is, do you think we're worth the risk? Because I do."

He shifted closer, his shoulder brushing against mine, the warmth sending shivers through me. "You make it sound so easy. But my past has a way of creeping in when I least expect it."

"Welcome to the club," I said, feigning a dramatic sigh. "We've all got ghosts. Mine just happen to be particularly chatty."

"I suppose that makes us ghost hunters," he quipped, a twinkle of mischief returning to his eyes.

I grinned. "Exactly! Together, we can face the unknown."

But just as the mood lightened, a sharp sound shattered our cocoon of safety—a loud crash echoed from the alley below, drawing our attention. We both jumped to our feet, peering over the edge of the rooftop, hearts racing.

"What the hell was that?" I whispered, adrenaline kicking in.

"I have no idea," Zane replied, his voice tense. "But we should check it out."

"Check it out? You mean, like, actually go down there?"

"Why not? We can't just ignore it."

"Okay, but if we die, I'm blaming you in my will."

He laughed nervously, grabbing my hand and leading me toward the fire escape. I hesitated for a moment, the rational part of my brain screaming that we were about to embark on a dangerous adventure. But the thrill of uncertainty was intoxicating, and I couldn't help but follow him, our fingers entwined like an unbreakable promise.

As we descended, my mind raced with possibilities—what could have caused that noise? Was someone in trouble, or were we walking straight into a scene from a horror movie? Zane glanced back at me, a reassuring smile on his lips, but I could see the tension simmering beneath his calm facade.

When we finally reached the ground, the air was thick with the scent of asphalt and something metallic. We stepped into the alley, our footsteps echoing against the brick walls. The alley was dimly lit, shadows stretching like dark fingers, and I felt a shiver run down my spine.

"What do you see?" Zane asked, scanning the area.

I squinted, adjusting to the low light, and my eyes landed on a broken crate strewn across the ground. "Just some trash and—oh, wait! Is that a backpack?" I pointed, a sudden surge of curiosity taking hold.

"Let's check it out," Zane said, moving toward it, and I followed closely behind, every instinct telling me to be cautious.

As we approached, I felt a pulse of dread. The backpack looked out of place, half-hidden behind a dumpster as if someone had abandoned it in haste. Zane knelt beside it, unzipping the bag with a slow, deliberate motion.

"Be careful," I cautioned, glancing around, feeling the weight of the darkness pressing in. "This might not be a good idea."

"Too late now," he replied, his voice steady but laced with apprehension. He pulled out a tattered notebook, its pages yellowed with age. "What's this?"

I leaned in closer, intrigued despite the unease creeping up my spine. Zane flipped through the pages, and my heart raced as he read aloud snippets of hurried writing: "The truth is out there," "They're watching," and "Don't trust anyone."

"Okay, this is officially getting weird," I said, my breath hitching. "Who carries around a creepy notebook like this?"

"I don't know, but we should take it."

"Take it? Are you kidding? What if it belongs to someone dangerous?"

"Or someone who needs help," he countered, determination shining in his eyes.

Before I could respond, a sudden noise echoed from the end of the alley, the sound of footsteps approaching fast. My heart raced as Zane and I exchanged worried glances. "We need to hide," I whispered, panic rising.

We ducked behind the dumpster, hearts pounding in sync as we strained to hear the voices growing closer. I could see shadows shifting in the faint light, a group of figures moving purposefully toward us. The fear coiling in my stomach tightened as I caught snippets of their conversation.

"It has to be here! We can't let anyone find out!"

"What if they do? We need to take care of this now."

Zane's grip on my hand tightened, and I could feel the tension radiating between us like static electricity.

As the figures neared, my heart raced, every instinct screaming that we were in the wrong place at the wrong time. With the weight of the notebook and the looming presence of danger, I had a sudden realization: we had stumbled onto something far larger than ourselves, something that could pull us into its darkness.

And just as I opened my mouth to warn Zane, the darkness swallowed us whole, leaving the echoes of our heartbeats as the only witness to the unfolding chaos.

Chapter 13: The Weight of the World

Sunlight streamed through the dusty window of my studio, casting an ethereal glow over the scattered sheet music and half-finished lyrics that littered the floor like fallen leaves in autumn. I brushed a stray curl from my forehead and took a deep breath, inhaling the familiar mix of wood polish and the faintest hint of paint. It was a scent that had once inspired me, igniting my creative spirit, but today it felt heavy, like an anchor dragging me down into an ocean of doubt.

I glanced at my phone, its screen flashing a notification. Another message from the artist I was working with, demanding changes to the track we had spent hours perfecting just the day before. "Can you make it more... I don't know, alive?" he had texted, followed by a string of vague metaphors that made my head spin. Alive? What did that even mean? Were we recording a song or performing a resurrection? My heart raced, not from excitement but from the weight of his expectations. It was as if I were juggling flaming swords, and every time I thought I had a handle on one, another would come crashing down.

As I sat at my desk, a symphony of frustration and anxiety playing in my mind, the door creaked open, revealing Zane. He leaned against the doorframe, arms crossed, a frown etched deep into his brow. There was something about the way he looked at me that day, a combination of worry and longing, like he was trying to piece together a puzzle that was missing its corner pieces.

"Hey," he said, his voice a gentle murmur, but it felt like a thunderclap in the silence that enveloped us. "How's the music coming along?"

I wanted to smile, to wrap my arms around him and pretend that everything was fine. Instead, I forced a laugh that sounded more like a gasp. "Just peachy! You know, it's all about the chase of artistic perfection. Or is it chaos? I can't keep track."

Zane's frown deepened. "You know you can talk to me, right? I'm here. You don't have to do this alone."

That was the crux of it, wasn't it? I had wrapped myself in a cocoon of self-reliance, convincing myself that asking for help was a sign of weakness. But the truth was, I was crumbling. I had poured everything I had into this project, and with every change the artist demanded, it felt like another piece of my sanity was being ripped away. I opened my mouth to respond, but instead, words jumbled together into a snarl. "You don't get it, Zane! You have no idea how it feels to be at the mercy of someone else's whims!"

His expression shifted, hurt mingling with confusion. "I'm trying to understand, but you keep shutting me out. You're working yourself into the ground, and it's not healthy."

It was a simple observation, yet it felt like a direct hit. The pressure was suffocating, and I was drowning in my own expectations, but lashing out at the one person who cared felt like the worst kind of betrayal. I didn't mean to snap, but my frustration erupted like a volcano, and the fallout was a hurtful silence that expanded between us, thick and impenetrable.

"I'm sorry," I said, my voice barely above a whisper as the reality of my outburst crashed over me like a wave. "I didn't mean that."

Zane ran a hand through his hair, the movement a mixture of exasperation and sadness. "You need to find a way to cope with all of this. It's not just about the music; it's about you. And me." He stepped closer, his gaze steady and earnest, the warmth of his presence a stark contrast to the turmoil inside me.

The gravity of his words settled in the air, heavy and unyielding. I could feel tears prickling at the corners of my eyes, the well of emotions threatening to spill over. But I couldn't let them flow; not now, not when everything felt so precarious. Instead, I took a deep breath, forcing a smile that felt more like a grimace. "I'll figure it out. Just... give me a little space, okay?"

His shoulders slumped slightly, a subtle shift that tugged at my heart. "I just want you to be happy," he murmured, and with that, he turned and walked away, leaving me alone in my chaos.

As the door clicked shut, I felt the emptiness wrap around me like a cold blanket. I retreated to my desk, fingers poised above the keys, but the music felt distant, elusive as smoke. I tried to focus, diving into the tracks that were supposed to be my escape, but the notes twisted and turned into a cacophony of anxiety. Each chord I played seemed to echo back at me with disappointment, taunting me with the reality that the spark I once had was flickering out.

Time slipped away, each hour melting into the next as I lost myself in a futile attempt to meet the demands that were spiraling out of control. I leaned back in my chair, closing my eyes, and for a fleeting moment, I imagined a world where creativity flowed freely, where every note fell into place without the weight of external pressures. But reality had a way of crashing back in like a tidal wave, reminding me that I was still here, still stuck in this never-ending cycle of self-doubt and frustration.

Eventually, the tension in my shoulders morphed into a dull ache, and I found myself standing, pacing the cramped room like a caged animal. I glanced out the window, watching the sun dip low on the horizon, painting the sky in hues of orange and pink. It was beautiful, a fleeting moment of peace that contrasted sharply with the storm brewing inside me. I needed to breathe, to escape this claustrophobic world I had built around myself.

With a sudden burst of determination, I grabbed my jacket and headed out the door. The crisp evening air hit me like a jolt, invigorating and sharp. I wandered through the streets, seeking solace in the rhythm of my footsteps, each step grounding me as I tried to shake off the suffocating weight of expectation.

As I walked, I felt my mind begin to clear, the noise quieting, and with it, the tension in my chest began to ease. But as I turned a corner, a familiar figure came into view—Zane, standing beneath a streetlight, looking for all the world like he was waiting for something... or someone.

"Hey!" I called out, a mix of surprise and relief flooding through me. As he turned to face me, I saw the flicker of hope in his eyes, and it made my heart race. Maybe I wasn't as alone as I had convinced myself I was.

As Zane's silhouette came into sharper focus, the streetlight haloed him in a warm glow, creating a moment that felt like an unexpected reunion after an eternity apart. I paused, caught between relief and a rush of uncertainty. "What are you doing out here?" I asked, my voice barely hiding the relief that bubbled just below the surface.

"I was looking for you," he replied, his tone a mix of concern and hope. "I thought maybe you'd take a walk. You know, just to breathe for a bit."

The sincerity in his eyes melted away some of the ice that had formed around my heart. "How did you know I'd need that?" I smirked, half-joking. "Do you have a crystal ball, or are you just a really good guesser?"

Zane chuckled, the sound a soft balm to my frazzled nerves. "Just intuition. Plus, I know you too well. When you go quiet, it's like the sun disappearing behind a cloud." He gestured toward the nearby park, an expanse of grass and trees that seemed to beckon us with promises of tranquility. "Come on. Let's get some fresh air."

We walked side by side, the sidewalk beneath us crackling with the remnants of fallen leaves, their colors muted in the dusk. Each step felt like shedding a layer of the weight I had been carrying, though I still felt the ghost of my earlier frustration hanging in the air like a forgotten melody. "So, how's the latest artistic crisis?" Zane asked, his voice light yet probing.

I let out a small laugh, the sound tinged with genuine amusement. "You know, just the usual chaos. If I didn't know better, I'd think my artist was training for the Olympics in last-minute changes." I rubbed the back of my neck, feeling the tension coiling like a spring. "I swear, he must have a secret handbook on how to drive producers insane."

Zane grinned, his eyes sparkling in the fading light. "Is it a thick handbook? Because I'd like to have a copy for future reference. Maybe I could learn a few techniques for our own creative endeavors."

His playful banter nudged me toward laughter, easing some of the tension that had settled into my bones. "I'd say it's a three-volume set. All highlighted and annotated with a side of stress-induced insomnia."

As we strolled through the park, the gentle rustle of leaves provided a soothing backdrop, a reminder that life continued its rhythmic dance around us. "You know," Zane said, breaking the comfortable silence, "it's okay to feel overwhelmed. We all have our limits. I get it, but pushing people away isn't the answer. Not with me."

His words were like a splash of cold water, invigorating and jarring all at once. "I'm not trying to push you away," I protested, though even to my ears, the sincerity felt strained. "I just thought... I don't know, maybe it would be easier if I handled this on my own."

Zane stopped walking, turning to face me fully. "And what makes you think it would be easier? Last I checked, this project of yours is eating you alive. The last time I checked, it was a team effort, right? You have me. Use me."

I met his gaze, and for a heartbeat, the world around us melted away. It was just me and Zane, standing under the fading light of day, a tangible connection that felt electric. "I know," I admitted, the truth bubbling to the surface. "I guess I just... didn't want to burden you."

"Burden?" He laughed softly, a sound that warmed the chilly evening air. "You could never burden me. But you know what is a burden? Trying to pretend that you're fine when you're not."

His words sank in like stones, each one rippling through my mind. "I just thought it would all settle down once we got the project rolling," I murmured, kicking at a stray pebble on the path. "But it's like trying to catch smoke with my bare hands."

"And here's the kicker," Zane said, stepping closer, lowering his voice to a conspiratorial whisper. "Even smoke can transform into something beautiful if you let it. It's about how you shape it, how you let it flow."

I couldn't help but smile at his metaphor, the weight of my worries lightening, if only for a moment. "You really have a way with words, you know that?" I replied, the warmth of our connection sparking like the first hints of dawn. "If you ever quit your day job, you could write greeting cards or something equally poetic."

"Please, that sounds boring," he shot back, his eyes dancing with mischief. "I prefer living out the real drama. Speaking of which, what happens next in your musical saga?"

I sighed, the burden of the project creeping back into my chest. "I'm supposed to meet with the artist tomorrow. I can only imagine what other demands he'll throw at me. Maybe he'll want to change the key to a different one because it 'feels more right.'"

Zane shook his head. "Or maybe he'll surprise you with something brilliant. You've worked too hard to let one person derail you. Trust your instincts. You know what you're doing."

The confidence in his voice pushed me forward, the first hints of hope flickering in the corners of my mind. "You're right," I conceded. "I can't let him dictate my creativity. I'll push back."

"That's the spirit!" Zane exclaimed, fist-pumping the air like he'd just scored a touchdown. "You're a force of nature. Show him what you've got."

I laughed, the sound rich and buoyant, chasing away some of the lingering shadows. "You make it sound easy."

"It's not easy, but it's worth it." He paused, his expression growing more serious. "And if things get too tough, just remember, you don't have to do it alone. Lean on me. I can handle it."

The sincerity in his voice settled over me, a warm blanket in the cool evening air. "Thank you, Zane," I said, my voice barely a whisper, but the gratitude was tangible. "I really appreciate that."

"Just doing my part to keep you from turning into a total musical hermit," he replied, nudging my shoulder playfully. "Now, let's get some ice cream. I think we both deserve a treat after today."

"Is this a bribe to get me to open up?" I teased, my heart swelling at the thought of our lighthearted banter returning.

"Hey, whatever it takes," he replied, the glint in his eyes making me smile. "Ice cream can solve just about anything. Plus, you need a sugar rush to fuel your next creative breakthrough."

With that, we turned toward the nearby ice cream stand, and as I glanced at Zane, I felt the weight of the world begin to lift, piece by piece. In this moment, under the soft glow of the streetlights, I realized that perhaps the journey ahead wouldn't be so daunting after all. It would be a ride, full of ups and downs, but I wouldn't have to navigate it alone.

The ice cream stand glowed like a beacon in the darkening evening, its vibrant colors and playful signage inviting us to indulge in a moment of sweet escape. Zane and I approached, the air tinged with the delightful scent of waffle cones and creamy concoctions. As we stepped in line, I scanned the menu, my mind still swirling with the day's tension but slowly uncoiling, like a spring releasing its pent-up energy.

"Okay, here's the deal," Zane said, his finger tapping the menu thoughtfully. "You can't take longer than thirty seconds to decide. Otherwise, I'm getting you the surprise flavor—beet and raspberry swirl."

I shot him an incredulous look, feigning horror. "Beet and raspberry? You're kidding, right? Is that even a real thing? I'd rather face the wrath of my artist than be subjected to that abomination."

His laughter rang out, genuine and carefree, a sound I had missed in the midst of all my worries. "Well, if that's your defense, I might have to start using it during our brainstorming sessions. 'Sorry, I can't do that—beet and raspberry!'"

"Touché," I replied, shaking my head, but my lips curled into a smile. "You've got a point. It's a strong argument. Still, I think I'll stick to the classic chocolate chip cookie dough. It's tried and true."

"Solid choice," he nodded, stepping closer as we neared the front of the line. "You can't go wrong with cookie dough. It's like the universal comfort food. Though, if I were you, I might consider shaking things up a bit. You never know what you might find."

"Are you suggesting I start branching out into the world of exotic ice cream flavors?" I quipped. "What's next? A lesson in bold living? 'Let's try goat cheese and fig, because life is too short to stick to vanilla!'"

"Exactly!" He beamed. "Life's too short. If I had to choose between my bland vanilla existence and a wild flavor explosion, I'd choose the explosion every time."

I rolled my eyes but couldn't suppress a laugh. "All right, Mr. Adventure. I'll consider it. But for now, I'm perfectly content with my cookie dough. It's the one thing in my life that doesn't require a last-minute rewrite."

After placing our orders, we found a bench nearby, and the ice cream was soon in our hands, melting slightly under the warm glow of the streetlight. As I took my first bite, the rich flavor enveloped me, a temporary balm to my racing thoughts.

"See? Isn't that better?" Zane grinned, his own cone disappearing far too quickly as if it were the last ice cream on Earth. "This is what life is all about—savoring the sweet moments."

I watched him, amused by his animated gestures as he recounted a story about a disastrous camping trip he had taken as a child. He claimed he had inadvertently angered a squirrel by trying to feed it granola, which had led to a chaotic series of events involving a missing tent and a very angry mother. His storytelling was infectious, and as I listened, I felt the weight of my stress slip away with each laugh.

"Okay, now I feel like I need to hear about your epic camping adventures," he said, licking his cone thoughtfully, his gaze playful. "Was it just as disastrous? Did you also face the wrath of the wildlife?"

I chuckled, the memories flashing through my mind. "Oh, I think I had a different kind of adventure. We once got lost on a hiking trail because I insisted we take a 'shortcut.' Spoiler alert: it wasn't short. We ended up hiking back in the dark, fighting off mosquitoes the size of small birds."

"Ah, yes. The infamous 'shortcut'—a classic blunder in the annals of outdoor misadventures," he teased. "I can see how that might've gone south. What happened next? Did you survive?"

"Just barely," I replied, leaning back on the bench. "We made it back to the campsite and decided to celebrate our survival with burnt marshmallows. It was, without a doubt, a very underwhelming end to our grand adventure."

Zane snorted with laughter, his eyes twinkling with delight. "You know, I think you need to start writing down these stories. There's a real charm to your disasters, and if anyone can turn a camping trip gone wrong into a bestseller, it's you."

"Maybe I should," I mused, my mind drifting to the half-finished drafts and forgotten notes scattered around my studio. "If only I had the time. Between work and the latest melodrama in my life, I barely have a moment to breathe."

He studied me, the teasing glint in his eyes fading. "What if you took a break? Just a short one, to gather your thoughts. You don't have to be all things to all people all the time. Sometimes, a little distance gives you the clarity you need."

"You make it sound so easy," I replied, feeling a flicker of rebellion against the demands of my world. "But it's hard to step back when everything feels so urgent. I'm worried if I let go, it'll all fall apart."

"Or," he countered, leaning closer, "maybe if you step back, you'll see the pieces more clearly. Sometimes, a little distance can help you put them back together. Besides, I promise to be here for moral support. Just think of me as your creative cheerleader."

The warmth of his words wrapped around me like a comforting blanket, and I found myself considering the possibility. Maybe he was right; maybe I needed a pause. A tiny rebellion against the chaos that had taken over my life. "Okay, you've convinced me," I said, half-serious. "Maybe a weekend getaway. Just a little one. I could use a little nature therapy."

"Excellent!" Zane's excitement was palpable, and he beamed at me, his smile lighting up the night. "Just us and the great outdoors. No deadlines, no pressure. We'll hike, we'll explore, and if we're lucky, we'll find that perfect, non-beet-flavored ice cream."

As we finished our cones, I felt lighter, as if the weight of the world had shifted ever so slightly off my shoulders. But just as I began to relax into the moment, my phone buzzed in my pocket, jolting me back to reality. I fished it out, and my heart sank when I saw the name on the screen.

It was my artist, and he was calling.

Zane watched me intently as I answered, my throat tightening. "Hey, what's up?" I said, trying to keep my tone casual.

"Listen," the artist's voice crackled through the line, tense and urgent. "We need to talk. I just had a revelation about the project, and it's crucial. I need you to meet me at the studio right away."

"Right away?" I echoed, glancing at Zane, who was now leaning in closer, his expression shifting to concern.

"Yes. I can't explain it all over the phone. Just trust me on this." The artist's tone left no room for argument, and my heart raced with anxiety.

"I—" I started, but he had already hung up.

As I lowered the phone, the weight of the conversation loomed larger than life. Zane searched my eyes, the worry etched across his face deepening. "What's going on?"

"An urgent meeting," I murmured, a lump forming in my throat. "He wants me at the studio... right now."

"Do you have to go?" he asked, the hopefulness in his voice faltering.

"I think so." I hesitated, glancing back toward the ice cream stand, a sense of dread swirling within me. "He sounded intense, like something has shifted."

Zane's eyes narrowed, concern rippling through his features. "Do you want me to come with you?"

I shook my head, but part of me craved his presence. "No, I need to handle this alone. It's just—" My voice trailed off, uncertainty creeping back in.

"Then go," he urged, his support tangible. "You've got this. And I'll be right here, waiting for you to fill me in. You're not alone in this."

As I turned to walk away, I felt a surge of apprehension mixed with determination. I would face whatever storm awaited me at the studio. But just as I was about to step onto the street, my phone buzzed again. I glanced at it, and my heart sank anew.

Another message from the artist.

"Meet me at the back entrance. We need to talk in private. It's important."

A chill raced down my spine. The air felt charged with anticipation, and as I looked back at Zane, the unease grew heavier in my chest. "I'll be back soon," I called over my shoulder, but the words felt hollow.

I stepped into the night, the familiar route to the studio now overshadowed by a growing sense of foreboding. Each footfall echoed louder than the last, and with every step, the world around me blurred, caught in the maelstrom of my thoughts. What could possibly be so urgent? What had shifted so drastically?

As I approached the studio, the streetlights flickered ominously, casting elongated shadows that seemed to pulse with uncertainty. I felt the weight of the artist's demand settling on my shoulders once more, and as I rounded the corner toward the back entrance, the air crackled with tension.

With a deep breath,

Chapter 14: Resounding Echoes

The venue buzzed with an electrifying energy, a tapestry of colors woven through the crowd, each person caught in a vivid moment of anticipation. Strings of fairy lights hung overhead like stars plucked from the night sky, illuminating faces with a warm, golden glow that contrasted sharply with the coolness of the early autumn air. The scent of freshly brewed coffee mingled with the slightly sweet aroma of pastries, each bite promising a taste of indulgence amid the nerves of the night. My heart raced, a frantic drummer marking time as I scanned the room, my eyes searching for familiar faces among the sea of strangers.

He strode in like a peacock flaunting its feathers, my artist, Eli, clad in an ensemble that could only be described as a kaleidoscope of fabrics and patterns. The jacket was a burst of color, each stitch singing its own note, while his pants shimmered in the light, an iridescent mirage that drew attention and admiration. The confidence with which he carried himself sent waves of pride through me, but it was quickly eclipsed by the shadow of anxiety that loomed larger than the crowd itself. I could practically hear the strings of his spirit vibrating, demanding perfection from the world around him.

"Make sure the spotlight hits my good side!" Eli's voice boomed across the space, a perfect blend of humor and urgency. The crew scurried around him like frantic ants, adjusting lights and equipment, trying to appease the creative tempest that was Eli. He had a knack for turning the mundane into the extraordinary, but tonight, as the moment of truth approached, that passion felt more like a ticking clock, each second echoing louder in my chest.

I forced myself to breathe deeply, to ground myself in the swirling currents of chaos. Music had been my sanctuary, a place where the world softened at the edges, and yet tonight, I felt it slipping away, unraveling like the frayed threads of my own hopes. The cacophony of laughter and chatter felt distant, muted behind the rhythmic drumming of my heartbeat. I had poured every ounce of my energy into this project, and yet as the final moments drew near, the exhilaration I once relished morphed into a tight knot of anxiety in my stomach.

The stage, a masterpiece of creative chaos, stood ready to birth something magnificent. The musicians milled about, their nervous energy palpable, fingers tapping against instruments as if trying to summon the right notes from thin air. Each one of them, a vital piece of the puzzle, but none more so than Zane. My Zane, the ever-steadfast presence in a world full of chaos. My gaze flickered to the crowd again, hoping to catch a glimpse of him, his easy smile a beacon in the crowded room. But he was nowhere to be found, and that absence echoed louder than any applause.

As the music began to swell, my breath caught in my throat. I leaned against the wall, my pulse quickening with each note that floated through the air. The performance unfolded like a vibrant painting, brushstrokes of sound weaving together harmonies and melodies that stirred the very essence of the audience. They swayed, their bodies dancing to the rhythm, lost in the spell Eli had cast. I felt the rush of applause, a tidal wave crashing over me, yet a sense of hollowness gnawed at my core.

The moment the final note hung in the air, the applause erupted like fireworks, filling the venue with a sound that should have ignited my soul. But instead, I felt like an actor caught in a scene of a play I didn't recognize. The cheers, the shouts of "Bravo!" echoed, but they felt like distant echoes, reverberating around a void that was growing inside me. I wanted to be swept away in the joy of the moment, to celebrate the culmination of our hard work, but the more I tried, the more I felt like a ghost haunting my own life.

"Can you believe it? We did it!" Eli's voice cut through my spiraling thoughts, pulling me back to the present. He was practically vibrating with energy, glowing with triumph as he basked in the adoration of the crowd. His laughter rang out, a melody I loved, yet all I could manage was a weak smile, the joy I should have felt choking in my throat.

"Yeah, we did," I echoed, the words tasting bittersweet. My heart sank deeper as I caught sight of the flashing cameras capturing every moment of his victory. The world adored him, and I couldn't shake the feeling that I had somehow lost myself in the process. The more he soared, the heavier my heart felt, a contrast that wrapped itself around my spirit like a shroud.

"I need a drink!" I exclaimed, the words spilling out before I could stop them. It felt desperate, but I needed a moment to breathe, to gather myself in this whirlwind of emotion. I slipped away from the crowd, navigating through the throngs of exhilaration until I found the bar tucked in a quiet corner. I ordered a drink, my hands trembling slightly as I clutched the glass, watching the ice melt with each passing second.

Just as I took a sip, a realization struck me like a bolt of lightning: I needed Zane. My heart ached for the comforting warmth of his presence, the way he could always see through my façades and lay bare the truth of my feelings. I glanced around, scanning the crowd again, searching for the familiar silhouette that had been my anchor in this storm. But the absence of his reassuring smile only intensified the emptiness that had settled within me.

A part of me wished he were here, sharing this moment with me, but perhaps I needed to confront this feeling alone. I leaned against the bar, the cool surface grounding me, while the distant sound of celebration faded into the background, merging into a symphony of unfulfilled expectations and lingering doubts. Would I ever reclaim that love for music that had once been so effortless?

The crowd surged with excitement, a living, breathing entity thrumming with applause and joyous exclamations. I stood at the edge of it all, a silent observer marooned on the island of my thoughts, where echoes of my discontent reverberated louder than the celebration surrounding me. Eli was soaking in the accolades, every shout of "bravo" another brushstroke on his already vibrant canvas of triumph. Yet here I was, clutching my drink as if it were a life raft in an ocean of confusion. The buzz of the crowd felt like an unseen wave, one that I couldn't quite ride, my spirit heavy with an unspeakable burden.

With a final cheer, Eli took a bow, his flamboyant outfit swirling around him like a cape of confetti. The applause crescendoed, a glorious cacophony that should have filled me with joy, but it only deepened the chasm within me. I turned away, unable to bear witness to his bliss while my heart twisted in knots. The bar was a sanctuary of sorts, though I doubted the bartender would appreciate my existential crisis alongside his cocktail creations.

"Hey, are you okay?" The voice startled me; I hadn't noticed anyone approaching. It was Delia, one of the musicians, her eyes sparkling with the remnants of adrenaline. She was a whirlwind of energy, her laughter infectious, yet tonight, even her warmth felt distant.

"Just peachy," I replied, trying to summon a smile. "Just enjoying the sweet nectar of success while I ponder my life choices."

"Ah, the old 'why am I here?' conundrum," she said, raising her glass in solidarity. "I've been there, trust me. The pressure can be a lot, especially when you're in the shadows. Want to join me for a toast? It's not every day we get to celebrate a rockstar like Eli!"

"Sure, let's toast to the guy who's currently basking in the spotlight while I'm here, drowning in my own introspection." I clinked my glass against hers, the sound sharp and clear against the backdrop of laughter and music.

"Okay, now that's an unfair comparison," she said, her expression turning serious. "You're more than just his right hand, you know? You're the glue that holds this whole thing together. It takes guts to stand in the background and make the chaos manageable."

"Glue is often overlooked, Delia. It's not exactly the most glamorous role." I sighed, watching Eli greet fans with the charm of a seasoned politician. "I feel like I've been sticking things together for so long that I've forgotten what it feels like to break free, to feel the music flow through me instead of around me."

"Then why not break out tonight? Celebrate yourself! You've earned it." She nudged my shoulder playfully, her eyes dancing with mischief. "What's stopping you? A little rebellion never hurt anyone. Go join him on stage!"

As tempting as the idea was, the thought of stepping into the glaring light made my palms sweat. "Yeah, that sounds like a great way to become a viral meme."

"Or it could be the start of a new trend. The unintentional stage-crasher," she laughed, her infectious spirit coaxing a reluctant chuckle from me. "But seriously, you should be up there. You deserve to shine just as much as he does."

Her words sank in, a whisper of encouragement nudging me closer to the edge of uncertainty. I had been so caught up in Eli's brilliance that I'd lost sight of my own. Music had been my sanctuary, my form of expression. Somewhere along the way, it had morphed into something that left me feeling empty and adrift.

"Thanks, Delia. I needed that," I replied, gratitude warming my insides. "But right now, I just need to find Zane. I think he's the only one who can really pull me back from this ledge."

"Good luck. If you find him, tell him to come back! He's the only one missing from the afterparty," she called over her shoulder as she maneuvered back into the crowd, a trail of laughter following her like confetti.

Taking a deep breath, I scanned the room again, the faces blurring together in my quest for Zane's familiar features. My heart raced with each passing moment, the void inside me expanding, fueled by the sharp pang of his absence. Where could he be? Had he stepped outside to catch a breath, or was he lost somewhere in the throng, perhaps engaged in conversation with someone else?

Pushing through the throng, I maneuvered past clusters of exuberant fans, each one waving their phones like flags of adoration, snapping pictures and shouting Eli's name as though he were some divine creature descended from the heavens. I stepped out onto the small patio that overlooked the city skyline, hoping the cool night air would provide some clarity. The view was breathtaking, the twinkling lights below reflecting the stars above, yet the beauty felt hollow without the one person who could truly appreciate it with me.

"Hey! Over here!" A voice rang out, familiar and warm, pulling me from my thoughts. I turned to find Zane leaning against the railing, a casual elegance about him that made my heart flutter. His hair was tousled by the breeze, and the soft glow of the lights illuminated the sharp angles of his face. He looked relaxed, at ease in the chaos, and it made my heart ache with a longing that felt both terrifying and exhilarating.

"There you are! I thought I'd lost you to the crowd," I exclaimed, rushing toward him as if he were the missing piece of a puzzle that had finally clicked into place.

"Lost? Nah, just observing. I've always preferred the sidelines to the spotlight." He offered a sheepish grin, his eyes sparkling with mischief. "Besides, someone had to keep an eye on you. You looked like you needed saving."

"Saving? I think I was doing just fine, drowning in existential dread and a cocktail," I replied, trying to sound nonchalant as I settled beside him. "You know, the usual."

Zane chuckled, the sound warm and inviting, wrapping around me like a favorite sweater. "I'm not surprised. Eli's quite the magnet for attention. It's hard to remember there's more to the show than just him."

"I've been trying to remind myself of that all night," I admitted, letting out a breath I hadn't realized I was holding. "But it's so easy to feel overshadowed."

"Don't let his shine dim your light," he said, his tone suddenly serious, almost solemn. "You have your own brilliance. You're the one who helped him get here. Without you, tonight wouldn't have been half as spectacular."

The sincerity in his words melted the tension coiling in my chest, and for a moment, I simply basked in the warmth of his presence, the comfort of knowing that he understood. The city twinkled below, a perfect backdrop to our quiet moment, but inside, I felt like the music was beginning to hum again, a soft melody in the depths of my heart, waiting to break free.

The night air was crisp, wrapping around us like an old friend, and the city twinkled below like a cosmic tapestry. I leaned against the railing beside Zane, the warm glow of the venue lights casting playful shadows across his features. His gaze drifted toward the distant skyline, a mix of admiration and contemplation. It felt good to be near him, to share this fleeting moment away from the revelry, yet the words that hung between us were heavy with unspoken feelings, lingering like a sweet, haunting refrain.

"You really did a fantastic job tonight," Zane said, breaking the silence. "The way Eli commanded the stage... It was something else." His tone was light, but I caught the undercurrent of something deeper, a hint of understanding that made my heart race.

"Thanks, but let's be real. Eli deserves all the credit. I was just the one behind the scenes, stitching everything together." I glanced away, feeling that familiar twinge of inadequacy, the nagging thought that I had become merely a backdrop in someone else's spotlight.

Zane turned to me, his expression softening. "You know, that's not how this works. You're not just an accessory. You're the reason this all happened. You have a gift for turning chaos into music, for making the impossible feel achievable." He leaned in closer, his voice low, as if sharing a secret. "I've seen you do it time and time again."

A small smile crept onto my lips, the warmth of his words soothing my frayed nerves. "You really think so?" I asked, half-wondering if I was fishing for compliments. But deep down, I craved the validation, the acknowledgment that I mattered in this whirlwind of creativity.

"Absolutely. And if you ever forget it, I'll remind you," he replied, a teasing glint in his eye. "Consider me your personal cheerleader, minus the pom-poms and questionable dance moves."

"Oh, thank goodness for small miracles. The last thing I need is a cheerleading routine from you." I laughed, but the sound felt foreign, a desperate attempt to shake off the lingering shadows of doubt.

"Why do you always sell yourself short?" he asked, genuine curiosity etched across his face. "You're brilliant, and it's time you embraced that. You could have your own spotlight if you wanted it."

I felt the weight of his words sink in, but doubt clung to me like a stubborn mist. "I don't know, Zane. The idea of stepping into the spotlight terrifies me. What if I fail? What if I crash and burn in front of everyone?"

"You won't. You've got the passion and the talent. Besides, failing is just another form of learning. If you're not willing to take a risk, you'll never discover what you're truly capable of." His conviction radiated through me, igniting a flicker of hope.

"But what if the music stops?" I asked, the vulnerability in my voice raw and exposed. "What if I lose that spark? I can't even remember the last time I felt... alive in this world of notes and melodies."

"You won't lose it. Music is a part of you, just like the doubts and fears. But it's also about rediscovering why you fell in love with it in the first place. Sometimes, you have to dig a little deeper to find that passion again." His gaze bore into mine, urging me to connect the dots between who I was and who I wanted to be.

"Easy for you to say. You're not the one wondering how to reclaim your rhythm after watching someone else steal the show." I sighed, looking down at the ground, feeling the weight of uncertainty pressing heavily on my chest.

"I might not be on stage, but I'm still rooting for you. You just have to let the music flow through you again." He reached out, brushing his fingers against my arm in a comforting gesture, and it sent shivers racing up my spine.

Just then, a loud crash echoed from inside the venue, the sound slicing through our moment like a jagged knife. We both turned, hearts pounding, as a collective gasp erupted from the crowd. I could see Eli's flamboyant jacket disappearing into the chaos as he rushed toward the sound.

"What was that?" I whispered, the sense of foreboding creeping in again, a dark cloud rolling in to obscure the night.

"I don't know, but it doesn't sound good." Zane's expression shifted, his earlier warmth replaced with concern. "Let's check it out."

We hurried back inside, pushing through the throng of people, the jubilant atmosphere now morphed into a whirlwind of confusion and alarm. As we entered the venue, the scene before us sent chills down my spine. The stage was littered with broken equipment, and several crew members were scrambling to regain control of the situation. Eli stood at the center, his expression a mixture of shock and fury.

"What happened?" I called out, trying to make my way to him.

"Someone tripped over the power cable," Eli shouted, his voice rising above the chaos. "We lost the sound system, and now we're scrambling to fix it before the crowd loses it completely."

My heart sank. The night had been so vibrant, so full of promise, and now it felt like it was spiraling into chaos. I could see the worry in Eli's eyes, a stark contrast to the exuberance just moments before. "We can fix this!" I yelled, determination surging through me. "We have backup equipment, right?"

"Yeah, but it's in the back room, and I need someone to grab it fast!" Eli replied, running a hand through his hair, frustration evident in every movement.

"I'll go!" I shouted, adrenaline coursing through me. Before I could second-guess myself, I dashed toward the back, weaving through the crowd and dodging the chaos that was brewing around me.

My mind raced as I pushed through the backstage door, the cool air hitting my face like a breath of fresh life. The room was dimly lit, the shadows long and foreboding. I spotted the equipment, neatly packed in a corner, but as I reached for it, I heard a strange sound—a faint, almost melodic humming resonating from deeper within the shadows.

Curiosity piqued, I took a tentative step toward the sound, the hair on the back of my neck prickling with unease. The humming grew louder, more insistent, wrapping around me like a silken thread pulling me closer. "Hello?" I called out, my voice barely above a whisper.

As I stepped further into the darkness, my heart raced with each echoing heartbeat. What was making that sound? I knew I should be grabbing the equipment and rushing back, but something deeper compelled me to explore, to uncover the source of this mysterious melody that seemed to beckon me forward.

Suddenly, the humming cut off, leaving a heavy silence in its wake. I froze, dread coiling around my chest. Just as I turned to leave, a figure stepped out of the shadows—an unexpected presence that sent my heart racing. I blinked, the realization hitting me like a cold splash of water.

It was someone I had never expected to see again. Someone who had vanished from my life without warning, leaving nothing but unanswered questions and a lingering melody that refused to fade.

"Surprise," the figure said, a sly grin spreading across their face. And in that moment, everything I thought I knew about tonight began to unravel.

Chapter 15: A Dance with Regret

The festival thrummed around me like the pulsating heart of a living creature. Laughter danced through the air, a symphony of joy intermingled with the heady aroma of fried dough and spiced cider. Lanterns strung high above twinkled like stars, casting a warm glow over the crowd as it ebbed and flowed, mirroring the swell of excitement in my chest. Yet, amidst this vivid tapestry of life and celebration, a shadow loomed over my spirit—a dark echo of my own insecurities.

Zane stood a few yards away, illuminated by the glow of a nearby bonfire, his laughter ringing out like a bell. He was surrounded by friends, their faces alight with the thrill of the evening. I watched him, a smile playing on his lips, and my stomach twisted into a tight knot. It should have filled me with warmth, this sight of him thriving, but instead, I felt like an outsider in a world I desperately wanted to inhabit. A pang of jealousy gripped my heart as I caught snippets of their conversation, the effortless camaraderie that seemed so far removed from my own tangled thoughts.

As I stood there, an invisible weight pressing down on me, I couldn't help but reflect on my own shortcomings. Here was Zane, charming and confident, the kind of person who made life seem easy, while I floundered in a sea of self-doubt. Every laugh that erupted from his lips felt like a reminder of my own inadequacies. Had I really pushed him away, or was I simply too caught up in my head to see the truth?

With each passing moment, my resolve crumbled. I took a deep breath, trying to steady the tremors that threatened to overtake me, and moved toward the group, adopting an air of casual confidence that I desperately hoped would disguise my internal chaos. "Hey there!" I chirped, forcing a smile that felt more like a grimace.

"Look who decided to join us!" Zane's voice was warm, pulling me into the fold. Yet, beneath the surface of his words lay a tension I couldn't ignore. The chatter stuttered, and I sensed the shift in energy, the unspoken acknowledgment of my awkward entrance.

I attempted to engage, throwing in a joke here and there, but my mind felt like a foggy haze. All I could think about was the distance I'd created between us, the walls I'd built as a shield against my own fears. Zane caught my eye, and something in his gaze shifted—an intensity that both thrilled and terrified me. He leaned in closer, his smile fading slightly as he noticed my struggle to keep up the façade.

"Can we talk?" he murmured, his voice low enough that only I could hear, yet heavy with a weight that promised no easy conversation.

I nodded, the words sticking in my throat like a stubborn lump. He guided me away from the laughter and light, toward a quieter corner of the festival where the music faded into a distant hum. The moment we stepped into the semi-darkness, the air thickened with unspoken tension, and I felt the familiar flicker of anxiety ignite within me.

"Okay, spill," he urged, his tone gentle yet firm, eyes searching mine as if he were trying to peel back the layers I'd so carefully wrapped around myself. "I can tell something's bothering you."

And there it was—his concern, a beacon in my swirling storm of doubts. But the fear of exposing my vulnerabilities loomed larger than the shadows around us. How could I possibly articulate the chaos in my mind? The words tangled on my tongue, and the silence stretched like a chasm between us.

"I—" My voice trembled, and I clenched my fists at my sides, grounding myself in the moment. "I'm just scared. Scared of losing you, scared of letting my past dictate everything." The admission slipped out before I could stop it, raw and unfiltered.

Zane's expression softened, and for a fleeting moment, I caught a glimpse of the boy I'd fallen for—the one who made the world feel lighter, who laughed with abandon and loved fiercely. "You're not losing me," he replied, stepping closer. "But you need to let me in. You can't keep shutting me out."

"I know," I sighed, frustration bubbling beneath the surface. "But it's so hard to shake off everything that's happened. I keep thinking if I let you see my insecurities, you'll run. That I'll become just another person who can't handle their baggage."

His brow furrowed, and he reached out, brushing a stray hair behind my ear, the simple gesture sending a shiver down my spine. "Everyone has baggage. It's what makes us human. But you're not just your past, you know? You're so much more than that. And I'm not going anywhere."

In that moment, a rush of warmth flooded through me, battling against the cold tendrils of doubt. I wanted to believe him, to accept that my past didn't have to define my present. Yet, the voice of doubt echoed persistently in my mind, whispering insidiously that my fears were justified.

"I'm trying," I managed, the words heavy on my tongue. "But every time I think I'm ready to move forward, something pulls me back. I just... I want to be the person you see in me."

Zane searched my eyes, a slow smile creeping back onto his face, a hint of mischief dancing in his gaze. "Well, then you've got to trust me. Let's make a deal: for every worry you share, I'll give you one of my own. It's a two-way street, right?"

I blinked at him, momentarily taken aback. "You want to share your worries with me?"

"Of course," he said, his tone teasing yet earnest. "But fair warning, mine are way worse. Like the time I accidentally sent a text meant for you to my grandmother instead."

My laugh bubbled up involuntarily, a sweet reprieve from the tension as I shook my head. "Okay, you've got me there."

With that, the weight on my chest began to lift, if only slightly. The vibrant sounds of the festival faded into the background as we stood together, two souls navigating the murky waters of vulnerability and connection, inching closer to a shore where fears could finally rest.

Zane's eyes sparkled as he leaned against the weathered wooden fence, the evening's vibrant colors casting a soft glow around us. I felt the rush of warmth in his gaze, a flickering flame of connection that made my heart flutter and my pulse race. The tension had ebbed slightly, giving way to a fragile sense of intimacy, and I was beginning to believe that perhaps we could navigate this labyrinth of vulnerability together.

But just as the atmosphere shifted, a ripple of commotion drew my attention. A group of festival-goers had gathered nearby, their excited shouts mingling with the sounds of an upbeat band that had just taken the stage. The music flowed through the air like a spell, lively and intoxicating. I could see people swaying and twirling, their faces flushed with joy. The contrast between their carefree abandon and my tangled emotions felt strikingly sharp.

"Dance with me," Zane said suddenly, his playful grin igniting a spark of mischief in my heart. "Come on! The band is amazing, and you can't just stand here and brood all night."

I hesitated, feeling the familiar pang of self-doubt creeping back in. "But I'm not a great dancer," I admitted, my cheeks flushing with embarrassment. "I might just trip and take you down with me."

"Is that a challenge?" He waggled his eyebrows playfully, and I couldn't help but laugh at his infectious enthusiasm. "Seriously, it's just dancing. No judgment here, I promise."

As he took my hand and led me toward the thrumming crowd, the warmth of his grip seeped through my skin, anchoring me in a moment I desperately needed. We plunged into the sea of movement, and for the first time that evening, I felt my worries fade into the background. The music enveloped us, pulsing like a heartbeat, drawing us closer together.

With Zane leading the way, I found myself letting go, even if just a little. I allowed my body to sway, the rhythm igniting a spark of joy I hadn't realized I'd been missing. He spun me around, a whirlwind of laughter and shared glances, and I felt the giddy rush of freedom fill my lungs. The world melted away, and for a brief moment, it was just the two of us, caught in the spell of the night.

"You're not half bad," Zane teased, his eyes gleaming as he twirled me again. I giggled, catching myself against him as he pulled me back in. "See? Just embrace the chaos. It's more fun that way!"

"Chaos is my middle name," I quipped, my cheeks sore from grinning. "At least, it should be."

Our laughter mingled with the vibrant music, and I found myself lost in the moment, allowing the worry to slip away like sand through my fingers. Yet, in the back of my mind, the memory of my earlier confession lingered like an unwelcome guest. How could I ignore the shadows that still danced around my heart?

"Hey, you okay?" Zane's voice broke through my reverie, and I glanced up to find him studying me, concern lacing his features. "You look a little lost."

"I'm fine! Just... thinking," I replied, trying to dismiss the weight that had settled back onto my shoulders. "You know, about how this festival is just as chaotic as my life."

"Then let's make it even more chaotic!" Zane declared with a grin, his playful nature bubbling to the surface once again. "I have a plan."

Before I could ask what kind of plan he had in mind, he tugged me toward a nearby booth adorned with colorful banners and twinkling lights. The air was filled with the scent of cotton candy and caramel apples, a nostalgic reminder of childhood fairs and carefree days. I couldn't help but feel a rush of excitement, a thrill coursing through me as I followed his lead.

Zane approached the booth, which promised a variety of games, and before I knew it, we were engaged in a fierce competition at a ring toss. The stakes were high: the winner would claim an oversized plush toy—a bright, absurdly fluffy unicorn that seemed to gleam in the fairy lights.

"You're on," I declared, my competitive spirit ignited. We tossed rings back and forth, laughter spilling from our lips with each failed attempt and triumphant success. The game was ridiculous, but every time Zane glanced my way, his laughter ringing in the air, I felt more at ease, the shadows receding further into the background.

After several comical rounds, I finally landed a ring over one of the pegs, a surge of exhilaration shooting through me. "Ha! Victory is mine!" I exclaimed, pumping my fist in the air as Zane feigned defeat, collapsing against the booth in mock despair.

"Fine, you win. But only because I let you," he said, his tone dripping with playful sarcasm.

"Sure, keep telling yourself that." I beamed, my heart soaring. The unicorn, an over-the-top creation of pastel colors and glitter, was mine for the taking. As I reached to claim my prize, I felt a rush of exhilaration. In that moment, it wasn't just the game I had won; I felt like I was reclaiming a piece of myself, shedding the layers of doubt that had wrapped around me like a cocoon.

But as I turned to face Zane, the triumphant smile on my lips faltered. His gaze had shifted to something behind me, a flicker of concern in his eyes that sent a shiver of dread curling in my stomach. I turned to follow his gaze, and my heart sank at the sight of a familiar figure standing just a few feet away.

It was Claire, my former colleague. She stood there, arms crossed, an unreadable expression on her face as she observed our antics. The last time we'd crossed paths had been less than pleasant, an awkward encounter loaded with unsaid words and unresolved tensions.

"Zane," I whispered, my heart racing. "I need to—"

"Just stay calm," he interrupted, squeezing my hand reassuringly. "You've got this. Just remember, you're not the person you were back then."

Taking a deep breath, I forced a smile, determined to face whatever was about to unfold. The unicorn felt like a weighty emblem in my hands, a symbol of my growth and newfound courage. I could either let the past dictate my present or take a step forward, embracing the messiness of life.

"Claire," I greeted, my voice steady despite the tumultuous emotions swirling inside me. "Fancy seeing you here."

The tension in the air crackled like static electricity, and I could feel Zane's presence beside me, a grounding force against the uncertainty. Whatever happened next, I was ready to confront my past, armed with the knowledge that I had a future worth fighting for.

The moment hung in the air, thick with unresolved tension, like the final note of a symphony waiting for its conductor to decide on the next movement. Claire's presence loomed, and the world around us faded into a distant murmur. The laughter of festival-goers and the upbeat melodies from the stage dulled into an unrecognizable hum. She looked every bit the picture of casual indifference, yet the sharpness in her gaze felt like ice slicing through the warmth I'd just begun to embrace.

"Fancy seeing you here," I repeated, the words rolling off my tongue with a forced casualness. I tried to catch a glimpse of Zane from the corner of my eye, hoping to find reassurance in his expression. His grip on my hand remained steady, a silent promise that I wouldn't have to face this alone.

"Not as fancy as it is to see you," Claire replied, her tone dripping with the kind of sweetness that suggested something bitter was lurking just beneath the surface. She glanced at Zane, assessing, and I felt an uncomfortable prickle at the back of my neck. "You've certainly found a new friend since the last time we met."

"Just enjoying the festival," I said, injecting a brightness into my voice that felt slightly strained. "How about you?"

"Oh, you know. Just here for the sights," she said, but her smile didn't quite reach her eyes. "And maybe to catch up with old friends. You do remember how we worked together, don't you?"

Her words danced between us like a blade, sharp and cutting. "Of course," I replied, trying to maintain my composure. "I remember everything, Claire. Some things are hard to forget."

Zane squeezed my hand tighter, and I could feel the warmth radiating from him. "We were just about to grab some food," he interjected smoothly, a flicker of irritation in his voice. "You're welcome to join us if you'd like, Claire."

I shot him a grateful look, appreciating his attempt to diffuse the tension. Claire hesitated, her expression morphing for a split second into something unreadable before it returned to the faux cheerfulness she wore like armor. "Oh, I wouldn't want to intrude on your little date. I just came by to say hello."

"Right," Zane said, his voice laced with disbelief. "But if you want to chat, I'm sure that's not a problem either. Just, you know, not too long. We have plans."

"Plans?" Claire's brows rose, genuine curiosity sparking in her tone. "What plans? I didn't know you two had any exciting escapades lined up."

I felt the heat of embarrassment creeping into my cheeks, but Zane remained unfazed. "Just some fun. You know how it is during festival season. Lots to see, lots to do." He flashed her a charming smile, the kind that would usually sweep me off my feet, but tonight it felt like a shield against the impending confrontation.

"Right," Claire replied, her eyes narrowing slightly as she considered her next move. "You're really enjoying this, aren't you? It must be nice to have someone to distract you."

The veiled jab cut deeper than I wanted to admit, a cold reminder of the insecurities I had been battling all night. I opened my mouth to respond, but Zane beat me to it, his voice firm. "I think it's safe to say we're both enjoying ourselves. And I'd appreciate it if you didn't make assumptions about what's going on between us."

"Assumptions?" Claire feigned innocence, but her smirk gave her away. "I'm just saying it's surprising. Especially considering how you two seemed to be struggling just a little while ago."

I felt a sharp intake of breath as I tried to process her words. Had I really thought we were on solid ground, just because we had shared a few moments of levity? The uncertainty crept back in like an unwanted guest.

"Struggling?" I echoed, my voice laced with confusion. "What do you mean by that?"

Claire tilted her head, an amused glimmer in her eyes. "Oh, come on. We both know what it's like to have personal baggage. To not be able to let go of the past. I just figured Zane would prefer someone a bit more... carefree."

The jab landed with the precision of a well-aimed arrow, and for a moment, all the joy I'd felt just moments before evaporated. I glanced at Zane, searching his expression for some sign of what he was thinking. His jaw tightened, but he held my gaze, reassuring me with a silent promise that he wasn't going anywhere.

"I'm perfectly capable of handling my own past, Claire," I said, forcing a smile that didn't quite reach my eyes. "And Zane doesn't need someone who's 'carefree' to enjoy himself. He's with me, after all."

Her eyes narrowed further, and I felt the thrill of adrenaline surge through me. Was I really standing up for myself? Had I come so far that I could confront the ghost of my insecurities with a strength I didn't know I possessed?

Claire shrugged, a nonchalant wave of her hand. "Just looking out for my old friend, that's all. You know how it is—people change, but some things never do."

"Like the tendency to make snide remarks?" Zane shot back, his voice sharp. The tension in the air had shifted from merely uncomfortable to electrifying, and I could feel the energy of the festival thrumming around us, almost matching the rapid beat of my heart.

"Touché," Claire replied, a flicker of surprise crossing her face. But it quickly faded, replaced by a thin smile. "I just want you to be careful, that's all. Not everyone can handle the weight of history. It can be quite the burden, can't it?"

The way she said it felt like a challenge, a taunt that hung between us like a dark cloud. My chest tightened as the words settled uncomfortably in the air. She was right—history had its claws dug deep, and I could feel the tension surging back, threatening to undo all the progress I thought I had made.

"Thank you for your concern," I managed, my voice steadier than I felt. "But I think I can handle my own life choices without your input."

Zane's expression was one of fierce support, a silent acknowledgment that this was my moment to reclaim my narrative. "We're happy, Claire. That's all that matters," he added, a note of finality in his tone.

With that, the atmosphere shifted once again, like a pendulum swinging wildly between confrontation and understanding. Claire's smile faltered, and I caught a glimpse of the hurt beneath her bravado. "If that's how you feel, I wish you the best. Just remember that not all fairy tales have happy endings."

The words hung in the air like a specter, dark and foreboding. As she turned on her heel and walked away, the music surged back into focus, but it felt distant and muted, the laughter of the festival-goers a hollow echo against the backdrop of my swirling thoughts.

"Wow," Zane said, shaking his head. "That was intense."

"Yeah, it was," I replied, my heart still racing. "I thought I was past that part of my life."

"You are," he reassured, stepping closer, enveloping me in his warmth. "But sometimes, the past has a way of sneaking up on you when you least expect it."

We stood in silence for a moment, the weight of Claire's words pressing down on us like an unwanted cloud. I glanced at Zane, searching for answers in his gaze. "Do you think she meant what she said? About fairy tales?"

Zane opened his mouth to respond, but before he could form the words, a commotion erupted nearby. A loud shout pierced through the air, drawing our attention. A group of festival-goers had gathered around a small stage where an announcement was being made, and the energy in the crowd shifted dramatically.

"What's happening?" I asked, feeling a flicker of anxiety rise within me.

"I don't know, but it doesn't look good," Zane replied, his brow furrowing.

We exchanged a glance, the unspoken understanding igniting a spark of urgency. I grabbed his hand, ready to pull him toward the growing crowd, when suddenly, a loud crash reverberated through the air, followed by a gasp that rippled through the onlookers.

And then, amidst the chaos, I caught sight of Claire again, her expression transformed from playful to something else entirely—a look of panic etched across her features. She pointed toward the sky, her mouth moving in rapid, frantic motion, but all I could hear was the pounding of my heart.

"Zane!" I shouted, but he was already pulling me closer to the commotion, and as we stepped into the throng of people, the world around us spun into a whirlwind of uncertainty and fear.

Then I looked up, and my breath caught in my throat. A dark figure loomed over the festival, silhouetted against the stars, and the sense of foreboding washed over me like a cold wave crashing into the shore.

And in that moment, as the crowd erupted into chaos, I realized that the night was about to take an unexpected turn—one that would challenge everything I thought I knew about myself, my past, and the very future I had fought so hard to reclaim.

Chapter 16: The Bridge Between Us

The festival lights twinkled like distant stars, illuminating the crowded square with a warm, golden glow. Laughter danced through the air, weaving itself into the crisp autumn night, a soundtrack to the festivities that were unfolding around us. The scent of caramel apples and roasted chestnuts mingled in a delightful concoction, tugging at my senses and urging me to let go of my worries, even if just for a moment. But I couldn't help glancing at Zane, his eyes reflecting the lights above like twin beacons of reassurance.

"I promise, I'm not going anywhere," he said, his voice low and steady, cutting through the cacophony of the celebration. I felt the weight of his words settle into the pit of my stomach, mingling with the flutter of anxiety that had become all too familiar over the past few months. It was a reminder of the battles I had fought, each one etched into the lines of my heart, but there was something different in the way he spoke. An unspoken promise, perhaps, that made the night feel less daunting.

We stood close, the space between us charged with a kind of electricity that sent shivers racing along my skin. It was as if the festival itself held its breath, waiting for us to bridge the chasm of uncertainty that had been lingering since my heart had been so carelessly shattered. In that moment, everything else faded away—the laughter, the music, the colorful booths bursting with life—leaving just Zane and me, suspended in time.

His gaze softened as he brushed a stray hair from my face, a gesture that felt both tender and monumental. "What if we write a song? Something that reflects all of this?" he suggested, gesturing toward the festival and, I realized, toward us—toward our journey, tangled and beautiful.

My heart raced at the thought. Music had always been my sanctuary, a refuge where emotions transformed into melodies. "You mean here? Now?" I replied, the idea taking root in my mind like a wildflower breaking through concrete.

"Why not? It's the perfect backdrop," he said, flashing a lopsided grin that made my stomach flip. "Let's capture this moment. The highs and the lows, the messy in-betweens."

As we wandered away from the crowd, I felt a stirring of excitement mix with the trepidation lingering in my chest. We found a quiet corner beneath a towering oak, its branches draped in twinkling fairy lights, casting a gentle glow around us. Zane pulled out his guitar, a well-loved instrument that had seen more of his heart than anyone else ever would. I nestled beside him, the familiar warmth of his body easing my worries, the notes of the guitar resonating in my bones.

"What should we start with?" I asked, feeling both exhilarated and terrified, like stepping onto a stage without knowing my lines.

He thought for a moment, the way his brow furrowed making him look achingly handsome. "Let's just start from the beginning. Tell me about the first time you felt... lost."

The question hung in the air, heavy yet freeing. I took a deep breath, letting memories spill into the space between us. "I was fourteen, sitting on the floor of my bedroom, surrounded by scraps of paper and unfinished songs," I began. "It was like the world was this giant puzzle, and I had lost the box with the picture on it. I didn't know how to put it together."

Zane listened intently, his fingers strumming lightly against the guitar strings, creating a melody that echoed the uncertainty in my voice. "And what happened?" he prompted gently.

"I wrote a song," I replied, my voice gaining strength as the memory unfolded. "It was terrible, but it was mine. That's when I realized that even in the darkest moments, I could create something beautiful."

The flicker of a smile danced across his lips. "See? You've always had that light in you."

As we wove our stories into lyrics, the lines began to blur between the past and present. I shared the darkness that had lingered in my heart, the moments when I felt utterly alone, while Zane opened up about his struggles, his aspirations, and the moments of doubt that nearly swallowed him whole. Our vulnerabilities lay bare, raw and unfiltered, binding us together in a way that felt almost sacred.

The song took shape in fits and starts, a testament to our intertwined journeys. With each chord, the tension of unspoken fears began to dissolve, replaced by an undeniable bond. Laughter punctuated our serious moments, especially when Zane's attempts at my favorite chord progressions went hilariously awry, his teasing banter lightening the weight of our confessions.

"Are you sure you're not secretly tone-deaf?" I shot back playfully, my heart soaring at his infectious laughter.

"Hey, I'll have you know, I've got perfect pitch!" he retorted, feigning offense before launching into a dramatically exaggerated rendition of a popular song, utterly off-key.

"Yeah, pitch black," I quipped, my laughter mingling with his, filling the night air with warmth.

As we poured our hearts into the music, the last remnants of fear began to fade. With every note, I felt myself healing, as if the melodies were stitching together the pieces of my heart, one chord at a time. Zane's presence was a balm, soothing the scars I had thought would never fade. I was learning that vulnerability was not a weakness but a bridge—a connection to the beauty of love, imperfect and real.

In the end, as the final notes drifted into the night, I realized we had crafted more than just a song; we had created a sanctuary of understanding and trust. It wasn't just about love; it was about growth, about finding a way to embrace the messy, complicated truth of who we were—together.

The last echoes of our new song lingered in the air, weaving through the thrumming pulse of the festival as the crowd around us began to disperse. With the fading notes, a sense of triumph washed over me, mingling seamlessly with the thrill of being so close to Zane. I tucked a loose strand of hair behind my ear and stole a glance at him. His face was illuminated by the warm glow of the nearby lanterns, and in that moment, he looked like an artist captured in a timeless painting—a perfect blend of passion and vulnerability.

"Do you think we should actually perform it?" I asked, half teasing, half hopeful. My heart raced at the idea, the prospect of sharing our creation with others both thrilling and terrifying. The thought of standing in front of an audience sent butterflies careening through my stomach.

Zane grinned, the kind of grin that made my heart do a little flip. "Why not? I mean, what's the worst that could happen? A few bad reviews?" His playful sarcasm always managed to ease the tension in my mind, like a gentle push against the door of my anxieties.

"Or we could be booed off the stage," I countered, rolling my eyes dramatically. "You know, my ego isn't quite ready for that kind of blow."

"Please, you have the ego of a thousand rock stars," he shot back, nudging me playfully. "Besides, if we get booed, I'll just take the hit while you serenade them with your dazzling charm." He leaned back, crossing his arms as if he had just handed me the ultimate compliment.

"Charm, huh?" I mused, trying to hide a smile. "Is that what we're calling it now? I thought it was just sheer panic that dazzled them."

Before he could respond, the thumping of drums and the strumming of guitars grew louder as the festival shifted gears into the evening concert. A crowd gathered around a makeshift stage where local bands showcased their talent. Music spilled into the night, infusing the air with an infectious energy that tugged at my heart.

"I say we give it a shot," Zane declared, standing up with a spark of determination in his eyes. "But we need to get ready. We can't just waltz up there looking like we've just come from the corner café."

"Speak for yourself! I happen to be a corner café fashionista," I retorted, rising to my feet with a flourish. "But if we're really doing this, I'll need a solid pep talk and maybe some lip gloss."

"Lip gloss?" He raised an eyebrow, clearly amused. "What are we, ten-year-olds at a sleepover?"

"Hey, it's the little things that matter!" I shot back, smirking. "A little gloss never hurt anyone. It's like my secret armor against the judgment of the world."

As we navigated the bustling crowd, I felt an exhilarating rush of possibility coursing through my veins. Zane's confidence was contagious, and I couldn't help but ride the wave of excitement he created. Each step toward the stage felt like stepping closer to reclaiming not just my love for music but my heart's rightful place in the world.

When we finally reached the front, I took a moment to soak it all in—the sea of faces illuminated by the festival lights, the sweet scent of cinnamon and sugar wafting from nearby stalls, and the distant sound of laughter intertwining with the music. It was intoxicating. As Zane nudged me forward, I could feel my nerves bubbling to the surface, but instead of succumbing to fear, I took a deep breath, letting the moment wrap around me like a warm blanket.

"Hey, everyone!" Zane called out, his voice ringing with an easy confidence. "We're here to play a little something special tonight." The crowd's attention shifted toward us, their faces eager and curious. "I promise we won't be terrible. Well, at least I won't be."

The laughter that followed eased the tightness in my chest, and I couldn't help but chuckle. "Yes, I take full responsibility for any musical mishaps," I added, trying to keep my voice steady.

A few chuckles rippled through the audience, and just like that, the stage became our safe haven. We exchanged a glance that sparked with determination, a silent understanding passing between us. With Zane's fingers poised on the guitar strings and my heart racing, we dove headfirst into our creation.

The first few chords flowed smoothly, the sound melding into the festival's rhythm. As I sang the opening lines, the words poured out of me, each note weaving our story into the night. The lyrics were honest and raw, echoing our journey, the struggles, and the laughter we had shared. With each passing moment, the audience transformed from strangers into our biggest supporters, nodding along, swaying to the music, and even singing the chorus back to us.

It was a revelation, the connection between us and the crowd blossoming like the first blooms of spring. As the final notes faded, a moment of silence hung in the air before the audience erupted into applause, their cheers ringing with genuine warmth. I glanced at Zane, who beamed with pride, and in that instant, I knew we had created something beautiful together.

"See? Not terrible at all," he said, breathless from the exhilaration of our performance.

"Okay, maybe I was wrong about the booing," I admitted, laughter spilling from my lips. "We might just have a winning formula here."

"Winning, indeed," he agreed, his eyes sparkling. "Just wait until we start charging for tickets."

But then, amid our playful banter, something shifted. I noticed a figure at the edge of the crowd, an unfamiliar presence that caused a tight knot to form in my stomach. A woman with striking features, dressed in a way that screamed sophistication, was watching us intently. There was something about her gaze that sent a chill down my spine, as if she saw through all the layers I had painstakingly built to protect myself.

"Hey, you okay?" Zane's voice broke through my thoughts, his brow furrowed with concern.

I forced a smile, though my heart raced with unease. "Yeah, just... someone I don't recognize."

"Let's not let anyone rain on our parade," he said, pulling me closer, his warmth grounding me. But as I glanced back at the woman, I couldn't shake the feeling that she was somehow connected to the shadows of my past, lurking just out of reach, waiting for the right moment to step into the light.

The applause faded like ripples on a pond, leaving a warm glow in the air that enveloped us both. As I basked in the afterglow of our performance, the crowd slowly dissolved, laughter and conversation blending into a backdrop of cheer. But that strange woman remained, her gaze steady and unyielding, like a lighthouse beam cutting through the fog of my happiness.

"Who is she?" I murmured, my eyes darting back to the figure that had unsettled me. I could sense Zane's tension, his protective instinct flaring up like a flare in a dark night.

"Not a clue," he replied, his voice a low rumble. "But she doesn't look like she came here for the cotton candy and karaoke."

My mind raced, conjuring shadows from my past that I had tried so hard to bury. Memories of failed relationships and opportunistic acquaintances sprang to life, and my heart pounded in response. "What if she's someone from my old life? You know, the life I left behind?"

Zane stepped closer, his presence reassuring as he tilted my chin to meet his gaze. "Then we'll figure it out together. You're not alone in this." The sincerity in his eyes anchored me, pushing back against the weight of my fears.

Just then, the woman moved, weaving her way through the dwindling crowd, her sharp silhouette striking against the warmth of the festival lights. I felt a mix of curiosity and dread. With each step she took toward us, the knot in my stomach tightened.

"Let's go grab some snacks or something," Zane suggested, glancing toward the food stalls. "Cotton candy always makes everything better."

As we turned to leave, the woman's voice sliced through the night like a knife. "Kira," she called, her tone smooth yet insistent. "I need to talk to you."

I froze, my pulse quickening. "You know her?" Zane asked, his body tense beside me.

"Not at all," I replied, shaking my head. "And I don't think I want to."

"Please," the woman urged, her eyes narrowing slightly as she stepped closer. "It's important. It's about your father."

The mention of my father sent a jolt through me, a mix of confusion and fear. "What do you know about my father?" I demanded, my voice trembling with a blend of anger and trepidation.

She took a deep breath, the noise of the festival fading into a dull roar as the world around us slipped away. "More than you think. He needs your help."

"Help?" I echoed incredulously. "After everything? He disappeared years ago. Why would I help him now?"

Zane's hand slipped into mine, his grip tightening as if he could shield me from whatever storm was brewing. "Maybe this isn't the time or place to discuss it," he said carefully, his voice low, but the determination was clear.

"No, I think it is," the woman insisted, her gaze unwavering. "You deserve to know the truth about what happened. You deserve to know why he left."

Every word she spoke felt like a punch to the gut. Memories flooded back—my father's hurried departures, the promises he broke, the loneliness that followed. I had buried those feelings under layers of resentment and pain, but hearing her mention him brought them crashing back to the surface, raw and jagged.

"Why should I believe you?" I challenged, fighting to keep my voice steady.

"Because you need to," she replied, her tone softened but resolute. "There's something you don't know, something that could change everything."

Zane shifted beside me, his presence a steady anchor against the rising tide of emotions swirling within me. "What do you want from her?" he asked, his voice low but sharp.

The woman's eyes flicked between us, assessing, weighing the tension in the air. "I want to help. There are things at play here that you both don't understand. Your father is in trouble, Kira, and the clock is ticking."

"Trouble? What kind of trouble?" I pressed, my heart racing as I took a step closer, intrigued despite myself.

She hesitated, a flicker of uncertainty crossing her face. "There are forces at work—people who want to keep the truth buried. But your father... he's fighting against them. He needs you."

"Why would he need me?" I shot back, anger surging within me like a tidal wave. "He made his choices. He walked away."

"I can't explain everything here," she said, glancing over her shoulder, her voice dropping to a whisper. "But if you want answers, you have to meet me. Tomorrow night, at the old warehouse on Fifth. I promise you, you won't regret it."

"Why should I trust you?" I demanded, my voice hard.

"Because I know things about you, things you don't even remember," she said, her gaze intense. "I'm not your enemy. I'm trying to help you find your father and protect you from what's coming."

My heart raced as I processed her words. There was a heaviness in the air, a weight that felt both ominous and tantalizing. Zane's grip on my hand tightened, and I could feel the heat of his concern radiating off him. "Kira, we need to think this through," he urged quietly.

But the woman had already begun to back away, her expression shifting to something more resolute. "Tomorrow night. You'll know what to do."

And just like that, she was gone, melting into the shadows of the festival, leaving behind a whirlwind of confusion and dread. I stood there, my heart pounding, grappling with the unexpected invitation that dangled before me like a forbidden fruit.

"What just happened?" I asked breathlessly, turning to Zane, who looked as stunned as I felt.

"I think you have a decision to make," he said softly, his eyes searching mine. "Whatever this is, it's not over. And you don't have to do this alone."

I looked back toward the direction where the woman had vanished, uncertainty twisting in my gut. Tomorrow night. The warehouse. The promise of answers mingled with the remnants of betrayal, and I knew deep down that I couldn't walk away from this. But as I looked back at Zane, the weight of the decision settled heavily on my shoulders.

"Let's get out of here," he suggested, pulling me closer. "We can figure this out together. No more surprises, I promise."

But as we turned to leave the festival behind, the echoes of the night hung in the air, leaving a lingering question: what truths awaited me at the warehouse? What had I just stepped into? The wind whispered around us, carrying with it the scent of uncertainty, and I couldn't shake the feeling that the past was clawing its way back into my life, ready to spill its secrets—one way or another.

Chapter 17: Reverberations of Truth

The bar buzzed with anticipation, a kaleidoscope of laughter and clinking glasses, all woven into the fabric of a Saturday night. Neon lights flickered overhead, casting playful shadows on the faces of the crowd, each one a story waiting to be told. I stood at the edge of the stage, a rickety wooden platform that felt as though it might wobble beneath me at any moment. The scent of beer mingled with the heady aroma of fried food, creating a symphony of sensory overload that seemed to pulse with the rhythm of the night.

Zane stood beside me, a steady force, his warm presence anchoring me amidst the chaos. The chatter faded as I adjusted the microphone, its metallic surface cool against my fingertips, and took a deep breath, the air thick with excitement and uncertainty. We had poured our souls into this song, a melodic tapestry woven from threads of our pain and resilience. It was more than just notes and lyrics; it was a declaration of our existence, a testament to the battles fought and won.

"Ready?" Zane's voice was low, laced with an electric confidence that seemed to spark something deep within me. I nodded, unable to find my voice amidst the thrum of adrenaline coursing through my veins. As the spotlight enveloped us, the audience blurred into a sea of silhouettes, and the world outside faded into nothingness.

I glanced at Zane, our eyes locking for a fleeting moment, a silent promise passing between us. Then the music began—a gentle strum of the guitar that swelled into something beautiful and haunting. My heart raced as I took a step closer to the mic, my pulse synchronizing with the beat. With each note, I felt the weight of my past dissolve, unraveling like an old sweater slowly coming apart at the seams.

We dove into the first verse, my voice rising and falling like the tide, the words spilling forth from a wellspring of emotions long kept at bay. The lyrics wove a narrative, painting pictures of heartbreak and healing, of the shadows that lingered and the light that broke through. Zane's harmonies wrapped around my voice, a rich counterpoint that filled the space between us, his smooth timbre contrasting with my more restless notes.

The crowd was entranced, and for the first time in what felt like an eternity, I felt truly seen. As the chorus hit, the energy in the room shifted. Bodies swayed, hands clapped in rhythm, and I could see smiles blooming like wildflowers across the audience. They were resonating with our story, sharing in our journey as if it were their own. I locked eyes with a woman in the front row; her gaze glimmered with understanding, a silent acknowledgment of the struggles we all faced.

And then, just like that, we reached the final chord. The last notes hung in the air, shimmering like fragile glass before shattering into applause that echoed through the bar, crashing against the walls and flooding our senses. I stepped back, breathless, the roar of appreciation washing over me, a tidal wave of pride and belonging. Zane grinned, his eyes sparkling as we took a bow, and I felt an exhilarating mix of triumph and vulnerability settle into my bones.

As the clamor began to fade, Zane leaned in closer, his breath warm against my ear. "Let's take this public," he whispered, the words tumbling from his lips with an urgency that sent a thrill racing down my spine. My heart stuttered, a wild drumbeat drowning out the ambient noise of the bar. The thrill of sharing our music with the world clashed violently with the sudden jolt of fear tightening around my chest.

"Public?" I echoed, my voice wavering slightly. The thought of letting others in, of exposing the raw edges of our relationship, sent a shiver down my spine. We had shared our story through music, but to declare it openly felt like standing on the precipice of a cliff, the ground crumbling beneath my feet.

"Yeah, I mean, why not? We could start a social media page, share videos, the whole deal." His excitement was palpable, a fire igniting in his eyes, and for a moment, I could feel the same flame flickering within myself.

"But what if it goes wrong?" I countered, my mind racing with a thousand possibilities. "What if people judge us or twist our story? What if we become... well, I don't know, a meme?" The idea made me cringe, images of our vulnerable moments being dissected and ridiculed by strangers swirling in my mind.

"Or," he replied, a smirk dancing on his lips, "we could inspire someone. What if our story helps others find their voices? We could be the soundtrack to someone else's journey." There was a spark in his eyes, a belief that what we had created could extend beyond the stage and touch lives in a way I had never considered.

The potential was intoxicating, yet the thought of putting our relationship on display felt like standing under a spotlight, completely exposed. I wrestled with my insecurities, the specter of judgment lurking just out of sight. But as I gazed into Zane's unwavering gaze, something shifted within me. Perhaps there was strength in vulnerability, a power in sharing our truth with the world.

"Okay," I found myself saying, the word spilling out before I could catch it. "Let's do it. But we do it on our terms." Zane's grin widened, illuminating the dimly lit bar, and my heart fluttered with a mix of fear and exhilaration.

In that moment, I understood: this was more than just a leap into the unknown; it was a chance to embrace every aspect of our journey, to turn our struggles into a beacon of hope for others. And as we stepped down from the stage, the applause still ringing in our ears, I realized that the real journey was only just beginning.

The bar had transformed from a crowded enclave of strangers into a sanctuary of possibility. After the performance, Zane and I found ourselves huddled in a cozy corner booth, the dim lighting casting a soft glow over our animated discussion. I could still feel the pulse of the crowd, a vivid rhythm in my veins, as we sipped on a pair of whiskey ginger ales. The warmth of the drink spread through me, bolstering my courage in the face of the bold move we were contemplating.

"Okay, so what's the first step in taking our relationship public?" I asked, teasing a strand of hair behind my ear. I could feel the thrill of the idea washing over me like a cool breeze on a hot day, yet the anxiety simmered just beneath the surface, a whisper of doubt that refused to be silenced.

Zane leaned back, a satisfied grin playing at the corners of his mouth. "First, we need to come up with a name for our musical duo. Something catchy, something that will stick in people's minds." He drummed his fingers on the table, his enthusiasm palpable. "What about 'The Heartstrings'? It's poetic and totally fits our vibe."

I snorted, half-laughing, half-choking on my drink. "Sounds like a support group for people who cry during rom-coms. How about something a little less... emotional?"

"Less emotional?" he echoed, his eyebrows shooting up in mock disbelief. "You mean we're not going for the heartfelt ballad vibe? Should we just dive into some hardcore punk instead?"

"Why not? Nothing says love like screaming into a mic about existential dread." I shot back, my heart racing at the thought. The banter between us flowed effortlessly, each quip a thread weaving our connection tighter.

"Okay, maybe not punk," Zane conceded, a glimmer of mischief in his eyes. "But how about something that combines our names? Z+S... Zane and Sunny! Like the sun and the moon. The universe's perfect pair."

"Or a bad sitcom starring us in the aftermath of a disastrous breakup," I laughed, rolling my eyes. "How about we just stick to our names for now? 'Zane & Sunny' has a nice ring to it. Simple. Straightforward."

He raised his glass in a mock toast. "To Zane & Sunny! The next big thing in music... or at least the next big thing at this bar."

"Don't sell us short! We could be legends," I replied, raising my glass to clink against his, the sound ringing out like a promise. As our laughter faded, I took a moment to really look at him—his enthusiasm, the way he leaned forward as if the world outside that booth didn't exist, just us and our dreams. I couldn't help but wonder what it would mean to share that with the world.

"Okay, but seriously, how do we navigate the public part?" I asked, my voice dropping slightly as the weight of the question sank in. "I mean, how do we make it clear we're not just a gimmick? I don't want people thinking we're some cliché story."

Zane's expression shifted, a more thoughtful look taking over his features. "Well, for starters, we can be honest about our journey. We're not perfect. We're figuring it out just like everyone else."

"Right. Perfectly imperfect," I mused, the phrase rolling off my tongue as if it were meant to be there. "But what if it gets messy? What if people scrutinize us?"

"We'll deal with it. Together," he assured me, his voice steady, a soft anchor amidst my whirlpool of thoughts. "Look, if we're going to do this, we have to commit to being vulnerable. That's what will connect with people."

His words hung in the air, heavier than the tension in the room. I could feel the weight of truth pressing against my chest. What did it mean to be vulnerable? Was I ready to lay myself bare for the world to see? The thought was exhilarating and terrifying in equal measure, like a roller coaster teetering at the edge of a steep drop.

Just then, the bar door swung open, a gust of wind trailing in behind a trio of newcomers. They were boisterous, full of laughter and reckless energy that cut through the reflective moment. One of them, a tall man with a wild mop of curly hair, strolled toward us, an easy smile plastered across his face.

"Hey, that was an amazing set! You guys rocked it!" he exclaimed, sliding into the booth opposite us. His friends followed suit, plopping down and draping their arms over the back of the booth like they owned the place.

"Thanks!" Zane replied, visibly brightening at the compliment. "We're just getting started."

"Oh, I can tell! What are your plans now? Going to be the next big stars?" the curly-haired guy asked, his eyes sparkling with enthusiasm.

"We're actually thinking about taking things public," I confessed, my heart racing. I had blurted it out without considering how it might sound to these strangers.

"Public?" one of the girls chimed in, her face lighting up. "Like, on social media? You guys could totally do it! I'd follow you."

My stomach twisted. The thought of someone I didn't know following our journey sent a ripple of unease through me. What if they didn't get it? What if they didn't see the depth behind the melodies?

"Yeah, we're working on that," Zane said, radiating confidence, while I silently willed the floor to open up and swallow me whole. "Just trying to figure out how to do it right."

"Just be yourselves! That's all anyone wants to see," the curly-haired guy said, a glint of sincerity in his eyes. "If you're genuine, people will connect. Trust me."

Trust. Such a simple word, yet loaded with implications. I stole a glance at Zane, who was already nodding along, his enthusiasm undeterred. He had that uncanny ability to find hope in the face of uncertainty, a quality that both inspired and intimidated me.

"I'll hold you to that," I finally managed to say, a wry smile creeping onto my lips. "But if I end up on some internet meme, I'm blaming you."

"Fair enough," Zane chuckled, a conspiratorial gleam in his eyes. "But just think about it: if we do become internet famous, at least we'll have a built-in fanbase to help us get through it. We'll be the poster children for awkward fame!"

The laughter that followed eased my tension, a gentle reminder that we weren't alone in this. As the conversation flowed, I felt the weight of my worries dissipate, replaced by the thrill of possibility. Perhaps stepping into the light wouldn't be so daunting after all. Maybe, just maybe, we could carve our own path in this wild world of music and relationships, side by side.

The booth grew louder as more friends joined the table, each voice blending into a harmonious buzz that filled the bar like an unwelcome chorus. I couldn't help but feel a swell of anxiety gnawing at my insides. What had started as a celebratory moment had morphed into something larger, something with expectations and pressures that felt foreign. The warmth from the whiskey ginger ale faded, replaced by the icy grip of doubt.

"Anyone want to hear another song?" one of the newcomers, a girl with a cascade of wavy hair, shouted, her excitement infectious. "I'm dying to hear more!"

"Absolutely! We're here for it!" Zane exclaimed, his grin broadening, an electric energy radiating from him that seemed to make the air crackle. I loved his enthusiasm, but my heart raced with uncertainty.

"Maybe we should keep it low-key tonight," I suggested, scanning the table filled with eager faces. "You know, savor the moment?"

"But you guys just killed it up there!" the curly-haired guy insisted. "You can't leave us hanging! We want more!"

A chorus of agreement echoed around the table, and the pressure began to mount. I glanced at Zane, searching for a hint of what he thought. The last thing I wanted was to disappoint anyone, but the thought of stepping back into the spotlight again felt daunting, as if I were about to dive into icy waters without a life jacket.

Zane leaned in closer, his voice low and conspiratorial. "What if we do an impromptu jam? Just us—no pressure. We can keep it casual." His eyes sparkled with mischief, and I felt my heart lift a little.

"An impromptu jam, huh?" I replied, raising an eyebrow, my lips twitching upward. "What's next? A surprise musical number in the middle of a supermarket?"

"Honestly, that would be epic," he said, winking. "But let's keep it to the bar for now."

With a deep breath, I found myself swept up in the current of excitement. "Alright, let's do it. But we keep it simple—no big theatrics, just music."

"Perfect!" he declared, and before I knew it, we were both standing again, the applause from before still echoing in my ears. Zane picked up his guitar, and I settled in beside him, feeling the familiar rush of nerves and adrenaline flood my system.

As we launched into a soft melody, the room quieted, the world narrowing to just the two of us. The song flowed from us like water, and the connection was palpable, a thread weaving us into a tapestry of sound and emotion. I glanced at Zane, his fingers dancing over the strings, his concentration etched into his features, and for a moment, everything felt right.

Just as we finished, a loud crash echoed from the bar's entrance, slicing through our moment like a knife. I turned to see a figure stumbling in, looking disheveled and frantic. A tall man, wild-eyed and panting, stood there as if the world had come crashing down around him. The lively atmosphere shifted, curiosity sparking through the crowd.

"What the hell?" Zane muttered, his expression morphing from joy to concern.

"Is he okay?" I whispered, my heart racing for entirely different reasons. The sudden intensity in the air was almost suffocating, an unsettling tension replacing our earlier merriment.

The man staggered further into the bar, swaying on his feet as if he were battling invisible waves. "Help! Someone, please!" he called out, his voice a raw mix of fear and desperation.

People shifted uneasily in their seats, and the jovial spirit evaporated like the last drops of my drink. Zane's brows furrowed, and without a word, he stepped forward, moving instinctively towards the stranger.

"Hey, man, what's wrong?" Zane asked, concern lining his voice. I wanted to follow, to keep that protective thread taut between us, but I hesitated, rooted to the spot.

"I... I need help," the man gasped, clutching his side as if the very act of breathing were a struggle. "I was... I was just at the diner down the street. There's a guy... he's in trouble. He—"

"What kind of trouble?" Zane pressed, his voice firm yet soothing. The crowd, which had been buzzing with anticipation, fell silent, hanging onto the stranger's every word.

"He's got a knife! You have to come quick! I don't know what he's going to do!" The man's eyes darted around the bar, wild and panicked, and I felt my heart drop.

Zane glanced back at me, his expression shifting, and I knew we had to decide, and quickly. Did we leap into action, risking everything, or do we wait and see what happened next?

"We can't just sit here," Zane said, determination etched into his features. "What if someone gets hurt?"

"Are you serious?" I shot back, a mixture of fear and frustration rising in me. "You're going to run off to a potential crime scene? We don't even know what's going on!"

"I can't just ignore it, Sunny! We can't!" He stepped closer, urgency painting his words. "What if it's really bad? What if someone is in danger?"

My mind raced, the implications colliding with my instincts. "And what if it's not? What if he's just some guy trying to stir up trouble?"

Zane hesitated, the tension between us palpable, and I could see the conflict in his eyes. But before he could respond, a shout erupted from the bar's back corner, a woman's voice shrieking, cutting through the air like glass.

"Get away from her!"

Instinctively, I jumped, adrenaline surging as I turned to see a scene unfolding in the shadows—a brawl, a struggle, bodies twisting in a chaotic dance. The air crackled with fear and confusion, and the bartender scrambled to call for help, his fingers fumbling over the phone like they were coated in sweat.

"Zane!" I shouted, my heart racing as I looked back at him. "We have to do something!"

In that moment, I realized I couldn't just stand by. I couldn't let fear dictate our actions. I took a deep breath, the weight of everything heavy on my shoulders, and steeled myself.

"Okay, let's go," I said, my voice firm, resolve blooming within me like a flower bursting through the cracks of concrete. Zane nodded, his expression shifting from uncertainty to determination, and together we moved toward the chaos, ready to face whatever awaited us, the world outside the bar fading into a distant memory.

As we approached the melee, a figure broke free, eyes wild, and for a heartbeat, everything froze. In that split second, I saw a flash of metal—sharp, glinting in the dim light. My breath caught in my throat, and everything around us fell away, a storm of uncertainty brewing just beyond the edge of my vision.

And then, the scream pierced through the air again, louder this time, echoing in the recesses of my mind, as I stepped closer, heart racing, bracing for the truth that awaited us on the other side of chaos.

Chapter 18: Crossing Boundaries

Every morning now, the sun filters through the sheer curtains, spilling gold onto the hardwood floors like a warm invitation. I stretch, letting the quiet hum of the city seep into my senses, the distant sound of honking cars and the murmur of life beyond my window intertwining like a gentle melody. Zane's side of the bed is a mess of sheets and blankets, evidence of our late-night chats that stretch until dawn, his laughter mingling with my sleepy murmurs as we batted around dreams like we were children tossing a ball back and forth. But beneath the comfort of our new rhythm lies an undercurrent I can't quite shake—a disquiet that flares like a misfired spark in my gut.

We had embraced social media with open arms, sharing snippets of our lives as if each post was a brushstroke in the painting of our relationship. Zane, with his effortless charm and that disarming smile that could make even the grayest day seem brighter, had become my muse. Our first concert together had morphed into a viral video of him singing a ridiculous duet with me, our voices weaving together in a hilarious cacophony that sent our followers into fits of laughter. The comments poured in, a stream of encouragement and adoration. "You two are perfect!" they wrote. "I can't get enough of your vibe!" The validation felt intoxicating, yet somewhere in that euphoria, a shadow lurked, waiting to cast doubt on our otherwise glittering facade.

One evening, I leaned back against the plush cushions of our couch, Zane perched beside me, a guitar resting in his lap. The living room was aglow with the warm light of a dozen candles, the air thick with the scent of vanilla and the soft twinkling of fairy lights strung around the window. I watched as his fingers danced over the strings, crafting a melody that seemed to echo the unspoken words dancing between us. He caught my gaze, his brow furrowed in concentration, a half-smile teasing his lips. "What's on your mind?" he asked, the playful lilt in his voice as familiar as the song he strummed.

I hesitated, contemplating whether to voice the gnawing uncertainty that had wrapped its tendrils around my heart. "Just thinking about how everything's changed," I replied, forcing a casual tone. "It's a lot to take in, you know? The music, the followers...us."

"Us?" Zane paused, his fingers stilling on the strings. "You mean in a good way, right?"

"Of course!" I chuckled, trying to lighten the mood. "You're not worried about how we look on Instagram, are you?"

A flicker of concern crossed his face before he laughed it off. "Nah, I'm just glad I get to be the lucky guy in your life. I mean, I'm an absolute star next to you."

We shared a laugh, but even as I smiled, a cold chill rippled through me. I had always prided myself on being grounded, immune to the superficial nature of social media, yet here I was, grasping for stability in a whirlwind of digital approval.

The next day, while scrolling through my notifications, a message caught my eye. It was from an anonymous account, a stark contrast to the usual supportive comments we received. "You really think Zane is in this for you? He's just using you for clout." My heart dropped as the words sunk in, their venomous bite igniting a firestorm of insecurities I had buried long ago.

I read and reread the message, the screen blurring as my vision faltered. I tried to rationalize it. Just another troll, right? Yet doubt wormed its way into my mind, a stubborn weed refusing to be uprooted.

When Zane returned from band practice, his laughter filled the room like sunlight, but it felt dimmer somehow, muted beneath the weight of my secret. I leaned against the kitchen counter, arms crossed, an invisible wall between us. "Can we talk?"

"Always," he replied, setting his guitar down, a hint of concern flickering in his eyes.

I steeled myself, pulling the phone from my pocket and turning the screen toward him. "I got this message. It's... it's not great."

He read it, his expression shifting from confusion to anger, the warmth of the room suddenly turning cold. "What the hell?"

"Do you think... do you think it's true?" I bit my lip, fighting back the tide of tears threatening to spill. "Do you see me as a stepping stone for your career?"

Zane's jaw tightened, and he stepped closer, closing the distance that felt like an ocean. "No. Absolutely not. I don't care about followers or likes. I care about you, and I thought you knew that."

The sincerity in his voice wrapped around my heart like a lifeline, yet the seed of doubt remained, its roots digging deeper. "But how can I trust that? With all this—" I gestured to the phone, to the buzzing world outside our quiet home. "It's hard not to compare, you know?"

His gaze softened, and he reached out, cupping my face in his hand. "You're not just some trophy for me, Jess. You're my partner, my friend, and the only person I want by my side. I wouldn't trade what we have for anything."

His words should have quelled my fears, but instead, they opened a floodgate of conflicting emotions. I wanted to believe him; I wanted to feel secure, but the vulnerability of our public lives made it difficult to discern truth from illusion.

As he pulled me into an embrace, warmth enveloped me, yet uncertainty coiled around my heart like a stubborn vine, refusing to let go. In that moment, I realized I was not just grappling with my insecurities; I was confronting the reality of our choices, the very foundation of what it meant to be intertwined in this unpredictable world. What if the next anonymous message shattered everything we had built? Would we have the strength to survive it together?

The weight of doubt felt like a storm cloud hanging over me, heavy and dark, as I navigated our day-to-day life with Zane. Each shared moment, once filled with warmth, now flickered like a faulty lightbulb, the glow intermittently waning beneath the shadow of that anonymous message. I tried to shake it off, but the lingering sting made everything feel slightly off-kilter, like I was living in a half-remembered dream.

The following Saturday morning, I woke to the smell of fresh coffee and the faint sound of Zane humming an unfamiliar tune. His morning rituals had taken on a new life; he brewed coffee with a flourish, danced a little while waiting for it to brew, and often whistled nonsensical melodies that made me smile. This morning, however, I felt like a ghost haunting my own life, drifting through moments without really being present.

"Good morning, sleepyhead," Zane said, glancing over his shoulder, a playful grin lighting up his face. The sunlight spilled into the kitchen, casting an ethereal glow around him, and for a moment, I lost myself in that vision. But then reality crashed back, and I blinked away the heaviness clouding my mind.

"Morning," I mumbled, forcing a smile that felt more like a mask than a genuine expression. He noticed. His brow furrowed slightly as he poured a steaming cup and set it down in front of me, the warmth radiating from the ceramic mug battling the chill in my heart.

"You look like you've seen a ghost," he said, a teasing note in his voice meant to coax me out of my funk. "Or worse, like you forgot to put on pants. Which would be quite a scandal, I must say."

"Hey, I've got pants on," I shot back, feigning indignation as I adjusted the blanket wrapped around my legs. "I just... I guess I'm still waking up."

Zane leaned against the counter, arms crossed, his eyes narrowing with playful suspicion. "You're telling me you're not brooding over that message again?"

The way he said it was lighthearted, but my heart thudded in my chest, caught between laughter and truth. "Maybe," I admitted, my voice barely above a whisper. "It just doesn't seem fair, you know? I'm trying to enjoy this. Us. And then something like that comes out of nowhere."

His playful demeanor shifted, concern settling in its place. "Look, Jess. We can't control what people say, but you know what? It doesn't matter. What matters is what we have."

"Do you really believe that?" I asked, studying his face for any hint of insincerity. "What if it's all an act for the cameras? What if it's not real?"

Zane moved closer, his warmth enveloping me as he took my hands in his. "You think I'd waste my time trying to impress anyone but you? This isn't a show for me; it's my life. Our life." His eyes locked onto mine, and the sincerity in his gaze almost melted the icy fingers of doubt clinging to my heart.

"Okay, okay. You make a valid point," I conceded, the corners of my mouth twitching upwards. "Just promise me if you ever decide to ditch me for a more famous Instagram model, you'll give me a heads up first."

"Only if you promise to take me back after my scandalous breakup," he teased, a glint of mischief lighting up his eyes. "I'd need a place to crash."

We both laughed, and for a fleeting moment, the storm clouds dissipated, revealing the blue skies of our shared laughter. But the laughter faded as the day wore on, and that gnawing uncertainty clawed back at me, persistent and insidious.

Later, we decided to hit up our favorite coffee shop, a charming little place with mismatched furniture and walls adorned with local art. As we entered, the familiar aroma of espresso enveloped us, stirring up warm memories of countless weekends spent huddled over steaming mugs, lost in conversation. I hoped this outing would provide a much-needed distraction from my restless thoughts.

"Two lattes, please," Zane ordered at the counter, his easy smile drawing the barista into a flirtatious banter that made my heart swell. I stood back, leaning against the wall, watching him with a blend of admiration and anxiety. He was magnetic, the way he moved through the world, and I couldn't help but feel the tight grip of insecurity as I wondered how I measured up.

As we settled into a corner table, Zane launched into a story about his latest band rehearsal. I listened, captivated by his passion, but my mind wandered, fixating on the unknown shadow that loomed over us. Just as I was about to respond, my phone buzzed insistently on the table, the screen lighting up with a new notification.

"Who is it?" Zane asked, his brow raised.

I hesitated, caught between wanting to share everything with him and fearing the weight of my unfiltered thoughts. "Just a message," I replied, dismissing the nagging feeling in my chest.

Curiosity danced in Zane's eyes, and I could almost hear the gears turning in his head. "Not from that account again, I hope?"

I shook my head, determined to project nonchalance. "No, it's just some group chat."

As we sipped our lattes, a playful conversation unfolded, filled with witty banter and teasing jabs. Yet, beneath the surface, the tension coiled tighter with each laugh, a silent dialogue echoing between us, rife with unspoken fears. I wanted to believe in the strength of our bond, yet I felt like I was balancing on a tightrope stretched precariously over a chasm of doubt.

After finishing our drinks, Zane suggested we take a walk in the park nearby. The sun hung low in the sky, casting long shadows as we strolled along the path, leaves crunching beneath our feet. A cool breeze rustled the trees, and for a moment, everything felt perfect, as if the universe had conspired to cocoon us in warmth and peace.

"Look at that," Zane pointed to a group of children flying kites, their laughter echoing like music. "That's pure joy right there."

I smiled, drawn into the moment, but my heart still drummed with unease. "Do you think we can be that happy? Just... without all the noise?"

Zane turned to me, his expression serious. "I think happiness is about what we make of it, not what the world tells us we should have. And I choose you, Jess. Always."

But as I leaned into him, feeling the solidness of his words, a shadow flitted across my mind, whispering doubts I couldn't quite ignore. The world around us shimmered with possibility, yet I felt anchored in place, straddling the line between love and insecurity. Would this happiness last? Could we withstand the turbulence of the outside world, or would it pull us apart?

The late afternoon sun dipped below the horizon, painting the sky in brilliant shades of orange and purple, as Zane and I meandered through the park, our fingers interlaced. It should have felt idyllic, a scene crafted for a postcard, yet the undercurrent of doubt lingered like a stubborn shadow. I could hear the laughter of the children with their kites, the echoing joy contrasting sharply with my own tumultuous thoughts. Zane, oblivious to my inner turmoil, chatted animatedly about a new song he was working on, his enthusiasm a bright flicker against my gray clouds.

"Okay, picture this," he said, his voice rising with excitement. "A ballad about love and uncertainty, with a bridge that really punches you in the gut. I want people to feel it, you know? Like they're standing right in the middle of it."

"Sounds profound, but how do you punch someone in the gut musically? Isn't that more of a physical endeavor?" I teased, a lightness sparking within me, grateful for the momentary distraction.

He laughed, the sound warm and infectious. "Well, maybe I'll throw in a dramatic pause. You know, build the tension, let them hold their breath." He paused, looking at me, his expression shifting slightly. "Just like life, right? Full of unexpected turns."

I felt the sting of that truth resonate deeply, a reminder of the unease coiling around my heart. "Yeah, full of unexpected turns." The irony tasted bitter on my tongue.

As we approached a small gazebo nestled among flowering trees, I stopped, my attention captured by a couple nestled on the bench, sharing whispers and soft kisses. It was the kind of moment I craved—an unguarded intimacy. But the sight twisted the knife of insecurity deeper. "Do you think we'll ever get to that point?" I asked, my voice barely a whisper.

Zane turned to me, his brow furrowing in thought. "What do you mean?"

"Just... that level of comfort. Where the world fades away, and it's just us. No doubts, no second-guessing."

He stepped closer, brushing a stray strand of hair behind my ear. "Jess, I can't predict the future, but I do know I want to be there with you, no matter what. We just need to trust each other."

"Trust is easier said than done," I replied, the edge of my voice betraying my simmering anxiety. "Especially when messages from trolls come out of nowhere."

"Are we really going to let some keyboard warrior dictate how we feel?" He crossed his arms, a playful glint in his eyes. "I'll make sure to put you in my next song as a 'gorgeous and witty muse who doesn't let internet drama affect her fierce heart.' How's that for a tribute?"

"Make it a rap, and I might consider it," I shot back, the tension easing slightly with our banter.

As we settled into the gazebo, the world around us softened, the distant sounds of laughter and music blending into a harmonious backdrop. Zane pulled out his guitar, fingers deftly finding the strings as he strummed a familiar tune. I watched, mesmerized by the way he lost himself in the music, his passion igniting a warmth within me.

But as the melody filled the air, a familiar unease returned, creeping back into my thoughts like an unwelcome guest. The message from the anonymous account had left a wound, and no matter how often Zane reassured me, I could feel the raw edges still there, sharp and unhealed. I glanced at him, the sunlight catching the angles of his face, and my heart twisted with conflicting emotions.

"Can I ask you something?" I ventured, the question tumbling out before I could stop myself.

"Anything," he said, pausing mid-strum to focus his attention on me.

"Do you ever worry that we're just living in a fairy tale? That once the reality sets in, it might crumble?"

Zane frowned, a flicker of confusion dancing in his eyes. "Jess, fairy tales are great for kids. We're creating our own story, and stories have ups and downs. They're messy and real."

"Right, messy and real," I echoed, trying to convince myself. "But what if the messiness makes it all fall apart?"

He leaned in closer, his sincerity overwhelming. "It won't. Because I'm not going anywhere. I'm right here, with you, dealing with all the mess together."

As he spoke, I felt my resolve waver, the warmth of his words wrapping around me like a blanket. But the nagging voice in the back of my mind remained stubborn. Would our shared moments hold up against the whispers of doubt that lingered like unwelcome specters?

Suddenly, my phone buzzed again, the vibration cutting through our intimate moment. I glanced down, my stomach dropping as I saw another notification from that anonymous account. My heart raced, fingers trembling as I tapped to open it. The words blurred as my anxiety heightened. "You're too good to be true. Bet he'll find someone better when he realizes it."

The words hung in the air, heavy and suffocating. I felt Zane's eyes on me, concern etching into his features as he reached for my hand. "What is it?" he asked, voice steady yet laced with worry.

"Just... another message," I muttered, trying to sound nonchalant, but the quiver in my voice betrayed me.

He leaned closer, peering at my screen, and his expression darkened as he read the message. "What the hell? Who even sends this stuff?"

"I don't know," I whispered, my heart racing. "But it feels like it's getting worse."

Zane clenched his jaw, his fingers tightening around mine. "We can't let this get to us, Jess. It's just noise."

I wanted to believe him, wanted to embrace his confidence, but the words gnawed at me, a relentless itch that refused to fade. The pressure of maintaining our public image felt like a suffocating weight, pushing me closer to the edge.

"I can't ignore it, Zane. What if there's some truth in it?" My voice quivered, a cocktail of fear and vulnerability spilling over.

He squeezed my hand, a grounding presence in the storm swirling inside me. "We're better than this. You're better than this. Look at what we have, what we've built. Don't let some cowardly voice in the dark steal that from us."

I wanted to fight back, to shake off the nagging voice whispering doubts into my ear, but as I looked into Zane's eyes, something shifted. A flicker of determination ignited in me, a spark pushing back against the darkness. "You're right. We won't let this tear us apart."

His face lit up with pride, but the moment was short-lived as a commotion erupted in the park. A group of people clustered around a small stage nearby, and I strained to hear the source of the ruckus. "What's happening?" I asked, curiosity piqued.

Zane turned to look as well, eyebrows raised. "Let's check it out!"

As we walked toward the crowd, I felt a sense of hope blooming in my chest, a reminder that life was still full of surprises. The air buzzed with excitement as we drew closer, anticipation crackling between us like electricity.

Suddenly, the crowd erupted in cheers, and I caught a glimpse of a familiar face on the stage—someone from our past. My breath caught in my throat, heart racing as I realized who it was.

"What the—" Zane began, but I was already stepping forward, propelled by a mix of shock and disbelief. The last thing I expected to see was my ex, Noah, taking the stage with a confident swagger, guitar in hand, looking every bit the rock star he always thought he could be.

A hush fell over the crowd, and as the spotlight illuminated his face, I felt the ground shift beneath my feet. My heart raced, the tension rising to a boiling point, and for a moment, everything else faded away. Would Zane's unwavering trust survive this unexpected twist? Would my own insecurities rise to the surface once more? In that moment, nothing felt certain anymore.

Chapter 19: The Fractured Melody

The dim light of the studio cast elongated shadows on the walls, shapes that danced and flickered like the fleeting thoughts in my mind. I paced back and forth, heart pounding against my ribs like a restless caged animal. Each footfall echoed in the cavernous space, a metronome marking the seconds of my spiraling anxiety. The walls, adorned with soundproofing panels, were a tapestry of my worst fears, and the music—a cruel, mocking melody that twisted in my ears—was now a cacophony of my own self-doubt.

"Can we take it from the top?" I snapped, frustration bubbling over like a pot left too long on the stove. The engineers exchanged furtive glances, their faces illuminated by the glow of their screens, and I felt my cheeks burn under the weight of their scrutiny. I could almost hear the whispers, could feel the judgment settling around me like a thick fog. My hands trembled, not from fatigue, but from the mounting pressure of expectations I had placed upon myself. The music, once my sanctuary, now felt like a vice, squeezing tighter with each passing day.

"Emily, it's fine," Zane interjected, his voice a low, soothing cadence that used to wrap around me like a warm blanket. He stood a few steps away, his brow furrowed with concern. The man was a paradox—his easy smile and effortless charm could lift the darkest of moods, yet here we were, trapped in a tempest of our own making. I met his gaze, and for a moment, all I could see was the chasm that had formed between us, vast and unsettling.

"I said from the top!" I barked again, a desperate attempt to mask the vulnerability creeping into my tone. The team shuffled awkwardly, the air thick with unsaid words. Zane's shoulders slumped slightly, and I cursed myself for it. This was not how I wanted to behave—not towards him, not in front of the team that had worked tirelessly to turn our shared dreams into tangible sound.

"We can take a breather," he suggested, stepping closer, the warmth of his presence a stark contrast to my icy demeanor. "Just breathe, Em."

"Breathing doesn't fix anything!" I shot back, each syllable laced with pent-up anger. "I'm tired of pretending everything's okay when it clearly isn't." The outburst felt like a release, but also a fracture—an irreparable crack in the fragile structure we had built together.

"Okay," he said, his voice steady, but I could see the hurt flash across his features. "But pushing everyone away won't help either. We're all in this together."

My heart sank at his words. Zane had always been the anchor in my tempestuous sea of emotions, but the more he tried to pull me back, the harder I fought against it. I took a deep breath, feeling the weight of my own stubbornness pressing down like a lead blanket.

"Why can't you just understand? I can't keep doing this!" I felt the walls closing in, the air heavy with unshed tears and unspoken fears. "I can't keep pretending everything's fine when I'm falling apart inside."

"Then don't pretend," Zane replied softly, stepping closer, his voice an invitation rather than an accusation. "Just be honest with me. You don't have to shoulder this alone."

His words hung in the air, a thread connecting us, but I was too tangled in my emotions to see it. I shook my head, the refusal bitter on my tongue. "I'm scared, Zane. Scared that if I let you in, I'll only push you away. That I'll ruin everything."

His expression softened, the lines of frustration and concern giving way to something more profound—understanding. "Emily, you're not going to ruin anything. But you're right about one thing; this isn't just about you anymore. We're a team. We need to communicate."

My chest ached at the truth in his words, a tightness that felt all too familiar. The music had always been a refuge for me, a way to express the things I couldn't say, but now it felt like it was drowning me instead. I had hidden my fears behind melodies and harmonies, but the façade was cracking, revealing the chaos underneath.

With a heavy sigh, I dropped my gaze, staring at the control panel like it held the answers to my myriad questions. "I just don't know how to fix this. It feels like the melody we're trying to create is fractured, and I don't know how to piece it back together."

Zane stepped closer, the warmth radiating from him like a beacon in my darkness. "Sometimes, the most beautiful music comes from the broken pieces, Emily. It's about finding the right way to stitch them together."

There it was again—the way he had of turning my doubts into hope, of weaving a thread of optimism through the tangle of my despair. I felt my defenses lowering, a slight crack in my emotional armor, but the fear still clung to me like a stubborn shadow.

"What if I can't?" I whispered, vulnerability cracking my voice. The words tasted like ash on my tongue, a bitter reminder of all the times I had failed before.

Zane reached out, brushing his fingers against my arm, a gesture both gentle and grounding. "Then we'll figure it out together. That's the beauty of collaboration—when one of us stumbles, the other is there to catch them."

I met his gaze, the sincerity in his eyes a lifeline pulling me back from the precipice. It was in that moment that I realized how far we had come, how much we had built together, and the thought of letting that slip away sent a fresh wave of panic crashing over me. But there was also a flicker of determination igniting within, urging me to fight for the bond we had nurtured.

As the music resumed, I took a deep breath, allowing the notes to wash over me, each one a reminder of the journey we had embarked on. Perhaps it was time to embrace the fractures instead of fearing them, to turn the dissonance into something beautiful. I would not let the shadows consume me, not when I had Zane by my side, ready to navigate the complexities of the melody we were meant to create.

The next morning greeted me with a heavy overcast sky, its gloom mirroring the turmoil that clung to my chest like a persistent ache. As I stumbled out of bed, the echoes of last night's confrontation replayed in my mind, each sharp word cutting deeper than the last. I made my way to the kitchen, the faint aroma of burnt toast wafting through the air like a ghost of my culinary attempts. Not that I could complain much; my culinary skills were as hit-or-miss as my emotional stability these days.

I flipped the switch on the coffee maker, the machine sputtering to life as I leaned against the counter, willing the caffeine to perform its magic. My gaze drifted to the window, where droplets of rain began to cascade down the glass like tiny tears. I knew Zane would be waiting at the studio, ready to dive into our next session, and the thought sent a fresh wave of anxiety crashing over me. What could I possibly say? Sorry? That felt utterly inadequate.

The coffee pot gurgled, and I poured myself a cup, its dark richness a small comfort as I took a tentative sip. My phone buzzed on the counter, a reminder of the messages I had avoided. I picked it up, half-expecting another message from Zane, but instead, it was from my sister. Her words were light and filled with random trivia about the benefits of singing in the shower—a topic that, frankly, had lost its charm in my world. "Singing helps release stress, you know!" she texted.

Rolling my eyes, I couldn't help but chuckle softly. Maybe my sister had a point; there was a time when singing was my escape, a way to drown out the noise of the world. Yet now, it felt more like a chore, a reminder of everything I was struggling to hold together. I replied with a thumbs-up emoji, then made my way to the studio, the rain tapping a soft rhythm against my windshield.

Arriving at the studio felt like stepping into a pressure cooker. The moment I walked through the door, I could sense the atmosphere shift. The team was huddled around the soundboard, their murmurs fading as they turned to me, the unspoken tension crackling in the air. Zane stood slightly apart, arms crossed, his expression a mix of concern and determination. I felt a pit form in my stomach, a familiar unease settling in as I faced the very people I had snapped at just the night before.

"Hey," I said, my voice barely above a whisper, trying to sound casual, though I knew I wasn't fooling anyone.

"Good morning, Emily," Zane replied, his tone cool, his gaze lingering on mine longer than necessary. There was a weight to his words, a hint of disappointment that made my stomach churn.

"Sorry about yesterday," I ventured, clinging to the hope that an apology would begin to patch the rift I had created. "I didn't mean to take it out on you all."

"Apology accepted, but let's focus on the music," he said, his smile not quite reaching his eyes. The dismissal stung, and I could feel the walls closing in again, the suffocating silence wrapping around me like a noose.

"Right," I said, forcing the words out. "Let's do that."

As we settled into our seats, I felt the tension hovering in the air like a storm waiting to break. I shifted my focus to the microphone, trying to channel the emotions swirling inside me into the notes I was about to sing. The music began, a gentle strumming of the guitar, but the melody felt hollow, a ghost of what it could be.

"More passion, Emily," one of the engineers called out, his voice laced with impatience. "We need to feel it."

I nodded, but it felt like a flimsy bandage over a gaping wound. "I'm trying," I bit out, frustration seeping into my voice again.

"Trying isn't good enough!" he snapped back. "If you want this to work, you need to dig deeper."

And there it was—the perfect storm brewing, the rising tide of my emotions threatening to break through the carefully constructed dam I had built around my heart. I could feel Zane's eyes on me, but instead of finding solace in his gaze, it felt like he was waiting for me to falter again.

"Can we take a break?" I blurted out, the words spilling from my mouth before I could stop them. The room fell silent, all eyes on me, and I felt my cheeks burn.

"Emily, we're on a tight schedule," Zane began, but I cut him off, desperate to regain some semblance of control.

"I need a minute!" I snapped, the frustration bubbling over. "You don't get it! This is—"

"Emily!" Zane's voice was firm, cutting through my spiraling thoughts. "You can't keep pushing us away. We're all in this together."

A sharp retort was on the tip of my tongue, but something in his tone made me hesitate. I could hear the hurt behind his words, the undercurrent of his own frustrations mingling with mine. I ran a hand through my hair, exhaling deeply, the weight of my emotions pressing down like a physical burden.

"I just... I'm trying to keep it together," I said, my voice trembling slightly. "And it feels like everything is falling apart."

"Then let us help you," Zane replied, his eyes softening. "That's what we're here for."

The sincerity in his voice cracked the walls I had been building, and I felt the tears prick at the corners of my eyes. I blinked rapidly, refusing to let them spill over. "I'm scared, Zane. I'm scared of messing this up. Scared of letting you all down."

He stepped closer, bridging the gap between us, and the warmth radiating from him was a balm to my frayed nerves. "You're not going to let anyone down. We're here to catch you when you fall."

A lump formed in my throat, the weight of his words sinking in. Maybe this wasn't just about the music; maybe it was about trust, about allowing myself to lean on others instead of bearing the burden alone.

I took a deep breath, feeling the storm inside me begin to settle, just a little. "Okay," I whispered. "Let's try again."

As I took my place at the microphone, I felt the energy shift in the room, a collective inhale as we prepared to dive back into the music. With Zane's unwavering support beside me, I was ready to confront my fears, ready to transform the fractured melody into something beautiful. The notes began to flow again, a delicate weave of harmony and vulnerability, and for the first time in days, I felt a glimmer of hope dancing on the edges of my heart.

The music swelled around me, wrapping me in its embrace, as I surrendered to the familiar rhythm. Zane's presence at my side was a grounding force, a reminder that I wasn't alone in this chaotic world. The first notes shimmered in the air, each one a tentative step toward rebuilding what had felt broken. The guitar strummed softly, weaving a tapestry of sound that filled the studio with warmth. I focused on the melody, letting it wash over me, cleansing the remnants of my fear and doubt.

"See? There's that spark," Zane murmured as I finished the first line, his eyes gleaming with encouragement.

"Maybe I just needed a little kick in the pants," I said, managing a small smile despite the lingering weight in my chest.

He chuckled, the sound rich and inviting, and I felt a flicker of something hopeful in the air. "Or maybe you needed to realize that nobody expects you to be perfect. Just be you."

"Easier said than done," I replied, the words escaping me before I could catch them. My voice dipped, vulnerability sneaking in, and I watched as Zane's expression shifted, a seriousness settling over him.

"Being you is more than enough, Emily," he said firmly. "You're the heart of this project."

His words sparked something deep within me, a resilience that had lain dormant under layers of self-doubt. The music surged again, and this time, I poured every ounce of feeling into the lyrics, letting them carry my story, my fears, my triumphs. Each note felt like a step toward liberation, a reclamation of the passion that had drawn me to this path in the first place.

The session flowed seamlessly, and with every take, I felt the tension among the team dissipate like fog under the rising sun. Laughter punctuated the air, a welcome sound that began to stitch together the fractures we had all been grappling with. It was as if the music was weaving us back together, note by note, creating a harmony that resonated not just in the studio but in our hearts.

"Okay, let's take five," one of the engineers called out, breaking the spell. I leaned back in my chair, panting slightly, exhilaration and exhaustion colliding within me. Zane approached, a triumphant grin lighting up his face.

"See? You've got this," he said, taking a seat beside me. "You really came alive in that last take."

"Thanks to you," I replied, my heart swelling with gratitude. "I wouldn't have gotten here without your... well, being you."

His laughter rang out, infectious and bright. "You're gonna make me blush."

"Good, you deserve it. Blushing Zane is a rare sight," I teased, nudging him playfully.

But as the laughter faded, a silence fell between us, thick with unspoken thoughts. I caught a flicker of something serious in his eyes, a moment of vulnerability that mirrored my own. "Emily, I—"

Before he could finish, the studio door swung open, and in walked Alex, our producer, with a look of urgency on his face. The energy shifted immediately, the lightness replaced with an undercurrent of tension. "Guys, we need to talk. Now."

My heart sank, unease prickling at the back of my mind. "What's wrong?" I asked, instantly wary of the shift in atmosphere.

"We've got a problem," Alex said, his tone clipped. "The label is unhappy with the direction of the project."

"What do you mean?" Zane asked, leaning forward, his earlier lightness vanishing.

"They're saying the sound isn't commercial enough. They want us to rethink the entire thing—more hooks, less soul," Alex explained, shaking his head in frustration. "And they want it done yesterday."

I felt a sharp pang of disappointment, as if someone had ripped the joy from my chest and tossed it aside. "You can't be serious," I blurted out, disbelief flooding my senses. "We've poured everything into this. It's about authenticity."

"I know," Alex replied, his voice tinged with irritation. "But they hold the purse strings, and if we don't deliver, we're toast."

A heaviness settled over us, the team exchanging worried glances. The very essence of what we were trying to create was now under threat, and the walls felt like they were closing in again. I glanced at Zane, searching for his reassurance, but his expression mirrored my own unease, a mix of determination and concern.

"So, what do we do?" I asked, my voice barely above a whisper, the air thick with uncertainty.

"We either compromise or face the consequences," Alex said, a note of finality in his tone that made my stomach churn. "I'm not sure we have the luxury of time."

"Compromise?" Zane echoed, incredulity evident in his voice. "We're not here to make something that sounds like everything else out there. We need to stay true to what we believe in."

Alex's face hardened, frustration evident. "You know it's not that simple. This is a business. If we don't play by their rules, we won't have a project at all."

The tension mounted, a palpable force that pulled at the edges of my sanity. "So, we just bend to their will? Change everything we've worked for?" My voice rose, each word laced with disbelief and indignation.

"I'm not saying it's easy," Alex countered, but the resolve in his eyes faltered. "But if we want this to go anywhere, we need to think strategically."

A silence enveloped us, heavy with the weight of his words. The realization settled in like a cold fog—our dreams were now intertwined with the demands of the industry, and I could feel the fragile threads of our passion fraying before my eyes.

"What if we... don't?" I ventured, my heart racing at the idea. "What if we take a stand? Create something real and authentic, even if it doesn't fit their mold?"

Zane's gaze locked onto mine, and in that moment, I saw a flicker of agreement in his eyes. "That's what I've been saying. We owe it to ourselves and to our art to fight for what we believe in."

Alex opened his mouth, likely to argue, but the fire in my heart surged. "What's the point of chasing after success if we have to sacrifice who we are? Let's show them what we can do, even if it's a risk."

"Are you both out of your minds?" Alex shot back, disbelief etched across his features. "You're talking about throwing away everything we've worked for!"

"Maybe what we've worked for isn't enough," Zane said quietly, a steely determination settling over him. "Maybe it's time to make something that's worth it."

The challenge hung in the air, electric and charged, and for a moment, I felt the rush of possibility flickering to life. But as Alex opened his mouth to respond, the studio's door swung open once more, and a tall figure stepped inside, soaking wet from the rain outside, their expression a mixture of urgency and dread.

"Guys, you need to see this. It's about the label..."

The words hung in the air, heavy with implications, and my heart raced. What new crisis awaited us? As the door swung shut behind them, sealing us in, I felt the tension tighten around us like a noose, and an unsettling feeling settled deep in my gut. Whatever was about to unfold could change everything.

Chapter 20: Shattered Reflections

The morning light filters through my bedroom window, illuminating the remnants of last night's arguments. Zane's absence is a void that deepens my sense of loneliness, echoing the turmoil I feel inside. As I scroll through social media, I come across a video of Zane performing at a benefit concert without me. My heart sinks as I watch him shine on stage, his effortless charm captivating the audience while I remain on the sidelines, feeling like a ghost in my own life. The ache of separation lingers, and I realize that I've allowed fear to drive a wedge between us. It's time to face my insecurities and reclaim the connection we once had.

The sun spills into the room, casting golden shadows that dance across the floor like fleeting memories. I catch a glimpse of my reflection in the mirror—tousled hair framing my face, eyes rimmed with the evidence of sleepless nights. I almost laugh at the sight; I look like a poster child for emotional upheaval. The remnants of last night's mascara smudge tell the story of tears that fell freely, a river of regrets I can't seem to cross. My phone buzzes, and I glance at the screen, half-hoping to see Zane's name flashing back at me. Instead, it's a notification from a friend about brunch plans. I consider it briefly, then shake my head, dismissing the idea like an unwelcome intruder. I can't bear the thought of forced smiles and small talk when my heart feels like it's being squeezed in a vice.

The day stretches ahead, an unwritten script filled with possibilities, yet I remain tethered to the past. The weight of silence lingers in the air, a tangible presence that wraps around me like a heavy cloak. I push myself off the bed, the floor cold against my feet, and shuffle toward the kitchen. The aroma of freshly brewed coffee greets me, offering a momentary distraction from the chaos swirling in my mind. I fill a mug, the warmth of the ceramic grounding me as I take a sip, letting the bitterness wash over my tongue, a stark contrast to the sweetness I crave in my life.

My thoughts drift back to Zane, to the laughter that once filled our shared moments like bubbles in champagne, effervescent and joyous. The memory of his smile, that goofy, infectious grin, tugs at my heart. I can almost hear his voice teasing me about my coffee addiction, how I'd turn into a jittery squirrel after just one cup too many. The laughter that used to roll effortlessly between us feels like a distant melody, a tune I can barely remember. I miss him, and the ache intensifies.

As I stand in the kitchen, my gaze lands on the small whiteboard we had hung above the counter. It was meant to be a space for notes, grocery lists, and reminders, but it had turned into a canvas of our dreams—concert dates circled in excitement, a vacation we had half-planned, even doodles of our future that seemed so vividly real back then. Now, it looks like a graveyard of forgotten aspirations. I grab a dry-erase marker, the scent of the ink filling my nostrils as I sketch a little heart in the corner. A small gesture, but it feels like a promise to myself to put effort into fixing what feels broken.

With determination bubbling beneath the surface, I decide to venture out, the idea of being trapped in my own thoughts suffocating. I throw on a light jacket over my pajamas, the fabric soft against my skin, and step outside into the crisp air. The world outside is alive with the morning hustle, the sound of distant laughter, cars honking, and the chirping of birds making their morning declarations. I stroll down the tree-lined street, the leaves painted in hues of orange and gold, nature's canvas reminding me that change, though often painful, can also be beautiful.

As I walk, I spot the local park—a vibrant patch of green where families gather, children's laughter ringing like music. I find a bench under a sprawling oak tree, its branches sheltering me like a protective embrace. I settle down, the wood cool beneath me, and let my mind wander. The chaos of my thoughts begins to ebb, replaced by a sense of clarity. I pull out my phone, the screen illuminating the details of Zane's concert. Each comment, each cheer from the crowd cuts deeper, a reminder of my absence. The reality is sharp, the pang of jealousy intertwining with admiration for his talent.

"Who knew Zane was such a heartthrob?" a voice interrupts my thoughts, playful yet sharp. I look up to see Jenna, my best friend, her blonde curls bouncing as she approaches. She plops down next to me without invitation, a half-smirk playing on her lips. "You look like you just survived a zombie apocalypse. Coffee and a day in the park didn't work its magic?"

"Maybe I'm the zombie," I reply, forcing a grin. "I'm just here, trying to reclaim my humanity one cup of coffee at a time."

"Let me guess—Zane?" she asks, her tone shifting from teasing to sympathetic.

"Always Zane." I sigh, the weight of the conversation hanging between us like a thick fog. "He was brilliant last night, and I wasn't there. I feel like I'm watching him from behind a glass wall, you know? Like I'm just... existing in his shadow."

Jenna rolls her eyes, ever the pragmatist. "You're not just existing. You're his partner, not his sidekick. You need to remind him of that."

"Easier said than done." I kick at a fallen leaf, sending it spiraling into the air. "I don't want to be the one dragging him down. What if he's better off without me?"

"Stop right there," she cuts in, her voice firm. "You're not dragging anyone down. You're both in this together. You need to talk it out. He can't read your mind, even if he is a rockstar."

"Rockstar," I repeat, the word rolling off my tongue like a bittersweet taste. "More like a distant star, and I'm just stuck on Earth trying to find a way to orbit him again."

"Well, maybe it's time to launch yourself into the stratosphere," Jenna suggests, her eyes sparkling with mischief. "Or, you know, send him a text, a bold one. Something like, 'Hey, I miss you. Let's talk.' No pressure, just a reminder that you're still in the same galaxy."

I contemplate her words, the tension in my chest easing just a fraction. Perhaps it's time to shatter the silence, to break through the glass wall I've built around myself. My heart races at the thought, anticipation mingling with fear, a cocktail of vulnerability that's both intoxicating and terrifying.

"Alright," I say, a sense of resolve washing over me. "I'll text him."

"Now we're talking," Jenna replies, her excitement bubbling over. "And if he doesn't respond, we'll unleash the ultimate friend strategy: ice cream and a rom-com marathon."

I can't help but laugh, the sound lightening the weight on my shoulders. Perhaps the day wasn't lost after all. With Jenna by my side and a flicker of hope igniting within me, I pull out my phone, ready to take the first step toward bridging the distance between Zane and me.

The moment I hit send on the text, my heart does a little flip, a tightrope act teetering between hope and dread. Jenna glances at me, her eyebrows raised, waiting for a reaction. "There it is! The digital carrier pigeon has taken flight," she teases, nudging my arm. "Now, we wait."

"Or we distract ourselves with overpriced pastries," I counter, an idea forming in my mind as the coffee buzz fades into the background. "Let's go to that new bakery around the corner. I hear they have croissants that might just change my life."

Jenna's eyes light up with delight, and she stands up, brushing imaginary crumbs off her jeans. "Croissants? Count me in! Plus, a good buttery pastry is the perfect armor for emotional turmoil. It's basically a hug in dough form."

As we stroll down the street, the early autumn air wraps around us, crisp with a hint of impending frost, a breath of freshness that invigorates my spirits. The city is alive, colors bursting from every corner—children laughing as they chase fallen leaves, their breath puffing out like tiny clouds; couples strolled hand in hand, their whispers lost among the chatter of the bustling morning. I feel a surge of warmth at the sights, yet an undercurrent of anxiety ripples through me as I wonder how Zane is managing his whirlwind life without me.

"I swear, if you see a pumpkin spice latte on the menu, we're getting it," Jenna declares, her pace quickening as we approach the bakery. "It's basically the law of autumn."

I chuckle, shaking my head. "How is it you can crave that stuff? It's like drinking a dessert that's also trying to be coffee. But hey, if it brings you joy, who am I to judge?"

The bakery stands before us, a quaint little shop with a whimsical sign swinging in the breeze. The scent of warm bread and sweet pastries wafts through the door as we step inside, my senses flooded with the promise of indulgence. My mouth waters as I scan the glass cases filled with treats—golden croissants, plump danishes, and cakes that seem to smile with sugar-coated glee.

"I'm telling you, they've got to have some kind of secret ingredient," Jenna says, eyeing a massive cinnamon roll with unabashed greed. "Maybe it's the tears of joy from every customer."

"Or butter—lots of butter," I reply, stepping up to the counter, where a cheerful barista greets us with a warm smile. I order the croissant and a simple black coffee, letting the comforting ritual ground me. Jenna orders an entire pastry platter as if we're hosting a brunch party for a dozen.

"Priorities," she grins as we find a cozy spot by the window, sunlight streaming in like a spotlight on our little moment of happiness.

As we dig in, the flaky pastry crumbles delightfully in my hands, and the taste is nothing short of divine. I can't help but let out a satisfied hum, the stress from earlier beginning to melt away with each bite. "Okay, you win. This is a life-changer," I admit, my voice muffled by a mouthful of croissant.

Jenna laughs, and I feel the familiar ease between us, the laughter smoothing over the rough edges of my thoughts. "So, what's next on your agenda for world domination?" she asks, tilting her head thoughtfully. "Rekindling the romance? Starting a bakery? Launching a space program?"

"Let's not get carried away," I say, savoring another bite. "I think I'll start with texting Zane back if he replies. I mean, I need to get my head straight before I can launch any missions."

Just then, my phone buzzes, vibrating against the table like a heartbeat. I snatch it up, half-expecting a standard reply, but my breath catches as I read Zane's name lighting up the screen. A quick glance reveals a simple message: "Hey! Miss you. Can we talk?"

My heart races, a mix of excitement and anxiety swirling within me. I can't help but smile, the words acting like a lifeline, pulling me back from the edge of despair. "He texted back," I whisper, disbelief mingling with joy.

"See? Told you! Now you have to respond. Use your best flirty emoji." Jenna nudges me, her eyes sparkling with encouragement.

I hesitate, my fingers hovering over the keyboard as I type and delete several responses, each one feeling too mundane or too exposed. After a moment, I settle on something simple but heartfelt: "I miss you too. Can we meet? I need to see you."

Before I hit send, I add a playful emoji—a little heart that feels like a timid offering of affection. I watch as the message zips into the ether, a small piece of my heart attached to it. The seconds tick by as I sit there, waiting for his response, an impatient rhythm echoing in my mind.

"You're going to turn into a statue if you keep staring at that phone," Jenna remarks, slapping her palm lightly on the table. "Just remember, he's probably as anxious as you are."

Just as the words leave her lips, my phone buzzes again. I fumble to grab it, my stomach doing a backflip as I see his reply: "Let's meet at the park in an hour? I'll bring coffee."

The world feels alive again, a burst of color flooding my senses as I nod, unable to contain my excitement. "It's happening! We're meeting! Oh my gosh, this is so nerve-wracking."

"Good! A little nervous energy will do you wonders," Jenna replies, her expression turning serious for a moment. "Just be honest with him, alright? Tell him what's been going on in your head. No more hiding behind texts or silence."

"I will. I promise." I take a deep breath, the weight of Jenna's encouragement settling in. "You're right. No more ghosts in my own life."

We finish our pastries, laughter filling the air as we plan for all the ways I could potentially sabotage my upcoming conversation with Zane. It feels refreshing, like a new beginning, and I can almost see the potential in it—a connection reborn, the shattering of the glass wall I've built.

After our feast, I head home to prepare. The walk back feels different, the sunlight warmer against my skin, the air sweeter. My thoughts swirl around Zane and the possibilities of what this conversation could mean. A million scenarios play out in my mind, from the tender moments to the uncomfortable silences, each one filled with a mixture of hope and fear.

As I arrive home, I take a moment to collect myself. The reflection in the hallway mirror greets me with a questioning glance. I straighten my shoulders, smoothing down my shirt as if I can iron out the wrinkles of doubt clinging to me. It's time to shed this lingering fear and face the person I've been avoiding—the one staring back at me with a mixture of excitement and trepidation.

Dressed simply but with purpose, I throw on my favorite cardigan, a cozy reminder of our shared moments, and step outside, feeling a surge of bravery coursing through me. Today is not just about reconnecting with Zane; it's about reclaiming myself, one conversation at a time.

The park blooms with life as I make my way to our meeting spot, the sun high in the sky and the air humming with the sounds of laughter and distant music. Children dart about, their playful shouts punctuating the serene backdrop, while couples lounge on blankets, sharing whispered secrets over picnics. I find myself caught in the bittersweet tapestry of it all, the vibrant energy reminding me of what Zane and I once shared—those carefree moments woven into the fabric of our relationship.

I glance at my phone again, the screen still glowing with Zane's last message, the anticipation coiling tighter in my stomach. With each step, the weight of our distance feels a little lighter, as if the sunshine has seeped into the cracks of my uncertainty. I catch sight of him under the sprawling branches of a nearby oak, his figure leaning against the trunk, a coffee cup cradled in one hand. He looks up, and for a moment, our eyes lock, a silent conversation flickering between us. That familiar grin spreads across his face, and my heart does an involuntary somersault.

"Hey!" Zane calls, pushing off the tree with an ease that seems to defy the tension hanging in the air. "You made it!" His voice is like a melody, resonating deep within me, awakening feelings I thought I'd buried.

"Of course! I wouldn't miss our chance to discuss your sudden rise to stardom," I reply, adopting a playful tone, though my heart races in response to the seriousness underlying our reunion. I move closer, the warmth of his presence beckoning me like a moth to a flame.

"I promise not to let it go to my head," he retorts, his eyes sparkling with mischief. He gestures to the bench beside him, and I sit down, the familiar creak of the wood grounding me. "How've you been?"

"Honestly? A little lost," I admit, my voice dropping slightly. "But I'm trying to find my way back."

Zane nods, the smile fading just a fraction as he takes a sip from his cup, the steam curling up like the lingering tension between us. "I've missed you. The stage isn't the same without my biggest fan cheering me on."

"Or glaring at you for not sending me a ticket," I tease, trying to lighten the mood, but the heaviness returns almost immediately. "I saw the video. You were amazing. It looked like the crowd was loving it."

"Thanks, but it was hard not having you there," he confesses, his gaze shifting to the ground, the vulnerability raw and palpable. "I felt your absence, like an echo I couldn't ignore."

An awkward silence settles between us, thick enough to cut, and I can feel the weight of my own words pressing down. "We need to talk about what happened," I say finally, my heart thumping in my chest like a war drum.

"Yeah, I think we do," he replies, his voice steady but low. "I don't want to dance around it anymore." He looks up, meeting my gaze, and I see a flicker of hope and uncertainty mingling in his eyes.

"Can we be honest? Because I've been a mess lately," I start, the floodgates opening as emotions surge forth. "I let my fears get the better of me, and I pushed you away instead of reaching out."

He leans forward, his expression serious. "You're not the only one. I felt like I was losing you, and instead of talking about it, I threw myself into work. It was easier than dealing with the discomfort."

A chuckle escapes my lips, bitter but real. "Isn't that just classic us? Running away instead of facing the music."

Zane laughs softly, the sound mingling with the gentle breeze rustling through the leaves. "Music is kind of my thing. But yeah, we need to change that. What do we do next?"

Before I can respond, a sudden commotion erupts a few yards away. A group of teenagers has gathered, their voices rising in excitement as they point toward the pond. "Is that a goose?" one of them shouts, while another insists it's a swan. Zane and I exchange amused glances, the laughter bridging the gap that had felt insurmountable just moments ago.

"Only in this park would a feathered creature cause such a stir," he jokes, and we both turn to watch the unfolding drama.

"Honestly, if it's a swan, it might just be the most glamorous goose I've ever seen," I quip, feeling the tension ease just a bit more.

The hilarity is short-lived. As we chuckle, a shadow crosses over us, and my heart drops as I look up to see a figure approaching—a woman with striking red hair, her expression fierce and determined. I recognize her immediately, a wave of unease crashing over me. It's Marissa, Zane's ex-girlfriend.

"What a lovely reunion," she says, her voice dripping with sarcasm as she eyes us both with an intensity that makes me feel exposed. "I didn't realize we were having a love fest here in the park."

Zane's posture shifts, a flicker of discomfort washing over him. "Marissa, what are you doing here?" he asks, his tone steady but laced with confusion.

"I could ask you the same thing. I thought we were done playing games." She crosses her arms, her gaze darting between us, an uninvited storm cloud hovering over our sunny moment.

"Games? This isn't a game, Marissa," he replies, his voice firm. "This is about us figuring things out."

"And what's that supposed to mean?" she shoots back, her frustration palpable. "Didn't you just perform at a concert? Maybe you should be focused on that instead of whatever this is." She gestures toward me, a flicker of possessiveness in her eyes.

My heart races, the earlier warmth evaporating into an icy dread. The tension in the air thickens as Zane shifts in his seat, the uncertainty flooding back like an unwelcome tide. "This isn't how I wanted things to go," he admits, his voice strained.

"What are you going to do, Zane?" Marissa presses, her tone almost pleading but edged with a sharpness that feels like a knife. "Are you really going to throw everything away for her?"

The words hang between us like a guillotine, and I can feel my breath hitching in my throat, the fear gnawing at my insides. I look at Zane, searching his face for a clue, for some sign of what he's thinking, but he's caught in the crossfire of his past and present, his expression a mix of regret and frustration.

"Marissa, this isn't fair," he starts, but she cuts him off, stepping closer, the air crackling with unresolved emotions.

"Is it fair to her? Is it fair to me?" she demands, her voice rising. "You can't just play with people's hearts like they're your songs!"

The world around us fades as I hold my breath, my heart racing. The laughter of the children, the rustling of the leaves—all of it feels like a distant memory as I brace for what's coming next. This isn't how I envisioned our conversation would unfold, and as the tension escalates, I can feel the ground shifting beneath me.

Zane glances at me, his eyes searching for reassurance, but all I can muster is a nod, a silent plea for clarity. "I need to figure this out," he finally says, his voice cutting through the storm. "And I can't do that while being pulled in two different directions."

Marissa's expression hardens, her lips pursed as if she's weighing her options. "You're going to choose? Just like that?"

The question hangs heavy in the air, and I hold my breath, the reality of the moment crashing down around us. Zane is at a crossroads, and everything I thought we had built feels precarious, teetering on the edge of an uncertain fate.

As silence envelops us, my heart races, anticipation lacing every moment. I glance at Zane, my emotions a whirlpool of hope and fear.

"What happens next?" I whisper, barely able to voice the thought echoing in my mind.

He opens his mouth to speak, but before he can form the words, a loud crash echoes from the pond, a startled goose flapping its wings, sending the teens into a fit of laughter. The moment feels surreal, the levity contrasting sharply with the tension that holds us captive. Zane's eyes dart to mine, a myriad of emotions flickering there, and in that instant, everything hangs in the balance.

Just as he takes a breath to respond, my phone buzzes again—an incoming call from someone I never expected. My heart drops as I see the name on the screen, the implications of the call suddenly looming large, overshadowing everything else.

And then everything changes.

Chapter 21: A Song for Healing

The studio was a sanctuary, a haven where melodies danced like sunlight on water. Shelves lined with vintage vinyl records towered over me, their spines worn and familiar. The smell of freshly brewed coffee hung in the air, mingling with the lingering scent of pine from the wooden beams overhead. I let my fingers glide over the piano keys, coaxing out a melody that felt like a balm for my soul. Each chord was a brushstroke, painting a picture of longing, sorrow, and the glimmer of hope that dared to take root in my heart.

As I closed my eyes, the world around me faded, replaced by the echoes of laughter and whispered promises shared in the moonlight with Zane. Those memories were both a comfort and a weight; they urged me to reach deeper, to confront the mess we had become. The lyrics flowed from me like a river bursting through a dam, raw and unfiltered, each line a confession, a plea for understanding. The song wove through my thoughts, taking on a life of its own, beckoning me to give it a voice.

I glanced at the clock, my pulse quickening. Zane would arrive any moment. Anxiety coiled tightly in my stomach, and I took a deep breath, trying to anchor myself in the moment. This was more than just a song; it was an invitation to bridge the chasm that had opened between us. I wanted him to feel every note, to understand the journey of my heart through this composition. Would he see my intention, or would he turn away, still shackled by the hurt we had endured?

The door creaked open, and there he stood, a silhouette framed by the late afternoon light. Zane was both familiar and foreign, a wild storm of emotions wrapped in denim and an old band t-shirt that clung to his well-defined shoulders. My heart raced, a rebellious rhythm that echoed the pulse of the music still lingering in the air. "Hey," I managed, my voice a shaky whisper.

"Hey," he replied, his tone even but with an undercurrent of something deeper, something waiting to be unleashed. He stepped inside, and the tension was palpable, a living thing swirling around us. We exchanged a tentative glance, one that held the weight of unsaid words and shared scars.

I motioned toward the piano, my sanctuary in this moment of uncertainty. "I've been working on something. I'd really like you to hear it." I could see the flicker of curiosity in his eyes, mingled with the apprehension that had become our constant companion. He nodded, stepping closer as I settled onto the piano bench, my fingers brushing the keys with a familiar tenderness.

The first notes resonated, filling the room with a warmth that momentarily chased away the chill between us. As I sang, the lyrics rolled out like a wave, crashing against the shores of our past, each line layered with vulnerability. "I'm sorry for the words that cut deep, for the nights we lost in silence, for the dreams that fell apart like sand slipping through our fingers." My voice wavered, but I pressed on, pouring everything I felt into this moment.

Zane's gaze held me captive, his expression shifting as he absorbed the music. I could see the way he leaned in, the slight furrow of his brow as he processed my offering. "It's beautiful," he murmured when I finished, his voice a low rumble that sent a shiver down my spine.

"Do you really think so?" I asked, the uncertainty in my voice betraying the walls I'd been trying to break down.

"Yeah," he replied, stepping closer. "It's... it's like you've captured everything we've been through, the pain, the hope." His eyes softened, a spark igniting that had been long absent. "You have a way of putting into words what we can't seem to say to each other."

I wanted to reach for him, to close the distance and weave our souls back together, but the moment hung between us, fragile and tentative. "I just want us to find our way back, Zane," I admitted, my heart racing with the truth of my confession. "I want to heal what's been broken."

He took a breath, a deep, steadying inhale that spoke of his own struggles. "Healing doesn't happen overnight. We can't just play a song and expect everything to be fixed." But even as he spoke, his body edged closer, drawn to the magnetic pull of what we shared.

"Maybe not," I countered, my voice stronger now, filled with conviction. "But we can start somewhere. I want to fight for us, to remind us of why we fell in love in the first place." The words hung in the air, heavy with promise and possibility.

With a swift movement, he closed the gap, wrapping his arms around me, pulling me into an embrace that felt like home. My heart raced, our breaths mingling as I nestled my head against his chest, the familiar sound of his heartbeat soothing my frayed nerves. "I want that too," he whispered, his voice a blend of warmth and uncertainty.

As we stood there, enveloped in the embrace of each other and the lingering notes of the song, I felt the walls that had divided us begin to crumble, one note at a time. Together, we dared to explore the landscape of our hearts, ready to navigate the treacherous waters of love, healing, and hope.

The warmth of Zane's embrace lingered, a protective cocoon that momentarily stifled the chaos of my racing thoughts. The world outside the studio felt muted, as if our small sanctuary had wrapped itself in a soundproof bubble, guarding us against the uncertainties lurking beyond. I pulled back just enough to look into his eyes, searching for the unguarded vulnerability I had seen before. "So...what do we do now?" I asked, my voice just above a whisper, the weight of my question hanging heavily between us.

His gaze held mine, a mixture of determination and uncertainty swirling like a tempest. "We take it one step at a time. But first, how about we let loose a little? You know, shake off the serious stuff." He flashed that charming, boyish grin that used to send my heart soaring. It was infectious, a flicker of mischief lighting up the shadows that had begun to gather around us.

"I can get behind that," I replied, the tension in my shoulders easing just a fraction. "What did you have in mind? Karaoke? A dance party?" I raised an eyebrow, fully expecting him to launch into a ridiculous song-and-dance number.

Zane laughed, the sound rich and genuine, reverberating through the space like the sweetest of melodies. "Actually, I was thinking of the ultimate classic: a game of rock-paper-scissors. Winner gets to pick the next song on the playlist."

"Ah, the age-old tradition of deciding fate with hand gestures. Truly a sophisticated method." I smirked, crossing my arms and adopting a faux-serious expression.

"Hey, it's a proven strategy. Just ask any five-year-old," he shot back, raising his hands in mock surrender. "Besides, it'll help us get back to just being us, without the heavy stuff hanging over our heads." He shifted his weight, a spark of hope lighting his features as he gestured dramatically. "So, shall we begin?"

We both stood, forming an impromptu arena in the middle of the studio. The air buzzed with a playful energy, the remnants of my song fading into the background as we prepared for our epic showdown. "Alright, on the count of three," I said, raising my hand, heart racing with anticipation. "One...two...three!"

"Rock!" he exclaimed, his fist closed tight.

"Scissors!" I cried, my fingers forming the requisite shape, victorious glee washing over me.

He groaned in mock agony, throwing his head back in exaggerated despair. "How could you? I thought you were on my side!"

"Clearly, I'm a traitor," I teased, reveling in the moment as I bounced on my toes, feeling lighter than I had in ages. "But I promise

I'll choose a good song for you. Maybe something really embarrassing, just to even the score."

Zane crossed his arms and raised an eyebrow. "You wouldn't dare. We had a pact about the whole 'no embarrassing songs' thing."

"Oh, sweet Zane, we both know that a little humiliation is good for the soul," I replied, my tone mischievous as I rifled through my playlist.

"Fine," he relented with a chuckle, "but I'm taking notes. Revenge will be mine."

As I scrolled through the options, I felt the barriers that had been weighing on us begin to dissolve, replaced by the warmth of shared laughter and inside jokes. I settled on a song, the upbeat tune echoing through the studio, and with a flick of a switch, the track filled the room.

"Here we go!" I declared, hitting play, and Zane's eyes widened in mock horror.

"No! Not that one!"

I danced in place, my body swaying to the infectious beat. "Oh yes, it's happening!"

He joined in reluctantly, laughter spilling out as he rolled his eyes. "You're enjoying this way too much."

"I can't help it! This is our jam!" I twirled, inviting him to follow, and soon we were both caught in the rhythm, forgetting the heaviness that had held us captive just moments before.

As the chorus kicked in, Zane let out a dramatic sigh, flinging himself across the studio, theatrically mimicking a music video. "I can't believe I'm doing this. My reputation is officially ruined."

"Welcome to the club! I've been here for years," I shot back, my laughter blending with the music, harmonizing with the joyous chaos we were creating.

The song carried us, lifting us above the worries that had shadowed our hearts. For a while, it was just the two of us, lost in a whirlwind of laughter and music, where the outside world faded to a distant hum. As the song reached its crescendo, I caught Zane's eye, and we both burst into fits of laughter, breathing heavily from the exertion and the joy of simply being together.

"Okay, that was actually kind of fun," he admitted, wiping a tear of laughter from the corner of his eye.

"Kind of? It was a masterpiece! We should go on tour!"

"Right after I find my dignity," he replied, feigning seriousness as he straightened up.

"Dignity is overrated," I laughed, grabbing his arm and pulling him back toward the piano. "Let's see if we can create a duet out of that last song. You know, just in case we ever need a career backup plan."

As I sat down, he leaned against the piano, watching me with that familiar spark in his eyes. The air shifted, and for a moment, I felt that old electricity between us flicker back to life, a promise of what could be if we just kept pushing forward.

"Alright, let's do it," Zane said, his voice lowering, imbued with a seriousness that sent a shiver down my spine. "But this time, we do it together. No hiding."

I nodded, my heart racing anew. With our voices interwoven and our souls laid bare, we stepped onto a new path, forging ahead together, ready to confront whatever lay ahead.

As we settled into the comforting rhythm of our impromptu duet, the tension that had once filled the room began to dissipate, replaced by the familiar cadence of laughter and harmony. Zane's voice blended with mine, weaving together like strands of a tapestry, vibrant and alive. I lost myself in the music, each note resonating with the unspoken promises we had made just moments ago.

"Okay, this is a lot easier than I thought," Zane admitted, a grin plastered across his face as he pushed through the chorus. "Maybe I should quit my day job and go for a reality TV singing competition."

"Right, because nothing says 'serious artist' like belting out ballads in your living room," I teased, nudging him playfully. "But seriously, you have a good voice. A little rusty, maybe, but we can work on that."

"Just wait until you hear my rendition of 'Total Eclipse of the Heart.' You might want to reconsider that compliment," he shot back, leaning closer as he delivered the next line with exaggerated emotion, his eyes wide and earnest, causing me to double over in laughter.

"Now I'm terrified," I said, wiping a tear from my cheek. "But I'll take that challenge. After all, what's better than a little melodrama to spice up our lives?"

He chuckled, the sound rich and full, filling the studio with warmth. "I think you just described our relationship in one sentence."

With the music still swirling around us, I turned my focus back to the piano, my fingers dancing over the keys. "Let's try that new song I wrote. We can tweak it together, see how it flows with both our voices."

"Deal," he said, straightening up, the playful glint in his eyes giving way to a more serious demeanor. "But I get to write the bridge. That's where the real magic happens."

"Sure, maestro," I replied, amused. "Just don't go writing any love sonnets that involve me running off with a pirate or something."

"Hey, if I'm writing a love story, you're getting the whole package. It's either pirates or time travelers. Take your pick."

"Time travelers, obviously," I countered, already plotting how to incorporate the absurdity of our banter into the song. "I'm definitely more of a 'Back to the Future' kind of girl."

Zane rolled his eyes, an exaggerated sigh escaping him. "Great, just what I need. A girlfriend who wants to travel through time. What are you going to do, bring me to see Shakespeare in the flesh?"

"Now that sounds like an excellent date idea!" I laughed. "Just imagine the conversation we'd have with him. 'Oh, hey, Will! So, about that whole 'star-crossed lovers' thing...'"

"Only for you to end up rewriting his works. It's genius," he said, shaking his head in mock disbelief.

The lightheartedness of our exchange carried us, infusing our music with an energy that felt almost electric. Each note seemed to fill the space around us with color, transforming the studio into a kaleidoscope of possibilities. It was in these moments, amid laughter and shared dreams, that I felt the possibility of rebuilding what had once been fractured.

As we wrapped up the song, I leaned back, a satisfied grin on my face. "I think we just created something special. Like, Grammy-worthy special."

"Or at least something we can proudly share at our next karaoke night," Zane quipped, raising an eyebrow. "That's bound to be a disaster."

"Nothing but the best for our friends," I replied, feeling the glow of camaraderie spark between us.

Yet, as the laughter faded, a silence fell, thick and almost oppressive, like a fog rolling in on a winter morning. I glanced up, only to find Zane's expression had shifted, his brow furrowing slightly as he looked away, lost in thought.

"Hey," I said softly, concern creeping into my voice. "What's going on? Did I say something wrong?"

He hesitated, the weight of unspoken words hanging in the air. "It's just... I've been thinking about the future, about us."

My heart quickened. "And?"

"And I want to be honest," he said, his voice steady but edged with vulnerability. "We've both been carrying a lot of baggage, and I don't want to pretend it's all fine when it's not. There are things we need to work through."

I swallowed hard, the familiar knot of anxiety tightening in my stomach. "I agree. But what do you mean? What's on your mind?"

"I guess I'm just afraid that we're on different pages," he admitted, rubbing the back of his neck as if the weight of his words was too much to bear. "What if we can't bridge that gap? What if we end up hurting each other more?"

"Zane," I said, my heart aching for the uncertainty that laced his words. "We've made it this far. I believe we can overcome anything together."

He met my gaze, searching my eyes for the truth behind my words. "It's just—"

Before he could finish, the phone rang, shattering the fragile moment we'd just begun to build. The shrill sound echoed through the studio, a stark reminder of the outside world. I glanced at the screen and my heart sank. It was my mom.

"I should probably get this," I said, my voice barely above a whisper. I felt a cold sweat break out on my skin, a sensation of foreboding settling in my chest.

"Yeah, sure. Take your time," he replied, his tone neutral, yet the tension had returned, thickening the air between us.

As I answered, the cheerful facade of my mother's voice collided with my apprehension. "Sweetheart! I have some news! You might want to sit down for this."

"Mom? What is it?" I asked, dread pooling in my stomach.

"Something's come up. Something important about your dad," she said, her voice faltering.

My heart dropped, the room around me fading as I tried to grasp the implications of her words. "What do you mean?"

"Just... please come home. We need to talk."

The seriousness in her tone sent a chill racing down my spine. I glanced at Zane, his brow furrowed in concern, the laughter of moments ago now a distant memory.

"Okay, I'll be there," I said, hanging up the phone, feeling as if I were standing on the edge of a precipice.

"What was that about?" Zane asked, worry etching his features.

"My dad," I replied, the words barely escaping my lips. "I have to go home. There's something wrong."

Zane's expression shifted to one of understanding, but also concern. "Do you want me to come with you?"

I hesitated, the thought of dragging him into whatever storm awaited me making my heart ache. "I... I don't know if that's a good idea. This feels like something I need to handle on my own."

He nodded, a shadow passing over his face. "Okay. Just know that I'm here for you, whatever you decide."

I felt the weight of that promise, a lifeline thrown in a turbulent sea. Yet as I gathered my things, the unease bubbled to the surface once more. I could sense that whatever awaited me at home could change everything, our fragile rebuilding teetering on the edge of uncertainty.

As I stepped out of the studio, Zane's eyes followed me, filled with a mix of support and apprehension. "Be careful, alright?" he called after me.

"I will," I promised, but deep down, a storm brewed, ready to collide with my resolve. And as I drove away, I couldn't shake the feeling that my life was about to pivot in ways I couldn't yet fathom.

Chapter 22: The Art of Trust

The desert sprawls before us, an endless canvas painted in earthy hues of gold and rust, dotted with the skeletal silhouettes of Joshua trees reaching skyward like arthritic fingers. The air is warm and dry, wrapping around us with the familiarity of an old friend. It feels as if we've stepped into another world, one where time slips away, leaving only the rhythm of our breaths and the crunch of gravel beneath our boots.

Zane walks ahead, his tall frame cutting a striking figure against the backdrop of the vivid landscape. There's a playful bounce in his step, a boyish charm that draws a smile from me, even as my heart flutters with both excitement and a tinge of apprehension. This isn't just a trip; it's a plunge into the depths of our relationship, an exploration of the uncharted territory between us. I catch up, matching his pace, and for a moment, we move in synchrony, the landscape alive with the vibrant pulse of possibility.

"Do you think the trees ever feel lonely?" I ask, trying to break the comfortable silence that has settled around us like a warm blanket. "I mean, they stand there all alone, just watching the world go by."

Zane glances back at me, his eyes crinkling at the corners as he smirks. "Lonely? Nah. They're too busy doing the whole 'I'm a desert tree, look at me!' thing. Besides, I bet they're just waiting for a tumbleweed to come by for a chat."

I chuckle, imagining a Joshua tree leaning in conspiratorially with a tumbleweed, gossiping about the wildlife that scurries beneath their shade. The whimsy of it sparks something in me, a flicker of joy I haven't felt in ages. It's in these moments, these small, shared laughs, that I find myself letting go of the guarded walls I've built.

As we continue our hike, the landscape shifts. Massive boulders rise like ancient sentinels, their surfaces etched with the stories of centuries, each crack and crevice a testament to the passage of time. We navigate around them, Zane's hand brushing against mine, igniting a spark that dances between us. I glance up at him, his expression focused yet relaxed, and I can't help but admire the way he seems to embody the spirit of this place—unfazed by the vastness around him, secure in his footing even as the ground shifts beneath us.

"I've never been here before," I admit, my voice barely above a whisper as I take in the surreal beauty of the scene before us. "It's more breathtaking than I imagined."

"Kind of like me, huh?" he quips, a teasing lilt in his voice.

I roll my eyes playfully, but warmth spreads through my chest. "Sure, but the desert has better fashion sense."

"Touché," he concedes, laughing. "But I'll have you know I clean up nice."

As the sun climbs higher, the heat intensifies, and I can feel the sweat trickling down my back. It's a discomfort that mingles with exhilaration, reminding me of the vulnerability I've been trying to wrestle with. Trust doesn't come easy for me; it's a delicate dance, a tightrope walk between wanting to leap and the fear of falling. But here, in the heart of the desert, surrounded by Zane's easy laughter and the mesmerizing landscape, I find a sliver of courage.

"Can I tell you something?" I say, my heart pounding against my ribs. "I've been thinking a lot about trust. It's hard for me."

Zane stops, turning to face me, the playfulness in his eyes replaced by a serious warmth. "I get that. It's not always easy to let someone in."

The moment hangs between us, charged with unspoken truths. I take a breath, feeling the weight of my confession. "I think I've built walls so high that I'm not sure how to bring them down. I want to, but—"

"But you're scared," he finishes softly, his gaze steady on mine.

I nod, feeling a swell of vulnerability. "Yeah. I don't want to get hurt again."

Zane steps closer, the distance between us shrinking to a heartbeat. "I promise you, I'm not here to hurt you. I want to be a safe place for you. But you have to meet me halfway."

His words resonate deep within me, stirring something I thought I had buried long ago. The desert stretches infinitely around us, a world unconfined, and here I am, trapped in my own fears. I swallow hard, contemplating his offer, my mind racing through memories of trust broken and promises shattered. But Zane's presence is steady, a lighthouse guiding me through the fog of uncertainty.

"I want to try," I finally say, my voice barely above a whisper. "I want to trust you."

His smile breaks through the tension, a genuine, softening grin that makes my heart leap. "Good. Because I'm not going anywhere."

With that, we resume our hike, each step feeling lighter than the last. The landscape transforms around us, the shadows stretching as the sun begins to dip low in the sky, casting long fingers of light across the rocky terrain. The air cools, and the desert starts to hum with life, a symphony of crickets and the distant call of birds echoing in the fading light.

As we reach a vantage point overlooking the vast expanse, the sun begins its descent, igniting the sky in a riot of colors—fiery oranges and soft pinks merging into deep indigos. It's a breathtaking display, one that feels almost sacred, and I stand there, breathless, my heart full. Zane steps beside me, his warmth radiating against the cooling evening air. We both lean against the boulder, our shoulders brushing, sharing this intimate moment of awe.

"Look at that," I breathe, utterly captivated. "It's like the world is on fire."

"Beautiful, isn't it?" he replies, his voice low and soft. "And it's only going to get better."

I glance sideways at him, curiosity piqued. "Better?"

He nods, a mischievous glint in his eyes. "Wait for it."

As if on cue, the horizon bursts into a final, dazzling display—a brief flash of vivid purple breaking through the orange and pink. I gasp, clutching at my chest as if I might burst from the beauty of it all, and I can't help but laugh at the sheer joy of being alive in this moment, here with him.

In the hush that follows, a quiet understanding blossoms between us, woven together by threads of honesty and hope. As the last light fades, I take Zane's hand, intertwining my fingers with his. It's a small gesture, but in that moment, it feels monumental—a leap of faith into the unknown, a promise to embrace whatever comes next together.

The desert night blankets us, softening the harsh edges of the day, leaving only a gentle warmth that lingers like the aftertaste of a fine wine. As stars begin to twinkle overhead, I find myself lost in their brilliance, each one a small beacon of light against the expansive canvas of the dark sky. The air is filled with the rich scent of sagebrush, and the distant call of owls echoes like a lullaby, wrapping around us as we make our way back to the campsite.

Zane's presence feels electric beside me. With every step, he chats about the constellations, his voice low and smooth, as though sharing secrets with the universe. I listen, half captivated by his enthusiasm, half engrossed in the way his hands animate the air as he gestures, describing Orion and his belt. There's a childlike wonder in his expression, a stark contrast to the complexities we've begun to navigate together.

"So, when you look up at the stars, do you ever wonder what they think of us?" I ask, my curiosity piqued. "Like, do they sit around judging our life choices?"

Zane laughs, a sound that reverberates through the stillness of the night. "Oh, absolutely. I'm pretty sure the stars have a council meeting about us every millennium. 'Can you believe these humans? Look at that one, falling in love in a desert!'"

"Right? They probably have a star-studded gossip session," I reply, grinning. "And we're the main topic of conversation."

He nudges me playfully with his shoulder, the warmth of his skin sending an unexpected thrill through me. "If we're the main characters in this cosmic drama, I hope we're at least interesting. Like, 'And then they stumbled through the desert, trying to figure out trust while dodging cactus spines!'"

"Cactus spines are a valid concern, you know," I tease back. "Trust may be hard, but I'd prefer not to get impaled while working on it."

With the campfire crackling behind us, the world feels larger than life, and somehow, so do we. We arrive at the edge of our campsite, where a flickering light dances against the rocks, creating an inviting glow. I find myself watching Zane as he moves, his silhouette framed by the firelight, each gesture infused with a certain grace that captivates me.

He stirs the embers, and I settle onto a log, allowing the warmth to wash over me. As the flames flicker and pop, I contemplate the journey ahead. We've shared laughter and vulnerability, but the road to trust still feels long and winding.

"Hey, do you ever think about what makes a person trustworthy?" I ask, wanting to dive deeper, to peel back the layers we've only begun to uncover.

Zane turns to me, thoughtful, his expression serious. "I think it's about consistency. Actions matching words. It's like that time I promised my niece I'd build her a treehouse. I didn't just talk about it—I got the lumber and spent weekends sweating under the sun, hammering away."

"A treehouse? Impressive!" I chuckle, picturing him with a tool belt, fully invested in the project. "Did she like it?"

"Oh, she loved it. Until she discovered she was terrified of heights," he admits, laughter in his eyes. "Now it's more of a 'look at it from the ground and pretend' house."

"That sounds like a tragedy waiting to happen," I say, unable to stifle my laughter. "But it's a great metaphor for trust, isn't it? You can build something beautiful, but if someone's not willing to climb up, it can all feel a little pointless."

Zane nods, his gaze steady. "Exactly. Trust is built, layer by layer, until you reach that point where you're not just looking at the structure but living in it."

I take a moment, absorbing his words. The idea of building something together, layer by layer, fills me with warmth, but it's also daunting. My mind drifts back to the last time I trusted someone wholeheartedly, how it felt to have that trust shattered. The memory flares like a match in the dark, and I blink, forcing it back into the recesses of my mind.

"Speaking of layers," Zane says, breaking into my thoughts, "I feel like we're not quite done peeling back ours. How about we play a game? Truth or dare?"

"Dare," I say without hesitation, the thrill of the challenge igniting a spark of spontaneity within me.

He leans closer, a playful glint in his eye. "I dare you to tell me the most embarrassing story from your past."

I groan, half-laughing. "Do you really want to hear about the time I tripped in front of my entire high school during graduation?"

"Absolutely," he encourages, grinning. "The juicier, the better."

"Alright," I relent, rolling my eyes but unable to suppress a smile. "So, picture this: I'm walking across the stage, and my parents are practically glowing with pride. I reach out to grab my diploma, and then... wham! My heel catches on the edge of the platform. I go down—hard. The diploma goes flying, and my cap is askew. My mom, bless her, jumps up like I'm in mortal danger, and my dad's just filming the whole thing."

Zane bursts into laughter, and I can't help but join him. "Oh man, that's the perfect graduation memory!"

"It gets better," I continue, enjoying the moment. "They announce my name again as I'm scrambling to my feet. The entire audience is howling with laughter, and I'm just trying to regain my dignity."

"Did you at least get the diploma?" he asks, eyes wide with mirth.

"Eventually," I admit, my cheeks flushed from the memory. "But it felt like I was chasing after my self-respect instead."

He leans back, shaking his head in disbelief. "That is both tragic and epic. Your parents must have been mortified."

"More like they relished every moment," I respond, laughing. "I swear my dad still has that video on repeat. It's family legend now."

"Okay, my turn," he says, his eyes sparkling with mischief. "Truth or dare?"

"Truth," I reply, curious about what he might reveal.

"Tell me the biggest secret you've kept from someone," he says, his tone light but his eyes probing.

I hesitate, weighing my options. The stakes feel higher, but this is a game designed to peel back the layers we've only just begun to understand. "Fine," I say, gathering my courage. "I'll tell you a secret I haven't even told my best friend."

Zane leans in, anticipation written all over his face. "I'm all ears."

"I once applied to a writing program in New York," I admit, my heart racing. "I got in, but I didn't go. I was too scared of failing."

His expression softens, genuine empathy reflecting in his gaze. "That's huge. Why didn't you tell anyone?"

"Because I didn't want anyone to think I couldn't cut it," I confess, the weight of the secret lifting slightly. "I didn't want to let anyone down, especially myself."

Zane nods slowly, as if processing the layers behind my confession. "That's not just a secret; that's a part of who you are. But you're here now, in the desert, sharing your stories. That's brave."

His words wrap around me, igniting a flicker of courage I didn't realize I needed. Maybe trust isn't just about overcoming fear; maybe it's about being seen and accepted, flaws and all. As the night deepens, we share laughter and secrets, building something fragile yet strong. The stars twinkle above, and the fire crackles softly, an orchestra of night sounds wrapping us in their embrace. In this moment, amidst the shadows and the light, I can feel the layers between us beginning to dissolve, revealing a foundation built on vulnerability and shared dreams.

The crackling campfire continues to dance in the night, casting playful shadows on our faces as we swap stories, but as Zane's laughter fades into the warm desert air, a deeper silence envelops us. We sit side by side on the log, our fingers still entwined, the warmth between us mingling with the gentle night breeze. A stillness settles over the campsite, the kind that makes your heart race with possibility.

"What's next, my daring adventurer?" he asks, eyes glimmering with curiosity, clearly not ready to end our game. "You're up again—truth or dare?"

I contemplate my options, feeling bold. "Dare. Let's keep this rollercoaster going."

Zane grins, a spark igniting in his eyes. "I dare you to make a wish on a shooting star."

I glance up, half-expecting the universe to comply with our whims. "Shooting stars? At this rate, I might as well wish for the moon, too."

"Fine, then. Wish for something outrageous," he challenges, laughter dancing in his voice. "You might just end up with a treehouse in New York!"

"Touché," I retort, leaning closer as if the universe might hear my desires whispered in the cool night air. "Alright, here goes nothing." I take a deep breath, close my eyes, and focus on what I truly want. "I wish for the courage to embrace whatever comes next, even if it scares me."

Zane's expression shifts, a softness entering his eyes that makes my heart flutter. "I think that's a perfect wish."

We sit in comfortable silence, the fire crackling as the scent of roasted marshmallows wafts through the air, reminding me of simpler times—camping trips as a kid, late-night confessions shared over flickering flames. I pull myself back to the present, realizing just how much Zane has become a part of my life, almost without my noticing. It's strange and exhilarating.

"Okay, my turn," I say, determined to keep the momentum. "Truth or dare?"

"Truth," he replies, a playful smirk tugging at his lips.

"What's the biggest lie you've ever told?" I ask, excitement bubbling within me at the thought of his response.

Zane leans back, contemplating, the glow of the fire reflecting off his thoughtful expression. "Alright, I'll tell you. I once pretended to be sick in high school just to get out of a history exam. I faked a cough and everything. The best part? My teacher totally bought it, and I ended up at home, binge-watching cartoons instead."

"Wait, you're telling me you pretended to be sick for a test?" I laugh, unable to contain myself. "What kind of rebel are you?"

"The coolest kind, obviously," he retorts, his eyes sparkling with mischief. "But to be fair, I didn't realize the history teacher would assign extra credit for showing up. So I basically sabotaged my own future."

"Classic Zane move," I tease, shaking my head in mock disbelief. "But hey, you could always use that on your résumé: 'Expert in Avoiding Responsibility.'"

His laughter rings out like music, and I can't help but wonder how someone so effortlessly charming could have also once been the kind of person who skipped exams. "Well, I prefer to think of it as 'Strategically Managing Stress,'" he says with a grin.

As the evening deepens, we watch the firelight flicker, the flames morphing into shapes that tell stories of their own. The world outside our small bubble feels like a distant echo, but the air shifts suddenly, a chill creeping in as the night deepens.

"I should probably start preparing for bed," I say reluctantly, trying to ignore the pull of the warmth from the fire. "I mean, we've got an early start tomorrow."

"Before you go, can I ask you something?" Zane's tone shifts slightly, a hint of seriousness threading through his playful demeanor.

"Sure," I reply, sensing the weight of his words even before they leave his lips.

"What if we took this beyond the weekend? I mean, not just a road trip, but really exploring what we have?" He looks at me intently, and the weight of his question hangs in the air, palpable.

My heart races as I process his words. The thought sends a rush of warmth through me, but it's accompanied by the familiar knot of anxiety. I open my mouth to respond, but before I can find the words, the crackling of the fire fills the silence.

"Zane, I—" I begin, but the sound of rustling in the nearby brush interrupts me. We both turn, the moment suspended in uncertainty.

"What was that?" Zane asks, his expression shifting from playful to alert as the rustling grows louder, punctuated by the unmistakable sound of something heavy moving through the underbrush.

I feel a shiver run down my spine. "Maybe it's just a rabbit? Or a raccoon?"

"Or something bigger," he murmurs, his brow furrowing as he stands, scanning the dark edges of the campsite.

As if on cue, a shadow flits just outside the reach of the firelight, a figure moving quickly through the darkness. My heart pounds, and I clench Zane's hand tighter.

"Okay, now I'm starting to get a little freaked out," I admit, my voice barely above a whisper.

"Stay here," Zane commands, taking a cautious step toward the sound.

"Wait, are you serious?" I protest, rising to follow him. "What if it's a mountain lion or something?"

"Then we'll outsmart it with our charm," he quips, but I can see the concern in his eyes.

The rustling grows louder, and just as he steps forward, a figure bursts from the shadows, sending us both stumbling back. I gasp, my heart in my throat, ready to flee, but Zane's grip on my hand keeps me grounded.

"Who's there?" Zane calls out, his voice steady despite the tension thrumming in the air.

A tall figure steps into the firelight, and my breath catches as I recognize the familiar silhouette. "It's me! It's Adrian!" he shouts, panting as he approaches, his eyes wide with urgency.

"Adrian?" I echo, confusion swirling in my mind. "What are you doing here?"

Before he can answer, the tension in the air thickens, an unspoken alarm resonating between us. Adrian glances over his shoulder, eyes darting nervously. "I need your help. There's something in the desert... something dangerous."

The laughter of the night seems to vanish, replaced by a chilling apprehension that twists in my gut. Whatever it is, it feels too close for comfort, and I suddenly realize that the trust we've begun to build might be put to the ultimate test.

Chapter 23: Notes of Conflict

The city of angels unfolded before me like a neon-drenched tapestry, familiar yet achingly distant, as I stepped off the plane and back into Los Angeles. The scent of the ocean mingled with the oily aroma of street food wafting from the food trucks parked outside LAX. I inhaled deeply, feeling the mixture of salty air and the distant echo of a guitar riff tugging at my heartstrings, but beneath that rush of nostalgia lay a gnawing tension that felt all too familiar.

The pressures of the music industry began to seep back into my bones as soon as I entered the studio, the sterile white walls a stark contrast to the vibrant chaos of my memories. My artist, a rising star with an insatiable hunger for the next big hit, was restless. I watched him pace like a caged lion, all energy and frustration, as he rifled through a pile of demos. Each beat that reverberated through the air felt like an accusation, each chord progression I'd brought to the table now tainted with the stain of failure.

"Dahlia," he called out, snapping me from my reverie. "I need something fresh, something that'll set the world on fire. This isn't what I signed up for." His voice dripped with an urgency that turned my stomach.

I nodded, my smile feeling more like a mask than a gesture of confidence. "I understand. Let's explore some new ideas together." But the truth was, I had poured my heart into those tracks. They reflected my artistic vision, the culmination of late nights and unfiltered passion, yet now they felt like shackles binding me to a moment of vulnerability I wasn't ready to face.

As I shuffled through my notes, the muffled sound of my manager's voice drifted through the glass walls. "She's struggling," he said, not knowing I was only a few feet away. "We can't afford to wait for her to find herself. We need hits, not heart."

The words struck me like a sharp knife, slicing through my carefully constructed facade. My stomach churned as anxiety clawed at my insides, each syllable igniting a firestorm of doubt. Had I truly failed? I felt the heat of shame flooding my cheeks, the weight of their judgment pressing down like an anvil, threatening to crush me under its enormity.

I slipped into the bathroom, my sanctuary, and splashed cold water on my face, trying to wash away the panic that was brewing just beneath the surface. My reflection stared back at me, hair a wild halo of curls framing my face, eyes wide with the fear of falling short yet again. "Get it together, Dahlia," I whispered, the words echoing back, a hollow reminder of my aspirations.

I needed to confide in someone, to peel back the layers of this burgeoning anxiety. I sent Zane a quick text, praying he'd be available. He always knew how to ground me, his laughter a balm for my frayed nerves. Minutes later, my phone buzzed—a response, followed by an offer to meet at our favorite café, a cozy nook tucked away from the glitz of Hollywood.

As I navigated through the bustling streets, the sun dipped lower, casting a golden hue over the pavement. The café was a refuge, a place where time slowed, and creativity flowed like the perfectly brewed coffee. Zane was already there, a disheveled mess of dark curls and an easy smile, the kind that made the world feel a little less heavy.

"Hey, sunshine," he greeted, his voice warm and inviting. "You look like you've been wrestling with a bear."

I laughed, the sound slightly strained but genuine. "More like a dozen industry sharks. They're circling, Zane. I feel like I'm losing my grip on everything."

He leaned forward, his expression shifting from playful to serious. "Talk to me. What's going on?"

I poured out my fears, the pressure from my artist, my manager's harsh words, the gnawing feeling that I was failing to deliver. Zane listened intently, nodding as I spoke, his brow furrowing slightly in concern.

"They want something fresh, but I'm struggling to balance their expectations with my vision. I'm terrified of what will happen if I don't come up with something spectacular."

"Dahlia," he said softly, "you're not here to mold yourself into someone else's vision. You have your own sound, your own style. Don't let their insecurities drag you down. You've come too far to lose sight of that."

His words sank in, a soothing balm on my fraying nerves. Yet, the shadows of doubt lingered, clinging to the edges of my thoughts like unwelcome guests.

"But what if it's not enough? What if I'm just not good enough?" I sighed, my voice barely above a whisper.

Zane reached across the table, his hand warm against mine. "You are more than enough. Remember when you wrote that song in a single night, and it blew everyone away? You have this magic, Dahlia. Don't let their fear define you."

The tension in my chest eased slightly, but the chasm between my vision and their demands felt more daunting than ever. I needed to find a way to bridge that gap, to remind myself of my purpose amidst the chaos.

"Maybe I just need to take a step back," I mused, the thought lingering in the air. "Revisit my inspiration, find what ignited that fire in the first place."

Zane smiled, a glimmer of mischief dancing in his eyes. "That's the spirit. And if it helps, I'll be your willing audience for any late-night jam sessions. I'll even bring snacks. How's that for motivation?"

I chuckled, the weight of my worries momentarily lifting. "You always know how to cheer me up."

As we left the café, the sun dipped below the horizon, painting the sky with vibrant strokes of orange and pink. For the first time that day, I felt a flicker of hope. Maybe, just maybe, I could reclaim my sound amidst the storm brewing around me. But as I walked side by side with Zane, I couldn't shake the feeling that the real challenge was just beginning, lurking just around the corner, waiting to test my resolve.

The morning sun spilled into my apartment like a spilled drink, scattering light across the mismatched furniture and vibrant art that clung to the walls like whispered secrets. I curled up on my favorite couch, a plush relic from a yard sale, with an old journal resting on my lap. This was supposed to be my sanctuary, a creative space where inspiration flowed freely, yet today it felt more like a cage.

Flipping through the pages, I spotted remnants of a time when ideas danced effortlessly, words cascading like melodies. I had written entire verses here, each line steeped in authenticity, but now they seemed like echoes from a distant past, tainted by the dissonance of expectations. I pushed the journal aside, frustration gnawing at my insides. What good was it to create if the only audience that mattered found my music lacking?

The phone buzzed, its shrill tone cutting through my spiraling thoughts. It was Zane, and I could almost hear the grin in his text. "Meet me at the beach? I promise sand, sun, and all the bad coffee you can drink."

I hesitated, the allure of salty air battling against the heavy weight in my chest. But Zane's offer was a lifeline, and before I could talk myself out of it, I replied with a simple "On my way."

The drive to the beach was a familiar one, the palm trees lining the road swaying gently in the ocean breeze as if waving me closer to the shore. The vibrant blue of the ocean was a sharp contrast to my tumultuous thoughts, a reminder that life continued to flow, regardless of my internal chaos. As I stepped out of the car, the sun warmed my skin, and I took a deep breath, letting the scent of the ocean ground me.

Zane was already there, seated on a blanket spread out on the sand, his legs crossed and a coffee cup in hand. "There you are, my favorite muse," he said, waving me over. "I was starting to think you were going to drown in those existential crises of yours."

I sank down next to him, a grin breaking through my worries. "I considered it, but then I remembered I don't float."

He chuckled, his laughter melding with the sound of crashing waves. "Well, I'm glad you decided to join the living. So, what's eating at you this time?"

I hesitated, watching the surf roll in and out, the rhythm calming my racing thoughts. "It's the new album. My artist wants something fresh, and I feel like I'm losing myself in all of it. I overheard my manager saying I'm not delivering, and it's... well, it's killing me."

Zane took a sip of his coffee, eyebrows raised. "Is this the same artist who thought it was a good idea to put bagpipes in a pop song?"

I couldn't help but laugh, the absurdity of it cutting through my tension. "Yes! But it gets worse. He wants to explore a completely new sound—something more... mainstream, I guess. And I don't know how to do that without compromising my style."

"Ah, the age-old battle between artistry and commercialism," Zane mused, tapping his fingers against the cup. "It's like trying to bake a cake with one hand while juggling flaming torches with the other."

"Exactly! And the worst part is, I want to create something that resonates, something authentic. But the pressure is suffocating."

He looked at me thoughtfully, his expression shifting from playful to serious. "Dahlia, you have to remember why you started making music in the first place. You're not a machine that churns out hits. You're an artist. If you compromise who you are, it'll show in your work."

"But what if they don't want me as I am?" I sighed, the worry creeping back in. "What if they want something that just isn't me?"

Zane leaned in closer, his eyes intense. "Then they're not worth your time. Your music is a reflection of you. The right people will appreciate that authenticity."

I took a moment to digest his words, letting them sink in like the sun warming the sand beneath us. "You're right. But the stakes feel higher this time. What if I fail? What if I'm just not good enough?"

Zane nudged my shoulder playfully. "Hey, if you were that bad, you wouldn't be here. You'd be trapped in a never-ending loop of writing elevator music or some other bland nonsense. But look around. You're not failing. You're just figuring it out."

"Thanks, but I think I'm more of a 'freaking out' kind of person right now."

"True, but remember, every artist has their crisis. Look at Van Gogh! Guy painted for like a decade before he got famous, and half the time he thought he was terrible. And then, boom—Starry Night!"

His analogy made me smile, a flicker of hope igniting in my chest. "So you're saying I'm basically on the verge of a masterpiece?"

"Exactly!" Zane's eyes sparkled with mischief. "You just need to channel your inner tortured artist. Maybe even go full Van Gogh. I hear ear piercings are all the rage."

"Ha! I'll stick to finding inspiration in my sound, thanks."

We both laughed, the sound mingling with the ocean breeze, lifting the weight from my shoulders just a little more. The fear was still there, lurking in the back of my mind, but at least for now, I felt a sense of clarity breaking through the haze.

"Okay, enough about me," I said, shifting the conversation. "What's going on in your world? Any new projects, or are you still avoiding adulthood?"

Zane leaned back on the blanket, an exaggerated sigh escaping his lips. "Well, there's a chance I might be roped into directing a community theater production. They need someone with vision and a sense of humor. Guess who's the only one who fits that description?"

"Are you seriously considering it? I can't imagine you giving up your freedom for rehearsals and stage directions."

"I know, but it could be fun. Plus, it's a chance to stretch my creative legs. Just imagine: 'Zane the Great' leading a ragtag group of actors through Shakespeare. It would be a disaster—and I can't wait."

"Just promise me you won't let them turn Hamlet into a musical. The world doesn't need more 'To be or not to be' set to a catchy pop tune."

Zane snorted. "No promises. I might be tempted to throw in a dance number for good measure."

We shared a laugh, the sun casting long shadows across the sand, and I realized how much I had missed these moments—conversations where laughter pushed worries aside, if only temporarily. Zane's presence was like a lifebuoy in a stormy sea, reminding me that even amidst the chaos of expectations, there was still joy to be found in creation.

As the waves lapped at the shore, I felt the stirrings of determination. I wouldn't let fear dictate my art. I would embrace my voice, my vision, and trust that the right sound would find its way to me, like the gentle tide returning home.

The sun hung low in the sky as I stepped back into the vibrant chaos of the city, the salty breeze from the beach still clinging to my skin. The weight of Zane's words lingered in my mind, a subtle reminder that I was more than the sum of their judgments. But with every turn of the wheel on my drive home, the familiar doubts crept back in, like a persistent song stuck on repeat.

My apartment felt both comforting and claustrophobic as I pushed open the door. The walls, decorated with my own artistic endeavors, felt like they were closing in, suffocating the very creativity I sought to nurture. I tossed my bag onto the couch, my fingers trailing over the guitar resting in the corner. It called to me, an old friend waiting to help me craft my next masterpiece—or perhaps a mere distraction from my current turmoil.

I picked it up, strumming a few chords that echoed through the silence, filling the room with a sound both haunting and hopeful. The notes danced in the air, teasing my mind into a state of inspiration. Maybe all I needed was to dive back into my music, rediscover the parts of myself that felt lost. But as I tried to focus, the ghost of my artist's expectations loomed larger than life, distorting the melody into something unrecognizable.

Frustrated, I set the guitar aside and paced the small space. My phone buzzed again, this time with a group chat notification from the band. The chatter was lighthearted, filled with inside jokes and banter, but my heart sank as I read the words. They were discussing rehearsal times for the next week, excitement radiating through the screen. A surge of panic gripped me—would I even have anything to contribute?

Taking a deep breath, I poured myself a glass of water and sank onto the couch, staring blankly at the wall. Maybe Zane was right. Maybe I just needed to find my own voice amidst the noise. But how could I do that when the very people I worked with seemed to doubt my abilities?

The late afternoon sun cast warm rays through the window, illuminating a notebook on the coffee table, its pages filled with unfinished lyrics and half-baked ideas. My heart raced at the thought of diving into it, of capturing something raw and real. Maybe I could craft a song that blended their desire for something fresh with the essence of who I was as an artist.

With renewed purpose, I grabbed the notebook and my guitar, settling into a comfortable spot on the floor. I strummed a few chords, letting my fingers guide me as I began to scribble down lyrics. The words flowed like water, raw and unfiltered, spilling out the frustration, the hope, and the fear that had been churning inside me.

Just as I was beginning to lose myself in the music, a loud knock startled me. I glanced at the door, my heart racing as I wondered who it could be. I didn't have many visitors—most of my friends knew better than to interrupt me during creative sprints.

"Dahlia!" It was Zane's voice, buoyant and insistent. "Open up! I come bearing gifts."

I chuckled under my breath, shaking off the heaviness as I scrambled to the door. Swinging it open revealed Zane, a paper bag crumpled in his hand and a wide grin plastered across his face.

"Did you bring donuts? Because that's the only way I'll forgive you for interrupting my creative flow," I teased, stepping aside to let him in.

"Better!" he declared, brandishing the bag as if it were a trophy. "I come with a promise of inspiration and a whole lot of caffeine."

I raised an eyebrow, intrigued. "Inspiration? That's a bold claim for a simple paper bag."

He stepped further inside, shaking the bag for dramatic effect. "You'll see. I have an idea for a new song. Something that might just get those creative juices flowing again."

I folded my arms, skepticism dancing in my eyes. "Your last idea involved a kazoo, Zane. You can't just toss the word 'inspiration' around without some serious backing."

"Trust me, this one's different." He plopped down on the floor next to me, the bag spilling open to reveal an assortment of colorful sticky notes, pens, and a surprisingly hefty thermos of coffee. "We're going to brainstorm, and I'll be your hype man."

I couldn't help but smile. Zane's enthusiasm was infectious, and I felt a flicker of excitement spark within me. "All right, you have my attention. But no kazoos, I swear."

"Deal. Now, what's your current struggle?"

As I shared my fears about the album and my artist's expectations, Zane scribbled notes furiously, his brow furrowing in concentration. "Okay, what if you turned the pressure into something good? Write about the expectations, the noise, the tension? There's power in that struggle, Dahlia."

I pondered his suggestion, the gears in my mind starting to turn. "Like, write a song that reflects the conflict I'm feeling? Something that embraces the chaos?"

"Exactly!" Zane beamed. "You could even weave in some elements of your artist's style while still keeping it distinctly yours. A fusion, if you will."

"Now you're talking. It could be like a sonic tug-of-war—capturing the essence of their demands while staying true to my roots."

"See? You're already thinking like a rock star!" He nudged me playfully. "Now, let's map this out. Grab a pen."

With a growing sense of purpose, I picked up a pen and began jotting down ideas, the sound of the scratching nib filling the room. Zane leaned in, tossing ideas back and forth, and with each passing moment, the weight of my anxiety began to lift. The collaborative energy ignited a spark within me, and suddenly the creative block that had felt insurmountable seemed within reach.

As we brainstormed, laughter filled the air, punctuated by the occasional sip of coffee or the crinkling of sticky notes. But just as I felt the rhythm returning, a sudden loud crash erupted from the street below, jarring us both. We exchanged a startled glance, our laughter freezing mid-sentence.

"What was that?" I asked, heart racing as I peered out the window.

Zane joined me, the joviality of the moment evaporating like mist in the morning sun. "I don't know, but it didn't sound good. Let's check it out."

I followed him cautiously down the stairs, a sense of foreboding settling in the pit of my stomach. As we stepped outside, the scene was chaotic—a delivery truck had toppled over, and people were milling about, some taking videos, others rushing to help.

Then, through the crowd, I spotted a familiar face—my artist, looking frantic as he spoke with a group of bystanders. His voice rose above the din, panic lacing his words.

"No, I need to get that album finished! This isn't the time for delays!"

My stomach dropped. What on earth could this mean for me? As I stepped closer, straining to hear, I felt Zane's hand on my arm, grounding me.

"Dahlia, we should probably—"

But before he could finish, my artist turned, locking eyes with me. The desperation in his gaze was palpable, and I could feel the weight of that moment pressing down on my shoulders, as if the universe had aligned to throw yet another curveball into my chaotic life.

"Dahlia! Thank God you're here! We need to talk!"

The world around me faded, leaving only the rush of my heartbeat echoing in my ears. In that instant, I realized this was no longer just about the album. It was about everything—the expectations, the pressure, and now the chaos unfolding around me. I felt as if I stood on the precipice of something monumental, and whether I would leap or fall was yet to be determined.

Chapter 24: Colliding Worlds

The walls of the studio were painted in muted shades of slate and cream, a canvas for the vibrant chaos that erupted from our collective minds. But today, those colors felt stifling, as if they were closing in on me, whispering doubts and insecurities into my ear. I stood in the corner, clutching my sketchbook like a shield, the pages filled with bursts of color and emotion that felt so far removed from the world around me. My artist, Leo, was in full swing, his voice booming through the space, drowning out any semblance of my thoughts. It was as if my contributions were mere whispers, barely registering against the grand symphony of his vision.

"Listen, everyone," Leo declared, throwing his hands up dramatically. "I appreciate the effort, but this is not the direction I envisioned." His words hung in the air like a heavy fog, chilling me to the bone. The room, filled with our eclectic team of designers and assistants, suddenly felt more like a gladiatorial arena. I could sense their eyes darting between me and Leo, a palpable tension brewing. A sinking feeling settled in my stomach as I realized that my ideas, the ones I had poured my heart into, had been reduced to a footnote in his grand narrative.

I bit down on my lip to suppress the surge of anger threatening to erupt. I had never been one for confrontation; it always felt like walking a tightrope, balancing the urge to speak out against the fear of falling into the chasm of conflict. But today was different. Today, I was tired of feeling small, tired of being overshadowed by Leo's towering ego. So I took a deep breath, clenching my sketchbook tighter, and found my voice.

"I think the vision could benefit from some..." My voice faltered as I searched for the right words. "...a little more color, a little more depth? My last sketch—the one with the layered textures—wasn't just a doodle. It had purpose."

The room fell silent, and for a brief moment, I felt a flicker of hope. But Leo's scoff cut through the tension like a knife. "Purpose? It's nice, but it doesn't align with the brand's identity. We're not here to reinvent the wheel, darling."

The collective gasp from the team felt like a physical blow. I could feel heat flooding my cheeks as embarrassment threatened to swallow me whole. With each word, Leo was dismantling my confidence, brick by brick. I opened my mouth to defend my work, but the words caught in my throat, suffocating beneath his domineering presence.

"Maybe if you listened to the input of the team," I shot back, my voice rising despite my instincts to retreat. "You'd see that it's not about the wheel. It's about the ride!" The moment the words left my lips, I felt a surge of adrenaline, like I'd just leaped off a cliff. But the thrill quickly dissipated as I watched Leo's brow furrow, his expression shifting from surprise to disdain.

He leaned back in his chair, crossing his arms with a smirk that sent my pulse racing. "The ride? Sweetheart, this isn't about joyrides. It's about crafting a masterpiece. And masterpieces don't come from half-baked ideas."

That was it. The dam broke. "You know what, Leo? You might be the artist, but this is a collaboration, not a dictatorship!" The words spilled out of me, wild and untamed. I felt liberated, yet terrified, as I stormed out of the studio, the door slamming behind me.

Outside, the world was a cacophony of sounds, the bustling city alive with energy that I barely registered. I needed to escape, to find solace somewhere other than this battlefield of creativity. It wasn't until I reached Zane's apartment that I began to feel the weight of my frustration lift slightly.

Zane opened the door, surprise etching his features. "Wow, you look like you've just fought a dragon and lost." He stepped aside, letting me in, and I sank onto the couch, exhaling a breath I didn't realize I was holding.

"More like I just tried to slay my ego and ended up on the floor," I muttered, running a hand through my hair. "Leo just ripped me apart in front of everyone. It was humiliating."

Zane settled next to me, his presence warm and grounding. "You know he doesn't define your talent, right? That man has a flair for the dramatic, but it doesn't mean he's right."

"I know, but it's hard not to feel like I'm just... invisible. It's like I'm constantly trying to shine while he hogs all the spotlight." I leaned back, staring at the ceiling as I let the words spill out. "I put so much of myself into this project, and for what? A pat on the head and a dismissal? It's infuriating!"

He listened patiently, nodding as I vented, his eyes steady and thoughtful. "Have you considered that your struggles in the studio might mirror something deeper? Like your relationship with Leo, or even with me?"

The question hung in the air, and I turned my head to meet his gaze. Zane had a way of cutting through the noise, laying bare the truths I often preferred to ignore. "What do you mean?"

"Relationships, whether artistic or personal, require honesty and vulnerability to thrive. You've built a world around yourself that lets you express who you are, but you need to let others see that too. Otherwise, they'll never understand the depth of your work." His words settled over me, heavy and comforting.

A flicker of realization danced in my mind. "I've been so afraid of being vulnerable, of exposing my true self. It feels safer to hide behind my work and let it speak for me."

"Maybe it's time to show them the real you," Zane suggested, a hint of mischief in his smile. "And while you're at it, maybe let me help you pull out the best version of your artistry."

The warmth of his presence, the gentle push of his encouragement, began to dismantle the barricades I had built around my heart. As I contemplated my next move, I felt a sense of clarity washing over me. I had to be brave, not just in the studio but in my relationship with Zane too. Standing firm in my artistry was non-negotiable, no matter the cost.

As I settled into the comforting embrace of Zane's couch, his presence felt like a buoy in a turbulent sea. I had stormed in like a hurricane, but now I was the calm after the chaos, with thoughts swirling like autumn leaves caught in a brisk wind. Zane's warm brown eyes searched mine, offering an understanding that wrapped around me like a cozy blanket.

"So, what's next?" he asked, leaning back with a half-smile that suggested he wasn't just here to be my sounding board. "Are we going to plot the downfall of Leo? Or perhaps overthrow him in a dramatic coup?" His playful tone broke through my tension, and I couldn't help but chuckle, shaking my head.

"I wouldn't mind throwing a paintbrush at his head," I replied, a teasing glimmer in my eyes. "But I think I'd prefer to channel that energy into something more productive."

Zane leaned forward, elbows resting on his knees, the way he always did when he was genuinely intrigued. "You know, they say every great artist has to wrestle with their demons. Maybe Leo is just your demon in this story."

"That sounds about right," I replied, frowning. "But I'm tired of wrestling. I want to create without constantly looking over my shoulder, waiting for his approval."

"Then stop seeking it," Zane said simply, his words slicing through the fog of self-doubt. "You're talented, and you know it. Own that. You've got to be your own biggest fan."

The spark of rebellion lit within me, igniting a fire I hadn't realized was smoldering. I thought back to the sketches I'd labored over, how they reflected not just my ideas but pieces of my soul. "You're right. I can't let his opinion drown out my voice. I need to fight for my work, even if it means standing alone."

"Good," Zane said, his smile broadening. "Now, how about we celebrate this newfound resolve? I happen to have a stellar bottle of wine that's just begging for company." He stood up, his energy infectious as he headed to the kitchen.

"Wine sounds like a plan," I said, letting the comfort of his words seep in. As he rummaged through the cabinets, I glanced around his apartment, which was a delightful mash-up of sophistication and cozy chaos—paintings stacked against walls, art supplies strewn about, and a collection of quirky mugs that seemed to whisper secrets of their own.

Zane returned with two glasses, the wine glistening ruby-red, reflecting the soft glow of the kitchen lights. "To the fierce artist ready to take on the world," he toasted, raising his glass. I clinked mine against his, the sound resonating like a promise.

As we sipped, a comfortable silence enveloped us, broken only by the soft clinking of ice in Zane's tumbler. The weight of my earlier frustrations began to dissipate, replaced by the warmth of connection. "So, tell me more about this Leo," Zane said, leaning back against the counter. "What's his deal, really?"

"His deal? Think self-importance with a dash of narcissism," I replied, rolling my eyes dramatically. "He's got talent, sure, but it's like he walks into a room expecting a standing ovation simply for existing."

Zane laughed, the sound rich and genuine. "Sounds like he needs a reality check. But what about you? Why do you keep putting yourself in a position where he can dismiss your contributions? You're not a background character in his masterpiece."

"I guess I've let myself be one," I admitted, setting my glass down and running my fingers along the rim. "For too long, I've waited for validation. I keep thinking if I just create something good enough, he'll notice. But maybe that's the problem—I'm creating for him instead of myself."

"Exactly," Zane said, his enthusiasm infectious. "Let this be the moment you stop trying to please others and start creating what brings you joy. Dive into your vision and don't look back."

I nodded, feeling a shift within me, a determination that felt both exhilarating and terrifying. "You're right. I need to find that spark again, the one that made me fall in love with art in the first place. It wasn't about others; it was about expressing myself."

"Then do it," Zane said, his voice steady and encouraging. "Let it out—don't be afraid to push boundaries. And if Leo doesn't get it, that's his loss."

I took another sip, the wine swirling flavors on my tongue, and I allowed myself to dream for a moment. What if I really leaned into my creativity? What if I crafted something bold and unexpected, something that challenged perceptions?

Suddenly, my mind flashed with an image, a vivid concept that filled me with excitement. "What if I create a series that juxtaposes traditional art forms with modern elements? Something that feels alive, that speaks to the tension between old and new?"

Zane's eyes lit up. "Now that's a powerful idea. You could incorporate mixed media—textures, layers. Make it a conversation, not just a presentation."

"Yes! I can use elements from the city—the graffiti, the textures of the buildings, even the natural decay of old structures. It would tell a story."

"See?" Zane leaned closer, his enthusiasm palpable. "That's the passion I'm talking about. Let your ideas breathe. And don't forget to take risks—sometimes the messiest work leads to the most beautiful outcomes."

I felt the walls of my insecurities begin to crumble, a breath of fresh air sweeping through my mind. "Thank you, Zane. Seriously. I needed this."

"Anytime," he said, his smile warm and genuine. "Now, how about we make this a little more interesting?"

"Interesting how?"

He grinned, mischief dancing in his eyes. "Let's have an art-off. We'll pick a theme and create something—whoever makes the most outrageous piece wins."

My heart raced at the challenge. "Are you sure you want to go up against me? I might have a few tricks up my sleeve."

"Bring it on," he said with a laugh, "I thrive on a little competition. Just be prepared to lose."

"Oh, is that a bet? Because I'm definitely winning this one."

With the stakes set and laughter filling the air, I felt a surge of energy course through me. The evening turned into a creative whirlwind, paint and ideas flying as we worked side by side, our playful banter igniting a fire within me. For the first time in a long while, I felt alive in my artistry, ready to break free from the chains of expectation and embrace the vibrant chaos of creation.

The air in Zane's apartment crackled with creativity and the slight chaos of paint splatters. With our art-off in full swing, the tension from earlier began to evaporate like mist under a rising sun. We had turned the living room into a makeshift studio, the floor strewn with colors and tools that hinted at the exhilarating mess we were about to create. I picked up a brush, my fingers tingling with anticipation as I looked at the blank canvas before me—a vast expanse of possibility waiting to be filled.

"What's your theme again?" Zane asked, tilting his head as he prepared his own canvas.

"Freedom versus confinement," I declared, channeling the energy from our earlier discussion. "I want to capture the tension of feeling trapped yet yearning to break free. How about you?"

He smirked, his eyes sparkling with mischief. "I was thinking of something more chaotic—'the vibrant clash of worlds.' You know, like if New York City were to wrestle with the Amazon rainforest."

I couldn't help but laugh. "That sounds like a disaster waiting to happen."

"Exactly! Bring on the chaos."

With that, we dove into our canvases. I started with bold strokes, layering deep blues and vivid greens, colors that whispered of growth and rebirth. My brush danced as I lost myself in the movement, the rhythm of creation flowing through me. Zane, on the other hand, was an explosion of energy. He splattered paint with abandon, a whirlwind of color erupting from his canvas like a vibrant volcano.

"This is what I'm talking about!" he shouted, a playful glint in his eyes as he flicked a splash of orange my way. It landed near my foot, a rogue drop of paint that only added to the atmosphere of frenetic creativity. "You're not actually going to let me win, are you?"

I narrowed my eyes, wiping my brush across my cheek as if preparing for battle. "Oh, this is far from over. You're about to see what happens when an artist refuses to be tamed."

The minutes flew by, our laughter and banter echoing off the walls. Every splash of paint, every stroke of the brush felt liberating. But beneath the joy lay an undercurrent of tension, a reminder of the struggles I faced in the studio. As I stood back to examine my work, a new idea struck me—a bold concept that melded the cacophony of my emotions into something visually arresting.

"Hey, Zane," I called out, shifting my focus from my canvas to his. "What do you think of incorporating elements of our earlier argument? The frustration, the conflict, the need for validation?"

"Now we're cooking," he replied, stepping back to take a look at his own chaotic masterpiece, which was morphing into a wild celebration of clashing colors. "Use it! Let it out. Channel that energy into your work."

As I added layers of texture, swirling together chaos and order, I could feel the remnants of doubt beginning to peel away. Each brushstroke became a catharsis, a release of everything I had bottled up during my time with Leo. In that moment, I was no longer an invisible artist. I was vibrant, alive, and unapologetically me.

"Look at this!" Zane exclaimed, pointing at a particularly bold section of his canvas where green splatters clashed with bursts of red. "It's like a city trying to breathe amid the madness."

"I love it!" I said, my voice a mix of admiration and excitement. "You're really capturing that push and pull. I think it's starting to come together for both of us."

He stepped closer to inspect my work, tilting his head in exaggerated contemplation. "Mmm, I sense a deep struggle here. Are you trying to escape from the clutches of a certain egotistical artist?"

"Who, me?" I feigned innocence, but the laughter bubbled up, escaping my lips. "Maybe I am."

Our playful jabs turned into deeper conversations about art, ambition, and the complexities of creative collaboration. With each passing moment, my earlier frustration transformed into something richer, a more profound understanding of my artistic journey. I realized how essential it was to embrace both my vulnerabilities and strengths, blending them into a symphony of color and emotion.

As the night wore on, the apartment filled with the smell of paint, and the music playing softly in the background began to shift to something more upbeat. The playful atmosphere was a perfect contrast to the intensity of our earlier discussion, and I felt a spark of something exciting—an electric charge of possibilities unfolding in my mind.

But just as I felt fully immersed in this newfound sense of purpose, Zane's phone buzzed on the kitchen counter, shattering the spell. He reached for it, his expression turning serious as he read the message.

"What's up?" I asked, sensing the shift in his demeanor.

"It's Leo," he said, his brow furrowing. "He wants to talk. Says it's urgent."

A knot tightened in my stomach at the mention of his name. "Talk? About what?"

"Not sure," Zane replied, his gaze flickering between the message and me. "But it seems like it has something to do with the project—and you."

"Great," I said, my heart racing. "This can't be good."

Zane set his phone down and stepped closer, his expression earnest. "You don't have to take it if you don't want to. We can just ignore him. Let's finish our masterpieces and call it a night."

"Tempting," I said, my mind spinning. Part of me wanted to turn my back on the whole situation, to revel in the artistic sanctuary we had created. But the other part—the part that had always sought validation—was curious. "But what if he wants to talk about my work? What if he wants to offer a collaboration?"

Zane raised an eyebrow, a mix of concern and support in his gaze. "Or it could be him trying to put you back in your place. Remember what we just discussed?"

"Yeah," I said, biting my lip, weighing my options. "But what if this is my chance to turn it all around?"

Before I could settle on a decision, Zane's phone buzzed again, this time with a follow-up message. He picked it up, and the look on his face sent a chill racing down my spine. "You need to see this."

"What is it?" I stepped closer, peering at the screen.

"It says... 'I need to meet tonight. It's about the direction of the project, and I think you'll want to hear what I have to say.'"

The words hung in the air, thick with tension and uncertainty. My mind raced as I felt the gravity of the situation pull at me. Would this be the moment that changed everything? Would I seize the opportunity, or would I let fear dictate my path once more?

Zane's gaze bore into mine, a silent question hanging between us. "What do you want to do?"

Before I could answer, the doorbell rang, echoing through the apartment like a thunderclap. My heart skipped a beat as I exchanged a glance with Zane, both of us frozen in a moment of shared realization.

"That can't be..." I whispered, my voice trailing off.

Zane nodded, tension rippling through the air. "It could be Leo."

And just like that, the warm glow of our creative sanctuary began to feel like a fragile bubble, teetering on the brink of chaos.

Chapter 25: The Power of Vulnerability

The studio buzzed with a chaotic harmony, a whirlwind of creativity that felt almost electric in the air. As I stepped through the heavy, graffiti-adorned door, the familiar scent of paint and varnish enveloped me, mingling with the sweet tang of lingering coffee. My heart raced with each step, a symphony of anticipation pounding beneath my ribcage. I was no longer the timid shadow that had tiptoed into this vibrant space weeks ago. Today, I wore my resolve like a second skin, and with it came the sharp clarity of purpose.

I found my artist, Morgan, hunched over a canvas splattered with colors that seemed to dance under the fluorescent lights. They paused mid-stroke, their brow furrowed in concentration, only to glance up, curiosity flashing in their eyes as I approached. "You're back," they said, a note of surprise coloring their voice, which was usually so controlled, like the tight lacing of a corset.

"Of course, I am," I replied, a hint of cheekiness slipping into my tone. "Did you think I'd let you get away with turning my dreams into a palette of pastel mush?"

Morgan chuckled, and that laugh unfurled something in my chest, loosening the tight coil of anxiety. "Okay, fair point. So, what's on your mind?"

I took a deep breath, letting the weight of my words gather before I spoke. "I want to reclaim my voice. I need to be part of this process, not just the canvas you paint on. I have ideas, and I need us to collaborate."

The air shifted as I laid out my thoughts, the gravity of my plea hanging between us like a bridge waiting to be crossed. There was a flicker of understanding in Morgan's eyes, a crack in the facade of professional detachment. "Collaboration, huh?" they mused, tilting their head, studying me. "You've been holding back."

"Like a dam bursting at the seams," I replied, my confidence rising like the tide. "This is my vision we're painting. I want to merge genres—take this music to a place where it feels truly me."

Morgan's expression morphed from surprise to intrigue. "That's bold. But what does that even look like? How do we mix the elements without losing the essence?"

The question hung in the air, and I seized the moment. "Picture it—an unexpected fusion. Classical strings underlaid with a gritty bass line, the warm embrace of jazz brushed with the electric thrill of rock. It's not just a sound; it's an emotion." My words flowed with newfound urgency, painting vivid images in the air between us, igniting the creative energy I had almost forgotten existed.

As we delved deeper into the brainstorming session, the atmosphere shifted from hesitant collaboration to a vibrant dance of ideas. Morgan and I bounced concepts off one another, crafting melodies that sparkled with life, layering rhythms like fine silk over a robust canvas. The studio transformed into a sanctuary of creativity, and I could feel the weight of my doubt lifting, replaced by a fierce exhilaration.

Hours slipped by, the golden light of the setting sun filtering through the high windows, casting a warm glow over the chaotic creativity of our workspace. The music we created seemed to echo off the walls, a sweet amalgamation of sounds that felt authentic, layered, and rich with texture. I could almost see the music flowing like a river, winding its way through every note, every beat, each one reflecting a part of me that I had hidden for too long.

"Is it too much?" I asked, hesitating for a brief moment, the specter of self-doubt creeping back in.

"Too much?" Morgan laughed, a delightful, rich sound that wrapped around me like a comforting blanket. "You've got to be kidding. It's electrifying! We're onto something here. Just look at what we've created!"

I felt the rush of pride swell within me, warmth spreading from my chest outwards. This was what I had been missing: the spark of collaboration, the interplay of ideas igniting like fireworks against the night sky. I wanted Zane to be part of this moment, to see me in this light—the light of someone reclaiming her narrative, her song, her spirit. I pulled out my phone, glancing at the screen, half-hoping for a message from him.

"Something on your mind?" Morgan asked, arching an eyebrow, a smirk tugging at the corner of their lips.

"Just wishing Zane could be here to see all this," I admitted, my voice softening, feeling a hint of vulnerability slide into the conversation. "He's been my rock through this whole mess. It feels like I owe him a front-row seat to my rebirth, you know?"

"Ah, the loyal sidekick," Morgan said, rolling their eyes playfully. "Every hero needs one, but you're the one in the spotlight now."

"True," I mused, a smile creeping onto my face. "But a hero without their sidekick can sometimes feel... incomplete."

The playful banter hung in the air like an echo, light and warm, bridging the distance between us. With each note we crafted, each idea we explored, I felt more whole, as if the pieces of me scattered across the past were finally weaving together into something beautiful, something vibrant.

As the clock ticked towards midnight, the studio buzzed with our laughter and the wild sounds of creation. The world outside faded, and in that cocoon of creativity, I could almost see the tapestry of my life unfurling, threads of vulnerability and strength interwoven, shimmering with promise. And in the quiet corners of my heart, a flicker of hope blossomed, urging me onward, daring me to embrace the beautiful chaos of becoming.

The rhythmic clatter of our creative exchange filled the studio, each idea spiraling into the next like a well-choreographed dance. It felt exhilarating to have my voice echoing off the walls, a melody in its own right, rising in harmony with the music we were crafting. As the sun dipped below the horizon, painting the sky in a palette of fiery oranges and muted purples, the atmosphere thickened with the scent of inspiration, heady and intoxicating.

With every note we layered, a rush of adrenaline surged through me, fueling my determination. Morgan leaned back, a paintbrush tucked behind one ear, and regarded me with a mixture of admiration and disbelief. "You're really onto something here. I didn't expect you to come in swinging like this. Where was this fire before?"

I shrugged, a grin tugging at the corners of my lips. "I suppose it was buried under layers of doubt and some well-meaning but misguided opinions. But like you said earlier, it's electrifying! I just had to dig a little deeper to find it."

Morgan chuckled, the sound vibrant and infectious. "Digging deep—sounds like you're gearing up for an archaeological expedition. Just be careful you don't unearth any ancient skeletons while you're at it."

"Oh please, I'd rather uncover lost treasures. Or at least something shiny," I shot back, laughing along with them. The room felt lighter, the barriers that once separated us crumbling like dust. We were artists, collaborating on something that pulsed with life, and it was an exhilarating sensation.

Just as we began to lose ourselves in the creative whirlwind, my phone buzzed on the table, breaking the spell. I picked it up, a surge of hope igniting within me, only to be met with disappointment—a message from a group chat I had forgotten about. A flurry of plans for the weekend that didn't include me.

"Everything okay?" Morgan asked, noticing the fleeting shadow across my face.

I forced a smile, though it felt a little brittle. "Just the weekend plans. Apparently, everyone decided to rally for some group outing without me."

"Ah, the classic social betrayal. You should start a support group for excluded friends," Morgan replied, their tone teasing but laced with genuine empathy. "Or better yet, throw a spontaneous party of your own. Who needs them when you have your music?"

"Good point," I mused, tapping my phone thoughtfully. "But I was really hoping Zane would be around to help me celebrate this new direction. He's been my biggest cheerleader through all of this."

"Sounds like a fun party waiting to happen. You could bring him into the mix; who knows, maybe he can lend his musical talents." Morgan's eyes sparkled mischievously. "And then we'll have a new genre altogether—'Zane and the Excluded.'"

"Zane and the Excluded? Now that's a band name that will really get the party going," I laughed, picturing Zane strumming a guitar, charming everyone with his wicked sense of humor.

Morgan's gaze turned thoughtful. "Have you told him how much his support means to you? I mean, really laid it out?"

The question caught me off guard. "I guess I haven't. It's easy to assume he knows, but I should probably be more explicit about it."

"Exactly," Morgan said, nodding vigorously. "People love to hear how they impact your life, especially when they're in your corner. A little vulnerability goes a long way, you know?"

Just then, I heard the familiar sound of the door creaking open, and a rush of cool air swept into the room. Zane stepped inside, his presence instantly brightening the dimly lit space. He had a casual charm about him—messy hair, worn jeans, and that smile that always felt like sunshine. "Hey, I came to see if I could steal you away for a moment."

"Oh, Zane, you're just in time! Morgan and I were just plotting world domination through music," I said, my heart fluttering with excitement at his arrival.

"World domination, huh? Sounds intense. Can I join? I'll bring the snacks," he joked, his eyes twinkling.

"Absolutely! You can be our lead guitarist," I declared, a warmth spreading through me at the thought of including him in this journey.

Morgan leaned back, arms crossed, a playful smirk on their face. "I don't know, Zane. Are you ready for the pressure of fame? We might need to hire a manager soon."

Zane laughed, a sound that filled the room with warmth. "Fame? Let's not get ahead of ourselves. I'm just here to support my favorite artist and her newfound vision."

"Support? That's an understatement," I countered, feeling my cheeks warm under his gaze. "You've been my rock through all this. I'm not sure I would have found my voice without you."

Zane's expression softened, the teasing glint in his eye replaced by something deeper. "You know I'll always be here for you, right? No matter how many late nights we spend in this chaotic studio."

"Exactly!" Morgan chimed in. "This one has the potential to become a masterpiece, and we'll need you to keep it grounded."

"Let's hope we don't drown in our own creativity," I quipped, smirking at Morgan. "But really, Zane, I want to thank you for always believing in me. It means more than I can say."

His gaze held mine, the world outside the studio fading as if we were cocooned in our own reality. "You're doing this for yourself, not for me. But I appreciate hearing that. It's nice to know I'm not just a background character in your story."

"Background characters can be pretty powerful, too," I replied, a playful lilt to my voice. "Like the quiet hero in a romantic comedy—stepping in at just the right moment."

Zane grinned, leaning against the wall, radiating that effortless charm that made my heart race. "Well, here's to you, our leading lady. Now, let's hear what this masterpiece sounds like."

With renewed energy flooding the room, we dove back into our work, laughter and creativity intertwining like a dance. As the notes soared around us, I realized that vulnerability, in its most potent form, had become a vital thread in the fabric of our collaboration. With each sound we crafted, I felt myself unraveling in the best way possible, a beautiful mess transforming into something extraordinary.

The energy in the studio swirled around us like a vibrant cyclone, a delicious blend of creativity and spontaneity. We had transformed this once-stifling space into a sanctuary of sound and laughter, and with Zane by my side, it felt like I could conquer anything. His casual leaning against the wall, casual yet engaged, brought an undeniable comfort. It was as if every chord we played was a step toward something monumental, a melody leading us to the edges of our imaginations.

Morgan plucked at the strings of the guitar, their fingers dancing nimbly, coaxing out notes that hung in the air like sweet perfume. "So, what's the next move? Where do we take this sonic adventure?" they asked, a spark of mischief in their eye.

"Let's add some layering, but not just any layering," I suggested, my pulse quickening at the thought. "What if we include some vocal harmonies that blend in and out, like waves crashing and receding on a shore? It could echo that feeling of coming back to oneself, you know?"

"Like a musical tide?" Zane chimed in, his smile wide as he leaned closer, enthusiasm bubbling. "I love it! It would give the track that push and pull, reflecting the struggle of finding one's voice."

"Yes! Exactly!" My excitement bubbled over, and I could feel a glimmer of hope blossoming in my chest. "And we could even incorporate spoken word sections, juxtaposing raw emotion with the polished sound."

Morgan's brow furrowed thoughtfully, but then they nodded, the gears clearly turning in their mind. "It's audacious, and I like it.

It could set the whole piece apart. But we'll need to be careful with how we structure it—too much, and it might drown the song."

"Drowning is not on our agenda," I quipped. "Only soaring!"

The laughter that erupted filled the room, a delightful cacophony that swirled into the air, joining the melodies we were crafting. With renewed vigor, we dove back into our creative whirlpool, time becoming a vague concept as the music enveloped us. Hours slipped by unnoticed, our collaborative efforts building upon each other until the piece began to take on a life of its own.

Suddenly, Zane's phone buzzed, a sharp intrusion into our world of sound. He glanced at the screen, and I watched as a flicker of concern crossed his features. "I should take this," he said, stepping outside to the hallway, his expression serious.

Morgan raised an eyebrow, their fingers still dancing on the guitar strings. "Everything okay?"

"Let's hope so," I replied, my gut twisting as Zane walked away. The energy shifted in his absence, like a light dimming. I couldn't help but wonder what news awaited him on the other side of that door.

"While we wait, how about we brainstorm some lyrics?" Morgan suggested, breaking the silence that had draped over the room. "We could find some key phrases that encapsulate what we're trying to say."

"Definitely," I said, trying to shake off the worry that had settled in my chest. "Let's dive into that raw emotion. We want to capture the essence of vulnerability without losing the strength that comes with it."

As we explored lyrics, my mind drifted back to my earlier conversations with Zane—his unwavering belief in my potential had been a beacon guiding me through the shadows of doubt. But what was going on with him? He had seemed distant lately, his texts becoming sparse, as if a fog had settled between us, blurring the lines of our connection.

"Do you ever feel like you're on the edge of something big, but there's a nagging voice in the back of your head telling you to pull back?" I asked Morgan, my voice barely above a whisper.

"Every artist has that voice, trust me," they replied, a soft understanding in their tone. "But sometimes, you have to silence it to let the music flow. Remember, fear is just a loud, annoying neighbor that thinks it can dictate the terms of your creativity. You've got to turn up the volume on your own inner soundtrack."

"Maybe you're right," I sighed, feeling a flicker of determination surge within me. "I won't let it hold me back anymore."

Just then, Zane returned, his expression a mixture of relief and concern. "Sorry about that," he said, running a hand through his hair, looking slightly ruffled. "It was just my brother checking in. Everything's good."

"Glad to hear it," I replied, though I couldn't shake the feeling that there was more to it than he let on. "We were just brainstorming lyrics. Ready to dive back in?"

Zane nodded, but there was something flickering behind his eyes, a hesitation that lingered just beneath the surface. "Actually, I've been thinking... maybe we should explore that fusion you mentioned earlier. Let's create something that really pushes boundaries, you know?"

Morgan and I exchanged a glance, both intrigued and a bit perplexed by his sudden shift in focus. "What do you have in mind?" I asked, tilting my head.

"I think we should take a risk. Let's invite someone else to collaborate. A fresh voice could bring a new energy, someone who can elevate the concept," Zane proposed, his enthusiasm almost contagious, yet his gaze drifted toward the window as if searching for something out there.

"Anyone in particular?" Morgan asked, strumming a chord thoughtfully.

"Yeah," Zane said, his voice dropping to a conspiratorial whisper. "I was thinking of reaching out to that vocalist from the other studio—her style is unconventional and raw. She could bring a unique edge to what we're doing."

A tingle of excitement shot through me, yet I couldn't ignore the nagging feeling at the back of my mind. "That sounds amazing, but do you think she'll be willing to collaborate? It could change the entire vibe of what we've created so far."

"I think she would," Zane said, confidence coloring his tone. "She's been looking for a project like this, something that blends genres and explores new territories. Plus, you'll never know unless you ask, right?"

"Right." The idea buzzed around my mind, invigorating yet terrifying.

As we continued to brainstorm, the atmosphere crackled with possibilities, but a shadow lurked at the edges of my excitement. Zane seemed more withdrawn, the conversation flowing over him like water as he remained focused on the lyrics but lost in thought. I wanted to reach out, to peel back the layers of his silence, but the moment felt fragile, like a spider's web glistening in the morning dew.

Then, just as we began crafting a chorus that resonated with all the emotions we'd been channeling, Zane's phone buzzed again. This time, he stared at the screen for a moment longer, the color draining from his face. My heart plummeted as a feeling of foreboding enveloped the room.

"What's wrong?" I asked, my voice barely above a whisper, sensing that whatever was on the other end of that phone call was about to change everything.

He turned to face us, his expression shifting from surprise to concern, and as he opened his mouth to speak, the studio door swung open again. The air turned electric with an unexpected tension, and my breath caught in my throat. There, framed in the doorway, stood a figure I had never expected to see—a past I thought I'd left behind. The figure's gaze locked onto mine, an unspoken challenge lingering in the air.

Chapter 26: Shadows of the Past

The phone vibrated on my desk, a persistent reminder of the life I thought I had neatly compartmentalized. I glanced at the screen, my heart lurching at the sight of the name that had become a ghost haunting my every waking moment. Jake's family. They wanted to meet.

Just when I believed I had finally stitched together a semblance of normalcy, the universe decided to yank the thread, unraveling everything in its wake. A wave of dread crashed over me, cold and unforgiving, as I remembered the weight of his absence—an absence that seeped into my thoughts like fog on a winter morning. For months, I had crafted a fragile fortress around my heart, convinced that solitude and distraction could keep the memories at bay. Yet here I was, facing the specters of my past with a single phone call.

I sank back into my chair, the leather creaking in protest, as I dialed Zane's number. He answered almost immediately, his voice a comforting balm amidst my swirling thoughts. "Hey, what's up?"

"Jake's family wants to meet," I said, trying to keep my voice steady. The words tasted bitter on my tongue, each syllable a reminder of the love I had lost.

"Have you called them back?" he asked, the concern palpable in his tone.

"No, I was hoping to avoid it forever," I admitted, the confession hanging in the air like a heavy cloud.

"Listen, you need to do this," Zane said, his voice firm yet gentle, like a soft hand on my back. "Closure is important. You can't keep running from it."

"Closure? Is that what we're calling it now?" I scoffed, unable to mask the sarcasm. "It feels more like stepping into a minefield blindfolded."

"Then take off the blindfold," he shot back, a playful edge creeping into his voice. "Look, I get it. It's scary. But what if this meeting brings you some peace? You owe it to yourself."

The irony wasn't lost on me. Here I was, terrified of confronting the ghosts that lingered in the corners of my mind, yet I had spent years chasing after resolution in other people's lives. I sighed, the air escaping my lungs in a rush. "Fine. I'll call them back."

As I hung up, a familiar melody floated through my thoughts, a song that had once danced between us, filling the air with laughter and promises. Jake had a knack for turning even the most mundane moments into something extraordinary, and now, with each memory, I felt like I was walking a tightrope strung between the past and an uncertain future.

The days passed in a haze of anticipation and dread, the date of our meeting looming like a storm cloud. I found myself lost in the mundane, trying to prepare for the inevitable while avoiding the flood of emotions that threatened to engulf me. The morning of our meeting arrived with a shroud of grey, the sky weeping soft, pitiful drops that matched the turmoil in my heart.

When I stepped into the café, the familiar aroma of coffee and freshly baked pastries enveloped me, a bittersweet reminder of the mornings Jake and I had spent here, our laughter mixing with the clatter of cups and chatter of patrons. My heart raced as I spotted his family at a corner table, their expressions a mix of anticipation and sorrow. They were just as I remembered, yet somehow altered by grief.

"Thank you for coming," Jake's mother said, her voice soft yet steady, like the warm embrace I had longed for but feared all the same. I nodded, my throat tightening as the words caught in my chest.

We exchanged pleasantries, the conversation starting as a cautious dance around the elephant in the room. Yet, the more we talked, the more I felt the walls I had built around my heart begin to crack. Stories of Jake spilled forth, each one a beautiful yet painful reminder of what had been lost.

"Do you remember the time he tried to serenade you?" Jake's sister asked, a hint of mischief in her eyes.

"Of course," I chuckled, the memory flooding back. "He was convinced he could sing, but I'm pretty sure even the coffee machine was trying to drown him out."

Laughter erupted around the table, and for a moment, the weight of grief felt lighter, like a fleeting cloud parting to let the sun shine through.

But as the conversation turned more serious, the laughter faded, replaced by the tension that lingered like the taste of bitter coffee. They wanted to know about my life after Jake, how I had coped, how I had continued without him. Each question felt like a knife twisting in my chest, exposing wounds I thought had healed.

"Do you think he'd be proud of you?" Jake's mother asked, her gaze piercing through my carefully constructed facade.

"I... I hope so," I replied, my voice barely above a whisper. "I tried to live the life he would've wanted for me."

As the words left my lips, I realized how true they were, yet the sadness that followed was a reminder of all the dreams that would remain unfulfilled. I had poured my heart into my work, my passion serving as both a balm and a distraction, but the ache of longing lingered, a shadow always at my side.

With each story shared, the ghosts of our past danced in the periphery, but there was also something new—a sense of connection, an unspoken understanding that grief, while isolating, could also weave people together in unexpected ways.

With each passing moment in the café, I felt the boundaries of my carefully constructed armor begin to blur, like watercolor on a canvas. Jake's family shared their memories with a tenderness that wrapped around me, the nostalgia a double-edged sword. Laughter spilled forth from their lips, each anecdote a reminder of what I had lost, yet it also knit together the frayed edges of our shared grief. They were not merely shadows of my past; they were pieces of a life that had intertwined with my own, their laughter echoing the joyful notes Jake had played.

"Remember the Halloween when he insisted on dressing up as a pumpkin?" Jake's sister said, shaking her head with a fond smile. "He spent hours perfecting that costume, only to realize he didn't quite look like a pumpkin, more like a confused beach ball."

I couldn't help but laugh, the sound genuine and warm. "I still have pictures of that monstrosity somewhere. I think it's time I framed one and hung it in my living room for all future guests to enjoy."

As the laughter faded, an uncomfortable silence settled around us. Jake's mother, her eyes glistening with unshed tears, turned the conversation toward more sensitive subjects, her voice wavering slightly. "How have you been coping since... since he left us?"

I shifted in my seat, suddenly aware of the weight of their expectations. I was supposed to have all the answers, to carry the weight of Jake's memory with grace and poise. But instead, I felt like a marionette with tangled strings, each pull an invitation to unravel further. "I keep busy," I managed, forcing a smile that felt more like a grimace. "Work helps. It keeps my mind from wandering too far into the depths."

Jake's sister leaned in, her expression softening. "We've seen your work online. You've been doing amazing things. I hope you know he would've been so proud of you."

Proud. The word hung in the air, heavy and bittersweet. I nodded, attempting to mask the lump forming in my throat. "I hope so," I replied, my voice barely audible, each word feeling like a pebble thrown into a vast canyon—too insignificant to bridge the distance of my grief.

But the sincerity in their gazes pulled me from the shadows of my mind, forcing me to confront the truth I had been hiding from. I had built a life that honored Jake, yet it felt like an incomplete puzzle, pieces forever missing. "I still think about him every day," I confessed, the admission slipping out before I could rein it back. "I see something funny, and I can't help but think, 'Oh, Jake would've loved this.' But then... it hits me that I can't share it with him."

A silence descended, thick and profound. Jake's mother reached across the table, her hand warm and comforting over mine. "You're not alone in that. We feel the same. It's hard to explain how much he's still a part of our lives, even though he's gone."

We exchanged stories of his quirks, his passions, the music that made him who he was. The laughter returned, but it was tinged with sorrow, a melody of what could have been. I felt the years of isolation slip away, replaced by a shared understanding that was both healing and heart-wrenching.

But just as I was beginning to find solace in our camaraderie, the conversation took an unexpected turn. "There's something we need to discuss," Jake's mother said, her tone shifting, the weight of her words palpable.

I braced myself, the air suddenly electric with tension. "What is it?" I asked, my heart racing as the walls I had just begun to lower sprang back up.

"We found something," she continued, her eyes flickering with uncertainty. "Something that Jake left behind. We think it's important."

My mind raced, panic clawing at my insides. What could it be? Had he left a message? A letter? Or something more tangible that could rip open the wounds I had barely stitched closed? "What do you mean?" I pressed, a lump forming in my throat.

Jake's sister reached into her bag, pulling out a small, worn journal. The cover was battered, the edges frayed, as if it had traveled through time. "He kept this. We found it after..." she hesitated, her voice cracking. "After he passed. We think you should have it."

The journal rested in her hands like a fragile relic, and I could hardly breathe as I reached for it. My fingers brushed against the leather, and a wave of memories rushed back—his laughter, his dreams, the late-night talks that felt like secrets shared under a blanket of stars. I opened the journal, the scent of aged paper wafting up, and my heart stopped at the sight of his familiar scrawl.

"What's in it?" I whispered, knowing that whatever it contained could either be a balm for my aching heart or a new wound I wasn't ready to face.

"Thoughts, ideas, dreams," Jake's mother said softly. "Things he never had the chance to share with you."

I flipped through the pages, my heart racing as snippets of his thoughts leaped off the page. There were doodles, half-finished songs, and rambling musings that danced between the profound and the absurd. And then, I found it—my name, written in bold letters at the top of a page filled with plans and dreams for our future together.

"Wow," I breathed, the weight of the words crashing over me like a tidal wave. I felt exposed, vulnerable, the raw emotion threatening to spill out. "He was planning... all this?"

"He had so many hopes for you, for your life together," Jake's sister said, her eyes shining with unshed tears. "And he believed in you, even in ways you might not have realized."

With each word I read, I could feel the pieces of my heart shifting, reassembling themselves with the weight of his love and expectations. But as hope fluttered within me, a bitter realization crept in—the paths we had envisioned would remain forever untraveled. "This is beautiful," I said, forcing a smile as the tears began to spill. "But it's also heartbreaking."

"We know," Jake's mother replied, her voice thick with emotion. "But we wanted you to have this, to remember that he believed in you, in your dreams. You deserve to carry that forward."

The heaviness in my chest morphed into a bittersweet ache, the love that filled the journal becoming a lifeline tethering me to a future that was no longer possible. I could feel Jake's presence in the pages, an echo of his laughter intertwined with my own joy and sorrow. I had lost him, but this—this was a piece of him that I could hold on to, a reminder that his love still lived on, even in the spaces where he no longer walked beside me.

As I sat there, the journal cradled in my hands, I felt the warmth of connection blooming between us—a family, bound by grief yet united in the love we shared for someone who had left an indelible mark on our lives.

As I sat at the café table, the journal open before me like a treasure chest brimming with memories, I was struck by the contrast between the hope it held and the ache of longing that weighed heavily on my heart. Each doodle, each unfinished lyric, seemed to resonate with the laughter and the love that filled my days with Jake. It was as if he had left breadcrumbs for me to follow, leading me out of the darkness that threatened to swallow me whole.

"This is incredible," I said, my voice wavering as I gestured to the pages filled with his handwriting. "He poured his heart into this."

Jake's mother and sister exchanged glances, a mix of sadness and understanding flickering in their eyes. "He always believed in living fully," Jake's mother said. "We think he would have wanted you to find your own way, even if he couldn't be there to see it."

Their words hung in the air, a bittersweet reminder that while Jake had envisioned a life filled with dreams, I was left to navigate the jagged path of reality without him. But the journal was a lifeline, a connection to his spirit, and the warmth of his love ignited something deep within me—a flicker of resilience I hadn't realized I'd lost.

"Can I take this?" I asked, cradling the journal like a delicate bird. "I want to keep it close."

"Of course," Jake's sister replied, her smile gentle. "It's meant for you."

As I tucked the journal into my bag, I felt an overwhelming sense of gratitude wash over me, mingling with the sorrow. It was a moment of clarity amidst the fog of grief, and for the first time in a long while, I felt ready to embrace the world beyond the confines of my heartache.

The conversation shifted back to lighter topics, and the laughter returned, filling the space like the aroma of freshly brewed coffee. We swapped stories about Jake's terrible cooking experiments and his ridiculous dance moves that could only be described as "enthusiastic." The memories flowed freely, and for a moment, I almost forgot the sorrow that had loomed like a shadow.

But just as I began to feel the warmth of belonging, the café door swung open with a dramatic flourish, sending a chill through the room. A man entered, his presence commanding immediate attention. He was tall, with tousled dark hair and a confident stride that seemed to pull all eyes toward him. My heart raced as I recognized him—Sam, Jake's best friend. The last time I had seen him, he had been a shadow at Jake's funeral, a figure haunted by grief.

"Hey, everyone," he said, his voice smooth yet strained, like a melody that had lost its rhythm. "Mind if I join?"

Jake's family exchanged hesitant glances before gesturing for him to sit. As he approached our table, I felt a mixture of excitement and trepidation. Sam had been a constant presence in Jake's life, a confidant and partner in crime. I could still picture them sprawled on the couch, debating the merits of various superhero movies, their laughter echoing through the room.

"Wow, it's been a while," he said, his eyes landing on me. "How are you holding up?"

"Like a deflated balloon, but I'm working on reinflating," I replied, trying to inject some humor into my voice, even as it wobbled. "Thanks for asking."

Sam smiled faintly, the corners of his mouth twitching in acknowledgment. "You've always had a way with words. I've missed that."

There was something in his tone that made my heart skip a beat, an unspoken understanding that lingered in the air. It felt as though he was searching for the right words, a delicate thread weaving through our shared grief.

Jake's sister shifted in her seat, breaking the silence. "We were just sharing some memories of Jake. It's been a nice way to remember him."

"Yeah, he would've loved this," Sam said, a distant look crossing his face. "He had this incredible ability to turn any mundane moment into something special."

We shared stories for a while longer, the tension slowly dissipating as laughter filled the air once again. But I couldn't shake the feeling that something was brewing beneath the surface, an undercurrent of unspoken words and unresolved feelings. Sam seemed different, as if he carried a burden heavier than the rest of us.

"I've been meaning to talk to you," he said suddenly, his gaze locked onto mine with an intensity that made my pulse quicken. "There's something I need to tell you, something Jake wanted you to know."

The room fell silent, the laughter fading into an expectant hush. My heart raced, the words hanging in the air like a fragile thread ready to snap. "What is it?" I asked, my voice trembling.

He hesitated, his brow furrowing as he seemed to weigh his words carefully. "It's about the time leading up to... you know. There were things Jake didn't share, things he kept hidden. I think he wanted you to have this information, to understand."

My stomach churned with anxiety. What could he possibly mean? "Sam, you're scaring me," I admitted, my voice barely above a whisper.

"I just... I need you to promise you'll hear me out before you react," he said, his expression serious. "Jake was planning something, something that would have changed everything for you two. But he didn't have the chance to tell you."

The weight of his words settled over me, a suffocating blanket of dread. I felt like I was teetering on the edge of a precipice, every instinct warning me to step back. "What are you saying?"

But before he could respond, a loud crash echoed from the back of the café, causing everyone to jump. A group of people had entered, their voices raised in angry debate, and the atmosphere shifted dramatically.

"Get away from him!" a woman shouted, her face flushed with anger as she pointed at a man who stood off to the side, his demeanor guarded.

"Who do you think you are?" the man shot back, a defiant glint in his eyes. "You don't know anything!"

Panic rippled through the café, patrons shifting uneasily in their seats. Sam's gaze flickered toward the commotion, and I felt the tension between us snap like a taut string.

"I'll tell you everything," he whispered urgently, leaning closer, but his words were drowned out by the chaos erupting around us.

Just as I opened my mouth to respond, the room went dark—a sudden power outage plunging us into an abyss of uncertainty. The hum of the café was replaced by nervous murmurs and the clinking of cups, while flashes of panic lit the faces of the patrons.

In the chaos, I felt a hand on my arm, pulling me closer. "Stay close to me," Sam said, his voice low but firm, as the darkness deepened, swallowing us whole.

As I squeezed the journal tightly to my chest, a knot formed in my stomach. I couldn't shake the feeling that the storm wasn't just outside but brewing in the shadows of our shared grief—a reckoning that had been long overdue. What secrets lurked in Jake's past, and what had Sam been holding back?

As the darkness settled around us, I was left hanging in the balance, unsure of what was about to unravel or who would emerge from the shadows.

Chapter 27: The Meeting

The café hums with life, an enchanting blend of soft jazz and the clinking of porcelain cups that creates a comforting cocoon around me. As I push the door open, a bell jingles overhead, announcing my arrival like a tiny cheer. Sunlight spills through the large windows, illuminating the rustic wooden tables, each bearing a unique character, their surfaces scarred by time yet polished with affection. I breathe in the scent of freshly ground coffee and baked pastries, and my heart beats a little faster. This place, with its mismatched chairs and walls adorned with local art, feels like a warm hug, even as the weight of my purpose settles on my shoulders.

I spot Jake's family seated at a corner table, their laughter bubbling over like the frothy lattes in front of them. I hadn't realized how much I needed this, how much I needed to see their faces, to hear their stories. They wave me over, and I make my way through the small space, each step stirring a cocktail of emotions in my chest. As I approach, I catch snippets of their conversation—a shared joke about Jake's awful singing and a heartfelt recount of his obsession with vinyl records. The air is thick with nostalgia and love, and I can't help but smile, even as a pang of loss ripples through me.

"Look who decided to join us!" Jake's mother, Clara, exclaims, her voice rich and warm like the chocolate croissant she offers me. Her eyes shimmer with a blend of joy and sadness, a reflection of the shared understanding that this meeting is both a celebration and a farewell. I take a seat, grateful for the comfort of their company, as I bite into the croissant, the flaky layers crumbling in my hands. The taste is buttery and sweet, a little piece of happiness amidst the bittersweet moment.

As we exchange stories, laughter flows like the coffee, rich and warm. Clara recalls the time Jake tried to cook for them and nearly burned down the kitchen with his "famous" pasta. "I think he mistook salt for sugar," she chuckles, her eyes brightening. "I've never seen anyone make macaroni and cheese quite like him." The laughter envelops me, and for a moment, I forget the heavy weight of grief resting on my heart. Instead, I'm transported to a time when Jake was here, his spirit alive in every joke and every note he strummed on his guitar.

I join in, sharing a memory of Jake's unforgettable birthday party, how he serenaded me with a clumsy rendition of our favorite song, his voice cracking yet full of passion. "He had a way of making even the most embarrassing moments feel special," I say, my voice a mixture of joy and sorrow. They nod in agreement, their faces etched with the same fondness I feel, as if the very essence of Jake still lingers in the air, urging us to cherish him.

As the afternoon wears on, the sunlight shifts, casting a golden hue across the table, bathing us in warmth. Each story we share is a thread woven into the fabric of our memories, pulling us closer together. I realize that this gathering isn't just about remembering Jake; it's about honoring his spirit by embracing the love he inspired in us all. And as the conversation deepens, I find a sense of peace settling over me. I understand now that my love for Jake doesn't negate the budding feelings I have for Zane. It's a delicate balance, one that requires both courage and vulnerability.

But as I sit there, I feel a flicker of uncertainty. Zane has been a steady presence in my life, a gentle force pushing me to heal, yet the thought of moving forward feels like betrayal. How do I honor one love while nurturing another? My heart wrestles with this internal conflict, a quiet storm brewing beneath the surface. Clara's laughter cuts through my thoughts, pulling me back to the table, where a story about Jake's high school band captivates everyone. The warmth of their memories fills the room, chasing away the shadows lurking in my mind.

"Do you remember that time he tried to impress you with that song he wrote?" Jake's sister, Mia, asks, her eyes sparkling with mischief. "He was convinced he'd win your heart with it." I chuckle, recalling the awkwardness of the moment, how Jake had been so earnest, so desperately hopeful. The memory feels like a soft blanket, wrapping around my heart and reminding me of the joy he brought into my life.

As the meeting begins to wind down, Clara reaches for my hand, her grip firm and reassuring. "You have to keep moving forward, you know. Jake would want that for you," she says softly, her eyes reflecting the deep well of love she holds for her son. "He wouldn't want you to be stuck in the past." I nod, the weight of her words sinking in. She's right, of course. Love doesn't have a shelf life; it transforms, evolves.

The café's bustle fades into the background as I take in their faces, a mixture of love and resolve swirling within me. I have a choice to make, and it's one I won't shy away from. I can carry Jake with me, a bright memory that fuels my heart as I step into the unknown future with Zane. I'm ready to honor Jake's legacy, to let his light guide me while I explore the budding relationship blossoming in front of me.

As I stand to leave, I feel lighter, a burden lifting from my chest. I'm stepping out of the shadows of grief, ready to embrace the love that awaits. The laughter of Jake's family lingers in my ears like a cherished melody, and with each step I take towards the door, I know I carry both love and memory in my heart, intertwined yet distinct. Today marks a new beginning, one that honors the past while bravely facing the future.

The café doors swing shut behind me with a soft chime, and as I step back onto the sun-drenched street, a wave of autumn air greets me, crisp and invigorating. The leaves, painted in vibrant shades of gold and crimson, dance in the gentle breeze, rustling like whispers of encouragement. With every breath, I feel the remnants of the afternoon's bittersweet nostalgia begin to melt away, replaced by a newfound resolve that blooms within me. I clutch my purse tightly, a talisman against the uncertainty that lingers on the horizon.

Zane had texted me earlier, his words a playful reminder of our dinner plans that evening. "Can't wait to see you! I hope you're ready for my famous pasta." The cheeky grin I could almost picture on his face made my heart flutter. I smile to myself, the thought of him a bright splash of color in my otherwise muted palette of feelings. He had a way of pulling me into his orbit, making everything seem lighter, as if we were cocooned in a bubble where only laughter and good food existed.

As I walk through Silver Lake, the familiar streets seem to hum with life. The charming boutiques and artisanal shops beckon me with their twinkling lights and cheerful displays. I stop briefly at a flower shop, where the scent of fresh blooms wraps around me like a hug. The vibrant dahlias and crisp white chrysanthemums catch my eye, and I can't resist picking up a small bouquet. Flowers are always a good idea, and today, they feel like a fitting tribute to both love and remembrance.

By the time I arrive at Zane's apartment, the sun has dipped low in the sky, painting the horizon in swirls of pink and orange. I take a moment to gather myself outside his door, the thrill of anticipation buzzing in my veins. Zane has a way of making the ordinary feel extraordinary, like a magician who pulls happiness out of thin air. With a steadying breath, I knock, my heart dancing a little at the thought of seeing him.

The door swings open, revealing Zane with his trademark grin, a bright, infectious smile that lights up his entire face. He wears an apron that's smudged with flour and hints of marinara, and his hair is a delightful mess, tousled from what I can only imagine was an intense cooking session. "You're just in time to witness my culinary genius," he declares, puffing out his chest with mock seriousness.

"Genius or disaster?" I quip, stepping inside, the warmth of his apartment enveloping me. It's a cozy space, filled with mismatched furniture and the faint scent of garlic that instantly makes my mouth water. "I could smell it from the hallway. Are you trying to woo me with spaghetti?"

"Of course! It's my secret weapon." He winks, and I can't help but chuckle. "You see, the secret ingredient is love—or at least that's what my grandma always said."

"Well, I hope she also taught you how to use a timer, or we might be in trouble," I tease, glancing around at the bustling kitchen. The stove is lined with pots and pans, all in various stages of chaos. "I didn't realize we were having a cooking competition tonight."

"Just wait until you taste it! I promise it will be life-changing," he retorts, a playful glint in his eyes. There's something about his energy that makes everything feel possible, as if he's casting a spell that's as potent as the aroma wafting from the pot.

I help him set the table, our banter flowing easily as we arrange mismatched plates and glasses, creating a cozy setting that feels both intimate and warm. "So, what's the plan for our next adventure?" I ask, my curiosity piqued. We had spent the last few weeks exploring the local hiking trails, and while I cherished those moments, I was eager to see where our journey would lead us next.

Zane leans back against the counter, crossing his arms with a mischievous smile. "I was thinking we could go to the art fair this weekend. They have a local artist showcasing her work, and I hear she's incredible."

"Art? You're stepping up your game! Are you sure you can handle it?" I ask, my voice teasing yet curious.

"Hey, I can appreciate the arts, you know!" he protests, his eyes sparkling with amusement. "Plus, I'll need an expert to explain the meanings behind all those abstract paintings."

"Ah, so you want me to be your personal tour guide? Well, I might charge for that service," I reply, smirking.

"Deal! I'll pay you in pasta." He gestures grandly toward the bubbling pot, and I can't suppress a laugh. There's a comforting rhythm to our conversation, an easy camaraderie that makes me feel at home. It's in these moments that I sense the budding layers of something deeper between us, something vibrant and thrilling.

Just then, the timer dings, cutting through our playful banter, and Zane rushes over to check the pasta. "Moment of truth!" he exclaims, pulling it from the heat with the flair of a game show host revealing the grand prize. "Drumroll, please!"

I join in, my hands mimicking a drumroll against the table. As he twirls the spaghetti onto plates, the sight is both impressive and comically chaotic, a noodle here and a splash of sauce there. "Not bad for a self-proclaimed chef," I admit, my mouth watering at the sight.

"Just wait until you taste it," he says, presenting the dish with a flourish. The steam rises, filling the air with a comforting aroma that is somehow both familiar and new.

We settle at the table, and the first bite is nothing short of delightful. "Okay, you win this round," I concede, my fork pausing mid-air as I savor the flavor. "This is amazing!"

"See? I told you!" he grins, leaning back in his chair, clearly pleased with himself. As we eat, our conversation flows effortlessly from one topic to another—our dreams, our pasts, and the little things that make us who we are. I find myself sharing more than I intended, the walls I had built slowly crumbling as the warmth of his presence washes over me.

Then, unexpectedly, the conversation takes a turn, and I can feel the air shift. Zane's expression becomes serious, his eyes searching mine. "Can I ask you something?"

I nod, my heart quickening as curiosity replaces the comfort we've built. "Of course."

He hesitates, as if weighing his words. "I know it's been a while since you lost Jake. How do you feel about... everything? About moving on?" His tone is gentle, laced with a genuine desire to understand.

The question hangs heavy between us, and I swallow hard, feeling the familiar pang of grief. "It's complicated," I begin, unsure of how much to reveal. "I loved him, and I always will. But I also know he wouldn't want me to be stuck. It's... it's like trying to find a balance between holding on and letting go."

Zane listens intently, his gaze unwavering. "That's completely understandable. But I want you to know that I'm here for you, whatever that means for us. I just—" he pauses, his voice softening. "I want you to be happy, even if that means I have to share you with Jake's memory."

His words hit me like a soft wave, soothing yet powerful. "I want that too," I admit, feeling a weight lift slightly. "I want to move forward with you, but it's like juggling two worlds. Sometimes, I'm afraid I'll drop one."

"Then let's find a way to balance it together," he suggests, his tone filled with sincerity. "I don't want to rush you, but I also don't want you to feel like you have to choose."

I nod, the tension easing a little, replaced by the warmth of understanding. "That sounds... perfect."

With that, the conversation flows into lighter topics once more, the lingering heaviness dissipating, leaving us with laughter and shared glances that promise something more. As we finish our dinner, I feel the world around us blur, the boundaries of past and present intertwining in a delicate dance, each moment building a bridge to whatever comes next.

The evening drapes itself over the city like a rich velvet cloak, its shadows deepening in corners while twinkling lights begin to punctuate the skyline. After dinner, Zane and I settle into the plush embrace of his worn-out couch, the fabric faded yet inviting, its well-loved surface cradling us in comfort. The glow from the table lamp casts a soft, golden hue over the room, where eclectic decor showcases glimpses of Zane's personality—artsy prints hanging crookedly on the walls, quirky knick-knacks gathered from various flea markets, and a stack of books precariously balanced on the coffee table. It's a reflection of his creative chaos, a mosaic of passions that instantly puts me at ease.

As we lean back, our plates cleared and bellies satisfied, I can feel the energy between us shift, the earlier levity giving way to a more intimate atmosphere. Zane grabs the remote and flicks through channels, glancing at me. "What's your guilty pleasure—rom-coms or horror movies?"

I laugh, the question surprising me. "Definitely rom-coms. Who doesn't love a good meet-cute?"

"Ah, so you're a sucker for predictable happy endings," he teases, a smirk playing on his lips. "How about we combine both? A rom-com with a horror twist? Like a wedding gone wrong, where the bride is actually a zombie."

"Now that's a plot I'd pay to see! You might be onto something," I respond, my eyes dancing with amusement. "But what happens when she meets her true love? Does he have to fight off her flesh-eating instincts?"

"Of course! Love conquers all, even the desire for brains," he quips, and we dissolve into laughter, the sound echoing warmly in the room. It's moments like these that remind me of the beauty in simplicity, the effortless connection that blooms when two people allow themselves to be truly present.

Just then, Zane's phone buzzes, vibrating against the coffee table with urgency. He picks it up, glancing at the screen before frowning slightly. "It's my sister," he murmurs, a hint of concern creeping into his voice. "I should probably take this."

"Of course, go ahead," I say, waving him off with a smile, though a tiny thread of curiosity tugs at me. As he steps into the kitchen, the clatter of dishes and his low voice fades into the background, leaving me alone with my thoughts. I take a moment to absorb the warmth of the space and the remnants of our earlier laughter.

A few minutes pass, and I can't help but eavesdrop just a little. "What's wrong?" I hear him ask, his tone serious. The silence that follows is palpable, thick with unspoken worry. My heart races as I wonder what could be causing such concern. Zane has always been the rock in our dynamic, the one who effortlessly brings light into any situation. Hearing him sound even slightly shaken unsettles me.

When he returns, the lightness in his demeanor has dimmed, and I can see the worry etched across his brow. "Everything okay?" I ask, concern knitting my own eyebrows together.

He sits back down, running a hand through his hair, which only adds to the tousled charm of his appearance. "It's my sister, Claire. She's had a rough day at work and called to vent. It's nothing major, just the usual chaos. But you know how it is. She always thinks the world is ending."

"Of course. Sisters can be dramatic," I say with a knowing nod. "I have a brother, and it's like an endless soap opera with him."

"Right? The drama never ends," he chuckles, though I can tell his mind is still partially elsewhere. "She's trying to manage a project that's falling apart, and I feel bad because I can't just jump in and fix everything for her."

"Sometimes just being there is enough," I reassure him, hoping to lighten his mood. "You know, like an emotional first-aid kit."

"An emotional first-aid kit, huh?" he muses, a smile breaking through the tension. "I'll keep that in mind for next time. Maybe I should just throw her a care package filled with chocolates and a nice bubble bath bomb."

"Now you're talking! Nothing soothes the soul like chocolate and a good soak. Add a rom-com and she'll be golden," I reply, pleased to see the weight on his shoulders lift a little.

As the evening continues, we meander through various conversations, but an undercurrent of something unspoken lingers. Zane leans closer, his voice dipping lower. "Can I ask you something a little more serious?"

"Serious? Are you sure you're ready for that?" I tease lightly, though a part of me knows this is a moment of transition.

He chuckles softly, then grows serious, meeting my gaze. "I mean it. I want to know where we stand. I care about you, and I need to understand what that means."

I swallow hard, the unexpected weight of his words settling in the air between us like a delicate balance. "Zane, I care about you too. But I'm still figuring things out. I want to be honest with you."

"Honesty is all I want," he replies, his expression earnest. "If you need time, I get it. But I don't want to play games. Life's too short for that."

A flicker of uncertainty dances in my chest, as I grapple with my emotions and the shadows of my past. "I don't want to rush into anything, but it's hard not to feel... something when I'm with you. You make me laugh and forget."

He nods, his eyes softening. "Then let's take it one step at a time. I'm here for the journey, wherever it leads us."

I'm about to respond when the sudden blare of Zane's phone cuts through the moment, its sound jarring against the warmth that enveloped us. He glances down, his eyes widening slightly. "It's Claire again. I should take this."

I nod, trying to push down the unexpected unease fluttering in my stomach as he walks back to the kitchen, leaving me alone with my thoughts once more. As I listen to him murmur reassurance, my mind races. Everything feels so fragile, like the delicate balance between past and present, love and loss, and the decisions that lay ahead.

Zane's voice fades as he talks to his sister, and I glance around his apartment, letting my gaze settle on the little details—the framed photos of his family, the vibrant artwork scattered on the walls, the way the light creates soft patterns as it dances through the window. But amidst the warmth, a sense of foreboding creeps in.

When he returns, the expression on his face has shifted again, and this time, it's marked by a furrowed brow. "Sorry about that. Claire's really in a tight spot now, and she asked if I could come over to help. It's kind of urgent."

"Of course. Family first," I say, though a knot forms in my stomach. The timing couldn't be worse; just as we were starting to delve deeper into our feelings, reality crashes in, pulling him away.

"Do you mind if I leave? I know it's last minute," he says, his voice tinged with regret.

"No, go. I totally understand," I reply, masking my disappointment with a supportive smile. "Just promise me you'll check in later?"

"Absolutely." He leans in, placing a soft kiss on my cheek, and my heart flutters with warmth.

But as he pulls away, the doorbell rings, cutting through the moment with an unexpected sharpness. Zane glances at me, a mix of confusion and concern on his face. "That's odd. I wasn't expecting anyone."

Curiosity piqued, I nod toward the door. "Do you want me to get it?"

"Yeah, sure," he replies, stepping aside. I rise, my heart racing as I approach the door, the sense of anticipation crackling in the air.

When I swing it open, I'm met with a sight that sends a chill down my spine—standing there is a figure cloaked in shadows, their face obscured by a hood. The streetlamp casts a flickering glow, illuminating just enough to reveal the glint of something metallic in their hand.

"Is Zane here?" the figure demands, their voice low and gravelly, sending a shiver coursing through me.

I glance back at Zane, who's frozen in place, an expression of alarm flickering across his features. "What's going on?" I ask, my voice barely above a whisper.

"Just tell him it's urgent," the stranger presses, stepping closer, the metallic object reflecting a hint of danger in the dim light.

Panic surges through me, the warmth of the evening replaced by an icy grip of fear. I don't know who this person is or what they want, but one thing is clear: whatever they've come for is about to change everything.

Chapter 28: Harmonizing Hearts

A gentle breeze tousled my hair as I settled onto the rooftop, the warmth of Zane's presence beside me igniting a sense of comfort that had felt elusive for far too long. The city sprawled beneath us, its lights twinkling like stars fallen from the sky. I couldn't help but marvel at the way the skyline seemed to pulse with life, a vibrant tapestry woven from dreams and struggles. Zane's laughter, rich and melodic, drifted through the air, pulling me from my reverie.

"I swear, the next time we're up here, I'm bringing popcorn," he said, leaning back on his hands, his gaze fixed on the constellations. "It's practically a crime not to pair stargazing with a good snack."

"Popcorn?" I laughed, shaking my head. "That's your grand plan? Next you'll be suggesting a movie projector. What do you think we are, a rooftop theater?"

His eyes sparkled mischievously. "Why not? We could start a trend. 'Starry Nights: Movie and Munchies.' Think of the Instagram posts!"

"Ah, yes, because that's what the world needs—more content of people shoving popcorn in their faces while staring at the cosmos." I nudged him playfully, feeling the spark of connection flaring brightly between us.

He turned to me, a smile softening his features. "You know, I think it's precisely that kind of ridiculousness that makes life worthwhile. Besides, this is our space now, right? We can make it whatever we want."

I felt a thrill at the thought of us defining this space together. There was something magical about the idea of turning this rooftop into our sanctuary, a canvas where we could paint our dreams without fear of judgment or interruption. "So, what do you want to fill it with?" I asked, letting the moment linger like the fading sunlight.

"Music," he replied, his voice laced with sincerity. "I want to fill it with music that tells our story—everything we've been through, everything we are now."

The weight of his words settled between us, heavy yet exhilarating. I could feel my heart quickening at the thought. The idea of recording an album was thrilling but daunting, an intertwining of our souls in a way that felt almost sacred. "You mean like...an album? Us, together?"

"Absolutely." He met my gaze, unwavering. "I want to blend our voices and experiences, the good and the bad, into something beautiful. We've both come from places that shaped us, and I think it's time to share that journey."

His eyes shone with a fervor that made my pulse quicken. Zane had this way of making every idea feel possible, like the stars above us were not just distant suns but attainable dreams waiting to be grasped. "But what if...what if it's terrible? What if no one likes it?"

Zane scoffed, his laughter ringing out like music itself. "And what if it's brilliant? What if it resonates with people in ways we can't even imagine? Besides, it's not about them; it's about us. It's our story, and we get to tell it however we choose."

His words wrapped around me like a warm blanket, and for a moment, the worries that had gnawed at me faded into the cool night air. I could see it now, our voices harmonizing like a symphony, echoing the melodies of our hearts. "You really think we can do this?"

"Together?" he said, his tone serious now, as if he were laying bare his soul. "Absolutely. We've faced everything life has thrown at us, and we've come out stronger. This will be no different. It'll be an adventure—a way to let the world in on what makes us...us."

A flurry of emotions surged through me—hope, fear, excitement. I had spent so long holding myself back, afraid to leap into the unknown, but now, with Zane by my side, the possibility felt electrifying. "Okay, let's do it," I said, my voice steady as I spoke the words that felt like they would change everything.

"Now you're talking," he grinned, a playful glint in his eyes. "We'll start with the lyrics. I'm thinking something along the lines of 'Life's Messy, But So Are We.'"

I rolled my eyes, fighting back a smile. "Charming. You really think that will fly?"

"Why not? It's authentic!" He laughed again, and the sound was like music to my ears. "We can write about everything—our first awkward date, the time I nearly knocked over that potted plant at your place, the night you took me to that dive bar and I thought I was going to get food poisoning from the nachos."

"Hey, those nachos were a culinary adventure!" I countered, feigning indignation. "You simply didn't appreciate their artistic merit."

"Ah, so now we're pretending they were gourmet?" He feigned a look of deep contemplation. "Perhaps we should add 'Culinary Catastrophes' to our album title list, then."

As laughter bubbled between us, I felt the tension in my chest dissolve, replaced by an exhilarating rush of possibilities. The stars above seemed to twinkle in approval, as if they were cheering us on, and I could already envision the first notes we would strum, the first lyrics we would craft. Together, we would weave our experiences into a tapestry of sound, each thread a testament to our journey.

"So, what's the first step?" I asked, eager to keep this momentum going.

"Let's write about tonight," Zane suggested, leaning forward with a spark of mischief in his eyes. "The stars, the popcorn, the rooftop theater concept—it's all ripe for poetic exploration. We'll make it vivid and lively, just like us."

My heart swelled at the thought. This was more than just music; it was our way of immortalizing this moment, a way to express all the hopes and dreams we dared to dream together. As we began to brainstorm lyrics, the night wrapped around us, our laughter mingling with the cool breeze, creating a melody of its own that resonated deep within my soul.

As the night deepened, the laughter between us turned into a comfortable silence, punctuated only by the distant hum of the city below. I leaned back against the cool, hard surface of the rooftop, staring up at the constellations as if they were old friends, waiting to hear our plans. Zane, ever perceptive, seemed to catch the shift in my mood. His expression softened, a hint of concern lacing his playful demeanor.

"What's going on in that beautiful mind of yours?" he asked, tilting his head slightly, a gesture that always made my heart flutter.

"Just thinking," I replied, absently tracing shapes in the cool concrete. "About how much we've changed over the past few months. I mean, remember when we barely knew each other? Now we're here, talking about recording an album like it's the most natural thing in the world."

"Change is good, isn't it?" he said, his voice low and thoughtful. "It means we're growing. And trust me, we're not done yet."

I felt a wave of warmth at his words, a mix of excitement and apprehension swelling within me. "It's just... I can't shake this feeling of vulnerability. Putting our music out there is one thing, but laying our hearts bare for everyone to see? That's a whole different ballgame."

"Hey," he said, turning to face me, his expression serious. "We're doing this together. That means every note, every lyric is a piece of us, and it's okay if it's not perfect. It's our journey. I want the world to see that."

His conviction wrapped around me like a comforting embrace, easing the knots of worry in my stomach. "You make it sound so easy, Mr. Philosopher," I teased, nudging him lightly. "But what if the world doesn't want to see it? What if it's too raw, too messy?"

"Messy is where the magic happens," he shot back, a smirk dancing on his lips. "Besides, if we wanted to play it safe, we wouldn't be up here planning a music career on a rooftop. I can practically hear the haters booing from a distance."

"Good thing we're only doing this for ourselves, right?" I replied, my heart racing at the thought of our dreams unfurling before us like the night sky.

"Exactly," he said, leaning closer, the space between us charged with an electric energy. "Let's not just dip our toes in; let's dive into the deep end. I mean, when was the last time you did something truly outrageous?"

"Outrageous?" I echoed, feigning contemplation. "You mean besides agreeing to write an album with you? Or singing karaoke while dressed as a giant banana last Halloween?"

"Now that was a showstopper." He laughed, the sound light and inviting, soothing the lingering doubts. "But seriously, I want to create something that reflects not just the music but who we are as a couple. Raw and real, with all the quirky bits included."

"Quirky bits? You mean like my embarrassing habit of singing the wrong lyrics?" I laughed, recalling a particularly hilarious incident where I had belted out a completely different song during a casual jam session.

"Exactly! That's the essence of who you are," he said, his eyes gleaming. "It's those little moments that create a connection. We'll write about those."

We began brainstorming songs, each idea sparking fresh laughter and creativity. As the night wore on, we poured our hearts into hypothetical lyrics, each line echoing the vibrant highs and melancholic lows of our lives. "Let's call one 'Banana Dreams,'" I suggested, biting back a grin, "with a chorus about the unpredictability of life and how sometimes you just have to embrace the silliness."

"Perfect!" he exclaimed, barely containing his laughter. "I can see the music video now—us, dancing on the rooftop in banana costumes, while the world watches in horror."

"Now that's a sight I'd pay to see!" I said, my voice bubbling with mirth. "We could put out a warning: 'Watch with caution; side effects may include excessive laughter.'"

The idea of recording such a fun, light-hearted song felt like a breath of fresh air. It allowed us to explore our identities beyond the struggles that had shaped us. "But what about the serious stuff?" I asked, tilting my head. "The parts of our journey that aren't exactly funny?"

Zane nodded, his expression thoughtful once more. "Absolutely. We need those moments too. Let's write about heartbreak and healing, about finding each other in the chaos. We can blend the light and the dark—show the full spectrum of our lives."

"Like a musical journey through the ups and downs," I said, feeling the pieces fall into place like a well-structured melody. "We could start with something light and fun, then transition into deeper themes. It would mirror our own experience."

"Exactly," he replied, his enthusiasm palpable. "We'll make it a rollercoaster of emotions, something that makes people laugh, cry, and think. That's what music does, right?"

"Right," I said, the weight of his words settling in my heart. "It connects us all. And I can't wait to share that with you."

As we continued to plot our album, the night sky slowly faded to a deep indigo, sprinkled with shimmering stars that seemed to twinkle in encouragement. Each idea flowed easily between us, our creative juices igniting a spark that fueled our passion. I found myself losing track of time, enveloped in the warmth of Zane's presence, as if the world around us had disappeared, leaving just the two of us and our burgeoning dreams.

"Okay, what about a love song?" I proposed, leaning forward, eyes alight with inspiration. "Something that captures that moment when you realize you're completely head over heels?"

Zane's eyes sparkled with mischief. "You mean like the moment I realized you were a karaoke-loving banana?"

"Hey, don't knock it. That was a pivotal moment," I shot back, laughter bubbling up again. "But really, I'm talking about that moment when everything clicks, you know? Like when we first started hanging out, and I thought, 'Wow, this guy is actually pretty amazing.'"

"I was thinking more along the lines of when I realized you were a walking disaster with the nachos." He winked, feigning seriousness, but his eyes twinkled with affection.

"Touché," I admitted, my cheeks warming. "But I do think there's something there. We should write about those moments—the ones that make you believe in magic."

"Agreed," he said, his tone softening as he looked at me. "Moments that take your breath away, that leave you a little speechless. We'll capture that feeling, the kind that makes you smile for no reason at all."

I could feel the excitement rising within me like a tide, pulling me closer to him. "I can already hear the melody in my head," I said, closing my eyes and picturing it. "A soft, gentle tune that builds into something bigger, something that feels like a hug."

"Yes!" he exclaimed, his enthusiasm infectious. "That's the magic we're after. We'll pour our hearts into this, create something that's a reflection of us—flaws, quirks, and all."

The realization washed over me like a warm wave, the thrill of what lay ahead propelling us into a world of endless possibilities. We were on the brink of something extraordinary, a creative journey that intertwined our lives and our voices.

With the cool night air wrapping around us like a comforting blanket, I could feel the momentum of our dreams propelling us forward. Zane and I continued to bounce ideas off each other, our excitement transforming the rooftop into a creative haven, a private world that felt entirely ours.

"What if we start the album with something that embodies our beginning?" I suggested, my fingers tapping the rhythm of an invisible beat on my knee. "You know, the kind of song that captures that initial spark—the thrill of meeting someone who completely throws your world into a tailspin."

Zane leaned in closer, his brows furrowing as if he were deep in thought. "Something like... 'First Glance, Lasting Chance'?" He grinned at the absurdity of the title, and I couldn't help but laugh.

"Okay, it sounds a bit cheesy, but I'm here for it," I admitted, shaking my head. "We could have a catchy hook that makes you want to dance, but the verses could be filled with those awkward, heart-stopping moments that make you want to crawl under a rock."

"Like tripping over your own feet while trying to impress me?" he teased, nudging my shoulder. "Oh wait, that was me."

"Right, right. Just keep digging that hole," I retorted, feigning exasperation. "But seriously, let's make it relatable. Everyone's had those moments where they felt utterly ridiculous in front of someone they liked. We could incorporate that sense of vulnerability."

"I love it," he said, his eyes lighting up. "We'll make it a rollercoaster—laughter intermingled with the sweet, shaky feeling of newfound love. It'll resonate."

"I can almost hear the guitars now," I said, a grin spreading across my face. "This is going to be the anthem of all the clumsy romantics out there!"

With each new idea, I felt the weight of my worries lifting, replaced by the exhilarating rush of possibility. It was as if every note we created was a thread weaving us closer together, forging an unbreakable bond. The rooftop became a sanctuary where our voices mingled, harmonizing with the distant sounds of the city below—honking cars, laughter from late-night revelers, the occasional bark of a dog.

As we planned, I felt an itch to share more than just our music with Zane. "You know," I said, looking out over the twinkling skyline, "there's something about this place that makes me want to lay it all out there. I feel like if we're going to do this, we need to be completely open with each other."

He turned to me, the playful glimmer in his eyes replaced by a more serious expression. "You're right. This isn't just about the music. It's about us. What's on your mind?"

"I guess... I'm still figuring out what I want in life, aside from this album," I admitted, my voice softer now, tinged with uncertainty. "After everything that happened with Jake's family, I've realized how fragile everything can be. One moment you think you have it all figured out, and the next, everything changes."

Zane's expression softened further, and he reached for my hand, intertwining our fingers. "We're all a work in progress, you know? I'm figuring it out too. I mean, I'm in this strange limbo between what I thought I wanted and what I actually want. It's terrifying."

I nodded, the truth of his words resonating deeply within me. "Right? And then there's this fear of what happens if we fail. What if this album doesn't turn out the way we hope? What if it changes everything?"

He squeezed my hand, his grip steady and reassuring. "But what if it does? What if it brings us closer together? What if it opens doors we never knew existed?"

"Those are some bold what-ifs," I replied, feeling a flicker of hope ignite inside me. "But they're also terrifying. What if we lay our hearts on the line, and no one wants to listen?"

"Then at least we've created something beautiful together," he countered, his voice firm yet gentle. "Something that speaks to us, even if it doesn't resonate with anyone else. That's worth the risk, isn't it?"

I took a deep breath, letting his words sink in. There was a certain wisdom in his perspective, one that reminded me of the magic that came from vulnerability. "You're right. It's just... I've spent so much time trying to protect my heart. Letting someone in feels like standing at the edge of a cliff, looking down into the unknown."

"Trust me, I get it. It's a leap," he said, his eyes searching mine. "But what if it's a leap worth taking?"

The weight of his gaze held me captive, and in that moment, I realized that perhaps the leap wasn't as terrifying as I had made it out to be. Perhaps it was an opportunity to embrace life's unpredictability, to dance in the chaos. "Okay, then," I said, my heart racing with determination. "Let's do it. Let's make this album and let the world see us—messy and all."

Zane's face broke into a brilliant smile, and the way his eyes sparkled made me feel like I could fly. "Now you're talking! We'll make it an adventure. No holding back."

Just as we were about to dive back into our brainstorming, a sudden commotion below interrupted us. A group of people had gathered on the street, their voices rising in excitement. "What's going on?" I asked, my curiosity piqued.

Zane leaned over the edge of the rooftop, peering down. "Looks like someone's making a scene. I think they're protesting something?"

I joined him, squinting at the commotion. A small crowd had formed, holding colorful signs and chanting slogans that echoed up to us. "It's hard to tell from up here, but it seems... passionate," I remarked, intrigued.

Suddenly, a loud crash echoed through the night, followed by a burst of shouts. Zane and I exchanged worried glances. "Should we go check it out?" he suggested, his brows knitting together in concern.

"Yeah, I think so," I agreed, adrenaline coursing through my veins. "Let's grab a couple of flashlights and see what's happening."

We hurried down the stairs and out of the building, the cool night air hitting us like a wall as we emerged onto the street. The noise grew louder as we approached the crowd, the atmosphere charged with a strange mix of excitement and tension.

"Did someone just throw something?" Zane asked, his voice laced with concern as we maneuvered through the throng of people.

I glanced around, taking in the colorful banners and the fervent expressions on the faces surrounding us. "I think so. This looks serious," I replied, trying to keep my voice steady despite the growing unease.

As we edged closer, the chaos intensified. I could make out snippets of conversation, a mishmash of anger and determination. Then, out of nowhere, a figure emerged from the crowd, eyes wide and frantic. "Help! We need help! They're trying to shut us down!"

My heart raced, and I exchanged a glance with Zane, both of us sensing the gravity of the moment. Before we could respond, the crowd surged forward, and we were swept along with it, the energy pulsating around us.

In that instant, the plans we'd just begun to sketch out seemed to fade into the background. The reality of the world outside our bubble crashed in, a reminder that life was unpredictable, messy, and often out of our control. And as we were pulled deeper into the thrumming heart of the protest, one thought echoed in my mind:

sometimes, the most significant moments are the ones you never see coming.

Chapter 29: A New Beginning

The sun hung low in the sky, casting a warm, golden hue that spilled through the studio's expansive windows, illuminating every corner with a comforting glow. I leaned back against the well-worn leather couch, the rich scent of aged wood and the faint trace of lingering incense wrapping around me like a cozy blanket. This was more than just a recording studio; it had morphed into our sanctuary, a space where melodies were birthed and dreams found their voice. Zane sat across from me, fingers dancing across the piano keys, coaxing out a tune that felt like it had been waiting for us, hidden beneath layers of uncertainty and heartache.

"Are you sure about this?" he asked, his voice a mix of genuine curiosity and that teasing lilt I adored. He shot me a sideways glance, a grin tugging at the corners of his mouth. "I mean, the world isn't quite ready for our brand of chaos, is it?"

I laughed, a light, airy sound that filled the room, cutting through the tension like a well-aimed arrow. "If they knew what we've been through, they'd either run screaming or throw confetti. Either way, it'll be a show." I let the words hang in the air, a playful challenge. There was something inherently beautiful about our shared journey, the way we had turned our struggles into songs, stitching together the threads of love and loss like a patchwork quilt.

Zane raised an eyebrow, that mischievous sparkle in his eye igniting the familiar flutter in my stomach. "So, a mix of redemption and a wild party? Sounds about right." He paused, letting the last note linger before lifting his fingers from the keys. "But seriously, are you ready to put all of this out there? It's... vulnerable."

The vulnerability hung between us, thick and palpable. I turned my gaze to the window, watching the trees sway gently in the breeze, their leaves whispering secrets I longed to uncover. "It's terrifying, but isn't that what life is? A series of terrifying leaps?" I felt the heat of his gaze, steady and unwavering, anchoring me to the moment. "This album isn't just a collection of songs. It's a testament to everything we've fought through. It's our story."

He nodded, the weight of my words settling into the space between us, binding us closer. "And it's one hell of a story. Love, loss, healing... you've lived it all." He leaned forward, resting his elbows on his knees. "What if the world loves it as much as we do? What if we're met with applause instead of crickets?"

The thought sent a shiver of excitement coursing through me. "Then we'll ride that wave, won't we? We'll let it carry us wherever it leads." I could see it, the glimmer of potential lighting up his eyes. We were standing on the precipice of something beautiful, and the thrill of it was intoxicating.

Zane's laughter danced through the air, bright and genuine, mingling with the sweet notes that still lingered from our last song. "You really think so? That we'll make it big and tour the world?"

"Why not? We're the perfect duo. You're the genius, and I'm the charm," I quipped, nudging him playfully with my shoulder. He feigned a look of deep thought, his expression exaggeratedly serious.

"Genius, huh? Is that what you call the ability to play three chords and hope for the best?" His smirk was contagious, and I found myself rolling my eyes, unable to suppress a smile.

"Hey, those three chords are magic!" I defended, waving my hands in the air dramatically. "Besides, it's not just the chords; it's the soul behind them." My heart raced with the truth of it. Music was everything to us, a language that transcended words, allowing us to express what lay deep within our hearts.

The gentle hum of the city outside began to fade as the sun dipped lower, casting long shadows that intertwined like our lives, forever entwined in this intricate dance of love and creativity. It felt like the world outside was holding its breath, waiting for us to take the plunge.

"Alright, one more time," Zane said, his voice steady and resolute, the playful banter dissolving into an electric focus. "Let's record that last track. I want it to feel like the world is exploding with joy." He settled back at the piano, fingers hovering above the keys, his body radiating a blend of anticipation and purpose.

With a deep breath, I nodded, feeling the familiar rush of adrenaline. As the music flowed from his fingertips, I closed my eyes, surrendering to the moment. Each note wrapped around me like a gentle embrace, grounding me in the reality of what we were creating. It was exhilarating and terrifying, a reminder that the path ahead was fraught with uncertainty, yet illuminated by the glow of possibility.

The room transformed, the air thick with our hopes and dreams as the melodies filled every inch of the space. I could feel the heartbeat of the song resonating within me, a rhythm that mirrored the flutter of my heart. It was a moment of pure magic—a tapestry woven with threads of our shared experience, stitched together with love, laughter, and the occasional tear.

As we reached the crescendo, I opened my eyes, finding Zane's gaze fixed on me, a fierce determination etched across his face. "This is it, isn't it?" he said, a spark of excitement igniting in his voice. "We're about to show the world who we are."

In that instant, I felt a wave of clarity wash over me. We were no longer just two individuals chasing dreams; we were partners, hand in hand, ready to embrace the unpredictability of what lay ahead. The scars of our past became badges of honor, symbols of resilience that would guide us through the storm. This journey was ours, and together, we would face whatever challenges awaited us on the horizon.

The echoes of our final notes faded into the corners of the studio, leaving behind a silence thick with promise. Zane leaned back on the piano bench, a satisfied grin spreading across his face, the kind that ignited a flutter in my chest. "So, are we officially rock stars now?" he asked, tilting his head in mock seriousness.

"Rock stars? Please, we're more like folk-infused troubadours with a flair for the dramatic." I couldn't help but chuckle, a sound that danced in the warm air like the last glimmers of sunset spilling through the window. It felt right to joke in this moment, a lightheartedness woven into the fabric of our shared experience, the kind that made all the heartache and uncertainty worth it.

"Folk-infused troubadours?" Zane echoed, raising an eyebrow, his smirk widening. "Sounds like the title of a failed indie band. We should definitely consider it."

I shot him a playful glare, a smile tugging at my lips. "Well, I suppose it's better than 'Dramatic Failures' as our fallback name. Maybe we'll add that to the merchandise line."

The thought sent us into fits of laughter, a joyous release that filled the studio, creating an invisible bond between us. It was in these moments, amidst the jokes and the music, that I felt the true depth of our connection, the way our lives intertwined in an intricate dance of vulnerability and trust.

As the laughter subsided, a sudden wave of seriousness washed over Zane. "You know, I've been thinking," he began, his voice dropping to a softer tone, each word carefully measured. "About how we're going to present this album. It's more than just songs; it's our story, our journey. It deserves to be shared with the world."

I nodded, feeling a familiar flutter of nerves. "You're right. But how do we even start? It feels so overwhelming."

Zane leaned forward, his eyes alight with inspiration. "What if we created an experience? Not just a release party, but a way for people to feel what we felt while making this music? Like an immersive journey through our lives."

My mind raced at the idea, already picturing the venue filled with soft lights and cozy nooks, a space where people could sip drinks and lose themselves in our melodies. "That sounds incredible," I replied, excitement bubbling beneath my skin. "We could have stations where guests could explore the stories behind the songs—photos, anecdotes, maybe even some live performances of the songs."

His eyes sparkled with enthusiasm, and I could see the gears turning in his head, crafting an elaborate vision of what this could be. "Exactly! We can create an emotional arc, guiding them from the heartache to the healing, showcasing every twist and turn we faced along the way."

The idea electrified the air around us, igniting our imaginations. It felt as if the walls themselves were cheering us on, encouraging us to take this leap into the unknown. "Let's do it," I said, a burst of determination swelling within me. "Let's turn this album into a celebration of life, love, and everything in between."

He grinned, the kind of smile that hinted at the adventures that lay ahead. "We'll need a team, though. You know, to help with the logistics and all that boring stuff. I mean, we can't very well set up our own fairy tale, can we?"

"Right, because that would definitely end in disaster," I agreed, feigning horror at the thought of our grand plans collapsing like a poorly built house of cards. "But who do we trust to help us create this magical event?"

Zane paused, his brow furrowing in thought, and I could almost see the cogs turning behind those dreamy eyes. "What about that girl from the café? You know, the one with the blue hair and the killer playlists? She seems to know a thing or two about organizing events."

A grin spread across my face as I recalled our conversations with her, her vibrant energy a perfect match for our vision. "Oh, Lexi? She'd be perfect! And maybe we could rope in some local artists to contribute to the experience. Make it a community thing."

"Now we're talking!" Zane's enthusiasm was infectious, and I felt my heart swell with hope and anticipation. "Let's set up a meeting with Lexi this week. The sooner we get rolling, the better."

With our minds racing, we began brainstorming ideas, our voices mingling with the fading light in the room. The more we envisioned our release event, the more the initial doubts melted away, replaced by the thrill of creation and the promise of a shared experience.

But as our plans began to take shape, a quiet voice in the back of my mind urged caution. What if the world wasn't ready for our truth? What if our vulnerabilities were met with indifference or scorn? I pushed the thought away, refusing to let it cloud the excitement building within me.

As night fell and the first stars began to twinkle in the velvety sky, Zane and I took a break, settling onto the couch, our laughter still lingering like a sweet melody. We shared stories, our dreams spilling out between us, revealing fragments of our pasts that had shaped us into who we were.

"Do you remember the first time we met?" he asked, a teasing lilt to his voice. "You were trying to convince me that your three chords could change the world."

I chuckled, rolling my eyes at the memory. "And you were the arrogant genius who dismissed me! I mean, who did you think you were?"

"Just a guy trying to survive in a world full of wannabe rock stars," he replied, a mock-serious expression on his face. "But I must admit, you were quite convincing."

We traded stories of awkward encounters and the strange twists of fate that had led us to this moment, building a tapestry of shared memories that felt as vivid as the notes we had just recorded. In this sanctuary of sound, where dreams danced like fireflies, I felt the weight of our journey transform into something light and hopeful.

"Whatever happens next, I'm glad we're doing this together," I said, my voice softening, filled with sincerity.

Zane reached for my hand, his touch warm and reassuring. "Me too. Here's to our chaotic, beautiful journey."

The promise hung in the air, a spark of magic that illuminated our path forward, inviting us to dive deeper into the unknown, hand in hand.

The days melted into one another like the vibrant hues on a painter's palette, each morning greeting us with a renewed sense of possibility. As our plans for the release event took shape, excitement surged through me like a current, electrifying every moment. Zane and I worked tirelessly alongside Lexi, our eclectic event planner with a flair for the dramatic. Her blue hair was always styled in wild waves, her wardrobe a delightful riot of colors that reflected her creative spirit.

"Alright, people," she declared one afternoon, her voice ringing with authority as we gathered in the studio. "We're going to make this album release a kaleidoscope of experiences! Think immersive art installations, acoustic corners for spontaneous jam sessions, and, oh, live art! I can get a local artist to paint a mural as the evening unfolds."

Zane leaned against the wall, arms crossed, clearly impressed. "A mural? That sounds incredible! A visual representation of our journey—our chaos—while we play. Genius."

"Exactly!" Lexi grinned, her enthusiasm infectious. "It'll be like creating a living, breathing art piece. And the attendees can watch it evolve while feeling the music."

I felt a thrill ripple through me, igniting a spark of inspiration. "What if we incorporate a storytelling session? We could share the backstories of our songs, allow people to feel the emotions that inspired each piece."

Zane nodded, a thoughtful expression on his face. "We can even invite some close friends to share their perspectives. They were there through the mess and the magic."

"Look at you two, turning this into a therapy session for the masses," Lexi teased, her eyes twinkling with mischief. "I love it! Let's add a little interactive element—maybe a 'confessions' wall where people can share their own stories of love and loss."

Our plans rapidly expanded into something far beyond what I had ever imagined. The studio buzzed with ideas, each suggestion weaving a thread of connection among us, drawing us closer as we crafted this immersive experience. It felt like a tapestry being woven from our lives, each stitch a testament to the vulnerability we had chosen to embrace.

As the weeks passed, the anticipation transformed into a tangible energy that hummed beneath the surface. We delved deeper into our rehearsals, transforming the studio into a hive of creativity. Zane's fingers glided over the piano keys with newfound fervor, and I poured my soul into every lyric, each line a piece of my heart laid bare.

One evening, as dusk settled and the first stars blinked into existence, I found myself standing in front of the expansive mirror that adorned the wall. My reflection stared back, a collage of excitement and apprehension. "What if we bomb?" I mumbled, biting my lip as I turned to Zane, who was sitting cross-legged on the floor, guitar in hand.

He glanced up, his expression a mix of amusement and concern. "What do you mean, 'bomb'? We're not launching a rocket here; we're sharing our story."

"I know, but what if people don't connect with it? What if they don't feel what we felt?" The anxiety clung to me, a specter that refused to fade away.

Zane set his guitar aside and stood, crossing the room to join me. "Hey, look at me." He waited until I met his gaze, his eyes steady and reassuring. "This isn't about them; it's about us. We're creating something genuine. If we connect with just one person, it's worth it. Plus, remember that time you almost fell off the stage? That was a bomb, and you survived."

I laughed, the tension in my chest easing just a fraction. "Okay, that was mortifying. But it's different. This is... personal."

"Exactly! And that's the beauty of it." He stepped closer, his presence wrapping around me like a protective cocoon. "You've poured your heart into these songs. If they don't get it, that's on them, not us."

"Wise words from a folk-infused troubadour," I teased, nudging him with my elbow, grateful for his unwavering support.

The days flew by as we finalized our preparations, Lexi weaving her magic with every detail, transforming our venue into a reflection of our journey. Soft lights hung from the ceiling like stars, each flicker casting a warm glow on the carefully curated installations. On the night of the event, the air buzzed with a blend of anticipation and nervous energy.

As the first guests began to trickle in, I stood at the entrance, my heart racing with each arrival. I wore a flowing dress that felt like it had been spun from sunlight, a warm yellow that mirrored my optimism. Zane looked stunning, his signature flannel shirt paired with dark jeans, an effortless blend of rugged charm and undeniable charisma.

"Ready to dazzle?" he asked, his voice a low murmur meant only for me, the corners of his mouth lifting in a lopsided grin.

"Only if you're ready to charm the crowd with your guitar," I shot back, unable to keep the flutter of excitement from my voice.

We welcomed guests as they streamed in, faces painted with curiosity and warmth. The vibe was electric, the room alive with conversations and laughter, each note of music blending seamlessly with the sound of connection. I spotted friends and familiar faces, their smiles reassuring me that we weren't alone in this venture.

Lexi flitted around, ensuring everything ran smoothly, her energy palpable as she coordinated the unfolding event. I couldn't help but admire her skill in transforming our vision into reality.

"Let the storytelling begin!" Lexi called out, her voice cutting through the chatter, and a hush settled over the crowd. My heart raced as I took my place next to Zane, the warm glow of the lights highlighting the connection we had forged through this journey.

We launched into our first song, the chords resonating like a heartbeat in the stillness, enveloping the audience. As I sang, I poured every ounce of emotion into the melody, inviting them into our world, a place painted with both shadows and light.

The room swayed, caught up in the magic of the moment, and for the first time that evening, I felt a sense of belonging. We were sharing something real—our story, our growth, our healing.

As the final notes of the song faded, a wave of applause washed over us, mingled with cheers that made my heart swell. It was intoxicating, a rush of validation that pushed the doubts away, even if only for a moment.

We moved into the next song, the narrative unfolding like a beloved novel, each note a turning point. Just as I was lost in the music, a sudden commotion near the entrance pulled my attention. I glanced up to see a figure standing in the doorway, silhouetted against the dim light.

My breath hitched in my throat as recognition dawned. A wave of emotions crashed over me, swirling through my mind like a tempest. There he stood, a ghost from my past, someone I had hoped would never cross my path again. The air felt thick, heavy with unsaid words and unresolved feelings as he locked eyes with me, a knowing smirk creeping onto his face.

"Surprise," he mouthed, his voice drowned out by the music, but the weight of his presence hung heavily in the air.

Panic coursed through me, twisting my stomach into knots as I wrestled with the sudden flood of memories that threatened to overwhelm me. How could this happen now, at the very moment I felt so alive?

The music faded into the background, a distant hum as my world narrowed to that singular moment, the room spinning with uncertainty. All I could focus on was him, the embodiment of my past, and the shadow he cast over my newfound beginnings. I felt Zane's hand squeeze mine, grounding me, but the storm inside me raged on, threatening to pull me under.

Milton Keynes UK
Ingram Content Group UK Ltd.
UKHW020756231024
450026UK00001B/65